THE FALL OF SOULS

THE BOOK OF KAN
BOOK ONE

R. A. MOREAU

P&P

First Edition

ISBN: 979-8986635392

"Whatever our souls are made of, his and mine are the same."
- Emily Brontë, Wuthering Heights

CHAPTER 1
ONIA

I never understood how people passed with such grace, welcoming the wings of Ma'at and giving themselves over to judgment without question. When I imagined my journey to the Hall, I saw myself fighting the Jackal for even one more breath. But perhaps others knew some secret of the gods. Perhaps they were so sure of their fate that they greeted the afterlife with open arms. Or maybe they simply accepted that something divine had come to claim them, and there was nothing they could do about it. I never imagined that, when my time finally came, I would go willingly.

Father had gone with grace, as most did. He didn't fight the fog as it crept into his mind, and he didn't resist the call when it finally came. For years I'd seen the signs, watching his ordinarily keen eyes become distant, gazing at the sun. Only to turn away from the strain and return a few moments later. His voice left him first. Then his mind had gone, and eventually, the sickness replaced his spark of understanding with a haze of confusion. I'd tried to find him some relief, but none of the sunu's remedies had slowed his descent, and by the time his call came, Father had little spirit left to fight with.

I glanced at his cloth-covered face and placed the stone scarab on his chest before sifting the sand over his body, scooping it up and spreading it over him in even layers until I'd covered the last of him. The sting of tears pricked my eyes, but they didn't flow. There probably weren't any left. I had done my share of crying years ago—when the last word had left his lips. Now I too had little spirit left in me.

The peasant family beside me was hunched over their loved one, wrought with emotion—tears streaming down their sun-rashed cheeks and clinging to each other desperately. It was easy to see their pain was fresh, unlike mine. Father's soul had passed through two days ago, but I'd been mourning his loss for over a year. I'd been alone from the moment his mind had gone. I wondered what it was like to share such emotion with someone—to be connected through loss and love. Was it easier somehow?

I kept my kan close, not wanting to intrude upon their souls in their time of mourning. Besides, I didn't need to read them to know what I'd find underneath. The pain of loss was as stifling as the thick blanket of heat covering the burial grounds, and I felt it press down on me as I stood to gather myself.

Ashwana was a few hours east, but the path back to the city grew dark and empty once the sun was gone. And it wasn't wise for me to wander the streets alone—especially when there would be no one to come looking for me. The sun was still high as I began my trek back to the eastern wall, but my load was significantly lighter now that I'd buried it in the earth for Father to carry. I'd managed to bring two jugs of wine, a loaf of bread, a decent helping of dates, and a pouch of bronze deben to ease his path. Hopefully, it would be enough. A soul's passage could be difficult, and he didn't deserve a harrowing journey—not after what this realm had granted him.

I stepped cautiously around the rows of freshly churned soil and tried not to disturb the huddled families as I passed. But I idled as I caught sight of a mother and daughter, clinging to one another as they knelt in the clay-colored dirt—their quiet sobs blending with the other families' around them. I bit down on my lip as I watched them with wistful eyes. Their spirits may be heavy, and they may know loss, but at least they weren't alone. A moment of shameful envy crept over me, and I buried it, pushing the thought from my mind to make my way back to Ashwana.

By the time I could see the high stone walls looming in the distance, the sun was barely peeking out over the city. But even in the dimming light, I could see the grand construction of Atem's form guarding the eastern wall. A reverent depiction of his human form stood in the center of the pillared entrance—arms crossed, a crook in one hand, a flail in the other, and a crown of light sprouting from the striped neme on his head. People shuffled around the base under his feet, pushing past one another to make their way home before the setting sun. I avoided his watchful eyes as I passed through. There were stories of the power Atem's eyes held. How he could trap you in the light of his vision, and you would wither away without a thought. I knew this was only stone, but I wasn't interested in testing the gods.

The symphony of the early evening streets met my ears as I crossed the threshold. The cool night air had summoned people from their homes, filling the streets with life. A fast staccato drumbeat sounded through the square, and a wide circle of dancers had already taken up their stance. A woman stepped into its center, shaking her hips and stomping her feet in time with the drummer's tune. A couple held each other close as they swayed together, and the shouts of women rose above the music as they bartered with nearby vendors.

Children dashed around their feet, kicking up dust until an elder dealt them a hollow smack. One child skidded to a stop to pout at her mother. With a huff, the woman waved her off, and she rejoined the flock of children sprinting through the stalls giggling. I smiled to myself. I'd never been quite that rambunctious. Father had always insisted I was well-behaved, but I distinctly recall giving him a hard time on more than one occasion.

A pang of loneliness struck me as I continued down the path and the drumbeat softened. The main road opened to a row of merchants still hawking their fare. The sweet scent of roasting dates and the sizzle of meat on an open flame sent my stomach churning and the emptiness flitting from my mind. I gripped my stomach as the sound of hunger reverberated through me. I hadn't eaten since the previous morning. Father's burial preparations had taken all my focus and, as was typical, I had neglected my own needs in the process.

I followed the savory-sweet scent to a nearby stall and opened my kan to the merchant's spirit. If I could get a read on the burly man, I'd have a better chance of keeping my coin up. The merchantmen tended to be more forthcoming when they were in a good mood and the sun was no longer beating down on them; the women were stern no matter the hour. I'd learned not to barter with *them* long ago.

I focused my kan, letting the rush of energy fill me, spreading into my arms and neck before pulsing in my chest. It'd taken some time to manage this feat and even more time to become acquainted with the sensation of my energy weeding through another person's soul. I remember the day I realized my kan was different from the other children. They never spoke about their kan the way I did— never mentioned how it coursed through them like a winding river and came to life with a gentle tug or how it would pour out of you to peer into the people around you. For them, kan was just the energy that fed their souls, but for me, it was so much more.

The day I told Father I could see into his soul was the day I learned about my "gift." He told me the balance had blessed me, and I shouldn't question it. But I'd spent years trying to ignore it, using all my energy to quiet the current in my mind rather than honing it. It wasn't until we needed my gift that I learned to use it in my favor. Now, almost five years later, I could read a person's soul to its core in a matter of minutes.

Pushing my kan forward, I waited until my energy reached the merchant before unraveling his spirit like a tightly wound ribbon. It took more effort than most, and I worried he might be a stubborn one. But as I waited in the shadows, a gentle stream of calm trickled out from the depths of his soul to blend with a subtle sense of frustration. I decided that was a temperament I could work with. I'd be hard-pressed to find a merchant that wasn't at least a touch angry at the end of the day. I stepped out of the shadows to try my luck.

"Evening."

I tried for a pleasant smile.

My appearance lent itself useful in these situations, that was, when men actually managed to find my face. Most of them lingered around my chest or hips. But I always found it easier when I offered them a smile, and coin was too scarce these days for me to play at being offended.

The man's eyes found my face after an agonizingly slow evaluation of the rest of me.

"Evenin'."

His tone was sharp, but I felt the jolt in his spirit at the prospect of a customer.

"Whadjya need, girl?"

"Bushel of dates and a half bushel of plums," I said.

"Fifteen bronze," he snapped and shoved an open palm in my direction.

I kept my hands to myself.

"Eight," I countered, folding my arms in front of me and reading his spirit carefully.

The current halted as if I'd hurled an insult, and I knew he wouldn't accept.

"Twelve," he offered, letting out an exasperated huff. But his spirit betrayed him, bubbling up with gleeful anticipation that told me he would walk away the winner if I conceded.

"Ten," I said.

His eyes darted to the pile of dates beside him as the current of his spirit slowed. After a brief silence, it dipped with a hollow acceptance.

I'd found it—the lowest number he'd accept without a fuss. It was a fair price, and it left me with enough coin for the next few days, at least until I could perform a few readings in the square.

"Uhgreed," he sighed.

I dropped my deben on the rug beneath him and snatched up my purchase before he could change his mind. He shouted a gruff "thank you," and I waved a grateful hand without turning back. As I stepped off the main road, I tossed a date in my mouth, enjoying the ooze of sticky flavor spreading across my tongue. Home was a ways away from the city center, and the crowded noise of the streets grew progressively quieter as I wound through the narrow backways to reach the edge of the western district. Once Father's mind began to fail him, the western district was the best I could manage.

But I was doubtful I could remain here much longer. I couldn't even give Father the burial he deserved. I'd set aside enough for his wrappings, but a sarcophagus had been out of reach, and I was forced to send him to the Hall without one. I would need to perform twice as many readings each cycle, and—though there was plenty of wealth to be had in the northern district—only the sick and dying ever sought my services. Even then, it was out of desperation. Few people were able to admit when death was around the corner.

I stepped out of the backway that ran behind our quarter and followed the carefully laid alabaster stones toward our row. The darkness of the road was accompanied only by the sounds of my feet and the beetles humming a dull tone. My body went rigid as our home came into view.

The wooden door hung wide open, creaking as it swayed gently on its hinges, and an imprint of large, leather-clad feet was pressed into the dirt where a man had been standing just outside the door.

I crept through the entry, raising the bag of dates above my head. I doubted they would prove a valuable weapon, but in a time of need, anything would do.

"Hello?"

My voice echoed across the low clay ceiling.

"Hello!" I repeated, trying to sound more sure of myself.

Padded feet shuffled across the rug-covered stone, sending me reeling for the nearest corner and pressing my back into the wall. A streak of ink-black fur shot out from the back room, along with a fast-moving current of rage at the back of my mind. I dismissed the foreign emotion and tossed the dates to the ground, hoping whatever wild thing that had wandered in would take the offering and leave me whole. The animal sprinted through the open door, ignoring me and my dates entirely, and I released the breath I'd been holding as I righted myself.

Sneaky creature.

I hurried toward the food stores, praying to the balance that it hadn't found them, and yanked the hatch open. Not a single grain out of place.

A polite creature then, probably seeking the cool of shade on a day like today.

It was bold to wander this far from the river, but I couldn't fault it for such desires. I'm sure I'd do much worse in the name of survival if I were him. I stepped outside to sweep away the footprints but found them erased by the shuffle of massive paw prints and the sweep of a long, bristled tail.

I shut the door and slid the latch into place, deciding the shoeprints belonged to someone come to pay their respects and instead tried to find some peace in the emptiness of our home. Now that he was gone, these stone walls felt suffocating.

Before sending him on his journey, I'd tried to clear away Father's things, but his parchments were still strewn about on every surface. Ink wells lined the ledge of the hearth, and the scent of his favorite beard oil still hung in the air. I hadn't the strength to move it all. After two and a half decades of his disordered clutter, the mess seemed more like a fixture, and I worried that once I cleared it all away, I would be all that was left. I popped a few more dates in my mouth and settled near the hearth to clear my mind. The weight of the day was beginning to wear on me, and I couldn't afford to rest into the morning. If I wanted to secure a spot in the market square, I'd have to be up before the sun.

CHAPTER 2

RA

An old merchant shouted a curse in my direction as I trotted down the street. I bared my teeth at him, standing my hackles up and thrashing my tail for good measure. He jumped back a few paces, shaking a fist at me, but I didn't turn around as he began shouting again. I had more important things to see to than angry old men. Although, if he wanted to keep his chubby little fingers, he had best leave me be at this early hour. Khepri hadn't even warmed the earth with his kan yet, and we were already trudging through the streets.

She had left while the sun was barely peeking out, and I had to shift quickly to catch up. Her long legs carried her through the streets as she munched on the dates she'd shielded herself with yesterday. I hadn't planned on entering her home, but the scent of death hung in the air, and my jackal had propelled me forward, fearing I was too late. Selfishly, I was relieved when I found the sickly scent tied to another. I maintained a great distance, trailing her scent as she strode through the city. Her aroma was easy enough to find and quite pleasant to follow—a sweet blend of lavender and sage mixed with parchment.

She skirted around a group of men lounging along the road,

9

and I watched their heads turn in appreciation as she passed. My jackal stretched to life inside me, ignited by the visceral urge to guard her. I stamped out the primal reaction as she tossed a fiery glare over her shoulder. They weren't wrong to admire her human form; you'd have to be blind not to. The balance had blessed her. Her thick hips swayed from side to side with each step as her bronzed legs stretched out in front of her—they could entice any man. Even *I* found myself looking longer than a guardian should.

I snarled as I passed the ill-mannered men. They screeched like children, jumping out of my way, and pushing at one another to scurry off into the surrounding backways. I followed her down the sun-bleached road until the sounds of life began to build, signaling we were nearing the city center. I pulled back as she stepped into the market square, waiting to see why we'd rushed here. Slipping into the shadow of a nearby building, I watched her settle under a large palm along the plaza's edge. Trees were scarce here, the shade they provided even more so. Three large buildings offered the illusion of ample shade, but once the sun reached up overhead, sunlight would bathe the square from corner to corner. She'd positioned herself well—one of the few spots that would retain a shadow well after the high heat.

She dropped a small, patterned carpet to the ground and knelt to make herself comfortable, leaning back to soak in the early morning sun as she pulled a plum from her bag. The golden light left a subtle glitter across her chestnut skin as it streamed through the palm leaves, and I had to smother the sudden sense of guilt as I looked at her.

She was beautiful—the soft curve of her face lifting into high-arched cheeks and the wide bridge of her nose sloping up to meet a delicate brow set with a small frown. She was unmistakably Ma'at's daughter. Whatever doubt I had dissipated once I caught sight of the knowing look in her eyes—a perfect mirror of her mother's. Save for the fire burning behind them.

She settled in to wait for the crowd to emerge. It would be a while before the other merchants began trickling in to take up their positions around the square, and it would be even longer before the bustle of patrons came flooding through. I claimed my place in the shadows, watching her from a distance and scanning the backways for any creatures that might be lurking.

I wasn't concerned with the earth-bound creatures—most of them had fled at my scent. The only creatures foolish enough to remain would be shabti. Their mindless servitude left them vulnerable to greater beings, but it also made them bold in a way that only stupidity could. Attacking in broad daylight, in full view of humans, was not beneath them.

Father was certain no one knew of her existence, but I refused to believe the Demoness wasn't willing to commit countless abuses to relieve someone of such information. Ma'at had hidden her well, but the Demoness was growing desperate, and we'd already lost too much at her hand. I would not make the mistake of underestimating her again.

The chatter of quiet conversation began to grow as merchants came bounding into the square. As was their way, wherever humans gathered, music and food followed, and soon there were performers in every corner, and the air was thick with the scent of garlic and figs. Several looks of indignation found their way to her as they spotted her taking up space in the shade. But she ignored their pointed stares, waiting in anxious silence.

Once the cool morning breeze was gone and the square had filled with people, an elderly man made his way through the crowd to stand in front of her. He lowered himself to sit and offered his hands. I waited with my ears pinned until she took them and shut her eyes. A moment later, she opened them to shake her head. Without a word, the man stood as she offered him her condolences. Deben dropped into her open palm as the man turned to leave with tears welling in his eyes, and I wondered what news she had given him.

I watched as people stopped before her, one after the other, each of them dropping deben in her outstretched palm before lowering themselves to the carpet and offering their hands. She would hold them gently, close her eyes, and her posture would soften while the person sat eagerly awaiting a response. Eventually, she would lift her eyes to their face to give them a swift nod or a gentle shake of her head, long, dark locs breezing around her face as she did. Most of them thanked her and left without further question.

She'd had a dozen visitors by the time the sun was high overhead. It seemed like a fair count to me, but she sat in the shade looking dejected—head craning upward and gazing at the sky as if she were pleading with Atem himself. If only she knew how useless he truly was, she wouldn't expect much from his selfishness.

The scent of her fear floated toward me as a warm wind swept between the buildings, and my kan pulled me to my feet. Father's stern words echoed in my mind. "Do not delay in retrieving her. She must be returned to the Hall whether it be of her own will or otherwise." I buried his words as I made my way into a dark alcove to reclaim my human skin. After completing my transformation, I stepped out into the sun to cross the square.

Her head snapped around to find me as I passed through the center, and the scent of fear intensified as she dropped her gaze. I continued through the throng of people—most of them moved without prompting, their spirits telling them to step away from me like mice fleeing from a cat. A few women idled in my path, gaping at me before skirting off to the side. Several of them were admittedly pretty and obviously willing, but my jackal paid them no mind. Its focus was drawn elsewhere.

Her scent shifted, and her heart beat faster as I drew closer—fear, curiosity, or maybe even excitement? A smile slid across my face; it was the perfect cacophony of feeling for what I needed—her trust.

CHAPTER 3
ONIA

A rush of spirit flooded my mind, and I sucked in a shot of air. Wild, passionate energy snaked through my thoughts, pushing past the barrier I'd erected to keep myself from intruding on the spirits of others and settling into a steady flame at the back of my mind. My head spun to find its source, and my eyes landed on a dark stranger towering over the crowd and moving swiftly in my direction.

His onyx eyes were already on me, and I dropped my gaze to force his spirit from my mind. I clamped my eyes shut, trying to find the point where I'd pulled him in. I sifted through my kan, looking for the connection I must have made, but there was no beginning or end. As I watched the flame grow, it became clear it had no origin. There was no push or pull—it was presenting itself to me without prompting.

The man was still watching me when I raised my eyes, and his spirit settled in my mind. Like a needle prick drawing blood, his energy grew stronger with every step, and I fought to tear my eyes away. But as they latched onto him, I was sucked in by his devilishly handsome features and the lethal look staring back at me. Bold tattoos covered his hands and neck, with a V inked into his forehead, coming to a point between his brows. Dark eyes, that looked as though they might swallow you whole if you stared for too long, gazed back at me, unblinking. I watched as hungry eyes followed him across the square. The old merchant women snickered as he passed their stalls. Several of the younger ones took up seductive poses, hoping to catch his attention. But none of them dared step forward. He was far too imposing.

His broad shoulders were thrust backward, burdened by a large leather holster lined with blades, and a black robe was draped over him, kicking up dust around his feet, adding to his overall intimidation. A small smile played along his thick lips, and his strong jaw was set tight with determination. He moved with certainty as he closed in on me, and I wondered if he knew I could see his spirit. If he did, he showed no sign of it. He was striding through the crowd without so much as a glance at the people around him. Bodies parted to give him space until he stood before me—flashing a wide smile and blotting out the sun.

CHAPTER 4

RA

Her emerald eyes blinked up at me as I disrupted the sunlight trickling through the palm leaves, and I was surprised by her penetrating stare. A subtle flush lay across her cheeks from sitting in the heat all day, and her perfectly supple skin glistened with a sheen of sweat from her head to her toes. I resisted the urge to reach out and touch it as a bead of sweat trailed between her breasts.

Her voice rose above the crowd and her face screwed up as I continued staring.

"Can I help you?" she asked in a tone that told me she would not be so easily persuaded.

I gestured at the carpet beneath her.

"May I?" I asked.

She hesitated, her frown deepening. But eventually, she smoothed her face, lifted her chin, and straightened her spine.

"Of course." She smiled sweetly.

She nodded toward the carpet in front of her, and I sat down to offer my hands as I'd seen the others do. She caught a perfectly plump lip between her teeth as her delicate fingers wrapped around my palms and the prickle of kan skirted across our skin—

our energy rising to meet one another. She jerked her hands back, gaping at her fingers. *She must not be familiar with the sensation.* Admittedly, neither was I. Kan rarely responded to one another so enthusiastically, but I managed to keep my face neutral.

"Sorry," she muttered as she tried to hide her surprise.

She reached for me once more. This time ignoring the mild tingle when our fingers met.

"What would you like to know?" she asked.

I paused. I still wasn't sure what she'd been doing here all afternoon. Was she giving fortunes? Surely, it wasn't fortunes. Few people valued the nonsensical mutterings of those who claimed to know the mind of Shai, and she'd had too many eager and pleased patrons for this to be mere fortune telling.

I shrugged and opted for vagueness.

"Whatever you can provide," I said, watching her closely to see if her face may tell me of her intentions.

Her eyes began to wander and take in the rest of me, stalling around my markings, to see where they ended. My robe kept her from following the pattern across my arms and down my chest, but her eyes traced the lines across the backs of my hands until they disappeared under the fabric. The heat of desire blossomed in her scent, and she averted her gaze, turning my palms upward to brush her thumbs across the center.

My markings weren't taboo by any means, but very few wore as many as I did.

She must like them.

I eyed her closely, suppressing an amused smile.

After a couple breaths it was clear she wouldn't act on it.

The jackal responded with disappointment, and I rolled my eyes internally.

It's not my place, I reminded myself.

"Very well," she said, closing her eyes and bowing her head slightly.

She repeated the process I'd seen with the others and sat silent for a long while. I was beginning to think she was playing an elaborate ruse when the sensation of someone prying at my spirit suddenly pricked me. Tendrils of warm energy lifted the layers, pulling at my seams, and searching for more.

Understanding sparked and I settled in to see what she'd find.

This was what people had so unknowingly sought from her—*a reading*—an assessment of their soul. Far more valuable than any fortune if you asked me. Every soul, human and divine alike, was weighed against the feather before making their final journey in the afterlife. She offered a chance to make that journey with certainty —to know your weight before you were judged by the scales and to avoid the fate of the Pit. It was grace she offered.

Of course, the humans wouldn't know. Most were too blind to their own spirits to understand the value of what she offered. They might feel their kan course through them on occasion—when their hearts fluttered as they locked eyes with a lover or when they felt that burning itch to run headlong into danger. That spark of life that raced through them in excitement. But they didn't know what it really was—they never would.

My eyes slid closed by the force of their own will as I savored the gentle separation. She was sifting through me like you would unfurl an aged papyrus, playing along the surface and laying it open for her to read. My kan responded in kind, reaching out to blend with her own wherever our hands met, and I stifled it— afraid she might pull away if the spark grew too loud.

She dove deeper, piercing through the shallow surface and reaching into the darkness underneath. Her kan continued its course, and I stiffened as she closed in on the shadow of my jackal. She was nearing the confines of its cage and would no doubt start prying at the bars if I let her. The jackal grew excited as she drew nearer, and I pulled my hands back. I might be curious about her, but not enough to risk the jackal running free.

She looked up at me with an apology on her plush lips.

"I'm sorry... I don't usually have to dive so deep. You have a great deal of spirit in you."

She fumbled for the right words, but she owed me no apology. I was foolish to think Ma'at's own daughter would be any less gifted. Even if she was half human.

"Well?" I prompted—eager to know her thoughts.

"You have a fierce spirit. Strong-willed and confident..." She worked a charm into her voice. "A wealth of pride and dignity and a deep devotion to your honor." *Shallow complementary words.* "It's a protector's spirit, very admirable," she added, gazing up at me with knowing eyes and blinking past her long lashes.

Smart woman. Aiming for extra coin.

"Well-balanced," she finished.

Her eyes darted away as if the lie tasted sour on her tongue.

Balanced, I certainly was not.

The jackal I kept tied down was indication enough that I would outweigh the feather when the time came. I'd worn us both ragged over the years—serving Father's selfish interests and biting back my own demons. It was undoubtedly heavy. If I died tomorrow, this life would be my last. I knew that.

But why had she lied? There was no use in sparing my feelings.

I stood, fishing in my pockets for the gold deben I carried, but never really found a use for, and dropped the totality of it in her hands. Her eyes grew wide as she clamored to contain the extra coins jostling in her grip and threatening to spill out into the dirt. I had no need for it, and soon she wouldn't either. But as she shoved the coins in her pouch, her scent shifted. The thick scent of fear fell away like a weight removed from her shoulders, and I decided it was well worth the loss.

"Thank you, sematawy," I said.

Her head snapped up to find my eyes as her brows drew together.

Her lips parted like she wanted to say something, but her mouth drew closed and she replaced the confused look with a gentle smile. Before she could dismiss me, I took her hand in mine, ignoring the sharp prickle of kan as our fingers met, and bowed at the waist. Her breath caught at my show of respect. But I continued, lifting her hand to my forehead, and pressing the back between my eyes.

When I finally pulled away, her eyes were wide with shock and heat had spread across her chest. She blinked back at me as I released her and turned to reclaim my place in the shadows.

CHAPTER 5
ONIA

I stood to watch the dark stranger retreat, following his broad shoulders until the crowd swallowed him up. The shout of barters faded into a loud hum as I stood there, waiting for the tingle in my hand to fade. A few of the merchant women were gaping in my direction—probably wondering why a man so handsome was bending to meet my hand.

I was wondering the same.

He had swept it up before I could protest, and by the time he was through, I hadn't the words to ask why. But that question paled in comparison to the one now beating in my brain.

Why can I still feel him?

There was a subtle ember of satisfaction winding its way through my mind—inexplicably foreign and involuntary. His wild spirit had licked up like flames crawling across hot coals, but a stillness like a veil had been carefully draped over the top, smothering the fire down until it was just a glimmer of what lay underneath—a pit of darkness where something powerful lay buried. It was far from balanced and heavier than the feather would ever be. I'd wanted to tell him as much. But as I finished my reading, the look on his face told me he already knew. So, I'd lied.

Maybe he could believe it for a few hours.

My legs moved me forward to the center of the road, and shoulders jerked me from side to side as people pushed past, throwing foul looks in my direction. I stared into the shadows he'd retreated to. Something pressed me to go after him, but my body grew stiff until all I could do was wait for the people to pass. I tried to push him from my mind once more, but his spirit wouldn't dissipate. Once he was well beyond my sight, the flame dimmed until I couldn't make it out anymore, and I was left to my own thoughts.

After a few labored breaths, I returned to my position in the shade.

The heavy clang of the coin in my pocket pulled my thoughts from him. Atem had heard my plea, and he'd given me more than enough for the day and the cycle if I planned properly. I wouldn't have taken it in ordinary circumstances. It was far too much for the simple service I rendered, and I didn't like the idea of being indebted to another's kindness. I'd learned long ago that the kindness of others was rarely freely given; it almost always came with repercussions. It was easier to rely on myself. So far, that'd been working well enough. But the stranger's spirit and his hands—the memory of the odd sensation crawling across my skin ran a shiver down my spine—had left my mind in a daze, and it was too late to go chasing after him.

I huddled under the shade of the palm for a few more hours, waiting until the sun began to dip behind the high city walls before collecting my things. My steps felt noisy as I made my way home, the weight of the deben swinging from my hips. But as I fingered the coins at my side, I somehow felt lighter now that the weight of survival had been lifted from my shoulders.

I took the backways home, not willing to risk the temptation of the merchant stalls and the fragrant lure of roasted garlic. The backways were narrow—built into the small space between large buildings and leading to the edge of the city in a zig-zag pattern—but quiet and clean from lack of use. Which meant I could make my way home uninterrupted.

I tossed a date in the air, aiming for my mouth and leaning back to find my target, but was met with the bitter taste of dirt as my face hit the earth.

I groaned, lifting my knee to my chest, and brushing the bits of gravel from my skin before spinning to face the culprit. A large divot lay in the stone beneath my foot, and I cursed myself for being so careless.

I dragged myself to my knees, enduring the sting of scraped skin as I righted myself.

The remainder of my dates lay strewn across the stone in every direction, and I dismissed them as a gift to the rats. My coins had rolled free of their pouch to lodge themselves in the stone's crevices, and I stood to collect them, swiping the sting from my palms and crouching down to pry them out with my fingers.

I sat hunched over the entrance where one backway joined another, picking at the coins as the light dimmed. Before I knew it, the sun was almost gone, and a slow, eerie scraping, like blades on stone, floated up from the darkness. I stiffened, pausing to isolate the sound. My breathing slowed as I listened.

Silence.

After a few shuddering breaths, I turned, dismissing it as one of the animals come to claim my lost dates, and continued fishing for my coin. As my fingers gripped the final piece, a scaly claw shot out from the darkness to sweep down my arm. Three long, shining talons tore through my skin, and I let out an ear-shattering shriek as I scrambled back on all fours, trying to distance myself from the creature now crouched in the shadows. Two glowing, yellow eyes bore into me, set deep into the skull of a dreadful animal. Scales, like rawhide armor, covered its head and wide crocodilian claws jutted out from its legs where paws would have been. Clutching my arm, I jumped to my feet as the creature passed through the shadows to join me in the narrow alley.

It crept forward, baring its teeth—long, pointed, and crowding in its mouth. I stumbled back as it fixed its massive, lizard-like head in my direction. Small horns dotted the ridges of its skull, giving it height and adding to its menacing presence. The creature paused in its stalking to be joined by two others of identical shape and size. In unison, they crouched low, preparing to strike.

The gashes running down my arm began to throb as the blood poured out of me in thick streaks.

I wouldn't be on my feet much longer.

I took my chance and hauled the heavy bag of deben over one's head. With a crack, it connected, and I spun to sprint for the end of the alley. I made it no more than four steps before a deep-throated snarl rumbled through the close quarters and a familiar flicker of searing hot rage flooded my mind. A giant, black jackal shot out from the dark, sprinting at me head-on.

I brought my arms around my waist, hugging myself and contracting every muscle as I braced for impact. But the jackal tore past me, leaping overhead, and clearing my height with ease.

It collided with the reptilian beasts before they could close in, scraping and tearing into the creatures' flesh without hesitation. The jackal darted around as the lizards lurched forward with talons extended. I told myself to move, but my legs suddenly felt weak, and my head felt like it'd been filled with the smoke of incense. I was dimly aware that the beasts were now tumbling in the dust—a blurry mass of scales and fur.

My legs gave way as I tried to run, and my hands came up to catch me. The skin on my palm tore open as I met the jagged edge of the stone, but I ignored the burning pain to crawl away from the bloodshed, dragging myself along the wall until I was as far from the creatures as the narrow space would allow.

I can't just sit here waiting for death to scoop me up. I need to run. Before one of them remembers I'm here.

Scraping a large chunk out of the nearest creature, the jackal moved with intention, darting between them, and striking where they couldn't see. The creatures were quick, but their hulking bodies were slow in comparison. The jackal struck with speed, meeting its mark before they could even follow the arch of its movements.

The jackal leaped into the air, and the creatures followed it up. But the lizards fell short of its height, colliding with each other and dropping back to the earth. I gaped as the jackal spread its limbs and its front legs stretched through the air, shifting into human appendages. Claws protruded from its fingers, and its torso solidified into chiseled human form while well-muscled legs stretched down to meet the earth. A jackal's head remained, creating a lethal-looking combination of man and beast.

He used his newly opposable thumbs to lift a creature up and tear through it with his jaws. My eyes scanned his familiar build as his teeth sank deep into its neck. An intricate design flashed across his swarthy skin, and my mind halted.

He tossed the dead creature aside, and it rolled to my feet with a stomach-churning slosh before dissolving into a cloud of sparkling dust. The man whirled on me, and my heart hammered in my chest as a pointed muzzle formed handsome human features. I scrambled along the wall, dragging myself backward and slipping as my legs shuffled in the dirt. My hand reached up to cradle my head as a stabbing blow ran through me.

The dark stranger from the market was standing before me with the creatures circling him, and his eyes fixed on me. His lips moved, but no sound came out. I clamped my eyes shut, trying to focus my mind. A shrill screech was ringing in my ears, and a dull thud was keeping rhythm with my heart as a spirit whispered my name...*Onia...Onia...*

"Onia!"

My eyes sprang open and landed on his face.

"Run!"

He ripped a clawed hand from deep within a creature's chest. His voice was interspersed with the guttural sounds of bone and flesh, and I tried to shut out the sickening noise. The body dropped, lifeless, and dissolved until nothing was left but a trickle of blood clotting in the dirt. I wanted to believe I'd imagined it. I might have if it weren't for the last of them still lashing out around his legs.

"Onia, now!"

My mind snapped back into place, and I struggled to get to my feet.

Home.

I righted myself and pushed clumsily out of the backway, slipping through the sliver of space and stumbling onto the road.

My head swam with fractured thoughts.

Door.

Close door.

Hide.

The earth tilted, and my feet tangled in one another.

You will make it home. You will not die in the street.

My legs pushed me forward until I slammed into the door. Using it to prop myself up, my hands fumbled with the simple latch until I pushed it open and collapsed onto the floor. With a grunt, I found the strength to kick it shut.

Something warm oozed down the right side of my face as I cradled my arm to my chest, hoping to bring back some of the feeling. I felt the dark stranger's rage grow into unbridled fury as he struggled with the last of them. I knew I couldn't lie here long. I could still hear the struggle through the thick clay walls. It was only a matter of time before the man was dead, and the creature followed the scent of blood to find me lying here.

I told myself to get up, to run back and help him, but my body protested. My head was suddenly filled with a thousand gold deben, and I fell back to the floor, giving in to the pain and savoring the cool stone against my skin. My lids grew heavy, fluttering closed even as I worked to keep them open. The sound of splintering wood sent my spirit racing and my energy surging through my body. Every part of me objected as I sprang upright.

CHAPTER 6

ONIA

The man stood just inside the threshold, staring down at me—his dark silhouette taking up what little light there was. He was hovering close, and his deep, midnight eyes ran over my body. I could still feel the embers of his spirit burning in my mind, and it immediately swelled as he took in the no-doubt sad state of me. He reached a hand in my direction, and I shuffled back a little, barely making space between us.

He bent at the knees, squatting low to meet my eyes.

For a moment, I was relieved to see his human eyes looking back at me. Something about them was warm and inviting, even as he stood before me covered in blood, but then I took in the rest of him.

The battle-torn version of him was even more overwhelming than the man I'd seen in the square. The claws and canine features had all subsided, replaced by his dark skin and dignified jaw. He was undoubtedly human again—or at least outwardly so. Long gashes that matched my own marked his chest and arms, and a crimson smear was staining his mouth—as if he'd tried to wipe away the evidence of his violence. The blades remained untouched, but streaks of blood now marked his shirt, where he'd hastily cleaned his hands.

"May I come in?" he asked gently, like you'd speak to a frightened animal.

Wise choice.

I was contemplating an escape attempt. Although, I doubted I would make it very far.

His hands hung limp, propped up on his knees, while he held my gaze as if we had all the time in the world. But my arm and head told me that wasn't true. So, I did the only thing I could. I reached out a hand, too weak to read him with my mind alone, and waited until he took it. His fingers curled around my palm and the prickling feeling crept across my skin, but I ignored it. I pierced his soul with my kan, diving past the surface of his spirit without a word.

The flames of his spirit burned at the edges of the veil, threatening to reveal what lay underneath, and something bitter swept through him in waves. He struggled to latch onto the tendrils still whipping through him as he tried to appear less threatening. But it wasn't working. No amount of carefully contained rage could hide the menacing spirit now coursing through him.

I pushed further this time, not hesitating when I reached the edge of the shadowed mass surging up from his core. The wicked force stretched within, eager to reach me as I followed the flame to see how deep the darkness ran. The energy surged but found its limit tied to the careful confines he'd placed it in. It yielded to its bindings.

Is this the beast I'd seen?

It grew farther and farther until, eventually, it was beyond my grasp. I still hadn't reached his core, but some spirits were more complex than others, and it would take much more than my simple probing to reach the heart of the man in front of me.

Yet, somehow, staring at him doused in blood, a stray thought broke through the smoke in my mind.

I'm safe.

I counted my instinct as more than enough reassurance and released him.

He had shut his eyes while I sat sifting through him, and as I pulled my kan back, they opened, revealing a tense but satisfied look.

"Well?" he asked, cocking a dark brow.

I managed a slight nod before my arm gave out, and my body found the hard stone beneath me. Without instruction or regard to my protest, he stood to his full height, ducking to keep from hitting the ceiling, and scooped me up to set me on the stool nearest the hearth.

My eyes drifted toward the open door, and with little more than a flick of his finger, it swung shut, and the latch fell into place. I dismissed it as another oddity of the stranger before me and chose to focus on keeping my brain between my ears.

"Don't worry; they're gone."

His voice echoed throughout the room, making his presence known, and I had difficulty discerning if he was lying to me. Usually, I would know without question, but my head was now pounding. His blazing spirit had subsided into a dim flame. I reached a hand to my head, hoping to ease the searing ache, but froze as something sticky and warm oozed across my fingers.

"They're not the ones I'm worried about," I said, watching the blood string between my fingers as I pulled my hand from my hair.

"Stop talking. You've lost a lot of blood."

My irritation sparked.

Who is he to speak to me like that? Especially now.

I may be injured, but I wasn't dim. It was becoming clear I may die tonight, and I didn't deserve his harsh words before I went.

I wanted to say as much, but my mind wouldn't clear enough for the words to form.

Lucky him.

My eyes fell on the floor where I'd been lying, and a gasp slipped from me. Blood was pooling at the entrance, seeping under the door and leaching into the rugs.

How am I still awake—or even breathing, for that matter?

The man knelt before me with concern carving up his chiseled face, and without touching me, began his survey of my wounds. He paid careful attention to the claw mark running down my arm and the blood collecting in my hair. He hesitated before lifting my locs away from my ear to assess the damage.

"There's a gash above your ear, and..."

His eyes fell on my blood-soaked arm—the rest of the damage was apparent.

"There's an old sunu at the edge of our quarter," I said, bracing myself to stand and make my way to the door.

The warmth of his hand met my chest, and a faint tingling spread across my skin as he lowered me back onto the stool.

"You're not going anywhere," he said.

As if the marks on my arm were no more than a minor scrape.

My brows lifted in response.

"Give me your hands," he demanded.

"I don't think—"

Before I could object, he took them, straightening my left arm and gripping my wrists. I sucked in a breath and shot him a look, but he continued without paying me any mind.

"I will give you my kan. Enough to heal you."

Give me kan?

"How are you going to—"

"Just be quiet. The more questions you ask, the longer until I heal you and the closer you are to the scales." He ground out between clenched teeth.

I fought the urge to slap him. Not that I could manage it even if I gave in. There was no sense in fighting him. I was at his mercy, and I would either be miraculously healed or die waiting for him to realize I required a proper healer.

With a tenuous glare, he turned my hands over, palms up. I fixed my expression, biting down so as not to wince at the movement. His grip moved up my arm, and I suppressed a cringe as searing hot pain shot through me. This time he stilled, giving me a chance to find my breath before continuing. Then began tracing small, lazy circles inside my wrists.

A dim, golden glow rose along his markings to seep into me, trailing across my skin as it followed the path of his fingers. The sensation was inviting and familiar, and I recognized it as the same spirit that persisted at the back of my mind—warm and wild, but well-tamed. The light moved through me, traveling up my arms and lingering in my shoulders. Year-old tension disappeared from my neck as the heat sloped down and settled into my chest. My heart slowed to a steady calm.

I hadn't noticed it was racing until it suddenly wasn't.

A warmth of my own was winding together in my stomach as his kan moved through me, touching every aching part of me and wrapping it in healing energy. My eyes fluttered closed, and I moaned an involuntary sigh of relief. I ought to have been embarrassed, but I couldn't find the feeling. I couldn't find *any* feeling other than a gentle calm coursing through me.

His energy was better than any remedy the sunu could ever offer. My body felt light in a way it hadn't in years, and I was skeptical of the man in front of me for eliciting such a response. In less than a minute, he'd managed to satisfy my body in a way no other man had, and he was barely touching me.

When I opened my eyes, another shock ran through me. The three ugly gashes were now three faint lines running the length of my arm, still visible but only a few shades darker than the rest of me, and not nearly as catastrophic. The blood had already dried in place, making the scars look angrier than they were. I reached up to feel under the clot matting my locs together only to find no evidence of my fall. Except for a fine, raised line just above my ear. The pounding in my head had stopped, and I gaped as the wound in my palm mended itself before my eyes.

I looked up to study the man's features. His focus was clear—eyes closed, shoulders dropped, his towering form leaning into me. He was a picture of serenity aside from the blood still covering him. The warmth began to recede then, retreating along the path it had taken, and I had to stop myself from gripping his hands to drink in more.

CHAPTER 7

ONIA

As the heat faded from my fingers, he straightened—the tension returning to his jaw, and we sat in silence for a moment. I had hoped his energy would silence the noise of his spirit in my mind, but the flame was still burning bright, flickering and twisting as he sat looking at me. I latched onto it, pulling it closer to examine. This time following its light to find myself face to face with the mass of darkness underneath. He'd smothered the torrent of energy in a masterful composure, but I found myself digging deeper once more—my curiosity winning out.

"Could you not do that?" he asked in a short, clipped tone.

I froze.

Is he talking to me?

He was speaking into the floor with his hands balled into tight fists.

"What?" I asked.

"Your surveying can be quite...jarring."

His hands flexed and released as they rested on his muscular thighs.

"I-I'm sorry," I blurted. "No one's ever felt my readings before. I didn't think—"

"Yes, well, I'd appreciate it if you kept your kan to yourself."

Says the man who was just pouring his into me with abandon.

I held my comment in and tried to remind myself to be grateful. If it weren't for him, my brain would probably be pouring out of my nose by now.

I pulled my kan back as far as I could, retreating from the depth of his spirit until all I could feel was the warm flicker of a single flame. But I couldn't douse it entirely.

I tried again, closing my eyes for added focus.

The flame wavered like a candle in the wind but stood strong, burning hot and steady.

I prepared myself to confess my accidental prying, but as I opened my eyes, he was no longer sitting with clenched fists and a tight jaw. His broad shoulders had relaxed, and he leaned back into the chair, stretching his arms behind his head.

"Better?" I tested.

"Yes, thank you."

I smiled to myself. He didn't know I could still see it. It wasn't the same depth of expression as a full reading, but it was enough to show me his intentions.

That should come in handy.

"How's your arm?" he asked, sitting up and leaning in close.

I tested it, holding it out and twisting it this way and that.

"Good as new, I think." I couldn't even feel the gentle tug of freshly healed scars. But that wasn't my main concern.

"What were those?" I asked, glancing past him to the blood on the floor.

"Shabti—soul eaters," he said firmly.

I almost laughed.

"The demons of the Pit?" I prompted, suppressing an incredulous look.

Shabti were the stuff of legends. Threats that mothers told

their children to send them off to bed at night or keep them from wandering off in the marketplace. Surely, they hadn't been lurking behind the city walls.

"You question your own eyes?" he pressed, gesturing between us.

Wide claw marks marred the fabric they'd savaged on his chest and my own scars glared back at me.

"No. I question strange men who shift from man to beast in the blink of an eye and tear through demons like parchment," I said, crossing my arms and daring him to lie to me.

A satisfied smile slid across his face as he matched my stance.

"I'm no stranger," he started. "And I'm no man." He eyed me with expectation.

I dropped my gaze. That much was clear. But I wouldn't give him the satisfaction of asking *what* he was. He was clearly having too much fun keeping me guessing.

I waited in silence until he saw fit to elaborate.

"I am Ra. Son of Anubis, Guardian to Ma'at, and protector of the dead."

He bowed his head slightly as he finished his introduction.

My heart raced. Guardian to *the* goddess? Son of the jackal?

His spirit was easy, and he spoke with pride in his voice—he was speaking the truth. But none of that explained his presence in my home or the persistent presence of his spirit in my mind.

"And why are you here, Ra, son of Anubis?" I imitated his tone of grandeur.

"I'm here to ensure you are safe," he answered simply.

I eyed him with open suspicion.

"Safe from what?" I pressed, my patience growing thin.

"Ammit, the Demoness," he said her name like a curse.

A shudder ran through me as the image of her crocodile head gulping down souls ran through my mind. A vision of Father's spirit slipping through her teeth left me cold. The Demoness was known by many names, but her most feared title was "The

Devourer of Souls." Every ailing person spent their time sorting the balance of their spirit so they wouldn't fail the test of Ma'at and meet the Demoness face-to-face. Most of my patrons came to me with such worries—questions about their souls and whether they'd struck a proper balance. Very few received a resounding "yes."

"What does she want with me? I'm still alive!"

Ra frowned at me.

"You need not play at ignorance. I know who you are. Your mother shared her secret with my father. He's sent me to bring you home," he asserted.

"My mother?"

His eyes rolled before they settled on my face to stare at me with open irritation.

"Yes, your mother—Ma'at, Goddess of the Hall and Justice of Souls?"

My heart hammered in my chest, and his brows drew together with a shock of their own.

"He didn't tell you?" He ran a tense hand over his closely shaved head and let out a sigh. "Damn," he cursed, and I didn't dare move an inch. "Your mother sent you to this realm for safekeeping. She left you with your father to watch over you—he should have told you this."

I continued with my blank expression. Father had never so much as mentioned Ma'at other than to tell me he would gladly go to her when the time came. The topic of my mother was equally as scarce. He only brought her up to tell me of her beauty and how she loved me with all her heart. I'd assumed she'd died by the way his eyes glistened when he spoke of her. But he'd never said, so I'd never asked. Believing her dead was easier than facing the alternative.

With a huff, Ra continued. "Onia, we don't have time. Ma'at passed through several days ago." He spoke solemnly, avoiding my eyes.

My eyes narrowed on him, fixing on his engulfing stare.

"My mother, the Empress of the Hall, judgment place of all souls, has passed through?" I asked, unable to hide my disbelief.

"Three nights ago, she was found murdered in the Hall. Old age may never kill us, but even we are susceptible to another's lust for power."

I ignored his pointed use of "we."

"You mean to say someone is trying to take her place? The Demoness?"

I used the honorary title rather than her proper name, as he had. He may go about provoking her spirit, but I would not.

Ra didn't answer immediately. Instead, he looked at me expectantly as if he was waiting for the tears to come pouring out of me. I suppose he'd anticipated more emotion, but I wasn't sure how I should feel. Surprised, scared, and vengeful all came to mind—she was my mother, after all. Perhaps the answer was some combination of the three. Although, I also wasn't particularly fond of crying in front of strange men, and I'd gotten used to the hollow feeling I felt each time I thought of her. I'd spent twenty-five years without her; this day was no different than any other. So, I absorbed his words without feeling—the tears could wait.

"Or keep someone else from taking her place..." His dark eyes turned sad. "Onia, you are your mother's rightful heir, her sole successor—"

I was up and across the room before he could stop me.

He continued quickly, trying to get the words out before I could run sprinting through the streets.

"Ammit has grown greedy; she wants the seat of Ma'at, *your* seat, to remain empty. She sent her shabti to ensure you don't return."

My mind was empty again, and I took up pacing in front of him.

"You're a reader, Onia. You can peer into a person's soul and see them for what they are. You know I'm speaking the truth."

He was right. I could see it in his spirit as he spoke. But his confession left me stunned—not the assertion of my birthright but the repercussions of an empty Hall. If the seat of Ma'at was empty, what would come of the souls that journeyed through? Where would they go if not to the Hall? Where would *Father* go? The image of his soul slipping through the Demoness's teeth struck me again. Raw emotion pricked my eyes, and I bit down on my cheek, stifling it as best I could.

"Onia, we must leave. I will answer any question asked of me, but right now, we can't stay here. They will return now that they've found you."

I continued pacing, ignoring his plea for action, but he snatched up my hand as I passed, pulling me to a stop. He jerked me around to face him, and I found him in a shocking stance.

With one knee on the floor, he held out a single unsheathed blade, offering it to me.

"As the next Empress of the Hall, my duty as Guardian of Ma'at now falls to you. I will protect you, but we must return to the Hall immediately. This realm is not safe any longer. Ammit knows you are here. They will return."

My legs felt stiff.

This man was knelt before me, asking me to abandon my home and flee from vengeful gods and hungry demons, but I couldn't move. This house was the last of Father's spirit, and leaving meant adding to that hollow hole inside me. The one that reminded me with every breath that I was all I had left.

Somewhere deep inside, I latched on to that feeling. I couldn't lose the memory of him too.

I'd seen myself through every other tragedy; this one would be no different.

"I have no plans of leaving here with you," I said, planting my feet and yanking my hand free. "Thank you for saving me and healing me, but I can take care of myself."

I did my best not to shout. I wasn't angry with him, but my

mind was racing. It was all I could manage not to shriek my defiance at him.

Ra's jaw clenched as he fixed his gaze on me and lowered his voice to a firm baritone that reverberated through the room.

"If you stay here, you will die, and I cannot allow that." A shiver ran down my spine as his dark eyes leveled me with a hard stare.

The word "die" hung in the air, making the already small space feel cramped and stifling, like someone had sealed every window and closed us in on a hot summer day. His spirit turned tense as he awaited my response.

"I-you..." I faltered, suddenly feeling hot all over.

"Onia?"

I paused, trying to catch my breath and wishing the room would stop shrinking.

"Onia."

Ra's deep voice was laced with worry, and I felt his spirit grow louder. My name mixed with a steady murmur at the back of my mind, fighting its way to the front.

"Are you—"

The voice droned as the murmur turned into a warbled throng —nothing distinct, just noise. My chest burned, and my breath caught as I swayed forward, reaching out an arm to balance myself. Black spots flooded my vision, sending me reeling. A dark hand reached across the empty space, and metal clanged to the ground as smoke filled my mind.

I tried to focus on him. The spark of his skin against mine, the tattooed lines across his hands, his encompassing stare...

But the spots took over, narrowing my vision to a needlepoint and making my knees soft. Then suddenly, I was floating.

The subtle scent of patchouli and musk drifted through my mind, and I reached for it. I wanted to wrap myself in it. To let it cradle me until my mind quieted. But I couldn't find it. It was calling me from deep inside, whispering with worry—unease rising from the depths of something dark.

CHAPTER 8
RA

I was holding her up before her body could slump to the floor, but I should have moved sooner. I'd heard the strain in her heart, but my knowledge of her half-human form failed me. I'd assumed it was just fear causing the sweat to collect on her chest. I cursed myself. I should have been more tender. But we didn't have time for tender words. We'd already spent too much time here. We needed to leave before the night was through.

I held her close, listening as her heart turned back to a steady, even pace and her breathing deepened. The jackal struggled against its restraints to pull her closer, and I took a moment to tighten its bonds before deciding what came next.

Father's words sounded in my mind, "her own will or otherwise," he had said, with a vicious scowl on his stubborn face. It wasn't a unique occurrence. He almost always looked that way, considering he let his jackal rule without question. But in this instance, he was right to be full of fury. If I didn't secure her, she would be...the Hall would be lost.

That wasn't an option.

My grip tightened around the curve of her waist, holding her up as I sorted through my options. Night had fallen in earnest as we sat arguing about the threat to her life. At this hour, no one would wander the streets this far from the city center, and few would notice my carrying a woman in my arms. Far darker things occurred in the eastern district of Ashwana after nightfall. Our blood-smattered clothes were more likely to turn heads.

I slid her body down, propping her against the wall to follow her scent into the next room. A wooden trunk lay at the foot of one bed—the scent of lavender and sage wafting out in thick waves. I stifled the urge to breathe it in and dug through the trunk, discarding the tops for something appropriate. Several piles of fabric lay by my feet before I pulled the dark linen kalasiri from the bottom. It was light, comfortable, and well-worn, but most importantly, it wouldn't garner unwanted attention. I set it aside to find myself something suitable. There was no other trunk in the room, only a small bed sitting opposite hers, steeped in the scent of death, and a singular tunic lying folded on top—a man's shirt, I was certain. Older, from the smell of it. Her father's. I hesitated to tarnish her memory of him, but the room was otherwise empty—it would have to do. Although, I would need to address the odor. I wrapped the kalasiri atop her blood-covered clothes and discarded my shirt for the one that reeked of death.

I'd been wrong about the dress. Even in the simple fabric, she was alarmingly beautiful. I simply had to hope that the cover of night was on my side, and we would go unnoticed. Her breathing was soft, and her kan prickled in response as I pulled her to her feet. I wound an arm around her waist and propped her up against me, making it look as natural as two lovers wandering the streets in a beer-soaked haze.

As anticipated, the streets were empty, and I only had to feign affection twice. When a group of young men bounded by, jeering at the sight of us, I ducked my head to her neck, covering her face and wrapping her in my arms until they passed. My jackal jolted as I pulled her closer, but I ignored its impulse. As we passed under

Atem's watchful eyes at the west entrance, I lifted her long legs into my arms.

At least this is easier than dragging her through the sand kicking and screaming.

I continued west until the sand met the water. The tall grasses along the bank provided ample cover from the elements and animals—shabti or otherwise. Bending the reeds beneath her, I laid her down, so she rested on a bed of grass rather than the hard, packed earth.

She stirred beside me as I set about removing the kalasiri to reveal the blood-soiled shift. My body stiffened, and my jackal whined, as the edges hiked up around her thighs, threatening to reach her hips. I steeled my nerve and pulled it from her blindly, using it to gather water and wash the crimson smear from her body until she was clean from the carnage and the scent of death only hung in the air. I avoided her more sensitive areas, too conscious of her beauty and the warmth of her coppery skin. I tried to ignore the tingling of her kan each time my fingers grazed her, but the foreign feeling was igniting my own, fueling some quiet craving I didn't know I had. It was a pleasant sensation. The question of its origins less so.

I dressed her quickly, not wanting to agitate my spirit any further, and made my way into the water to free myself from the filth of demons.

The memory of her scream surfaced as I scrubbed at the patches of blood, and I smothered my rage. I'd run sprinting through the streets at the sound—I wasn't willing to fail her, not again—but I was too late, and she hadn't made it out unscathed. Her heart was withering when I burst through the door. I guessed the strength of her spirit was the only thing keeping her on this side of the Fall.

I was confident I'd restored her fully—perhaps even more so. Once I'd opened my kan to hers, it'd been difficult to stop. The urge to heal every aching muscle and strained tendon was hard to ignore. In the end, I'd given her more of me than I had planned.

I glanced down at her body curled in the grass. The air was thick and warm. Even in the dead of night, the glisten of sweat was budding on her face. Then, as if Shu had whispered beside me, a cool breeze swept across the bank, gently tousling her hair.

I'd have to thank him for his timely nature when I saw him next.

Her delicate brow was set with determination, even as she slept, and I knew she would run when the opportunity arose. I settled beside her and draped an arm across her body, tucking her close. She might not take kindly to my nearness come morning, but I was sure she'd prefer it to being bound with grass, so she didn't flee in the night.

Her tall frame had been shaking with rage as she spouted her defiance, and the image of her screeching at me when she realized I'd removed her from her home left me mildly amused. But she would not deter me. So long as she made it to the Hall, she could loathe me all she wished.

CHAPTER 9
ONIA

The sound of rushing water met my ears, and the scent of sweet grass wafted up from somewhere beside me. I stretched, savoring the softness of my bed, and trying to burrow deeper. My hands gripped the fabric beneath me, only to find dust under my fingers. I shot up from my place on the ground.

The glare of light striking the water stung my eyes as I tried to take in my surroundings. It was early morning, the sun was just peeking out over the horizon, and the earth was beginning to warm. I squinted and pushed up on my arm before panicking and remembering the slice of bony claws tearing through my flesh. I snatched my arm back, cradling it to my chest before the pain came coursing through. But the memories came trickling in instead. Images of demons lunging for me. The scent of musk washing over me as my eyes slid shut. A tender sensation and a handsome man holding me tight to his chest.

He had to be nearby—his sizable form was hard to miss. I straightened to peer over the grass, scanning the bank until I found him—crouched low, bare-backed, and working something in his hands. The ridges of his shoulders deepened as the muscles flexed under the pressure of his concentration. I eased myself to my knees, wondering if I could sprint through the grass in time to hide before he turned around. The grass grew dense and high here, stopping at my hips. It would be a trudge to make it to the grove of palms further down, but if I made it, I could hide among them.

I anchored my legs, rocking back until I sat crouched in the grass, balancing on the balls of my feet.

"I wouldn't if I were you." Ra's deep voice called from the bank, and I bolted, hiking my knees up to my chest and pushing through the grass with as much speed as my legs would allow. I'd expected a deep ache in my muscles but found them surprisingly lithe and loose. I silently thanked him for whatever he had done to aid in my escape.

Dried grass crunched beneath my feet as I tore down the bank. My arms pumped in time with my legs. Air whipped through my hair, sending my locs flying out behind me. The flame of his spirit burned hot with irritation as I pressed on.

The sound of my steps ceased as strong arms lifted me from the earth, carrying me backward.

"Put me down!" I shouted.

"I asked you not to." Ra's voice reverberated through me, and my eyes rolled of their own volition.

"No, you *told* me not to... There is a difference," I sassed.

His spirit responded with interest, only to be stifled quickly with mild anger.

"*Please*, do not run," he corrected with a huff, and I had a feeling his eyes were rolling too.

He waited patiently for my answer, holding me to his chest even as I slapped at his arms. I was still kicking and flailing as his impatience grew. Eventually, my limbs grew tired, and I let my body go limp.

"Fine!" I shouted after a minute of dangling above the grass.

"Thank you," he muttered. Although, I wasn't sure it was really to me.

He pulled away, and I contemplated another attempt. He was eyeing me like he *wanted* me to run. Something told me he had enjoyed our brief chase. But he stood silent, waiting for me to decide.

My pride told me to run, and he tensed as I took a step back, preparing himself for another sprint. I narrowed my gaze, craning my neck to face him. I was reminded of his impossible height as I had to work to meet his eyes. Most men hardly met my chin. Then again, this wasn't a mere man before me.

He turned to make his way back to the water, and I watched the red-orange tint of early morning sun light his skin. The warmth made his deep color look rich, and my eyes wandered as I studied the markings across his back. The intricate design wasn't just along his hands—it was everywhere. Across every limb, black lines spread out from a uniquely shaped ankh between his shoulder blades. The handle was formed from a hawk's wings, arching up to meet a simple depiction of the sun, and a small scarab beetle sat in the cross-section with its outstretched wings forming the bar. Lines spiraled out in every direction, reaching up and over his shoulders, then down the length of his arms. It was a masterful work of art, more elegant than his hands would lead you to believe and beautiful enough to draw you in.

The source of my distraction was snuffed out as creamy linen draped over his skin, and he turned to face me.

"Where did you get that?" I asked.

It was the same shirt Father had worn on his final day, and my face scrunched up to hide the pain.

"Ah, this was all I could find, and mine was no longer suitable to be seen in public."

He motioned absentmindedly to the pile of fabric lying by the bank. His blood-soaked shirt lay folded atop a red-tinted fabric that I recognized as the shift I'd been wearing. I glanced down at myself for the first time since my escape attempt.

Gone was the simple shift.

I now stood perfectly wrapped in my favorite kalasiri. The pleated folds were draped with care, sloping down in a V-shape along my front and the skirt wrapped loosely around my waist to join in the back, leaving my sides bare. It was a traditional draping that I hadn't worn before, but it was beautiful and comfortable. But none of that excused the fact he had stripped me bare in my sleep.

"Did you—"

"Yes," he interrupted. "My senses are quite keen; you'll find I don't need my eyes for much." He shot me an uninterested look in the process. I bit my lip, ignoring the disappointing sting. He was handsome enough to share a bed with. *More than handsome enough.* Under different circumstances, I might not mind what he'd seen. But his easy dismissal of that prospect was surprisingly hurtful.

"You had no right!"

My screeching didn't faze him.

"Would you rather I left the blood to dry in your hair?" he asked pointedly.

"I would have *rather* you not carry me off while unconscious!"

He continued his work without acknowledging my presence or my plight.

"You gave me no choice. Father requires your presence, and you are remarkably stubborn for someone with death knocking on her door."

His refusal to match my anger drove me deeper into my own, and I lashed out, latching on to the cold and bitter feeling that surfaced in his spirit as he mentioned Anubis.

"And I suppose you always do as your father asks?" I snipped.

His spirit reacted then, flames flaring high and the darkness threatening to spill out of its cage. I took a step back. He followed, bringing his face close to mine and glaring at me over his wide nose.

"As your guardian, my duty is to you and the Hall. Both of which will suffer if you are not returned to your rightful place!" He was shouting now, and a thick vein came to life in his neck. "So, yes, in this instance, I will do as my father demands. But do not mistake me for a mere pawn," he finished, and his jaw set tight as he went about clenching his teeth in silence.

The image of him propped on one knee, blade outstretched, surfaced from my memory.

Before I could say anything, he trudged off to return to his work near the water.

Fleeing wasn't out of the question, but I wasn't particularly fond of the idea. I doubted I'd be successful. His height alone meant he outpaced my stride easily, and I knew he was far from reaching his limit. *I* would likely fall victim to the heat within the hour. The sun was already streaming over the dunes to the east, and the cool morning breeze had ceased. Even sticking to the shade along the river, I wouldn't stand a chance at outrunning him. But even if I could, I wasn't sure I wanted to.

Ra's confession was enough to leave me wanting more—a chance to know Mother, to know myself...I'd come to terms with the mysteries of my life long ago, but now that he was here, offering me a chance to know, I was hesitant to abandon the opportunity. If I let it pass me by, I was sure I'd regret it. Not to mention Father's spirit finding its final resting place in the Pit. There was also the very real possibility that I'd be killed by demons before I could take even five steps without him.

A chill crept down my spine at the memory of their yellow eyes and pointed teeth. I glanced back at my ill-mannered rescuer as I made my way to my makeshift bed. The indentation of my body was still pressed into the grass, along with a larger, more defined version close beside it.

Argh! Does he know no boundaries?

What may be the worst of it all was that my body had betrayed me. Somehow, I'd managed to have the deepest sleep in over a year, lying here in the dirt, next to a man who'd kidnapped me. But I suppose it could have been worse—he could have been ugly.

"I've decided to stay," I said as I came to stand beside him.

"Praise Isis, the heavens will weep," he muttered under his breath.

My teeth ground together as I forced myself to ignore his comment.

"But—" I began. If he thought I would simply go along without question, he was sorely mistaken. He blew out a puff of air and pressed his fingers to his eyes. "You will answer my questions."

"I believe I've already agreed to those terms," he responded with an amused smile tugging at his lips. My kan sparked as it took in the fire in his eyes, and I stamped out the heat swelling in my core. I would not be falling for his glittering smile and chiseled face, not after what he'd done.

His words crept up from my memory—"I will answer any question asked of me."

So he had...

"What happened?" I asked.

"You fainted," he said, lifting his fingers to hover near the side of my face. His eyes turned heated as he dropped them and added, "I think your spirit was overwhelmed. I didn't mean to give you so much. But I couldn't risk the alternative. Forgive me."

I blinked in response.

Was that an apology?

As I stood stunned, for what felt like the hundredth time today, he turned to bend down into the dirt.

"Your spirit should be at its full strength now. You shouldn't have anything to worry about."

His hands were working deftly to untie a makeshift netting he'd woven from the fibers of dry grasses. Beside him, several fish lay flat in the sun while another lay lifeless in his net.

"I thought you might be hungry. It's no roasted dates, but it will have to do."

He flayed the fish and removed the bone before roasting them in a wrapping of palm leaves.

Eventually, I sat beside him and fixed my eyes on the water in front of me. When he was satisfied that they'd been cooked through, he began picking at the steaming white flesh and dropping it in my palm. After I'd collected three pieces in my hand, I pulled away.

"What are you doing?" I asked, confusion contorting my face.

"It's very hot," he answered simply.

"I am not a child," I snapped, snatching the palm leaf from him, leaving his hands empty.

"No. You certainly aren't, sematawy," he grumbled as he got to his feet.

My head whipped around—there was that name again.

"Why do you keep calling me that?"

My knowledge of Kemi, the old tongue, was limited to the more common words and phrases I'd translated in Father's work. But "sematawy" was a name he'd called me since I was a girl. It meant "Lady of the Two Lands." I'd just assumed it was a nickname he'd conjured up.

Ra was glaring at me with open irritation but answered anyway.

"You are of two lands, no?" He paused, watching me closely. "This land." He pointed to the earth beneath his feet. "And that one." He gestured toward the open sky.

He meant my divine parentage, joining together with a mortal one to create me—a spirit straddling two realms. I swallowed my temper. It was an apt description, I must admit, and another piece to confirm what I now knew was a long-held secret on Father's part.

"I suppose," I said, hating that I had to admit he was right.

"Then stop frowning," he ordered, throwing the words over his shoulder as he stepped away to eat in isolation.

CHAPTER 10

RA

My kan had settled after my outburst. I wasn't in the habit of letting my spirit wander unchecked, but it lit up every time she questioned me, and as much as I enjoyed the challenge of her heated words, we did not have time for her defiance. Ammit would not wait for a time that was convenient to her, and we had more significant concerns than quibbling over boundaries. The journey to Mahatnaten was long, and it wouldn't be easy. The northern desert lay between us, and the sun could be cruel on long journeys, even along the Nile.

My jackal wasn't pleased with my decision to leave her sitting in the sun alone, and as I moved closer to the bank, the kan in my legs became stiff as it fought against me.

You are not in charge here, I thought as I snuffed out the fire it was stoking.

It'd taken long enough for me to gain control of my jackal's power. It sought out its every whim, making for a wild spirit when left to roam freely. Shu was the one who taught me how to draw from it and use it to my favor. Once I'd managed to gain a hold on it, my jackal and I had been as one ever since. I couldn't say the same for Father or the others. Father called on his for every minor inconvenience. So much so I sometimes wondered who he'd be without it. When I did call on mine, it was not for slight reason. The power it harbored was so great it often destroyed all that was in its path. Hence, the strong bonds I'd placed it in.

But this woman had brought it to life—with her smart mouth and heated glares. My jackal was fighting its bonds to reach out to her. It was excited at the prospect of their play, but I couldn't allow its fickle affections to cloud my judgment. Her survival must come above all else.

The soft scent of lavender blew across the bank, and my head followed the wave back to her. She was sitting in the sand with her legs folded under her, eating absentmindedly—the same gentle frown taking up space on her beautiful face.

Does she ever stop? At this rate, she could give Father a run for his money.

Her eyes came up to find my face. For a brief moment, her brows softened, then she turned from me, jutting her chin out and focusing her gaze on anything other than mine.

I couldn't blame her.

My actions had been brutish, but it was for the best. The shabti would be crawling the city looking for her, and even I could only handle so many. She would simply have to go on frowning.

<hr>

ONIA

I ate quickly. The sheer force of hunger gripping my stomach had me scarfing down the simply cooked fish as it if were honey-soaked fig bread.

I twisted around to peer behind me. The high walls of the city were far from view. We were at least a few hours' walk from the nearest entrance, and the closest village was almost two days away.

Where are we planning to go? Surely, the shabti were capable of following us across the desert sands.

As if he could hear me, Ra called from the bank.

"We will go to Mahatnaten. That is where we will find the nearest entrance to the Hall."

The sacred city of Ma'at? How would that give us passage to the divine realm?

I turned to see him watching me, and he was ready with an answer before I could ask.

"To enter the Hall, we must go the way of the dead."

"To die?" I gasped, choking on the chunk of fish I'd just stuffed into my mouth.

A broad grin spread across Ra's face, and a dimple peeked out on his left side, softening the sharp lines of his face.

"You think I'd lay demons at your feet just to let you die at the gates of the Hall?" He suppressed a laugh, and his smile spread wider, but he didn't dwell on my embarrassment. Instead, he added quickly, "No, only humans must die to pass through to the Hall. We are gods. It will not reject us."

He spoke with the confidence I wished I had. But my anxiety was weighing on me. I wasn't keen on relying on strangers. I much preferred to place my life in the hands of someone I could trust— me.

We started on our journey in silence, slogging through the sand and speaking only when necessary. The ground was hot on my feet, but I didn't mind it. It pressed me to move quicker than I otherwise would, and the sooner we reached the Hall, the sooner I'd be free of Ra and his overbearing nature. I took a position a few paces ahead of him, occupying my thoughts with the scenery. Not that there was much to see, other than cubits and cubits of sand. Walking along the water, there was a bit more variety, but even the animals knew better than to breach the surface at this time of day. I wrapped my bloodied shift around my face in a feeble attempt to keep the sun from beating on me. But once the sun was overhead, it was no use. Its rays reached me at every angle, and I resigned myself to sweating through the makeshift headdress.

CHAPTER II

RA

We left before the sun was too high, and the creatures began to stir. Before setting out, I watched her hand come to her chest as she said her silent goodbye. But then as if she'd been replaced entirely, her delicate features hardened like smooth stone and her resolve came to the front. I had to commend her for the effort to conquer her fear. Someone less observant might have believed it. But her teeth had taken a gentle hold on her bottom lip, betraying her. Guilt pierced my spirit as I recalled the night that had led us here.

The Hall was dark, and the sound of mangled cries erupted through the rotunda the moment I stepped through my passage. The tinge of copper hung heavy in the air, and my jackal was rising to the front, but I dampened it. I jerked backward before two blades crossed in front of me, aiming for my neck. They locked with one another, and I turned my attention to the guardians wielding them. Abraxas and Nejeri glowered at me before realization dawned, and they lowered their weapons.

"What happened?"

"Brother." Abraxas began with a worried look, but I shouldered past him, pushing toward the scales where the copper smell gathered into a thick fog.

"Brother, he is angry," he warned, barely a whisper, only for my ears.

I grunted in response and continued past the soul pool. My steps echoed loudly in the empty corridor, ringing in my ears as I stepped into the rotunda. Guardians stood under every arched entrance. Heads swiveled in my direction, and the slosh of blood sounded under my feet as I stepped under the scales.

Whose blood was this?

Father surged to his feet, and the thought was torn from me as he screamed in my face.

"You dare to shame this house!" he roared.

He raised a wide, clawed hand, and I didn't flinch away from him. I'd seen this look of madness before. Avoiding it would only worsen my fate. I braced myself.

Claws scraped down my chest in a brutal arc.

Mother rushed to place herself in Father's path, but he battered her aside. She clawed at him, pleading—clinging to him as tears streamed down her face. Then she collapsed to the floor in a heap. I was confused why she didn't fight for me as she did Amon.

Her shouts echoed through the chamber as Father's hand cut across me again—

"Goddess, can he walk any slower?" Her soft, honey voice jerked me back to the present. The words were hushed, not meant for my keen ears. But they met them anyway, and the jackal perked up at her clever tongue, chipping away at my sympathy.

"This pace is for your benefit, sot nesu," I called out.

She turned, kicking up dust as she skidded to a stop.

Her chest burned hot as she realized I'd heard her, and I stepped in close, forcing her to lift her chin to meet my eyes. My control faltered as her emerald eyes looked up at me, and the words rolled off my tongue before I could stop them.

"In fact, it may be faster if I carried you."

"You wouldn't," she said, issuing her challenge in return.

I lifted a brow in response—unable to resist. Part of me wanted to see how far she'd go in the name of her stubbornness. Her arms crossed in a show of defiance, and I had to admit, she was stunning when angry—eyes ablaze and sheer determination surrounding her like armor.

As expected, her pride kept her from backing down, but she didn't know me very well. Guardian or not, she wouldn't continue throwing barbs from that wicked mouth of hers. Not so long as they were directed at me.

She was over my shoulder before her bitter words could leave her lips.

I continued at my "leisurely" pace as she pounded her discontent into my back. The jackal's spirit surged as it witnessed her defiance, and the spark in my hands heated until a vibrant hum played along my fingers. I drank in the feeling, savoring the simple touch more than any guardian should.

CHAPTER 12
ONIA

R a had slung me over his shoulder, and I'd been hanging there ever since. I'd ran out of fight after a few hours. It would have been a nice break from marching through the endless sand if it weren't for the fact that I was about to lose my breakfast—not to mention the precarious placement of his hands.

He balanced my weight with a hand splayed across my bare thigh and another round my waist, sending our kan bouncing back and forth in a frenzy. The sensation left me willing to remain hanging over his broad back indefinitely, but I wouldn't give him the satisfaction. He'd already carried me off from Ashwana; I didn't want him lugging me all the way to Mahatnaten as well.

For the fifth time that hour, I demanded my release.

"Ra. Put me down."

To my surprise, he answered.

"What happened to 'ask, don't tell,' sot nesu?"

"What happened to *no kidnapping*?" I shot back.

He paused for a moment, and I held my breath.

"Point taken."

With a quick pat on my thigh, he lowered me to the earth. I

righted myself, straightening my kalasiri and trying to brush the sensation of his hands off my skin. Once I was sure my breakfast was secure, I swung my hand. It connected with his cheek in a dull smack. He blinked in surprise, a flicker of amusement sweeping across his face.

"I am not your princess!" I yelled. "I am not some feeble-minded woman that needs her guardian to carry her every step of the way!"

The flame of his spirit burned a little brighter as his eyes landed on me, desire inking out before he rushed to smother it, and I took a step back, trying to separate myself.

"Sot nesu, only a fool would think you weak. A demon's claw is no easy opponent. Some full-fledged guardians would have succumbed to your injuries before the first drop of their blood hit the floor. And garnering power to perform a reading in such a state? Your mind is anything but feeble," he said with a deep frown as if he couldn't possibly understand what had given me such an idea.

"I call you 'princess' because, as the daughter of the late Empress, that is what you are to me and the rest of our realm. Not because I think you weak. In truth, I find your resilience quite impressive." I bit down hard on my lip, feeling foolish and rash.

Impressive?

I hadn't considered he meant it as anything other than an insult.

"And I never said anything about you being *mine*," he corrected, flashing the delicious dimple before fixing his expression.

Hadn't he? Or had that been my own shameful thoughts creeping in?

I dropped my gaze, hugging my chest a little tighter as my embarrassment threatened to swallow me.

The thought cooled my temper, but that didn't excuse his boorish behavior.

My lips turned up in a sneer as I remembered how he'd tossed me over his shoulder without a thought, and I turned on my heel to continue as if he'd never existed.

I'll find my own way to Mahatnaten.

The thought was nothing more than my anger talking. But I held on to it as I trudged through the sand, following the river upstream and only looking back when I was certain he was otherwise occupied. His spirit flicked with anguish, but he let me be, and I was glad for the moment of solitude even if it wasn't real. Maybe, if I were lucky, he would tire of me and leave me to my quiet seething until we reached our destination.

CHAPTER 13

ONIA

We continued walking at what *Ra* had deemed a reasonable pace. After three days of hugging the bank, we'd agreed to a mutual respect. I'd decided to forgive him for his tactless handling of me, provided he abide by our arrangement. I could remain at my position in the front so long as I listened to Ra's direction, and I would refrain from slapping him so long as he stopped making demands.

Each morning, I woke to a trickle of his kan skirting across my calf as he gently coaxed me awake, and I was surprised that someone so gruff could manage such a gentle touch. We would walk a few hours before the sun crept over the hills, myself stepping out in front with Ra close behind. Every few hours, he would bark out an order or a change in direction and I would wait for the begrudging "please" before I complied. A few times, I'd been too tired to fight him on it, and I'd moved anyway. But I was sure to let him know he shouldn't get used to it. To which, he'd respond "Sot nesu, I wouldn't dream of stripping you of that stubborn independence." Despite his insistence on calling me princess, I'd felt a traitorous shiver run up my spine.

I did my best to keep my distance, but his spirit was working a knot in my mind that I couldn't get rid of. Even as we walked in silence, I could feel his quiet concentration building and the spark of intrigue each time he looked at me. More than once, I wished I could keep myself from prying. Every time I caught him looking at me, I thought about telling him. But I was too fearful of his response—too scared we'd go back to our bitter silence.

Instead, I would brush away his hand each time he reached out to steady me, but only to avoid the rush of feeling each time we met. His touch sent my kan alight and my spirit was beginning to take to his with ease. Each brush of his hand or tap of his fingers filled me with a tender warmth that unnerved me. His spirit was calling to me as it had that day in the square, and if I had any hope of ignoring it, he would need to keep his hands to himself.

I did my best to occupy him with my questions. Questions meant I was too busy listening to his answers to pay attention to his spirit shifting and changing. He told me of the Hall and the other guardians—how they protected the Hall and the spirits as the assessors weighed them against the feather to test their balance. He painted a glorious picture of divinely carved stone and heavenly light. I could feel him censoring his words but decided not to press the matter. I wanted to believe the lie of divine peace. Although my encounters so far told me it was nothing but myth.

Whenever the topic of House Anubis came up he would turn the subject elsewhere before the heat of anger rose in his spirit. All I'd managed to learn was that Ra was the eldest, after his late brother, Amon, of the House Anubis children. It was hard to believe given he looked no older than I. Most of his siblings were now scattered across the realm, leaving only him and two others in the Hall. Any more information was closely guarded, and I eventually stopped asking.

He didn't press me to share my life with him. At first I appreciated his lack of prying, but then a thought burned into my mind that I couldn't rid myself of—what if he didn't ask because he didn't care?

One night, as we sat along the bank eating another helping of freshly cooked fish, I asked.

"Why don't you ask me any questions in return? Do you not wish to know me?"

The idea was surprisingly upsetting. I hadn't realized before I said it, but his answer meant more to mean than I wanted it to. I waited with bated breath.

He turned to me with a curious frown, his midnight eyes fixed on me as if he was trying to peer inside.

"Of course, I wish to know you, sot nesu. How can I not? A woman so bold must have many stories to tell. But I will not press you to share your life with me. You will tell me when you are ready." He shrugged with a soft smile curving his lips.

The next day, I spent the better half of the afternoon telling him of my childhood in Ashwana. How I used to sit by the hearth as Father scribed, scribbling my own nonsense on a spare piece of papyrus. How he'd insisted that reading was an essential skill for any woman. How he'd always been supportive of my kan. Even when I was convinced it was a curse from Shai.

I fumbled my way through Father's illness when Ra asked how he died. Only finding the words when he settled a warm hand on my shoulder. As I spoke, he watched me with a longing that I tried to ignore. He worked hard to cover it with a broad smile as I moved on to brighter tales.

"But roasted dates were our favorite!" I called over my shoulder as I finished recounting Father's insistence on cutting through the market each time we journeyed to the priests in the northern district. He'd always been convinced their dates were grown by the gods, claiming that the impossibly sweet flavor couldn't come about naturally.

"Yes, I'd noticed," he said, eyeing me playfully, and I remembered the bag I'd been carrying that night I found him in our home. My stomach grumbled as I glanced back at him. I'd been craving a glimpse at him, but I was denying myself in hopes of ignoring him. He was walking through the sand, his powerful legs making it look easy. This time he smiled up at me from the base of the hill, waving me onward.

As I crested the top, a barely blooming sycamore came into view in the valley below. I could see the plump, sunset-colored figs peeking out between the leaves and my mouth began to water. Before I could stop myself, I was racing down the hill. Ra hollered after me and I shouted in response but didn't slow until I reached the base of the tree.

CHAPTER 14

RA

It'd been days since my "kidnapping," and she was no longer throwing daggers with her eyes each time I looked at her. I was beginning to miss the heat in her stare, but she no longer argued when I reminded her to pace herself, and I would say "please" even when I didn't feel it necessary. I should have known better than to expect a woman as determined as her to relinquish all control without question. I'd decided to let her keep her place in front. It seemed to bring her a peace of mind that I had no desire to disturb, and if this small act allowed her to feel some sense of control, I would gladly relinquish it. Besides, I could guard her just as well from behind.

I was watching the switch of her supple hips, and trying to avoid all thoughts of her round bottom in my hands, as she ambled up the side of the hill. She offered me a soft smile as she tossed her locs over her shoulder, looking for me with a hand shielding her eyes. I inclined my head, telling her to go on without me. My senses told me it was still just the two of us out in these sands, and the smile that cracked across her face was well worth it. She hustled up to the crest of the hill, and I immediately regretted my decision as she broke out into a run down the other side.

"Sot nesu, where are you going?" I shouted, throwing my hands in the air. "I thought we were past this!"

Why would she run now? We were much too far from any point of civilization for her to think I wouldn't find her.

I broke out running as her dark hair disappeared over the hill and she called out, "come on!"

My hand reached for my blade, but before I could pull it free, my eyes found her in the valley below, shimmying up the base of a tree and reaching her slender arm into the sparsely growing leaves. Gently, she shook a few figs free and looked over at me, grinning wide—clearly satisfied with her own ability. I came to stand in the shade of the tree as she shimmied higher until she sat straddling a branch.

"Careful, sot nesu!" I called up from my place on the ground. Her eyes rolled with heavy exaggeration.

"You worry too much," she chided.

Of course, I did.

She should have waited for me. I would much rather be the one in the tree, and not only because I was having difficulty focusing on anything other than her bare thighs gripping a branch between them.

She was too precious to risk.

The reminder of Father's anger crept up, but as I watched her teeter along the branches, I knew there was a greater reason for the knot of tension in my chest. One I had to abandon.

I shook off the thought and tore my eyes from the warmth of her brown skin.

She braced herself to drop from the tree, and my instinct pushed me forward, reaching a hand into the branches. To my surprise, she took it, letting my other hand rest along her leg for added balance. She was too eager about the prospect of something other than fish to shy away from my nearness as she had been.

But I realized my mistake too late.

My kan had opened up as I stood gawking at her and a rush of feeling spread across my hands, shooting up her leg as her fingers wrapped around mine. My jackal lit up with anticipation, and she sucked in a quiet breath. But she didn't pull away. Instead, her hand clamped down on my own and her balance faltered, causing her to tumble from the tree like a flightless bird.

A panicked, little shout burst from her chest as we crumpled to the earth.

"Sot nesu!"

I ran my hands over her, suppressing the urge to hold her tight to me. She'd fallen flat out of the tree, but I'd managed to break her fall, and she was lying crushed against me from the force.

"Are you alright?"

Her emerald eyes locked on mine, heating as her chest heaved. My spirit breathed a satisfied breath as she lay pressed to me. But our kan was still surging, and she pushed away trying to get to her feet in a hurry.

"I was! I don't need your help," she ground out, her face scrunching up in anger as she stumbled trying to right herself. I reached out a hand. But she denied me.

"Just, stop touching me!" she shouted, turning her face into the wind.

The scent of sweat and shame swept past me as the breeze caught her hair.

My jackal twisted in agony as it watched her turn from us, and I smothered the aching longing as I looked at her.

Her shoulders rose with a steadying breath before she turned back.

"I'm sorry, the sensation of your energy is...stronger than I anticipated." She sighed before dropping her gaze and moving to scoop up the fallen figs. "I suppose I'll have to get used to that."

Unlikely. Her kan seemed to have taken an interest in me, and I doubted it would react the same with all others. Selfishly, I hoped it wouldn't. But I wasn't about to tell her that. It would only turn into more questions. Questions I didn't have the answers to.

Instead, I let her gather the figs in silence, keeping my hands to myself.

The sun set quickly, and the harsh winds of the evening desert began to beat against her skin, sending her hair flying around her face. I offered my body to shield her, draping my robe around her shoulders, but she responded with a scolding look. That bright, angry glare that I'd learned was just for show. I tucked the robe over her shoulders, ignoring her protest, and eventually left her to her frantic swiping.

Wind never killed anyone—not that it couldn't. Shu just didn't have it in him.

As we crested another hill, movement sounded from the west and I stilled. My arm reached across her chest to keep her from taking another step. The wind was too loud in my ears; I needed stillness to focus on the noise drifting in from the water. Her breath hitched and she shot me a look. Her stubbornness faltered as she caught sight of my face, and she quieted. After half a heartbeat, a familiar scraping met my ears—a heavy shuffle concealed in the whistle of the wind.

CHAPTER 15
ONIA

Ra's muscular, tattooed arm cut into my path, knocking my breath from me. I opened my mouth to voice my frustration, but as I turned to him, his usual look of mild irritation had disappeared, replaced by a dark and threatening shadow.

I'd seen that look before—only once—that night in the backway.

"What is it?"

"Shh. Listen," he whispered, eyes boring into me with urgency.

His head was tilted into the wind, waiting for the sound to carry across the current, and I followed suit. I lifted my chin and turned my head to the west to focus my senses. The sound of something slow and big marching through the sand drifted from the bank, and a chill ran through me. Ra turned back, barking out hushed orders before I could even blink.

"Hide!"

"What?" I tried to keep my voice to a whisper as panic flooded my spirit.

His eyes were scanning the horizon, fixing on a point in the distance, but I knew I wasn't seeing what he could. A thick curtain of night hung a few cubits ahead of us, with nothing visible beyond it. When he turned on me, his commanding tone took on new life. His dark eyes heated, and his spirit grew frenzied.

"Onia, now is not the time. As your guardian, I am ordering you to slide down the slope and stay out of sight. We can argue about my manners later."

I shook my head. I wanted to comply, but fear had my feet sticking in the sand.

"What if they find me? I can't fight them alone." The words were rushing from me, one after another, forced out by fear as I recalled the searing pain of their claws and the splatter of my blood spraying across the stone. "What if I—"

Before I could continue my downward spiral, Ra took my face in his hands, forcing me to meet his eyes. I watched as the guardian slipped back and the man stepped forward. When he spoke again, his voice was tender.

"Onia, I promise you, they will not find you. They'll have to make it through me first, and I'd sooner meet the scales than sacrifice you to Ammit. You must trust me."

The thought brought me no comfort. I wasn't sure I could handle another loss, even if it was a surly guardian like Ra. I drew in a shaking breath and nodded.

Sharpness pricked the back of my neck as his hands pulled away—lethal claws already protruding from his skin. The darkness in his spirit made its way to the front, and he loosened his hold to let it seep through to the surface. Long pointed ears began taking shape on Ra's head, and a grimace snuffed out his handsome features as a muzzle pushed out from his face.

"Go!" He snapped, nudging me forward, still stuck between man and beast.

I raced down the slope without looking back, pressing myself into the dirt as I tried to conceal my presence. Stars blinked back at me in the night sky, and I hoped the balance would weigh in our favor.

A terrifying screech erupted from the darkness, a cross between a rumbling crocodile and the hiss of a viper—the unmistakable sound of shabti. Metal cut through the air as Ra unsheathed a blade, and a knot lodged in my throat. His spirit was wild, the darkness blazing a path through him as it tried to break free, and I knew what I'd see if I looked over the sandy ridge. Soon the shabti would fall, and he would return a blood-beaten mess, just as he had before.

Guilt gripped my stomach as I sat listening to the crunch of bone and the tearing of flesh. I counted the thud of falling bodies, waiting for Ra's spirit to calm and the last shabti to dissipate. The night grew still. Metal clanged to the earth, and my body jolted as Ra let out an agonizing scream. The shock of his pain pierced my mind, and I was scrambling up the slope before reason could stop me. I raced over the crest, praying for what I'd find on the other side.

Ra stood doubled over—blood dripping from a now limp arm —his blade was discarded in the dirt a few steps ahead and five piles of blood lay in the dust at his feet. Three giant shabti, larger than those in Ashwana, were circling his bleeding body.

"Ra!" I called his name, hoping he was only gathering himself. His kan was fiercer than any I'd seen. It would heal him—it had to. Otherwise...I couldn't think about what would happen otherwise.

After three shallow breaths, Ra was still hunched over, and the shabti continued their stalking, taunting him as they paced in front. Before they could turn their hulking bodies in my direction, I sprinted for the blade, swiping it up and cutting through the air in a wild arch. Something in my kan jerked awake, and I latched onto it, following its pull as it surged and pulsed in my legs, sending me darting to the left. The demon jerked as it pivoted to keep in front, but my kan moved me forward, and my energy rushed down my arm. I acted without question, slicing through the air and watching as metal connected with flesh.

Blood smeared across the demon's hide, but I didn't wait for it to return the favor. I sprinted across the sand until I practically tumbled into Ra. Blood was now pouring out of him in a heavy stream. His arm had been torn to the bone, hanging from his shoulder in ribbons. He groaned his discontent, and I knew he would have shouted at me if he could.

I spun, facing the shabti and placing myself in their path.

"Ra! Stand up!" My voice turned pleading when he didn't respond. "Ra! Please...please!"

He turned on me—his mind jerked awake by my piercing screams. His face twisted with rage as his eyes latched on me, but I ignored it, pulling against his hand, trying to move him to action. If he didn't recover, we would both be at the Hall much sooner than we'd hoped. Tears streaked down my face as my spirit grew desperate. I reached for him, gripping his good arm until my nails dug into his skin. With a jolt of my kan, Ra's blazed to life.

The darkness broke free of its hold, rushing to the front and tumbling out of its cage to swallow his control, flooding his spirit with rage. His deep onyx eyes glazed over, replaced with smokey grey irises the color of white sage. The markings along his body began to glow a golden hue. Our spirits tangled in my mind until I couldn't separate the threads. Passionate anger and desperate longing knotted together into a singular thought.

Ra.

I pushed it from my mind, trying to find him under the deafening noise of the darkness now filling his spirit, until I realized it wasn't just some elusive darkness. It was his jackal—its spirit normally lay buried beneath his, but it was stepping to the front to take his place.

His arm wrapped around my waist, pulling me tightly to him as he let out a guttural snarl—a singular warning to the demons still circling us. His markings brightened, and the shabti jerked to a halt—the light reflecting in their hollow, reptilian eyes. His kan was gathering in his core, causing the spark of our touch to intensify until his hands felt like hot coals on my skin. I struggled to pull away, but his grip only tightened, drawing me back into him. The heated touch turned tender as his kan poured into me. Warmth spread through me, his energy mixing with my own, filling me with strength until I cried out.

A whip of golden light burst from his core in a wide circle, passing through me and slicing through the beasts on either side. Sparks scattered in every direction and their bodies shattered before they could meet the earth.

This time there was no blood, only clusters of ash spreading through the warm wind.

I stilled in his arms. His searing touch began to cool, dissolving back into the mild tingle I'd grown used to. But the strength of his kan lingered in me. I spun to face him.

Midnight eyes met mine and a more human form slumped toward the earth. Panic seized my chest, and I followed him down.

"Ra?" My hands scrambled over him. "Ra! Can you hear me?"

I knelt in the dust, prepared to read his spirit thoroughly. The shallow glimpse I could see wouldn't suffice. Not now. I needed to know that death wasn't still looming over him.

Gripping his hands tight, my kan burst open. Eager to find him, it latched on, diving deep and waiting for the flames to return to their usual ebb and flow. His thoughtful energy was working to right itself—anger fighting to cage the darkness once more. A satisfied groan tore from his throat, and his hands gripped me back.

Oh, fate! Thank you!

I sent my praises to the heavens and waited in silence as he pieced his spirit back together.

After several agonizing minutes, the warm grate of his voice pulled me from my panic.

"Forgive me, sot nesu."

His voice was hoarse and low. Whatever he'd done had taken more energy than before, but that didn't stop the rush of relief that washed over me as he lifted his face to meet my worried eyes.

"Oh, praise Shai! You scared the spirit out of me," I muttered, throwing my arms around his neck and hugging him close.

One muscular arm draped around me, and I held him for a moment, feeling betrayed by my affections and the tears clogging my throat. But after seeing him bent over, a breath away from the Hall, I didn't much care about my pride. It'd disappeared once I came sprinting over that hill.

"I'm sorry. I'd hoped to spare you from the extent of my jackal's power."

"What?" I said, rocking back on my heels to look at him.

"Ra, I thought you were dying. When the jackal took over I—"

His thumb brushed my cheek, sweeping away an errant tear. His eyes met mine, soft and understanding, and impossibly caring for someone who'd just been torn to pieces—all for the sake of me. I thought to tell him then that I could see a hint of his spirit, that it was always there with me and I'd felt the searing pain just as he had. But my nerve faltered.

"It's alright. My jackal and I are on friendly terms. He steps in when I need him. Although, he isn't quite as gentle as I am. Are you hurt?"

I swept a fist under my eyes.

"Why would I be hurt?"

He was the one collapsed in the dirt. I felt fine. Come to think of it; I felt more than fine. My kan was humming loudly, and a comfortable warmth had settled in my chest.

"You screamed," he said, his eyes fixing on my face as if he wanted to pull me in close again. But his hands fisted in his lap, and I made an effort to keep mine to myself.

"That wasn't from the wave, it was..." I paused, trying to remember what he'd done. It was an overwhelming sensation. It'd built in my core only to flood through me in the next moment.

"My kan. I passed it to you so you wouldn't meet the same fate as them." He nodded toward a pile of ash still sitting in the sand. "You may feel the effects for a while. I gave you a great deal. I hope it didn't pain you too much."

His kan had flooded me with a feeling unlike anything I'd ever known, and I wasn't sure how to tell him it hadn't been a cry of pain, so I kept the truth to myself.

"I'm fine. You should have kept more for yourself," I said.

"My kan will recharge in time," he answered simply.

"Still, I'm worried about you. Your arm..." I confessed. Part of me wanted to throttle him, but the rest of me wanted to pull him in close and let him hold me until sunrise—just to know he was still alive.

He lifted a brow.

"Is that so?"

Is he teasing me? Now?

"The jackal's power is good for many things." He lifted the arm that had been hanging limp and shredded to the bone. It was now covered in his smooth, ebony hue with a few more scars cutting through the collection of intricate markings. "And he seems to have taken a liking to you. He doesn't show his face for just anyone," he added, eyeing me with interest.

"One of two isn't bad odds, depending on who you ask."

I tried for a smile, but I couldn't really manage it. There was too much blood crusting his skin to feel much more than relief.

"Two of two," he corrected, brushing a loc over my shoulder, a finger grazing my flushed skin. "Although, it may not matter if you keep endangering yourself, sot nesu." His jaw set tight once again, and his eyes were unyielding. But I wasn't going to let him shame me for my actions.

"I heard you...and then I saw you hunched over..." The memory replayed in my mind. But it was all a rush of kan and choices. "I didn't know what else to do."

We may be two equally stubborn mules trudging through the desert, but I wouldn't leave him for the beetles.

"So, you decided fighting demons was the wisest choice?"

He sounded amused, but his spirit knotted with concern, and there was a cold stare in the depth of his eyes.

"There was no wisdom in it. I wasn't going to let you die."

His strong brow bent up in confusion.

"First, I wasn't *dying*. My kan was doing its work. Second, it is my duty. If anything else happens to you, I couldn't... Father will be—"

"I don't care about your father," I interrupted. His jaw flexed, surprised by my honesty. "He isn't here risking his life for me...you are." My spirit swelled, and I choked back emotion. I'd cried enough for one day. "You may be my guardian, but I won't sit idly by and watch you sacrifice yourself for me." A deep frown formed on his face, turning the V on his forehead into a poorly scripted W. My chest tightened, bracing for my shameful confession. I'd spent half my life garnering my fierce independence, draping myself in it like a shield. But now, I was helpless, and anger threatened to overtake me as he sat staring back in confusion. Before he could spew any more nonsense about his duty, I let it flow free. "I wouldn't be here without you. If you go, I will be next."

CHAPTER 16

RA

Her face sank as she confessed her truth, and I cursed myself, suddenly feeling like I'd crushed a blooming lotus.

"Stand up," I commanded as I got to my feet.

A frown formed on her soft face, and my jackal whimpered at the sight.

Ugh. Between the two of them, this is making for a difficult journey.

"Onia, you don't need to be in control all the time. Just stand up."

She stared up at me, gaping at the sudden shift in my attitude. After the night we'd had, I figured we could set our egos aside. I reached down to grip her wrist and pull her to her feet.

"What are you doing?" she yelped.

"Making sure you live...even if I don't."

Her heart lurched at my words, beating hard and fast in her chest.

In one swift movement, my arms encircled her, holding her tight and daring her to break free.

"Aye! What are you—"

Her face was mere inches from my own, and my groin grew hard as her piercing eyes gazed up at me. I loosened my hold, hoping she wouldn't feel it pressing into her. I doubted she would take kindly to my affections, and I forced myself to calm as she stood blinking up at me.

"If you insist on defying my every order, you should at least be prepared for the consequences."

Her eyes brightened, but she only nodded in response, and I was glad for the break from her sharp mouth. My control was beginning to falter, and I'd had enough of my own yearning for one night.

"If someone takes you from the front, aim for the stomach. The fleshy part, right under the bone."

I showed her where to aim, pressing my fingers beneath her ribs before spinning her around and holding her back flush to my chest.

"From behind, aim for the leg. Use your elbows...and your head. It seems quite thick; it may make a good weapon," I teased, and she wiggled, trying to get free.

The hum of kan sparked everywhere our skin met as she struggled against me. The sensation was louder than before, but neither of us paid it any mind.

"Ra, you just—"

"Don't worry yourself with me, sot nesu."

She jerked as I whispered the hated words, and her resolve came rising to the front.

Her head slammed back, connecting with only air, and her elbow jabbed at my sides as she thrust her hips back for good measure. I loosened my hold, and she pushed free. I pretended not to see the glint of excitement in her eyes as she spun to face me.

"You will not fall," I said.

"How do you know?" she asked, a flicker of doubt creeping through the fierce confidence.

"Because I won't let you."

I pulled a small blade from the row of knives strapped to my chest and offered it to her.

"Keep this in the folds of your dress, and we shall hope you never need it."

She reached forward, and I placed it in her palm, folding her fingers around the leather-bound hilt. It was small compared to my others, intended for throwing rather than close combat, but in her hand, it looked lethal. She took to its weight as she held it away from her body.

"For it to be of use, you will need to know how to handle it."

I stepped backward, beckoning her forward and asking her to strike me.

"Show me," I commanded.

She shifted on her feet, unsure.

"Ra, I've never—"

"Do not doubt yourself. It only leaves space for failure. Follow your kan; it will guide you." I stepped forward, bringing her target closer.

"Now, show me."

After a moment's hesitation, she called upon the armor I'd seen her wear. The same one she'd donned before we left Ashwana; a smoldering look that called upon her strength and buried her every weakness. It suited her, transforming her beautiful features into a fearsome determination. Truly, I wished she didn't need it. If it were up to me, she'd have no reason to shield herself. But the balance had spoken, and she would need it now more than ever.

Before I could dwell on it any further, she sprang forward, swiping at me as my arms came around her.

CHAPTER 17

RA

She was as intuitive as I'd anticipated, her defiance serving her well in this role. Each time I tightened my grip, she fought harder; even as we moved to different holds, she corrected quickly, finding her openings and striking without hesitation.

She waggled her brows at me as she bounced back and forth on the balls of her feet, feeling as if she were exceeding my expectations. Which, to be fair, she already had—days ago in Ashwana, and every day since. She had taken each step begrudgingly, but she did it with her head held high and her shoulders thrust back as if she would defy the will of Shai if it meant she would live another day.

The armor was still clear on her face, but she moved through the sand with ease. The tension in her shoulders dissipated, and her eyes were bright as a smile played at the corner of her full lips. She was enjoying this, no matter how hard she tried to convince me otherwise. I continued my role as her captor until she was bent over, hands propped on her knees, and breathing hard.

Father would not be pleased to see her injured. Anything further, and he'd throw one of his tantrums that ended with rolling heads. Even now, we risked his wrath. Training her ran counter to his plans, but I hoped we could rely on his arrogance to overlook her as a threat. Besides, if it meant she stayed on this side of the celestial plane, I would gladly take the risk. Father might be head of my house, but Onia's life was in my hands.

Eventually, she flopped down into the dirt, gasping for breath with her arms and legs splayed out like the stars of Orion. I stared down at her as she drew in labored breaths. The rise and fall of her chest told me she was fine but spent. I dropped down beside her, offering a fig, and she took it eagerly.

"Are you going to tell me how you did that back there? With the shabti?" she asked after her breath returned to normal.

I chuckled. I'd been hoping she would forget. Naturally, she hadn't.

"It's not something I often do. It takes a significant amount of energy."

Guilt crossed her face, and I wished I could soothe it. But we both knew why the jackal had taken such measures. Her life was a treasure with which we wouldn't barter.

"It was beautiful," she said, fixing her eyes on my markings as if she expected them to glow again. I covered the smug satisfaction as the jackal took in her words.

Fickle beast.

"I'm glad you think so. It's been known to cut men in two." I laughed, unable to hide my amusement at her casual comment.

Only fools stood near when the jackal was in command, and very few lived to tell of its glory. But not her. She'd braced herself with the stubborn independence she displayed so openly. She might be reckless, but there was one thing of which I was certain—Onia was no fool.

"Could I do that?" she asked.

I nodded, enjoying the twinkle in her expressive eyes.

"Our kan is unlike that of any human," I said, waiting for the hum of beetles to quiet before I continued. "A human's kan is merely food for their soul. But ours…is capable of great power and great destruction." I pushed a current of my kan from my body, letting it bump up against her. She rocked back slightly, and her eyes grew wide. "Many of us can will it from our bodies; others can affect your spirit with a single touch. Some of us carry death itself in our fingertips," I continued, not wanting to dwell on the image of Osiris's touch finding its way to her. "Your readings come most naturally because of your house and your lineage from Ma'at. There are those of dual spirit like myself. I carry the spirit of the jackal because of my father, and its energy gives me great strength and heightened senses. The power of kan is different for every soul. But I imagine you could do much more than even me." Her lips formed a soft O as she sucked in a breath, and I stifled the image of myself parting them with my tongue. "Ma'at was one of the most revered of our kind. Her kan is legendary. Yours may be just as powerful." Before I could finish, she propped herself up on her elbows to bring her face closer.

"Could you teach me?" she asked—eyes bright and eager.

"Unfortunately, no. You'll need a teacher much older than I."

"How old?"

"Older than dirt," I said.

Ma'at was of the ennead, a primordial deity older than the dust beneath our feet. Any power Onia held would be far greater than my own, and I had no idea what gifts she held inside. She would need a teacher of equal footing before she could wield it properly.

Her bright smile broke through my focus as she burst into laughter. She was smiling at the stars with her head thrown back, laughing loudly into the sky, and I couldn't deny myself the pleasure of seeing her without the armor. Even if only for a moment. It was a sweet sound, like milk and honey, and I let it roll over me, not stopping when my spirit reached out to touch her.

My hand brushed her cheek, catching a joyful tear as it rolled free.

"I'm sorry." She wheezed.

I wasn't. Although, as she sat smiling at me, I had a feeling I soon would be.

"It's just—I'd assumed you were as old as dirt with how cranky you are. Like an old man with a permanent scowl on his face." She laughed again, leaning into my palm. "So, you aren't an old man, then?" she quipped.

"Far from it."

"How old then?" she asked with hungry eyes.

"Time flows differently in our realm, but I am only twenty-nine of your human years."

"Good," she said, and if I wasn't mistaken, there was a lust in her voice as she said it.

* * *

Beside me, she had a fitful sleep. Her head tossed, and her body jerked back and forth as she confronted her dreams. I didn't disturb her for a long while, but my ears perked at every movement until I could no longer ignore her restlessness. I *would* carry her to Mahatnaten if needed, but apparently, she didn't prefer it. We had at least half a day before we reached the northern desert, and once we did, she would need every ounce of rest she could muster.

I reached across the sand to offer her some comfort. Her body stilled as my fingers found the rise of her hip, and her fingers wrapped around mine as she clung to me. I tried for a moment to separate myself, but as I looked down at her restful face, I couldn't bring myself to send her back into whatever horrible vision she'd conjured.

My eyes slid shut only to snap back open as she rolled over, draping an arm across my chest and curling her face into me. I stiffened—the current of kan spreading across our skin, causing me to bristle. She'd ignored my brief touches after our ordeal. The emotion of another attack had stripped us both of our stubbornness, but I didn't know if she would wake in anger when she found herself here.

I thought to peel her off, but after careful consideration, I decided it best to risk her wrath rather than disturb her. I would eagerly accept my punishment. My body was hers to do as she pleased. If this was the cost of her peace, then so be it.

CHAPTER 18

ONIA

Patchouli and musk filled my senses as a warm hand stroked down my back. I could feel the sticky film of sweat that had covered me in the night and a gentle breeze blowing through my hair. I shut my eyes tighter, burying my face into the soft fabric to avoid the bits of sand stirring around me.

"Onia." A gentle voice prompted, accompanied by a deep vibration.

I ignored the call of my name, focusing instead on the tingle beneath my fingers—savoring the sensation.

"Onia?" The voice called again, tickling my cheek as it reverberated back. "Onia."

My vision blurred as I pried my eyes open, and the broad planes of Ra's chest stared back at me. My head and arm lay across him as he tried to coax me awake, and I stiffened. He chuckled, a deep rumble sounding under me.

"It's alright; the desert winds can be unforgiving."

He laughed, brushing a hand down my arm and sending sparks flying in his wake. Some guilty part of me craved the feeling, drinking it in and wanting more. But the part of me with sense told me I shouldn't. Less than a day had passed since I'd demanded that he stop touching me. Yet here I was, seeking him out in my sleep. Even now, I didn't want to let go. But embarrassment settled in my chest, and I couldn't face it.

"Sorry...if I disturbed you. I didn't mean to," I muttered as I pushed away from him.

"Not at all. You seemed to be having unpleasant dreams." His jaw ticked with frustration, but his spirit told a different story as a flicker of longing swept through my mind. "I would have let you rest as long as you needed, but we must be going."

I turned to see the sun sitting well above the horizon. The red and orange hues of early morning had already shifted into a golden yellow.

"Balance! It's already mid-morning. We should have left long ago," I said, feeling guilty for having kept us behind schedule.

Ra stood, brushing dust from his clothes and flakes of dried blood from his arm. I did the same, straightening the folds of my kalasiri as I swiped the dust from the fabric. I slid the small blade he'd gifted me into the folds just below my right breast. Once it was properly concealed, I turned to him.

His brow furrowed, and his head cocked in amusement as I stood staring.

"Are you...*waiting* for me?" he asked, confused.

I couldn't blame him. I'd spent the last several days walking a few cubits in front, too stubborn and too distracted by his spirit to stand so close. At a distance, it was quieter, and I didn't have to feel every flare of emotion as he looked at me. But Ra had spent the night bolstering my strength, and in the midst of it, his spirit had become more of a comfort than a disturbance. A gentle reminder that I wasn't alone. I was glad to feel the warm flame burning in my mind.

"And if I am?" I retorted.

"Then I'd call it a disappointment."

My heart sagged a little. I'm not sure what I expected him to say, but I was beginning enjoy Ra's company, and I hadn't expected him to dismiss me so quickly.

"My view has been rather pleasant these last few days," he added, eyes hooding and a playful smirk drawing across his fierce features as he looked at me.

My teeth drew in my lower lip as I covered a cheeky grin.

"Mm, a true loss," I joked and watched as his dimple came out in full force.

A rush of pleasure filled me as I looked at him, and I turned my face toward the river, shocked by my own reaction.

"You should clean the blood from your arm before we leave," I said in a feeble attempt to turn my mind elsewhere. But watching him barebacked, squatting by the water with muscles flexing as he washed away the taint of demons, only reinforced my sordid thoughts.

After scrubbing his arm clean, he nodded north as he had every other day since Ashwana. But today was different. We walked in lock step—my desire to push ahead had dissipated. Instead, I leaned into the comfortable silence and the quiet current of his spirit flowing freely through my mind and, for the most part, he kept his hands to himself. He still managed to steal a few touches as he reached out to help me over rough terrain. I accepted his arm without argument, telling myself I was simply too tired to find my own way but secretly enjoying the ripple of his kan across my skin.

He was being particularly cautious, even glancing up to watch the ibis flying overhead as if the shabti would come dropping in from the clouds like rain. For all I knew, they could, so I hadn't said anything. As we crested a hill, he stepped out ahead to survey the stretch of earth beyond.

"It's not too far. We'll reach Harmon soon," he called.

"Harmon? The province of Anubis?"

I tried to ease my excitement, but Harmon was the first town we'd crossed paths with on our journey, and I was growing tired of eating fish and half-dried figs.

"Yes," he said, stepping down the bank and offering a hand to ease me down the slope.

I took it.

"The people of Harmon are kind; we will be well taken care of," he added.

"They know your human form?" I asked, falling in step. Neither of us moved to free our hands as we reached the bottom.

"The people know me, but not as the son of Anubis," he said. "They will provide us with what we need."

"Couldn't we just *buy* what we need?"

"We could if we had any deben to barter with."

"What happened to your coin? Last I saw, you had plenty," I teased.

More than plenty.

"You may recall, I gave it to you."

Ra's voice was firm, and I paused, coming to a stop.

"Yes, but surely…" His dark eyes were watching me, waiting for me to make the connection, and I pulled my hand from his grip. "You mean to say you gave it *all* to me?" I asked, hoping I was mistaken.

My question was met with a silent confirmation. I replayed the moment I launched the weighted satchel at the demons before darting out of the alley. An image of some lucky street rat finding the glittering coins in the road flashed in my mind.

"What? Why?" My voice was tight, and I tried to hide my judgment. But if I had to guess, I wasn't doing a very good job. Ra's brows bent up as he stood glaring at me.

"I didn't need it." He shrugged. "And you did."

"And you didn't think to stop and pick it up as you were carrying me off into the desert?"

I was growing loud, but I couldn't help it.

Who disregarded such security? Who stepped over coin lying in the street? After months and months of careful spending, he'd handed me comfort I hadn't known in a long while—not since Father's mind was still with him, and now it was gone.

He stopped then, his anger twisting through my mind.

"You'll have to forgive me for prioritizing your *life* over the treasures of man." His voice was pointed and condescending as if such "treasures" weren't the very difference between life and death for most people.

"Right, and now we are facing begging in the street." I threw my response at him.

A deep frown took up space on his face. "*Begging?*" he asked with disbelief.

He had no intention of succumbing to such a thing. Good. Because neither did I.

"Why do you care so much? You'll have no use for it where we're going," he said when I didn't respond.

My insecurity came tumbling out of my mouth before I could stop it. "Because those '*treasures*' mean safety. They mean food and shelter. And I've worked *too* hard to see that I don't go without them. Now we have none. And I'd rather not wind up indebted to a stranger for a few dates!"

I knew I was yelling, and I knew I shouldn't be. Ra was right. The struggles of this realm wouldn't follow me into the next. But his response went against everything I'd ever known.

It wasn't greed. It was survival. Too often, I had to make the hard choice between food and water, and I knew what happened when you relied on others—how their greed would consume them. I worked tirelessly to never face that again. Ra reached out a hand, and I took a step back. Now was not the time to be distracted by his alluring touch. I looked past him, trying to bury my insecurity back where he couldn't find it. I may be the reader, but he was perceptive in his own right.

He paid my boundary no mind and snatched up my hand to hold it firmly to his chest.

"Onia. You will want for nothing. The human realm may

balance life and death against a man's wealth, but the balance certainly doesn't. You will be well cared for in the Hall. Even if I must serve you myself for the rest of my days." A bitter ember sparked to life in his eyes, blending into a flame of sorrowful sadness I hadn't seen before. It was something hollow and deep like shame, but not quite as self-centered...it was guilt. "I promise you."

My heart hammered at his words. Ra's effortless declaration left me stunned, and I wished it were more than just his duty talking.

"Why give it to me then? If the coin is so useless, why give it to me?"

Ra's lips formed a tight line as he released me. "To ease your spirit." He heaved a sigh. "You will face greater trials than filling the city coffers or meeting a monthly quota. I had peace I could offer you, so I gave it." I felt my cheeks burn as his flame danced with a mixture of frustration and yearning. "And no, I don't regret it."

My mouth fell open with an apology on my lips, but before I could manage it, he stepped in close and lowered his voice to a deep and commanding tone.

"Do not apologize," he ordered, sweeping up my hand and tugging me after him.

CHAPTER 19

ONIA

I'd heard of Harmon from the merchants after their annual journey along the lower Nile. The legend of the people told that Anubis himself led a wealthy merchant out of the desert to the spot where Harmon now stood—inspiring its founder to build a place in honor of his savior, calling upon his spirit to shield them from harm. In response, Anubis sent dogs to act in his stead. Now they roamed free, cared for by the people as a collective.

The town walls came into view shortly before the sun reached its high point, and I was grateful for the shadow of the buildings as we stepped through the entrance. Pillars flanked us on either side, each standing six times my height with an intricate relief of Anubis's half-human form carved into the limestone. The jackals' heads sat on broad shoulders, with bronze wesekhs lying across their chests and a neme draped over top. One carried a golden ankh and the other a staff.

Ra groaned as we passed through, rolling his eyes and ducking under the archway.

Aside from the chorus of dogs that ignited every few minutes, Harmon's streets were quiet. The children here seemed more occupied chasing after the dogs than their mothers. I guessed the women preferred it to the constant pestering I'd seen in Ashwana because they didn't holler for them to stop. Unlike the street dogs I'd known, which usually went from merchant-to-merchant begging and looking starved, the dogs of Harmon were happy and well fed, even friendly enough to pet. Ra entertained my breaks to play with them, stopping every once in a while when they came trotting up. We stuck to the shade as best we could, only stepping out into the sun when the crowds grew too dense.

Heads turned as we pushed through the people, craning to see us.

"Is there a reason everyone is staring at you?" I whispered, glaring at an older man who was watching us intently.

Ra laughed—a deep and throaty sound.

"It's not me they're staring at," he said, and my head swiveled to catch a man gaping at me from behind. I was thankful for my brown coloring to hide my embarrassment as a rush of heat filled my cheeks. I rolled my shoulders and sloughed off the feeling. It was nothing I wasn't used to.

"I thought you said the people here were *nice*," I pressed, doing my best to shoot daggers from my eyes as a man met my gaze. To his credit, he quickly dropped his eyes and hustled off.

"They are. It's not their fault you wear that draping so well." He chuckled. A flutter swept through my stomach and I swatted him in the arm. "Here." The heat of his palm settled against my hip as he draped an arm around me and tucked me in close. My kan sparked as he brushed against my waist, and I squirmed. Being pressed together in my sleep, when I couldn't possibly be blamed for my weakness, was one thing. Letting him lead me through the streets with a possessive hand gripping me tight was another.

Ra peered down at me and I tried to quiet the pounding in my chest as his eyes hooded.

"Would you rather I pluck their eyes out?" he asked, his chiseled face deadly serious. "I'd be happy to oblige. Although, you are uncommonly beautiful. It may take a while." His head scanned the crowded street, and I caught at least four men and three women gaping in our direction. I suddenly remembered myself hanging over Ra's shoulder with my arse waving in the wind, and I decided I didn't want to test his resolve.

I rolled my eyes with a huff and leaned into his hard body as he tightened his grip on me.

Ra led me down the slate stone path deeper into the heart of town until we reached a tall building with colorful awnings lining the roof. Gruff and muffled shouts drifted from inside as he jerked the door open. Eyes landed on us before a chorus of excitement erupted, and men pushed forward, taking Ra's hand in greeting. He shook them in turn, performing the same ritualized and rhythmic motion known throughout Nubia. All the while keeping his hold on me. Moving from one man to the next, Ra guided us toward an oversized wooden chair at the back of the room. It was three sizes too large for any human man, with the Harmon Merchant Guild crest etched into the head—a hawk carrying a snake in its clutches. A few women stepped out from the crowd to bow their heads in our direction. They offered me small smiles that didn't reach their eyes and promptly turned cold as they saw Ra's arm still draped around my hip.

A hoarse and commanding voice rose above the others as we greeted the last of them.

"RA! Back to torment us already?" A short, bearded man with a singular braid swaying at his back pushed up from the makeshift throne to shove past the men who'd huddled around us.

"Harmon!" Ra shouted with a broad smile.

Harmon? *The* Harmon? The Merchant King?

"Good to see you, old friend!" Ra exclaimed as Harmon pulled him into a fierce hug, beating on his back with enthusiasm. Harmon returned the sentiment, and they pulled away to look at each other with broad smiles before turning their sights on me.

"Who is this dove you've brought with you?" Harmon asked.

His question was for Ra, but I offered a hand, which he took without question.

"Omari," I proclaimed and was glad when Ra didn't so much as blink. I didn't know if we had anything to fear in this town, but I wasn't willing to take the chance.

A wide smile spread across his face, and the glint of gold flashed in his mouth, several teeth catching the light. They were a fine compliment to his deep copper skin and joyful eyes, adding to his overall friendly face.

"Happy to have you with us, Omari. I hope you'll find our town welcoming during your stay," he said, bowing slightly. "How long can we expect to entertain you?"

"We'll be leaving at nightfall. But we could use food and water skins if you can spare them," Ra said.

"Of course, my friend. Come! My dear, some wine while you wait," Harmon said, gesturing to a dark woman with a closely shaved head and gold bracelets lining her arms. She immediately poured out a sizeable cup, and my tongue slid across my lips as I realized the thirst I'd been harboring. I turned to make my way to her, but Ra's grip pulled me back until I was pressed against his chest. I sucked in a breath as his lips came close to my ear.

"I won't be far," he whispered.

His spirit wavered, growing hesitant, and I caught a trace of need cross his face. I nodded and he turned to follow Harmon through the crowd of men. They were all laughing loudly over something one of the women had said. His spirit dimmed in my mind. But over the past few days, it'd grown clearer than before, and I could still feel a whisper of him even as he disappeared around a corner.

I ambled over to the giant goblet and swiped it up to make myself comfortable on a long wooden bench. I squeezed in beside two men arguing about the cost of a calf and drank as slowly as I could manage. Wine spilled out over my lips in small dribbles as I tossed it back. The bittersweet tang covered my tongue, and I was grateful for the woman's heavy-handed pour.

"Would you like some help with that?" A harsh voice called from somewhere on my left.

As I turned, I came face-to-face with a staunch man breathing down at me with beer on his breath.

"No," I snapped with a grimace creeping up.

I turned in my seat to return to my liquid bliss, but my arm was caught in his bony grip and wine sloshed over the rim onto the floor.

"Aye!" I yelped, ripping my arm free.

Ra's spirit flared at the back of my mind as the word left my lips, swelling into a blazing fury.

The two men beside me barked out an angry shaming, their voices overlapping as the man reached for me again.

"Aye, how dare you!" one said as he jutted his arm out in front of me, forcing the intruder to take a step back. "We don't tolerate that here!" the other shouted.

Several men got to their feet, disgust and anger splashed across their sun-beaten faces, but I knew Ra was already moving in my direction. His spirit grew stronger as he neared, and before I could turn to find him, a hand wrapped around the stranger's throat, lifting him from the floor in one swift motion. The man dangled in the air as Ra held him at arm's length—spirit pulsing with a closely guarded rage.

My hand landed on Ra's straining arm, but he ignored me as the man clawed and kicked in a panic. The crowd cheered, and the men settled back into their seats, waiting for Ra to dole out justice.

"Apologize," Ra demanded through gritted teeth.

"I-I didn't know she was yours," the man choked out.

My anger flared, and I turned my attention to him. He wasn't the first man to be so brazen with me. I knew how to handle him; Ra would have to wait his turn. I reared back to slap the man, but Ra held him beyond my reach.

"She's not. Nor is she *anyone's*, but that's no excuse. Now, apologize."

"Sorry..." the man gasped as his lips began to turn an ashen grey.

Ra's grip tightened.

"Not to me, you fool!"

The man twisted in Ra's grip, trying to face me.

"Forgive me, madam." He managed to close his eyes in what I assumed was a bow, given his compromising position. But I wasn't paying him much attention. I was too busy studying the hard profile of Ra's relaxed face. His chin was lifted high, cutting into the air with purpose, a picture of peace entirely at odds with the vicious fire blazing inside.

His spirit burned bright, and a flicker of adoration blended with his anger. Warmth blossomed in my chest—the stranger forgotten. But I was quickly pulled back as I realized the room had fallen silent, and the crowd was now staring at me, waiting.

Waiting for what?

Ra's dark eyes found my face, and he lifted a brow.

"Do you require anything else, sot nesu?"

A shiver rushed through me as the power in his voice swept over me. When he said it like *that,* I didn't mind it as much.

As I stared into the depth of Ra's eyes, I knew he would do as I said. For a moment I considered turning the contents of my cup out on the man's head, but I couldn't bear to waste the wine. I shook my head, and Ra released him, not caring where he landed. The women giggled as the man crumpled onto the ground before turning and scrambling through the door.

"Travelers don't always understand our code. He will learn. If he hasn't already," Harmon called by way of apology, a hint of amusement in his voice.

The crowd returned to their boisterous chatter, and Ra turned to face me, his anger subsiding.

"I could have handled that myself," I said.

For all that it was true, I was secretly glad I didn't have to. As it turned out, I much preferred watching Ra handle it on my behalf.

"I'm well aware of that," he said, reaching out a hand to brush a drop of wine from my lip. "But have you considered that I enjoy acting as your sword and shield?" His eyes found mine as he brought his thumb to his mouth, dragging it across his tongue.

My eyes rolled to hide the fire he was stoking between my legs.

"You're my guardian; you have to say that."

"I know of no such rule," he said, flashing his sweet dimple, and brushing his thumb across my cheek. "Perhaps my charge is just too precious to me."

His eyes flicked to my lips, and he idled a moment—as if he were contemplating more than this simple touch. My eyes fell to the floor, unable to withstand the heat in his gaze.

"I need a few more minutes with Harmon," he said, cupping my face in his big hand. His spirit was full of need, and I watched him smother it as he took a singular step away from me. "Will you be alright?"

My stomach clenched as I realized I wasn't ready for him to pull away, but I nodded, and he turned away to finish sorting out our wares.

I sat, drinking my fill, and watching the people come and go. A bubble had opened up around me. No one dared step into it after what they'd just witnessed, and I counted it another positive to having a guardian like Ra.

"Ready?" he asked, emerging from the back room dangling a fragrant bag of roasted dates in front of me.

I jumped to my feet and grinned to keep myself from squealing. The dimple winked back at me as he dropped the bag in my hands. This time I didn't balk when his arm came around my waist, but I did curse the traitorous feeling that settled into my chest. I did my best to stifle it by filling myself with food.

Ra led me out of the main square through the shaded alleys until we reached a quiet corner that bordered the boundary wall.

I spotted a few street dogs creeping out from adjacent alleyways, and Ra let out a low whistle, calling them forward. He stooped down to gather some radishes, pulling them in half and tossing them in every direction, making sure to throw them in a wide arc.

"Their instinct won't let them come close enough to take them," he explained in a hushed tone. He tossed a few more halves toward a bristly, tan dog with black-tipped ears and a curious face. "My jackal makes them nervous. It's taken ages for them to do even this."

He crouched down and held out a half to entice the curious dog. It inched forward with its ears pinned but kept its distance. Eventually, Ra released the radish, saving the dog from the emotional torment.

"You like them, don't you?" I asked, watching how he was careful not to make sudden movements as they crept up to snag a bite.

He cracked a wide grin.

"Yes, but as Shai would have it, *they* do not like *me*."

"Couldn't you ask him to change that?" I asked—only half joking.

An amused puff of air left his lips, and I lifted a brow. It didn't seem like an outrageous request. How consequential to the balance could it be?

"The god of fate is not so easily swayed. Although, his daughter *is* somewhat fond of me. I doubt even she could change his mind."

He laughed in earnest at his joke, a deep and thunderous laugh, startling the dogs that had managed to linger. He stood, using the corded muscle of his thighs, and dusted his pants before unfurling a small bolt of fabric and laying it on the hot stone beneath us. He settled onto the mat with his legs outstretched and his strong arms propping him up. And for a moment, in his casual display, he looked almost human.

"Harmon was very generous," I said, noting the expensive fabric as I sat beside him.

"Yes, he's always very welcoming when I visit."

"Does your father, uh, Anubis," I was still getting used to that idea, "visit the town too? They've erected quite the memorial in his honor." I gestured toward the entrance where he stood watch.

Ra scoffed.

"Father would never. He doesn't care for humans. He sees them as fickle and fleeting."

"But...the legend. He saved Harmon."

A sly smile spread across Ra's face as he avoided my eyes. He dropped a date in his mouth, chewing slowly, and savoring the moment of my confusion. When he swallowed, the smile was still plastered to his face.

"Harmon has always been quite generous. I found him wandering only a few hundred cubits from the river. But he was too disoriented to find his way. He followed me out of delirium, and by the time we were close enough to feel the breeze of the river, he'd passed out, and I had to carry him to the water. He awoke a few days later and was kind enough to feed the stray jackal that had led him there." He shrugged. "Once he was well, he made his way home, only to return and build a province in the name of the jackal-headed god that was his savior," he raised his hands over his head in mock praise, "calling on Father to watch over his people. Of course, Father dismissed it and didn't see the need. So, I sent the dogs in his place. They've been here ever since. Although, I think they've gotten too comfortable to be of much use." A soft grin pulled at his lips and threatened to reveal his attachment to the misfit canines.

"You mean this town was built in reverence for...*you*?"

He feigned insult before straightening his expression and whispering, "Yes, but they don't know that."

"Why do you let your father claim the victory as his own?"

"What would you have me do? Tell them who I am? They'd

chase me past the town walls for defiling the name of their savior." He spat the word "savior" out in disgust, but I couldn't tell if he meant their pretend savior Anubis or their true savior. "Knowing the town is cared for is enough. I do my best to visit. A few years ago, the people across the river took to killing dogs in revenge for some stolen fish. I resolved the issue on behalf of Harmon and helped bury the bodies. I'm glad to see the pack is filling out again." His head dipped down, and he went back to the dates. "Now, I tend to handle the *unique* problems that arise every so often."

"It's a beautiful town. And the people *are* nice...mostly," I muttered.

CHAPTER 20
ONIA

We lolled in the shade for a long while, waiting for the sun to go down. Ra was stretched out on the ground with his eyes closed. I tried for a moment not to stare but eventually gave up, figuring he wouldn't mind what he didn't know. His muscular form looked somehow stronger in the relaxed pose, like a crocodile lying in wait, and my eyes wandered over him, noting all the little details I'd missed before. Like the strip of skin peeking out above his pants. The bold tattooed pattern was different on his chest and stomach than I'd seen on his back. Words, in the old language, were inked along the intricate design to tell a story—one I suddenly wanted to know. I leaned in close to read the small symbols.

"Would you like to see them?"

I jolted back, feeling a flush rising on my cheeks.

"Oh, I didn't mean to—" I began, but he interjected.

"Do none of the men in Ashwana have markings?" he asked.

His eyes hooded as they flicked over me, and my mouth went dry.

"A few...but none like this..."

My eyes focused on his taut abdomen. I told myself to look

away, but he was already reaching behind and pulling his shirt over his head.

"Feel free..." he offered, stretching out an arm and laying it in my lap—an invitation to study him.

The prickle of kan skirted across our skin, but I'd grown used to the strange sensation, so I didn't hesitate as I brushed my fingers across the back of his hand.

"Why so many?" I asked.

There was hardly any open space along his arms and hands. His chest was full but not so closely packed, and they shared space with various scars. Most of which were faint and faded, save for four lines moving diagonally from shoulder to hip. They broke up the words climbing across his middle, and I sucked in a sharp breath.

"Ra, what are these?" I asked, breathy.

My hands wandered to his chest, and I splayed my fingers across his hot skin, tracing the angry lines. His hand came to rest on top of mine and his eyes slid closed.

"Those are not for you to worry about," he chided.

I forced my mouth to close before he opened his eyes again, but he didn't. He just carried on, holding my hand to his chest, and speaking in a husky tone.

"The markings guide my kan through my body like a shepherd leading his ox. They allow me to concentrate my energy and reinforce my strength or speed. I mostly use them in combat. Although, there are some things I've marked for sport."

I caught the chiseled V disappearing beneath the waist of his pants, and warmth filled my cheeks as my imagination ran off.

I wonder what those markings look like.

I tore my eyes from the hard ridges of his chest, wishing he would put his shirt back on, but too curious to deny myself. The symbols twisted over sculpted muscle, winding up to his chest to join the design that ran across his arms and back, ending below his collar.

As I translated, my fingers slid across his swarthy skin, and Ra let out a tortured groan. A heated satisfaction settled between my legs at the sound, and I continued.

"A soul torn in two..." The angry scar disturbed the rest of the phrase, and I moved to the next one. "For those without...light to guide the way, the journey through a thousand nights is treacherous."

Ra lifted his head to look at me.

"Where did you learn to read the old language so well?" he asked, not bothering to hide his surprise.

"Father," I said, continuing my translation in silence.

The ink mentioned great power and great betrayal, hearts torn in two and spirits mended. A lot of it was broken, disjointed from the four jagged lines running through them. But I could piece some of it together. When I raised my eyes from his hard body, he was watching me, waiting for an explanation. I drew in a deep breath before opening the old wound, and focused on the stone beneath us, unable to speak it to his face.

"When Father's mind started to go, the symbols stopped forming words on the page. I hadn't learned to control my kan yet, but Father couldn't scribe like before, and eventually, our coin ran dry. Some of the wealthier men in our quarter offered us aid and we accepted, thinking they did so out of generosity. But then they came demanding repayment. And when we couldn't meet their demands some requested my hand instead...while others requested my bed." Ra's spirit danced with anger and a low growl sounded in his chest. "Of course, Father refused. But he spent quite a few evenings begging in the street before I started to scribe in his place. I took on his clients in secret. I'd use his old scrolls to translate, and eventually, I didn't need them anymore."

Ra's big hand was suddenly gripping my thigh.

"Onia, I—"

I continued without giving him time to speak. I had to get it all out now, or it might stay locked away forever.

"Once I honed my kan, I realized I could care for him just as he'd done for me. For the past five years, I've spent my days giving readings in the marketplace and my nights scribing. It took months to perfect Father's script. I lost a handful of his customers in the process. But once I'd solidified the basics of the old language, they were none the wiser." I heaved a breath as I felt a weight lifting from my chest. "There was little spare time in between, but I never saw Father in the streets again. At first, I think it pained him to watch me do it. But eventually, he forgot my face, and it didn't hurt as much." Tears stung my eyes, and I pushed them back. "I would rather do it all myself than watch him suffer even one more day."

Ra's lips parted, and I knew what was about to come. So, I continued my translation, not wanting to dwell on my past suffering.

"The..." *Sun?* Another scarring line disrupted the path and I guessed. "Sun shall rise...for light may only be born of darkness."

The story ended along his stomach, just below his navel.

I felt the rough callouses of his hand brush across my skin as he squeezed my leg, trying to get my attention.

"Onia, I didn't know—"

"You couldn't have," I said, shrugging and offering him a small smile.

He had no hand in our suffering. I wouldn't berate him over it. Shai or Mother, on the other hand—if I ever saw *them*, they would get more than an earful.

"I would never ask anything of you," Ra said. "You must know that."

I nodded, an overwhelming sense of security pouring over me as he rubbed small circles across my skin. I chanced a look at him. His dark eyes sucked me in until I couldn't look away if I wanted to. "Those eyes are payment enough," he said.

The heat between my legs intensified, and I pressed a trembling hand to my thighs to dampen the sensation. A knowing smile settled on Ra's face, but he didn't fight me as I changed the subject.

"You chose these words?" I asked, glancing back at his chest.

"No, sematawy, they are conjured by your spirit when you are marked."

I ignored his pet name. I had no right to be angry over that one.

"Marked?"

"It requires a powerful renewal of your soul. It takes some time to master. Some go centuries without obtaining a single one."

My brows lifted as my eyes ran over him once more.

"What do they mean?"

He shrugged, relaxing into the earth, unconcerned with the hot air beating against his skin.

"Most claim it's a gift from the balance—a whisper of your fate. But few lead lives that follow their markings. Éshe doesn't place much stock in them, and she's about as close to fate as one can get. So, I don't pay them much mind."

Her name slid off his tongue with a sweet trill, like he was speaking of a flower, and my stomach tightened. I bit down on my lip, trying to suppress the flush of irritation as it blossomed under my skin.

"Who's Éshe?" I asked, trying to hide the pit of jealousy that had just opened in my chest.

Immediately after the words left my mouth, I wished they hadn't. It was foolish. I had no right to be jealous. I was in no position to grow possessive. Ra was my guardian. But that didn't stop the sour taste at the back of my mouth as I said her name.

"Éshe is the eldest daughter of House Shai. She takes very closely after her father and is a very gifted oracle. Though she doesn't take kindly to that word. She says, 'fate is a fickle thing, and even *she* can't be trusted.'"

I offered him a silent nod and stifled the bitter taste in my mouth. To which he let out a soft sigh.

"She is a very dear *friend*," he explained, and I knew I hadn't hidden my distaste well enough.

I didn't say anything more. His reassurance settled the sour feeling in my stomach, and I laid down beside him, staring up at the cloudless sky. Eventually, I fell asleep curled against the warm earth with my hand wrapped in his—a blanket of comfort draped over me as I dreamt of what fate had in store.

CHAPTER 21

ONIA

I woke to Ra's kan drifting down my arm and struggled to pull myself from a deep sleep. I'd been dreaming of him. The kind of dream that left my legs loose and made me wish he was speaking of other things when he whispered, "Come, sot nesu."

The moon had risen and was peeking out over the rooftops as we gathered ourselves. Ra was issuing terse commands followed by hushed "pleases" as we made our way out of the town walls. After I'd pet all the sleeping dogs, we set out over the sand dunes, trudging quietly through the night.

Ra was keeping closer than usual. Even by the moonlight, I could see the muscles in his shoulders tensed and ready. The darkness had him on edge. It was a shame he couldn't enjoy it. I preferred the desert at night. Not simply because it meant avoiding the depressing heat, but because it was the only time it came alive. In the day, you could walk for hours without the chirp of even a bug. But at night, a symphony of sounds floated along a cool breeze, reminding you that life prevailed, even here.

Ra paused to breathe in the air, and I stilled, preparing for the worst. His hand came around mine, pulling me gently toward him.

A single finger slid over his lips, and he nodded his head in the direction of the wind. My question caught in my throat as I spotted a jackal perched atop the hill beside us. Its head tilted as it pondered our presence. A moment passed, and it flattened its ears, tossing its head back and letting out a wailing howl. The unexpected sound pierced the still night air, and I started as Ra responded in kind. A pair of arrow-point ears peeked out over the dune as another jackal came to sit beside the first.

"Where are the others?" I asked in a whisper.

"It is only the pair. They are solitary, monogamous creatures," Ra answered.

"Hmm, must get lonely."

"Not necessarily. You see, they bond for life. Those two will roam the earth together until the very end," he said, his thumb absentmindedly stroking across the back of my hand.

We watched the pair trail down the hillside until the ink-black night swallowed them up.

Ra turned to me; spirit alight with a burning longing, searching my eyes in the darkness. I tensed, afraid of what it meant if I didn't pull away. This man, with eyes like the night, had somehow managed to draw me in so deep that I could no longer resist. As we stood in the dark with our fingers laced together, it felt like a secret had blossomed between us. One that both of us were itching to tell but too stubborn to speak aloud.

We held each other's gaze for a long while, and I waited, hoping he would take action when I couldn't. A glimmer of desire crept up his spirit, but he promptly replaced it with confusion and a frown.

He stepped away from me, and my heart sank.

"Care to dance?" he asked, reaching for a blade and assuming his position.

I couldn't bring myself to speak my need, so I simply hitched a brow to hide my disappointment and set my sights on him.

CHAPTER 22

RA

The craving in my spirit was prepared to swallow me whole, and I needed something other than the smooth curve of her body and the touch of her skin to occupy my mind. I'd scarcely made it through Harmon in one piece. Hungry eyes had followed her through the streets, and I was itching to pull her close. I was grateful when she let me, and I couldn't help but bask in the feeling of her body melding to mine. Leaving her in Harmon's beer hall had been harder than I anticipated. I feared he might think me rude after I'd muttered several agreements in response to his polite conversation. In truth, my mind had been elsewhere. I was listening to the steady thump of her heart in the other room, and it took all that I was not to tear the head from that leech of a man.

Her smoldering eyes told me she wouldn't mind if I did, but I wouldn't subject her to such things. So long as she was satisfied, I would be too. But it didn't stop me from pulling her close as we left.

I thought the sweet words and teasing touches would be enough to satiate my need. But my desire had grown into an irrepressible hunger, and my resolve was wearing thin. Her silken skin was too divine to deny myself. But I knew it couldn't go on any longer.

The look on her face as I unwound our fingers pained me. If the balance struck me now, I'd welcome it. At least then, my torture would end. Her fiery eyes were too great a distraction. Feeling her curled against me in the night had sent the blood rushing to my groin. I'd dreamt of her body welcoming me, and now I ached to know if she would take me well. But no matter how badly I wanted her, she wasn't mine to have. Training would give her a reason to keep beyond my reach.

She was dancing around me as I sped in and out of her grasp and a cunning smile flashed as she lunged for me. She'd unsheathed her blade and was holding it with purpose—I wondered if she intended to use it.

She answered my unspoken question, striking out as I stood distracted by the bounce of her breasts and imagining how perfectly they'd fit in my palm. A mild sting swept across my arm, and I looked at her. Her eyes grew wide as they landed on the dribble of blood seeping from my arm, and her hand shot to her mouth. She'd managed to place a shallow cut along my bicep. I stilled, watching her chest rise and fall as the glint in her eyes grew bright with pride until something inside me broke.

My claws emerged and a subtle glow built under my skin. I sprang forward, and she lurched back, but she wasn't fast enough. I dashed around her, closing the distance before she could blink. She sucked in a breath as I snatched her up from behind—my arms encircling her. Holding her body tight to my chest, I let my fingers find the flesh at her sides, spreading them out to take in as much of her as possible. Her kan rose to meet me, and I bent, answering her need with my own and pressing my lips to the smooth column of her neck.

The rhythmic beat of her heart slowed as I lingered to savor the sensation. Her body responded—the sweet scent of desire perfuming the air. But she rushed to cover it, turning her face to hide from the moonlight. I loosened my hold, and when she didn't pull away, I continued, trailing my mouth up to her ear.

"Forgive me," I whispered.

"For?"

"For being so bold...I shouldn't. But your body calls to me..." My breath trailed across her skin, and she trembled in my arms. "Your skin begs for my touch."

She twisted around, trying to find my face in the dark. A pretty pout settled on her soft lips as her eyes found mine, and I knew she was about to argue. I kept my smile to myself. If she knew how much I enjoyed her stinging tongue, she'd only press harder, which wouldn't end well for either of us.

"You are too bold. I beg for no one," she snipped, a playful note in her voice.

Her kan rose to the surface in a frenzy, and I watched her stifle her own desires as she snatched her lip between her teeth.

"We'll see about that."

I pushed my knee between her legs, and her sweet body yielded, parting to make room for me. My blatant arousal pressed tight to her sex, and I relished in the little sound of excitement she made. But she was stubborn as usual.

"How about now?" I asked.

She shook her head deviously, locs bouncing around her face.

I reached down, snaking my hand through the fabric of her dress, and gripping the flesh beneath her butt.

She gasped as our kan ignited.

"Now?"

Her pink tongue swept out over her lips. But she shook her head.

Very well, then.

I leaned forward until my lips grazed her ear and spoke in a low whisper.

"I would worship at your altar. All you need is ask..."

Her green eyes glistened with an irresistible need, and her lips parted.

"Ra..." She moaned in response, causing my shaft to stiffen like iron between her legs.

"Balance, help me," I pleaded.

CHAPTER 23
ONIA

His mouth was on me. I pulled him in deeper, stretching my arms around his neck and bending his large frame to meet my own. He kissed me slowly, drawing me in closer and savoring the heat of our embrace as I melted into him. A quiet grunt slipped from him, and his hands fisted in my dress, trying to restrain himself. My tongue ran across his lips, spreading my kan over his skin before I opened to him. His tongue snaked into my mouth, and the smoky taste of his kan poured into me. It trickled down my throat and settled in my chest, before creeping lower and lower until it felt as if I might unravel at that very moment.

I leaned into him, finding the evidence of his affection pressed between my legs and wishing he'd lay me out under the stars. His mouth grew demanding, nipping at me when our kiss suddenly wasn't enough, and my hands moved lower, encouraging him. A low growl vibrated through him as he took a possessive grip on my thigh. His claws protruded and I cherished the little pinch as they poked into me. I imagined myself screaming his name into the night sky, and a tortured moan escaped me.

"Tey sot nesu..." He groaned in answer—*my princess.*

And at that moment, I was. I was *his*.

"Damn." He cursed, breaking away, and trailing his hands over me as if trying to commit it all to memory.

"What?" I asked, running my hands across his chest.

"We can't," he muttered with agonizing pain in his voice.

I swallowed the knot climbing up my throat.

"I understand if you think this is a mistake, but—"

"Mistake? Onia, you could never be a mistake," he said, brushing a longing hand down my neck. "But you set my spirit on edge, calling it after you, and tearing at my resolve. Every time that smart mouth gets the best of you, every time you meet the challenge without question, and every time you look at me like...like that," he said, and I blinked back in surprise. "I've tried to ignore it, but it pries at me. Every glance pulls me apart until suddenly my duty is disregarded, and I'm craving the touch of your skin. I'm afraid my heart will not know balance without you." His dark eyes dipped down as he studied me. "But that doesn't mean I can have you."

He steadied his breathing and took a concentrated step back.

"I am your guardian. Your wellbeing is my priority."

I drew in a ragged breath and tried to quiet the yearning. But it felt like a gaping hole had opened up in my chest, and all I could do was fist my hands at my sides. I didn't care about his duty, or mine, or the Hall. All I knew was Ra was feeding the hole in my heart, and I didn't want to return to the hollow, empty feeling, and neither did he. I could see it in his spirit. It was eager and hungry—frantic with need.

"Of course, you can. I don't care about your duty—" I began, but he cut me off.

"Princess, having you would bring you into the realm of everything that weighs on me. Not just my duty—my demons, my house—"

"Your house?"

He paused, dragging a hand down his face as he let out a terse sigh.

"If it were up to me, you would never meet them. Except maybe a few. The House of Anubis is not gentle, Onia. My mother is not kind, and my father is not loving. They are selfish and cruel. Nothing like the life you've known, and I have no desire to see you suffer at their hands for my sake. I would never be so selfish."

I pulled my arms in around myself, trying to keep my heart from spilling out of the hole that had opened in my chest.

"Why would I suffer for a kiss?"

He gripped my shoulders, forcing me to meet his eyes.

"Do not play at being naïve. You're much too observant for that. This isn't just a kiss. It never could be."

My heart sank; he was right. We'd been circling this moment since the day he stepped into the square. But now that it was here, it felt like so much more.

His hands found my face as I fought back tears, but he continued trying to make me see reason.

"My father demands my unwavering loyalty. He will see my feelings for you as nothing more than a distraction and a threat to my duty, to my house, and to him. And Mother....well, she is not one I'd ever wish to see you cross." He dropped his hands. "But it doesn't matter because this won't happen again."

I stepped away to widen the gap between us.

"And that's your decision to make?" I snapped.

"Yes," he said with grim finality. "I have promised to protect you. Even from the likes of me."

"Because of your *duty*?" I shouted, and he jerked back as if my words had reached out to cut him.

"It is my duty, yes. But make no mistake, I would lay down my life for your love alone. But the balance has frowned upon us, and it cannot be."

The hole in my chest cracked open wider, and I choked back a sob.

Why had he done this? We could have gone on resisting one another. I would have been fine never knowing. But now we'd faced our desires, and we were meant to go back to guardian and guarded without a thought? As if it never happened?

"If giving you up is the price I must pay for your life, I shall gladly pay it."

His eyes turned sad as he took a decisive step away from me. A cool desert breeze swept between us. I pulled my arms around myself, striding off into the sand.

"Onia!"

I ignored him, unsure of what direction I was headed. But I couldn't find it in me to care. I was too busy trying to wipe away the stinging emptiness.

Everywhere he'd touched, my skin burned with a need I hadn't imagined possible. A wealth of pleasure had opened up inside me when his lips met mine, and I drank him in without question. Only for it to be ripped from me a moment later. I tried to bury the hurt with anger. It was all I could find to keep me from crying. So, I latched onto it. I wasn't even sure I had a right to be angry. How could I be? When he was so willing to sacrifice his wants in favor of my life. But I was still seething quietly when the morning light made its way over the horizon.

My feet began to drag as the morning turned to the sweltering heat of mid-day. My body sang the praises of Atem when Mahatnaten's towering spires came into view from across the valley. This far from the river, I wondered how the people lived even a minute without shade. Sweat poured between my breasts and thighs, reminding me of the sun's ever-present rays with each step. Ra offered me his robe as we crossed the valley. But my anger stopped me from letting him drape it over my shoulders, and I stepped beyond his reach. I pretended not to hear his frustrated grunt as I denied him.

CHAPTER 24
ONIA

Mahatnaten was unlike any place I'd ever been. Shouts echoed off the walls—men and women, some in pain or anger, and a few with the distinct sounds of pleasure. Beggars huddled in every corner, and no children could be seen sprinting through the market with innocent laughter. The street dogs looked sickly, and Ra tossed the rest of our food into the road as we stepped through the south entrance. Dogs and men scattered across the ground groping for a piece.

A frail-looking man shot out from the shadows to grip my arm with a slick smile and several gaps in his mouth. The scent of urine and other unknown fluids wafted from his clothes, and I recoiled. Ra stepped in front of me, slicing a shallow cut in the man's arm as he yanked me closer to him. I gasped at his hasty punishment but was glad for his intervention.

"That will teach him to keep his hands to himself," Ra said coolly, draping an arm over my shoulders and pulling me close.

I bristled at his touch and twisted out of his grip. His hands were more than I could bear after last night.

"I thought that was forbidden," I said, indignant.

His jaw ticked.

"Mahatnaten is nothing like Harmon or Ashwana. The people here will not hesitate to cut you down where you stand. So, until we reach the temple, we'll just have to behave ourselves," he said, clenching his fists and speaking mostly to himself.

I rolled my eyes and let out a huff but didn't bother to argue. Ra was persistent when it came to my safety, and I knew he wouldn't move an inch until he was satisfied.

He led me through the streets, glaring at every man and woman whose eyes dared to pass over me, but his blades remained firmly strapped to his chest. We stayed on the main road, following the filthy, shaded pathway straight into the rear boundary. Mother's temple sat at the opposite end of the city, up a steep hill that turned steeper with every step. I watched it grow closer in the distance—a massive pyramid jutting out from the horizon, marking the end of the city bounds. It was bigger than the pyramids we built in Ashwana, wider at the base than the big buildings in the northern district. The pyramids of Ashwana were more decorative than they were functional—smaller and less ostentatious. Mother's temple looked as if each stone required ten men to carry, and I couldn't help but wonder how a city so barren had erected something so marvelous.

Eventually, we reached what felt like the top of the city, and Ra stopped to gesture toward a small wooden door embedded directly in the side of the pyramid.

"This is it," he said, waving me forward.

I stepped gently over the incense laid along the steps and eyed the plate of dried dates and bronze deben by the door.

Would it be improper to take an offering for my own house?

I decided against it, passing through the threshold only for my breath to be stunted as I set foot on the other side.

A deep, hollow cavern had been carved out of the structure's core to erect a monument in Mother's name. A testament to her power and a feat of almost inhuman construction. The entrance was deceiving, but nothing could have prepared me for the temple of stone reaching high overhead and bathed in intricate carvings.

Warm amber light illuminated the symbols running along the columns—prayer and praises in the old language designed to bless those who entered. Mourners were etched into the base, huddled together with their loved ones. I recognized the common depictions of Anubis as he guarded the dead on their journey, the scales deciding a path, Ammit devouring those who failed, and Osiris as he received those who succeeded to start their journey anew. At the end of the hallway, standing tall among the masterful engravings, in stone relief, was Mother—wings thrown open wide, spanning from wall to wall, and an arm outstretched holding the scales— waiting for you to submit yourself.

My legs ushered me forward until I stood under the scales gazing up at her. Her legs alone were thrice my height, and her head reached up high into the ceiling, so I had to crane my neck to see her face. A gentle look with high, arching cheeks and round, watchful eyes stared back at me. It was a face shockingly similar to my own, but I still found myself questioning the similarities. A goddess of such magnitude couldn't possibly be my mother.

"That's how I knew it was you." Ra's voice echoed through the vaulted chamber, reminding me I wasn't alone.

"Your eyes, I mean. They have the same allure. It's an impossible look of knowing that I've only ever seen in Empress Ma'at. Like you're looking into my very spirit with every glance."

A muffled "hmm" was all I could manage.

The sculpture, however detailed, couldn't convey what he'd just described. But I knew what he meant. Father had mused about my eyes in the same way, remarking whenever the opportunity arose that he saw Mother looking back at him. He'd always meant it to be endearing, but for some reason, it always left me feeling like a vessel for her memory.

"They're not exactly the same, though," Ra added, pulling my attention back to him.

I turned to see him staring up at Mother's stone-carved face.

"There's a ferocity in your eyes, like someone tossed emeralds on a fire... It's quite mesmerizing actually, watching you draw on it. A man could get caught in them if he's not careful." A smirk spread across his face, and the dimple threatened to reveal itself. So much for behaving himself.

"What was she like?" I asked, shifting the conversation, and trying to ignore the flutter in my chest.

"More powerful than any I knew and more loving than her own capacity would allow. She cared for my siblings and me as if we were her own. If it weren't for her, I think Father would have been even harsher than we knew." He paused, drawing in a ragged breath. "Now that she's gone, who knows what he'll become."

"How am I meant to measure up to that?" I wondered aloud.

"You aren't," Ra answered without hesitation. "You aren't your mother, Onia." My face scrunched up. "But you aren't meant to be. You are meant to be Onia—brave and bold and more capable than even you seem to understand. And when you are ready, you will claim your place as Empress."

He shrugged as if it were so simple.

Empress? Could I truly ever be worthy of such a title?

I went back to gazing up at Mother's heavenly form. Ra had settled against a pillar waiting for me to conclude my marveling. But an unfamiliar warmth was spreading through his spirit, deeper than I'd felt in the past few days and more persistent. I thought of reaching for his hand but sided against it as I remembered his decision against us. After a long and pregnant pause, he pushed away to stand beside me.

"Are you ready?" he asked.

I nodded, feeling the wonder begin to wear off and the sorrow creep in.

His fingers closed around my hand to lead me deeper into the cavern, but we spun as coins clattered across the stone floor. I unsheathed my blade to grip the handle until my knuckles paled. Ra's grip on me tightened, and he stepped out in front, unveiling a clawed hand as he turned to address the intruder.

The wooden door creaked open, and a hand, clad in gold rings, reached around the frame before a tall, slender woman with glistening toffee skin stepped into the light.

"You're losing your touch, darling."

The woman's voice was quiet, even as we stood so far apart. She knew Ra would hear just fine. His spirit responded to the husk in her voice, a wave of anger crashing against his composure, but he didn't move. Instead, his kan swelled to a peak before leaking out of him in a steady stream. A shroud of golden light began to press against my back, and I glanced behind me. Ra's kan had poured out of him to form a round opening wide enough to hold us both.

A passage.

"Onia, go. I'll be right behind you." His easy return to that commanding tone grated on my nerves, and I tightened my already impossible grip on my blade. We'd done this once before, and it hadn't ended well.

"I'm not leaving without you," I said.

"Sso, thiss is Onia..." the woman hissed.

Her tawny-brown skin shimmered as she swayed on her delicate feet, causing light to ripple over her and bounce back. She held the S's in her words a little too long, like a child imitating a snake. I peeked around Ra's broad shoulders to get a better look, but he sidestepped, cutting me off.

"Chishi," Ra spit her name out. "Leave before you regret crawling out of that pit you call home."

A playful pout formed on her beautiful face as she flicked her long braids over her shoulder. The tips brushed past her butt, and a gentle tinkling sounded as golden beads clashed together.

"Rabasssam," she whined his name like a lover, and my head whipped around to find his face.

Rabassam? Who in the balance was that?

A snarl echoed in his chest, and my spirit flooded with irritation at her overly familiar tone.

Who is this woman? And why is she so comfortable with his name in her mouth? A name I didn't even know he had!

A pit opened in my stomach as I pushed around him. I shot him a look, knowing he would catch the general sentiment.

"Aww, she's jealouss, darling. Can't you ssmell it? Just give her to me, and I'll put her out of her misery," she said, goading him into action.

"Chishi, don't make me do this," Ra warned.

Her mood shifted, and the playful look disappeared from her face, replaced by a bored and unaffected stare.

"Mother requestss otherwise," she said, her tone dripping with disdain.

This was Ammit's daughter, come to collect her mother's prey.

"You're not taking her," Ra barked.

"Isn't that jusst like him?" Chishi addressed me. "Always the protector. But I didn't ssay anything about *taking* her."

She took up an innocent smile as shabti crept through the entrance and around the pillars on either side.

"Go home, Chishi!"

Ra turned, gripping my hand and dismissing her. But before we could take a singular step, she stood before me, rage in her eyes, and a bony hand latched around my throat. I caught the distinct trace of markings running up her legs, as her dress settled around her ankles. She jerked me forward, bringing my face close, and blinking at me with her head tilting at an unnatural angle. A secondary lid swept across her eyes, and she stood eyeing me hungrily. I let out a strangled scream as she carried me backward, slamming me hard into a nearby column.

"Rabasssam, your tasste really has declined you know!" she called over her shoulder, glaring at me.

The shabti had descended on Ra, keeping him and his blade

thoroughly occupied, and all he did was growl in response. His kan swelled, and I watched as the jackal crept closer to the surface. I knew Ra would let the jackal out if Chishi kept her hands around my neck much longer, and I didn't want to find out what Mother's temple would look like once he'd forged his path. Seconds passed, and my breath escaped me, filling my mind with a thick haze.

Chishi was staring at me with her mouth hanging open about to say something more, but I didn't wait for her to speak. Still gripping my blade, I steeled my nerves, and let my kan surge and pulse into my arm as I raised it high. I cut across her arm. A slice of flesh fell away, and she stumbled back, gaping at my boldness. I pushed away from the column and sprinted for the passage.

Ra was still cutting down demons in the center of the temple. His spirit was growing frenzied, the jackal lurking, and I knew it was time to leave if I wanted Mother to remain standing. I skidded to a halt in front of the light and spun to find his face.

"Ra!" I shouted.

His head jerked in my direction, and I threw out a desperate hand, asking him to abandon his vengeance. His midnight eyes found the pleading look in my own, and he broke away from the fray, speeding toward me. Chishi righted herself, prepared to cut him off, but Ra was faster—his markings lending him greater speed than her own. Before she could take one step, he was diving across the expanse to envelop me in his arms. All at once, we collided, his momentum pulling me off my feet and carrying us backward through the light.

CHAPTER 25
ONIA

We were falling in a tangled mess—our bodies rolling over one another as the warmth of Ra's kan surrounded us. We met the ground on the other side with a loud smack, and my body groaned as I slammed into him. He lay underneath me with his arms wrapped tightly around my waist. I planted my hands on his chest, pushing hard to break his hold, spinning to look toward the passage behind us. But the space we'd fallen through had been replaced by a clay-brick wall.

"It closes once its creator passes through," Ra answered in response to my confusion.

I glanced down at him as his palms came to rest on my thighs and he shifted under me. An ember of pleasure sparked deep within his spirit, and a firm prodding pressed between my legs. I scrambled to get to my feet.

"Sorry," I murmured.

"You really should stop doing that," he said, standing to straighten himself and peer down at me with anger in his eyes.

"What? Letting you save my hide?"

"No...apologizing." His voice was gruff, but the glint in his eye betrayed his seriousness. He turned away to stride down the corridor, and I followed, matching his pace as I tried to take in every detail.

We'd landed at one end of a wide rectangular corridor with a glittering pool of water running the length of it, and I slowed as I gaped at the structure around me.

"You did well back there." He called over his shoulder.

"Well, it was either that or get mauled again."

"*Or*, you could have gone through the passage as I asked." The musculature of his back tensed and released as he spoke, but he didn't get to scold me. Not again.

"Oh, is that so, *Rabasssam*?" I hissed, doing my best to imitate Chishi's flirtatious tone.

He turned, yanking me to a halt and speaking through clenched teeth. "Do not call me that."

"Is that not your name?" I asked, cocking a brow.

His face hardened into stone and his eyes threatened to devour me. "Not to you, it's not. Only those I have no love for call me by that name. And I certainly don't count you among them," he said with a tick of anger in his jaw.

My chest tightened at his words, and I faltered. My feet stumbled as I tried to get them moving again, coming dangerously close to tumbling into the pool in the center. Ra swooped in to balance me—the spark of our kan feeling more like a cursed reminder than the comfortable energy I'd grown to enjoy.

"Careful, sematawy. You wouldn't want to fall in there. It'd be a long while before I could fish you out," he said, releasing me before our kan could become too excited.

I stared at the water as he continued down the path. It was still, like a sheet of glass, with clusters of light moving beneath the surface in a disordered fashion. Some shone brightly with a golden hue while others were a dull blue-grey, and some an inky-black color devoid of light. My kan stretched inside my limbs, drawn to the water, itching to read them. These were souls gathered beneath the surface, waiting to be weighed. But where did they feed from? I couldn't see the bottom of the pool as I peered over the edge.

It must run deeper than my eyes can see.

Ra's spirit began to dim in my mind, drawing further from me. I glanced up to see him near the end of the corridor and hurried after him, clutching my skirt in my hands as it breezed around my legs. My pace slowed, and my mouth fell open as I stepped into the center. The ground changed underfoot from smooth polished marble to a natural limestone, and I blinked as I stepped into the light streaming from above. Archways lined the rotunda, four on each side, tall and pointed with the image of a feather stamped into the top. A pedestal sat in the middle—the scales of Ma'at mounted atop in a bold brass sheen, large enough to balance twelve men. The room was otherwise empty, and my steps echoed loudly as I turned to find Ra.

He was standing in front of the scales and his spirit was suddenly stiff.

"Come here, sot nesu." He ordered, not bothering to abide by our agreement.

I opened my mouth to demand he do so, but the heavy clomp of angry steps had me skirting back to his side—my bold defiance dwindling.

Feet echoed through the rotunda as a tall, dark man with a jackal's head entered through the archway furthest to the left. Three others flanked him. Two men, stepping in unison with fierce looks on their faces, and a full-figured woman struggling to keep up with their long strides. Ra straightened as the group closed in, and I felt his kan dim as he pulled apart from me. A whisper of hurt flitted through my mind, but I wasn't sure if it was mine or Ra's, so I buried it, swiping the dust from my dress, and pulling my shoulders back.

"Father." Ra addressed the man in front.

I didn't need an introduction to know who he was. The jackal's head was telling enough. Anubis's jackal looked nothing like Ra's. Ra's was all night and smoke; Anubis's was a greying iron with a bolt of lily-white fur scraping between his ears and down the back. An angry-looking scar covered one eye, and his ears sat too close together on his head—like a rabbit more than a jackal.

"Rabassam, I see you were successful," Anubis returned in greeting—if you could call it that. The voice felt unnatural, speaking through razor-sharp teeth and strong jaws. Neither reached forward to greet one another properly, but Anubis continued. "Although, I expected her to remain unharmed." He growled with a disinterested sneer.

"We ran into—"

"I do not wish to hear your excuses!"

Anubis's voice ricocheted off the domed ceiling, each word bouncing back three-fold. But no one so much as flinched at his outburst, and I resisted the urge to turn to Ra.

Anubis spoke about me as if I wasn't standing before him, and he hadn't so much as looked at me. What did he know of my injuries? Ra was the one risking his soul for me. Ra's kan dipped at the accusation that he had somehow failed me, and my anger boiled up.

"Ra has done more than enough," I asserted, not waiting for an introduction.

"Onia." My name sounded rough on Ra's tongue, a flicker of fear in his spirit, but he didn't do anything more to stop me.

"I wouldn't be here without him. He was kind enough to share his kan with me, and I owe him my life," I said, feeling the pride in Ra's spirit spark a little, and suddenly I didn't care what Anubis thought of me. "Perhaps more than one."

Anubis stared at me blankly. The men behind him exchanged a knowing glance, and the woman dropped her eyes to stare at her feet. This was no way to greet someone, human or otherwise. I dug up a polite smile to hide my irritation. Anubis raised what I assumed was an eyebrow, and eyed me from head to toe and back again before grunting a breath too close to my face. A subtle glow emerged beneath his long robes, and his features began to soften, returning to a more human form. Dark skin, the same shade as Ra's, covered his face, and thick locs fell just past his shoulders. But his vicious teeth remained as he settled into his human face with a look of bitter disgust.

I couldn't help but drop my gaze, glancing at Ra instead. His eyes were focused on his father, but his kan had returned to its even flow. His subtle amusement pricked my mind, but he was otherwise unfazed. My words hadn't bothered him.

"Father, may I present Onia. Head of House Ma'at, heir to the seat of the Hall, and soon to be Empress." Ra gave my name the same tone of grandeur he managed with his own, and I felt the weight of his words as he spoke them aloud. I didn't offer my hand, and Anubis didn't reach for it. Instead, he only offered a slight bow of his head, a silent signal of his superiority.

"Anubis, Master of the Dead Guard and head of my house." His voice was flat. "You are a mirror image of her, your mother," he murmured. His face softened for a moment before returning to a stony look, as if he suddenly remembered it wasn't Mother he was looking at. "Although, your mouth is quite unlike hers." He glared at me over his thick nose, eyeing me with distaste. He stepped closer, and I held my ground as he dipped his head to whisper. "We are pleased to have you returned to your rightful home. But you will do your best to remember your place here, young Onia. You may be our next Empress, but this Hall does not belong to you." He rested a rough hand on my shoulder. Ra's spirit bristled then, his hands fisting as Anubis leveled his threat. "Seraya here will show you to your quarters," Anubis ordered, dismissing me as he righted himself.

He gestured to the woman behind him, and she nodded, bending at the waist with one foot forward in a more formal display. She motioned toward the entrance opposite the one they'd taken. As much as I craved the comfort of a bed and freedom from my sandals, I didn't move. Ra's kan had grown agitated, leaving me hesitant to follow the young woman, and Anubis's dismissive tone made me slow to comply. I looked to Ra, waiting for any inclination that I should remain where I was. He might have left me to his father's callousness, but if there was one thing I knew after our journey together—I trusted him with my life.

He turned to face me, and his hand moved to rest on my arm, but he quickly reconsidered, dropping it to his side as he remembered whose company we were in.

"I'll find you after I've spoken to Father." With a slight nod, he offered his reassurance.

I waited for a few beats, holding his gaze to see where his mind had gone. The tense knot I sensed dissipated until his spirit returned to its usual calm. Only then did I turn to leave. I followed after the woman, feeling more like a scolded child than an Empress to-be but satisfied with Ra's assurance that I wasn't being led to my death. As Seraya led me through the pointed archway, I could hear Anubis's voice echoing through the vaulted chamber, saying something about obedience.

CHAPTER 26
RA

"She appears obedient to you." Father's voice carried, and I looked after her to see whether she'd caught his words. Listening to her soft footfalls, I waited until she was at least a few cubits away before answering him.

"Yes, that's not unusual after an ordeal like hers."

I didn't challenge his assumption, even though it was far from the truth. I found amusement in the idea that Onia was somehow submissive to me. The thought of her doing as I said without question would burn her pride to its core, but Father needn't know that. The more unassuming I could make her, the better off she would be.

"Good, that will be of use to us. We will need her sooner than expected." He responded as anticipated, with little regard for anyone's interests other than his own.

Before I could respond, his hand came across my face with a stinging slap as his claws trailed down my cheek.

The guardians stiffened, daring only to look directly ahead. I simply blinked back in response. I'd watched his hand rear back. I could have stepped aside, but I'd learned it was easier to heal it than run from it long ago. So, I'd simply stood my ground. When he was finished, he turned, moving toward the archway he'd appeared from, and the guardians skirted out of his way.

"What happened? You were to be here two days ago!" he shouted.

"Shabti. They were waiting for her." It wasn't an outright lie. But the shabti weren't the reason we'd been delayed. I simply wasn't willing to push her past her limits.

Father spun at my words, causing the guards to take a noticeable step backward. "Impossible!" he bellowed, bringing his face mere inches from my own.

I stood before him, the novelty of his anger had worn off long ago and I'd since grown impervious to his outrage. The guards had my sympathy, though. I didn't recognize them by name, but they were different than the two he'd had before I left. I wondered what the previous pair had done to earn themselves the demotion. At least, I hoped it had only been a demotion.

"They already knew of Onia's existence. The shabti were close behind the entire journey. Chishi even graced us with her presence. Someone has divulged Ma'at's secret." I flattened my tone to keep from sounding accusatory. Father's selfishness might be his base nature, but his devotion to Ma'at and his duty as her guardian were a close second. She was the only soul he'd never so much as raised his voice to. He would not have betrayed her.

"She assured me she told no one else!" he shouted, causing the flame sconces to flicker and falter.

The scent of fear wafted from the guards. I doubted they would last long. Father would grow tired of their whimpering before the month ended. His brows knitted together, and a flash of insult crossed his face. I recognized the sting of betrayal as he realized Ma'at had lied to him.

"They were waiting for her in Ashwana. Someone has betrayed House Ma'at," I reiterated, hoping to break through his denial.

Had he already forgotten that the threat to Onia's life still lingered? "Ammit may—"

"Ammit is no match for me! That snake of a woman wouldn't dare to enter this Hall uninvited. And when I find whichever of her subjects is responsible for the loss of Ma'at I will return their head to her in pieces!"

I only nodded, leaving him to revel in his pride.

"What does the girl know?" he asked, once he'd calmed.

"Very little. Her father shared nothing with her. She knows nothing of her mother, her kan, or duty."

"Typical human ignorance," Father interjected, but I continued.

"She will need time with Shu," I added.

If anyone was equipped to meet her inquisitive nature, it was Shu, and he was aged enough to help her strengthen her kan.

"Yes, yes." Father waved a hand, dismissing my suggestion. "Just see to it. And see to it she learns some manners. I will not have her questioning my order. She may be the heir, but she holds no power here," he barked.

Interesting words for a man who'd crowned himself in Ma'at's absence.

I didn't bother to tell him of Onia's stubbornness. He would likely find out soon enough. Her subtle defiance in the rotunda should have been his first clue, but I wasn't surprised he hadn't seen it for what it was. Father wasn't accustomed to a spirit like her's. Very few defied him openly. Or rather, very few defied him openly and continued to walk this plane. Many times I'd been made to deal out his justice.

"Yes, Father," I said as we came to the fork that divided the east and west wings.

"And do not let her wander alone. Keep a close eye."

Finally, a demand I supported in earnest.

We'd been making our way through the inner circle, and we

parted without saying anything more. Father continued east, heading for his den, and I headed for the west wing. The urge to rid myself of demon blood drove me directly to my chamber. I tried to ignore the echo of her soft sobs floating through the Hall toward my sensitive ears. She deserved a moment's peace. She'd been wearing that armor since we left Ashwana, and I didn't want to be the reason she donned it again.

I entered the dark of my chamber to change and wash quickly. Her scent was clinging to me, and I wished I could hold onto it, but she deserved some memory of her Father. I tossed the blood-soiled shirt aside before hunting down a guardian to have it cleaned.

"This must be spotless, do you understand?"

I hadn't seen the guardian's face before, and while I may not know every guardian by name, I certainly knew every face.

"Yes, Lord Rabassam," the young guardian muttered.

"Do not come back to me with a shirt that is anything less than spotless," I demanded.

He shifted on his feet, staring at the blood I'd collected during our last encounter with the shabti. As he stood there questioning the value of the garment he held, I was reminded of the fear wafting off Father's personal guard.

"This garment is very important." I corrected my tone. "If you have trouble, let me know."

"Yes, my lord."

"Your name?"

"Tarik, my lord," he offered with a bow of the waist.

"Thank you, Tarik. I trust you will do your best."

Tarik nodded, turning on his heel to make his way to the guardians' chambers.

"And Tarik!"

He spun, stopping short.

"If anyone questions why you're doing laundry, send them to me."

With a nod, I sent him on his way and turned to collect our newest resident for dinner.

CHAPTER 27
ONIA

Seraya had led me through a labyrinth of stone walls, leading further and further from the rotunda. I tried to make sense of the passages as we went, but we entered corridor after corridor, plunging deeper into the Hall until the walls began to look identical and I couldn't be sure we hadn't gone in several circles. The paths were lit by the warm flicker of flame sconces, and the limestone floor echoed lightly against the sloped ceiling as we walked in silence. The scuffle of people moving about drifted from the adjacent pathways, but we didn't cross paths with a single soul, and I wondered just how large the Hall was.

Seraya was moving quickly, turning down each corridor without hesitation and only checking twice that I was still in tow. After the fifth turn, I started to understand the layout. I wasn't imagining the circular path we'd taken. Rings of passages rippled out from the main rotunda, connected to the initial corridors like spokes on a wheel. Some spokes were interconnected through a direct path and others led into an outer ring through another set of complex pathways. Eventually, I gave up counting the passages to make note of the rooms.

There was a small, empty-looking room with an altar at the far end lit by candles of various sizes and the scent of incense floating out into the hallway. We passed a deep room with a wide table running down the middle, long enough to seat sixty people. I saw what appeared to be a library in perfect replica of the rotunda with the addition of rows and rows of leather-bound texts reaching high into the rafters.

Eventually, Seraya stopped in front of an ornate wooden door with a deeply engraved pattern swirling up from the bottom, and I prayed there wasn't another hallway on the other side. To my surprise, she swung the door open to reveal a meticulously crafted room in various shades of natural linen. A spacious four-poster bed draped in a sheer canopy sat to the right, and painted palm leaves climbed the walls, prompting you to look up at the artful detail on the ceiling.

It was a room designed for relaxation, and from the looks of it, its purpose was well achieved—a quiet cocoon calling my name.

"A bath has already been drawn, and there are clothes on the bench. They should fit you fine." Seraya's voice pulled me from my marveling, and I turned to see her hovering near the doorway just on the other side of the threshold.

"Thank you," I said. I tried to find more words in my quiet disbelief, but ultimately, that was all I could manage.

"Someone will be back to collect you for dinner." She moved away from the door, closing it softly behind her as she left.

I crossed the room to slide the heavy latch into place and propped myself up against the warm wood. My shoulders sagged as I released a labored breath that I must have been holding for days, maybe years. Death hadn't caught me yet, and for the first time since Ra had found me in that backway, I knew it wasn't lurking around the corner. I waited for the initial shock to wear off—not daring to sit down for fear I'd ruin the rich fabrics—and wished I wasn't so desperate for what came next.

Tears welled in my eyes, burning to be free, and I let them pour out of me without concern for my appearance. My shoulders jerked from the force of them, and my chest tightened as a knot lodged in my throat. Hiccups wracked my body as I struggled to find my breath. Eventually, I left them to stream down my face in silence as I made my way to the deep copper tub opposite the bed. Tendrils of steam crept up from the bath and suddenly my body ached all over. I pulled myself from the fabric of my kalasiri, ignoring the flecks of blood around the skirt, and hitched a hip on the wide rim.

I sank beneath the surface, letting the water cover me completely, and sat submerged, wishing I could bottle the stillness. When my lungs began to burn, I came up for air and waited until the water calmed before starting the process of washing the dust and dirt from my skin.

By the time I stopped scrubbing, my skin felt raw, and the tips of my fingers resembled dried dates. But as I stepped out, I already felt lighter. I draped myself in a silken robe that Seraya had laid on a wide settee flanking the tub and began sifting through the selection of clothes. I ran the rich fabric between my fingers, touching them all like a child in the market square. Each item was crafted from fine linen and stitched with bold embroidery in different hues. I settled on a long cream-colored skirt with a slit running up each leg, a singular panel draped down the center, and a matching top. The skirt sat just above my hips, and the neckline curved across my chest, leaving my arms and shoulders bare. It was comfortable, familiar, and a perfect complement to my brown skin. All I needed was something to pull my hair away from my face.

Days in the desert had left it frazzled, and I was tired of it hanging in my eyes. I checked the usual places—the small desk beside the bed, the mantle over the hearth, and the chest lying in the corner. Then I checked the unusual places—under the pillows, behind the tub, the underside of the bed. All I found were a pair of silk shoes to match the dressing gown and several ink quills. I was prepared to give up when my fingers ran over a faint indentation along the front of the desk. A rectangular groove lay on the front, barely discernible to the touch. I stepped back to see how I'd missed it. Dark green leaves shadowed the fine outline of a drawer, providing the perfect camouflage, practically invisible unless you were looking for it.

I knocked lightly against the wood until I heard the pitch change. The sound signaled a hollow space on the other side, but there didn't seem to be a handle or lock on its face. I pressed against it, hoping to jostle it open, and felt the tiny spark of my kan before the drawer gave way.

I reached in, hoping to find a ribbon or something otherwise useful. But all I was met with were stacks of papyrus—some with writing, some blank, and others only having scribbles on them. I shuffled through the pages and noticed a familiar, bold script running across several of them.

Father's handwriting covered page after page, but I didn't stop to read them. I fumbled through the stacks until I found the beautiful sweeping script I'd seen first. I gathered a handful; each of them signed "With spirit and love, Mother." I ripped a sheet from the stack and began reading before I lost my nerve.

My Treasured Onia,

I've taken to writing these in hopes of bringing myself some sense of peace. I know not whether it is working. Only time will tell. As I write to you, I know you may never see these words, but if you do, I hope I am the one to deliver them to your hands.

I want so desperately to be the one to tell you how your mother loves you so, and how she fights for you—even now when you're so far from reach. But the balance may not grant me such a kindness. In fact, it may look poorly on us both.

If a day shall come when I am no longer here, know that I have loved you as only a mother can. And if you should find yourself in this Hall, hold fast to your spirit and your heart.

With spirit and love,
Mother

I settled against the chair, preparing myself to read through the rest when a soft knock sounded at the door. I snatched up the pages, feeling as though I'd been caught prying, and tucked them back inside, doing my best to shut it as swiftly and quietly as I could manage.

"One moment," I called as I straightened myself in the golden mirror.

My skin was still flush with emotion, and my eyes had grown swollen from tears, but I could blame it on the vigorous scrubbing and the heat of the bath if need be. Even so, I hoped my face would calm before I reached the dining hall. I didn't care for anyone's pity. I might not have much left, but I'd made it across the desert with my life, and for that, I would applaud myself.

I crossed the room quickly and pulled the door open.

Ra's broad stature was taking up most of the doorway, and I took a step back. I was so engulfed in Mother's letters I hadn't noticed the whisper of his spirit return to my mind. But now that he stood before me, it was stark clear as ever—a heated flame as his eyes scanned me. My own spirit settled as my eyes fell on the warm, ebony shade of his chest peeking out from under fresh linen. But the feeling quickly turned sour as my eyes found his face.

"Ra!" I reached for him on instinct. "What happened?"

Shallow cuts were healing along his cheek, barely visible. But I'd spent a week straight with only his face to keep me company, and I could see the faint lines. My fingers settled on his cheek, and he leaned into my palm, the usual spark of our energies calming him.

"It is nothing I have not faced before. It will not scar," he said. *As if that's what I'm worried about.*

"Anubis did this?" I asked, hoping I was wrong, but already knowing the answer.

"Yes, and far worse will come to us both if he finds you in my arms."

As he said it, I registered our compromising position. I'd stepped in too close. Ra had snaked an arm around my waist and was brushing slow circles across my skin in the gap between my skirt and top. I stiffened, glancing past his broad shoulders out into the hallway. Empty. I'm sure he knew; he wouldn't have let me come so close otherwise. But he pulled away, regardless.

I felt the sting of rejection, and my eyes fell to the floor as I stepped back. I reminded myself our time in the desert was ended, and we couldn't continue down this path. Ra chose to idle in the doorway—fists clenching at his sides.

"I told Seraya I would escort you myself. She asked that I give you these," he said, holding out a few vanity items gathered in his big hand. There was a skin balm, some hair oils, and a few incense.

"Oh, thank the balance!"

I hastily ran the rose oil through my hair until I was satisfied I no longer looked like I'd been wandering the desert. I checked my reflection once more and took a deep breath as I smoothed the fabric around my thighs. When I turned, Ra was propped against the doorframe, arms crossed, watching me with a pensive stare.

"I'm ready," I said.

"Are you sure?"

"As I'll ever be." I gave him the best answer I could. I knew that if we waited until I was truly ready, we'd likely die in this doorway.

CHAPTER 28

RA

I'd caught her without the armor again—as she should be, shoulders light and free. But then she'd spotted Father's handiwork, and it all fell back into place. We'd been in the Hall for less than a day, and already he was driving her from me.

I cursed the balance for having placed her in Father's path. He would take this opportunity to bend Onia under his thumb, to achieve greater power for himself—of this, I was sure. He'd never been so brazen with Ma'at. She'd been too powerful a match for him, but it hadn't stopped him from craving it. I doubted anyone else had noticed. Mother always turned a blind eye, and my siblings spent so little time in his presence, whether that be voluntary or otherwise, they hadn't learned to see Father for what he was.

Holding her chin high, she brushed past me, grazing my chest as I reached for the door. The fabric of my shirt saved me from the heated stroke of her kan. But even it couldn't protect against the sweet scent of roses as she swept through the doorway. I grit my teeth, remembering my promise to her.

When I turned back, she was staring at me with a question on her lips.

"Go ahead. Ask," I said, coaxing it out of her.

"Are you alright, truly?"

"Onia, it is only a scratch—"

"Not that." Sad eyes blinked up at me through her thick lashes, and I cursed Father for making her feel this way. "You seem angry. Angier than usual..." Her eyes dropped to her feet as words failed her. "I'm just worried, is all."

Her perceptiveness never failed to amaze me. Perhaps I was angrier than usual. Father's presence always grated on my nerves, but I wouldn't burden her with that.

"Do not waste your energy worrying over me, sot nesu."

Her arms folded across her chest, in that way that I loved, and a stern look of determination settled on her face.

"You're the only one who gets to be worried?" She grumbled.

I urged her forward, hovering along her lower back, careful not to touch her. Our circumstance called for distance. Control would do me no good when even the scent of her chipped away at it.

"Yes," I said, hoping she would leave it alone.

Her head snapped around, her mouth turning down in a fierce pout.

"Why?"

"Because I am not worthy of your worry," I said.

"Why would you say that?" she asked, her eyes burning into me.

"It is not your concern, Onia." I ground out the words. Her persistence was pulling at my spirit, stoking my desire, and I needed her to leave it be.

"I disagree! Give me one good reason I shouldn't be allowed to care for you?" She quipped, cocking her head.

"Because Onia! I am the reason you are here!"

She flinched at my outburst.

Damn.

How could she ever think I was a danger to her? I'd sooner fall on my own blade. But I gripped my spirit tighter, reigning in the heated anger. She did not deserve my shouting, and I would not allow this Hall to turn her against me.

"Forgive me, sot nesu. I didn't mean to shout. Being home makes me rather uneasy…"

I didn't tell her what it was that had me on edge. It would only add to her stresses, of which she already had plenty.

"What does that mean? *You're* the reason I'm here?" She asked, eyeing me closely.

I took a deep breath and found her piercing, emerald eyes. Could I bear the look in them after I said it?

"I am the reason your mother is dead."

Her frown deepened as she skidded to a halt.

"I don't believe you," she said, stubborn as always.

I sighed. I was hoping to avoid this.

"Father stepped down from his post as Ma'at's guardian long ago. He left it to me. The night of Ma'at's passing, after she'd gone to bed, I left the Hall to…cater to my own weakness." Steps echoed in the distance, and I lowered my voice. "When I returned, she was gone, and no one had heard or seen a thing." I touched the place on my chest where Father's claws had cut deep. Even now, they were still healing. I think he meant to kill me, and I would have welcomed it. But Abraxas and Ananiah held him back. Her eyes blinked back tears and my hands fisted at my sides. "Her life was in my hands, and I failed her. I failed *you*. So, do not worry about me. It is a waste."

"Ra." My name sounded sweet on her lips, and I braced myself for her words.

"I couldn't possibly blame you. How could I? You weren't here."

"But I *should* have been. I should have been there. And now, all I can do is ensure I don't make the same mistake. I will stand by your side in whatever way you need." If I thought it would make a difference, I'd have let her cut me down there in the hallway. But it was too late. She was here. And if she were going to stand a chance at resisting Father's hold, she would need someone prepared to lay down their life for her. "You have greater concerns than me—I am not deserving of your worries."

"Ra, I will not toss you aside for your mistakes. You're all— you're the only friend I have left." Her words burned me—to be only a friend was a cruel fate—but somehow, they soothed the searing pain of guilt I'd felt since that fateful day in the square. "And you are more than deserving. Your spirit is more tender than you believe. I've seen the warm embers of your heart. I know you would have gladly given your life for her. But we can't rewrite the past. So, you shouldn't berate yourself any further. I won't have it," she demanded, her foot stomping the floor as she stalked off in front of me—not a clue as to where she was going.

"Turn left!" I called as she veered too far in the wrong direction.

I could practically hear her eyes roll as she huffed and pivoted.

Apparently, she'd decided the topic was settled. I would abandon it, if only to keep from troubling her any further, but I caught her hand as the towering doors of the dining room came into view.

"Onia, please don't use your kan at dinner. Some don't agree with your presence here, and they won't take kindly to your examining." I made sure to phrase it as a request, lest I face her "wrath." But we both knew it wasn't.

Several groups were seated at the banquet table, and their heads swiveled in unison, followed by frenzied whispers. I met their stares, shielding her from their curious eyes with my body. With a hard look and wordless orders, I offered my ultimatum—stop now or bear the consequences. The assessors corrected themselves quickly, tearing their eyes from her as we passed by, and the few guardians seated knew better than to linger. They were out the door before it creaked closed behind us.

The family was already seated at the far end nearest the hearth, and Abraxas pushed up from the table to come bounding toward us with his arms spread open wide.

"Brother!" His voice boomed.

Beside me, Onia slowed a fraction of a step, and her heart quickened its pace.

Oh, Brother. Now is not the time.

Abraxas was the most uninhibited spirit of all my siblings. I liked to think it was the lack of Father's influence. As the youngest, he had come at a time when Father was already infatuated with someone or something else, and he hadn't possessed the desire to torment Abraxas as he had done me and the others. But it also meant he was less observant than the rest of us. The years of brutal training had left us with keen and discerning senses that he now lacked.

Still, I envied him at times.

I stepped out in front to take the brunt of his embrace and correct him with a harsh whisper.

"Do not push her," I said, gripping his arm.

With a grunt, he heeded my warning.

"How was your journey to the plane of the living? I heard you fought off the Demoness's servants." The speed at which gossip spread through the Hall always astounded me. "Even danced with the Princess of the Pit." Abraxas chuckled at his joke, jabbing me in the rib.

Onia's lip flinched at the mention of Chishi, and I shot him a look, which he promptly ignored.

"I see you've brought a beauty back with you."

His eyes hooded, and I grit my teeth as he swept up her hand and pressed it to his forehead. So much for not pushing her.

"Onia, this is my brother, Abraxas."

"Nice to meet you," she said.

"The pleasure is all mine, *tey nubian*."

I let out a low growl at his overly familiar words and his hand roaming up her arm. His eyes widened in surprise, and I met them unwavering. I might not be able to have her, but that certainly didn't mean I would stand by idly as he tested my patience. But before I could correct him, she spoke.

"I'm not your *golden one*." She threw back, her lip curling.

"You speak Kemi?" Abraxas blinked at her in surprise.

"Enough to know when a man is overstepping his bounds," she declared, snatching her hand back.

Pride flooded my chest, and I had to resist the urge to drape a possessive hand over her hip. Abraxas stood gaping at her, taken aback by her sharp tongue. I was familiar with the feeling, but all I could offer him was a shrug. She was no more at my whim than his. As if on cue, she spoke, proving my point.

"Although, that seems to run in this family," she added, throwing a glance in my direction before striding forward.

"HA!" Abraxas laughed, clapping his hands together and jutting a thumb in her direction. "I like her."

I marveled at her from behind.

Balance, she is going to make this difficult.

CHAPTER 29
ONIA

Ra's kan flared with excitement as I pushed past him. He idled for a moment but was already moving at my side within a few steps. I tried not to look at him as his spirit struggled to contain itself. I knew I shouldn't pull at his control, but seeing the mild shock cross his face had been worth it. Besides, who was he to growl over me? Especially after what he'd done. I wouldn't allow him to reject me and lay claim to me all in a single breath.

As we reached the end of the table, he swept an arm out, gesturing toward the group that sat before us.

With a nod to the woman closest to me, he said, "Onia, this is my mother, the Hall's resident healer, Nephthys."

Nephthys?

I hid my shock as the woman stood to cross her arms in front of her.

"So you are the trouble that has kept my Rabassam away for so long."

So long? Was a week "so long?" Then I remembered Ra's comment about time moving faster in this realm. Perhaps he had been gone a while.

"Mother, it has been a long journey. Leave her be."

"Oh, of course, dear. I was just wondering what all the fuss was about."

She offered me a half smile, framed in a red-orange tint, that didn't quite reach her eyes.

I glanced back at Ra, skeptical he'd introduced me to the right deity and trying to reconcile the stories with the woman before me. Her tight auburn coils sat in a pile on her head, spilling over a silken-gold headdress accompanied by a tight-fitting kalasiri in a matching fabric. Beaded bracelets rolled over her arms and down her neck, making her look perfectly polished. She was petite with a delicate frame and no markings that I could see, and I wondered if she could even crush a fly.

This must be why they called her "The Housewife."

People often mistook Nephthys as the goddess of the home, gentle and helpful, nothing more than a housewife. But I knew better—as did any woman who ruled over a home. Nephthys was no homemaker; she was the first guardian, guardian of children, and the first Pharoah. Father had translated the old stories for the priests back home in Ashwana, and they all spoke of her spirit— like fire, vicious and dangerous, and known to protect her own.

Suddenly, Ra's spirit made more sense. It wasn't Anubis he'd inherited his protective nature from, it was Nephthys.

I opened my mouth to apologize, then remembered Ra's request.

"The Demoness slowed our journey, but Ra took care of it," I said.

"Yes, well, let's hope you were worth it," she said, the smile fading into bored indifference.

"Doubtful..." The muffled voice came from the young woman beside her.

"Ananiah!" Ra shouted—his sister.

My heart went out to him as her lip curled in response. His family was turning out to be exactly who he told me they were.

Glancing at Ananiah, the relation was clear among them. She had the same thick dark hair as Ra and Abraxas, except hers floated down to her shoulders in ringlets, and her eyes were a deep-set almond shape with amber irises—a perfect echo of her mother's. I glanced back at Ra, realizing he was the only one that hadn't gotten Nephthys's sunset eyes. But neither Abraxas nor Anaiah had the same engulfing stare as Ra or Anubis. In that, Ra took after his father.

"Nice to meet you," I offered, doing my best to ignore her snide remark.

"I'm sure," Ananiah responded, not bothering to meet my eyes.

"Ananiah, that's enough." Ra urged her to watch her words, but she didn't heed the warning.

"What? She shouldn't be here, and we all know it."

"I'm not so thrilled about it either," I shot back—unable to compose myself. After being dragged across the desert, I wasn't in the mood for her misplaced judgment. I hadn't asked for any part of this.

"Then maybe you should go back to the human realm," she smarted.

"Enough!" Ra bellowed, and he didn't need to say anything more before Ananiah quieted. It was a commanding tone that silenced everyone in the room involuntarily—even the assessors at the opposite end quieted. "Onia is here to take her rightful place, and you will show her your respect. Whether you deem her worthy or not, is immaterial." Ra's anger was beating against his composure, threatening to spill out, and my spirit swelled in appreciation.

The flame settled as he glanced down at me, and a silent "thank you" passed between us. He nodded as he flexed his hands, and I knew he was having a hard time keeping them to himself. He redirected my attention to a bald man across from us.

"This...is your uncle Shu, our record keeper." Ra didn't wait for my thoughts to catch up. "Shu tracks the souls as they pass through the Hall—to keep the balance in order."

The burly man with a clean-shaven face and a smile that crinkled the corners of his eyes stood, jutting out a hand for an enthusiastic greeting.

"Hello," I said as I stood gaping.

The god of peace looked like someone's grandfather without the wrinkles and greying beard, and I found it fitting, albeit different from what I'd imagined.

"Goddess, you are her spitting image," Shu said, clapping his meaty hands together in awe. His voice was a smooth baritone, and I thought to myself how well it fit his gentle disposition. "Bit more spirit in you, though," he said with a wink.

"I didn't know mother had siblings."

I probably should have said more, but, not for the first time today, I couldn't find the right words.

He sucked his teeth in disappointment.

"I'm not surprised. Considering how little she and your father shared with you..." He let the rest of his thought die, deciding it wasn't an appropriate dinner topic. "No matter." He waved it off. "If you ever have questions, please do not hesitate. The library is always open."

Shu wavered for a moment, as if there was more he wished to say. But he thought better of it and settled back in his chair.

Ra waited until I settled in my seat before placing himself between Ananiah and me. A wise choice considering she was still quietly seething in her chair.

Plates clanged as people filed in with fragrant food, and I glanced around to see that a few groups had already left since we entered.

"Where is everyone?" I asked as I scanned the room.

The rest of the table was now empty, aside from a group of chatty women at one end and a couple sitting fairly close together in the middle. Seraya looked up from her intimate conversation with a nice-looking man to offer me a soft smile. I returned the sentiment, but her face fell as she looked past me, and she dropped her gaze.

"The assessors eat in shifts, and I have increased patrols for the foreseeable future," Ra said.

"You?"

"Yes, *I*. Father is Master of the Guard, but I am their commander. They follow my order. Other than his personal guard, he rarely bothers to speak to them."

A grunt of agreement sounded from Ananiah, and the rest of the group shot her a look that she didn't seem to mind.

"How are the shabti these days, brother? Still dumb as dung?" Abraxas quipped, tactfully changing the subject.

"Unfortunately for them, yes," Ra said, a hearty chuckle rising in his chest.

"Those poor souls," Shu muttered.

"Souls? I thought they were demons," I said.

"They are, but they were once living," Ra answered carefully as if trying not to upset me.

Too late.

My face must have paled because Ananiah barked out a haughty laugh at my shock.

"Ammit offers those that fall into the Pit more time in exchange for their service," Ra explained.

"And there is only *one* way to leave her service," Nephthys chimed in, holding out an elegant finger tipped with long, pointed nails.

"That's awful."

"It's quite ingenious, actually," Nephthys added, musing over it as she pushed her food around her plate.

Suddenly the fragrant meat didn't seem so appetizing, and I picked at it—disinterested.

We ate in a mixture of comfortable and tense silence until

Abraxas pushed away from the table, mumbling something about scratching an itch. Ananiah was next to leave. She hadn't said much all night, and her exit was more of the same. Eventually, Nephthys excused herself, leaving Ra, Shu, and me to finish our meal in peace.

True to his legend, Shu wasn't the kind of person that felt the need to fill the void with noise. So, the three of us sat quietly for a long while, and I found myself watching him closely, trying to find hints of Mother, or even myself, in him. For a moment, I contemplated reading his spirit, but Ra's voice echoed in my mind, and I suddenly felt conscious of the possibility that Ananiah wasn't the only one that didn't want me here. A whisper of worry crept into my mind as I sat looking at him.

"No need for such anxiety, my dear. You're home now," Shu mumbled around a bite of bread.

Home?

Shu's thick hand covered my own, and a calm fell over me, clouding my mind and loosening my grip on my kan. My body relaxed, and my mind slowed as the thoughts fell away. Before I could smother it back, my kan melted into a soft haze and opened itself to read him.

"You may not want to do that, my dear."

Shu's voice was deep, but it wasn't scolding. Instead, he sounded rather amused. But I jerked my hand back, realizing my intrusion.

"Forgive me! I didn't mean to—" I offered, keeping my voice to a tense whisper.

"Not to worry. That may have been my doing. You're likely sensitive to my kan because of your lineage." He spoke matter-of-factly, not realizing I wasn't following. "Your mother, I mean. She could read you to your core with the briefest glance. I imagine your power is the same?"

I nodded. Shu's eyes were bright with excitement as he recalled Mother's power. I couldn't imagine accomplishing such depth with a simple glance. It had taken me ages of fearful practice just to pierce the surface. Now I could peel the layers back in a few moments, but I doubted I would ever attain such precision.

"She must have been very talented."

"She was truly a wonder," Shu said solemnly.

My spirit sank a little further as I was reminded once again how I'd been cheated out of her memory. Shu met my eyes with a small, sorrowful smile, and it struck me that he was mourning too. Perhaps, they all were. Somehow the thought didn't give me much comfort. Instead, it drove me deeper into my loneliness. Shu may have joyous memories of her, but I had none. I'd forever be tied to another's vision of her—never to have my own.

"May you know balance in your time of mourning." I spoke the rites as I'd heard so many times since Father's passing. I knew it wouldn't give him the comfort he needed; it never did. But unfortunately, it was all I had to offer him.

"Thank you, your mother was a treasure among us. There are not many left like her. Most of us have grown jaded over the centuries, but she was a light we soon won't forget."

"How did she do it? How did she read people so easily?" I asked, eager for a chance to know her, even secondhand.

Shu opened his mouth to speak, but Ra shot him a look from across the table.

"This is neither the time nor the place," Ra said, using his dark eyes to point out the group of assessors still seated several rows away.

The chatter had all but died, but a few guardians had taken a place at the far end of the table, and Shu eyed them wearily.

"Young Ra is correct. Please, come by the library tomorrow. We can discuss anything you'd like. We will have more privacy there."

"Thank you," I said, hoping he understood the depth with which I meant it.

After a few moments, he excused himself, leaving Ra and me

to sit in silence. It was a sound we'd grown accustomed to—a comfortable silence devoid of stress. I saw us sitting over an open flame again, picking at fish and splitting figs. He'd become tense the moment we stepped in the Hall, and I couldn't help but wonder if the man beside me was different than the man I'd known by the fire.

<h1 style="text-align:center">CHAPTER 30</h1>

ONIA

I paid close attention to the path we took back, counting each turn and marking the general direction in my mind, but sleep was calling to me, and I struggled to keep up, eventually losing count. Ra led me through the maze just as Seraya had—swiftly, without hesitation, and as if he could find any room blind. I wouldn't be surprised if he could.

"I apologize for my family's behavior," he said once the shuffle of people faded and it was only our steps echoing through the hallway.

"Your mother isn't as brutal as you or the legends make her out to be," I said.

"You do not know her as I do. She protects herself to a fault. They both do," he said, gazing down the path before us with pain marring his spirit.

"What is that supposed to mean?"

"It means you are not to trust them, either of them. Father's only goal is to rule this Hall as his own, and Mother only wishes for him to notice her."

"And Ananiah? It's clear she doesn't think much of me."

Ordinarily, I wouldn't mind her distaste for me. But I'd

already seen the questioning looks as we entered the dining hall—a room full of gods, gawking at the lost woman who'd wandered home. I hardly had a place here, and I doubted adding Ananiah's animosity would help matters any.

"Don't concern yourself with her. She knows this is your rightful place. She's just upset about the state of things." His kan shifted toward anger before righting itself, reminding me of his demand as we entered the dining hall.

"I don't *examine*, by the way."

There was a hint of frustration in my voice that I hadn't planned on, but I didn't care. Did he think I went around peering into every soul that passed me by? I always did my best not to pry, and when I did, it was for good reason. He was a singular exception.

"Excuse me?" he asked.

"Earlier, before dinner, you asked me not to *examine* anyone. I don't read people all the time. I always avoid it unless absolutely necessary. Shu was an accident, and with you I can't seem to quiet it. But its not on purpose." I'd grown distracted searching the corridors, and the words came quickly before I knew what I'd said. I clamped a hand over my mouth as my confession came tumbling out.

"Why would you need to quiet my spirit?" he asked, drawing his brows into a frown as he tried to hide the surprise in his voice. As if that would keep it hidden from me.

I hesitated. Ra wouldn't take kindly to being so open, especially when it wasn't within his control...or mine. But my heart was in the way. I didn't want him thinking I'd been reading him maliciously.

My eyes fell to the floor and I sucked in a deep breath.

"I can read *others* when I *want* to. But with you...your spirit is different. It's always here." I tapped a finger to my temple. "Not all of it, just a hint of you. Always coursing through my mind. I've tried to block it out since that day in the market, but nothing's worked. Even before I saw you, I felt it. And it hasn't quieted since..."

He answered my confession with silence, and when I looked at him, I wished those dark eyes would swallow me up and save me from my misery. I could see the distress on his face, and worse, I could feel a clotted knot of unease rising in his spirit. My stomach clenched as I realized I may have just secured my loneliness.

We turned down the path to my room, and I suddenly wished we had much further to go.

"Interesting," he said, continuing as if we were just making idle conversation.

Interesting? That's it?

"That's all? Aren't you the least bit curious as to why? Aren't you upset I've been invading your spirit?"

"Not particularly," he lied, but I couldn't tell about which part.

"You have nothing else to say?"

He paused to think a moment.

"What's it like?" He asked, and I blinked back at him.

"*That's* what you want to know?"

"I suppose." He shrugged. "And don't say it's 'a wealth of pride and dignity.' There's no coin in it for you this time," he said, smiling down at me.

I stifled a laugh. That hadn't been a lie, but it was a bit dramatic.

I looked at him and his broad shoulders, tense with emotion and covered in markings. I knew exactly, what he felt like.

"You're like fire," I said. "Warm, and soothing. But dangerous."

"Hm." He grunted.

I knew I should say something more. Something witty and sharp to jerk the truth out of him, but my mouth clamped shut, stunned into silence at his easy acceptance.

"Rest. You will need it," he said, stepping away and forming tight fists with his otherwise gentle hands.

I watched him retreat through the corridor, the comfort of his spirit growing fainter with every step.

"Sot nesu!" he called over his shoulder as I reached for the door. "Please, do not wander."

I nodded. I had no intention of traversing this maze at night. I stepped into my room and a mild panic set in as the door shut behind me. I'd known this was Mother's room the moment I set foot inside, from the gentle colors and the warm sensation permeating the air. It'd been a relief at first. But I quickly realized her legacy was even grander than I'd imagined, and I was woefully out of my depth. I pulled her letters from the drawer that seemed to respond to my kan and set about sifting through them. If I were lucky, Mother's words would be enough to guide me.

CHAPTER 31

RA

I t'd taken every ounce of resilience not to follow her, shut the door, and feast upon what I knew would be an oasis between her thighs. She'd unknowingly granted me a gift—to have her see me always without constraint or composure; it was a freedom I'd never known. Father had demanded I hold tight to my spirit, else my weaknesses be displayed for the whole realm to see. But knowing I didn't need to hide from her, *couldn't* hide from her, left me aching to return her sweet gift. It also meant I couldn't ignore my suspicions any longer. I thought it was my heart playing tricks on me. But now I knew it was more than that, and there was only one man I trusted to tell me the truth.

The light of the library was dim as Shu sat at his bureau sifting through aged scrolls. As usual, he was hunched over his papers, focusing on whatever knowledge he hoped to glean, but this time it wasn't the peaceful, curious Shu that sat behind the desk. This time, he was shuffling through them in a frenzy, the sweaty scent of anxiety pouring out of him in waves.

"Everything alright?" I asked from my place by the door.

He hadn't noticed my entrance and his head snapped up.

"Ah, Ra, yes. Certainly, just something your father needs quite urgently," he said as he swept the pages aside. "What can I do for you?"

"Cast your shroud," I demanded.

He frowned but didn't question it. Instead, I felt the blanket of his kan spread over me and the commotion of the Hall fall away. A quiet unlike any other draped the room as Shu's peaceful energy swept over me. Leaving us to a deadened silence, separated from whatever lay outside the doors. He waved a hand, beckoning me to speak and signaling that his kan's work was complete. We were alone. This conversation would be heard by no others.

"I need your knowledge on a matter concerning O-Lady Onia," I began.

Shu's brows lifted into his would-be hairline. "She is safe and resting," I assured him. "But I wondered what you could tell me of soul tethers."

"Ra, you know as well as I how a tether is made."

"Yes, but how do you know when a tether was created in a *past* life? How does a pair know of one another without the memory to tell them?"

"The spirit knows. It always knows," he said solemnly.

His mind drifted away, and I knew he was remembering Tefnut. Pain flashed on his face, and I couldn't help but pity him for the loss of something so sacred.

"In what way?" I pressed.

"In every way. Your kan will remember the sensation of being one; it will crave the connection. It may even try to obtain it. Why do you ask such things?"

For a moment, we stared at each other in weighted silence. I waited until his brows crinkled and understanding sparked. As he leaned back in his chair, I told him of my evidence. The way our kan reacted at a single touch, the aching desire that weighed on me, and how my spirit opened to her against our will.

"And what of your jackal?" he asked after I'd finished.

"It longs for her. It fights for her with ease, unlike anything I've ever felt before. It resists its bindings to reach out to her—as if it knows her."

"Perhaps because it does," Shu said, shrugging. A wide smile spread across his face as my fears were confirmed.

"It appears you and the Lady Onia tied the knot that cannot be broken."

I sighed.

Our souls had been bound together in a past life, and now we were facing its remnants.

"No one must know," I commanded. "Not even her." *Especially not her.*

A tethered soul was loyal to one above all else, and while Onia was my only concern, Father would see it as weakness. I suspected that was his reason for rejecting Mother's pleas to tether himself to her after all these centuries. His selfishness would suffer in the wake of a tie to another. Instead, he'd given her children, hoping our love for her would stand in his place. But try as Mother might, we were never what she needed—all she'd managed to foster was a thorough resentment from each of us, save for maybe Ananiah. While I would gladly lay down my life for Onia, I would not see her do the same for me. She was stubborn beyond compare, and Father would see fit to confine her to the lower levels if he thought my loyalties lay elsewhere. Heir or not, he had done worse for less.

Shu's big hand came to rest on my shoulder.

"My boy, a tether is not something you simply *ignore*."

"But it *can* be."

Shu knew that better than most. His treatment of Tefnut had cost him her affections, and he'd never been the same since. She'd abandoned their soul tie after centuries of his disregard for her wishes. The entire realm knew that they both continued with a gaping hole where the other used to be. The tether could never broken, but it could be forgotten.

"True, a reborn tether need not be reknotted, but the cycle of rebirth does not smile on many. To find a soul tie in the next life is a gift from the balance. There are those of us that wander about with a hole in our spirit, wondering why it can never be filled and never knowing it is for lack of a missing piece. A tether is a beautiful gift...to willingly neglect it is..." He couldn't bear to speak the rest.

"I will not endanger her. This remains between us," I ordered.

"I fear it may not be that simple."

"Father took Amon's life for a crime less than treason. I will not wait to see the lengths he will go to maintain control of this Hall. You will not speak a word of this." This time I spoke as commander of the guard and not the young boy who'd spent so many hours among these scrolls under Shu's gentle guidance. He sat back and looked at me as if I were nothing more than a fool. He might think so, and he might even be right, but that didn't mean I would place her in the path of Father's vengeance.

Eventually, he raised a hand in defeat.

"Shu, she will need the strength to withstand him. I will see to it her body is well trained, but she will need your help to hone her kan. She is quite impressive for having no instruction, but I will not leave her life to chance."

Shu nodded. "I will see to it."

I bowed at the waist before standing to make my exit.

His shroud began to fade and the noise of people wandering through the hallways trickled back into the library.

"Ra!" he called as I stepped up to the wide double doors. "Congratulations, my boy!" he teased with a wide grin.

I shook my head.

"Goodnight, old man!"

I could still hear his burly laugh echoing through the hallway as I shut the door behind me.

CHAPTER 32
ONIA

I woke to a soft tapping at the door and shot up from the bed to stuff Mother's letters back into their hiding place. I'd spent the night sifting through her things, but there were enough letters tucked away to take up two lifetimes. I only managed to make it through two before falling asleep with paper strewn across the bed.

I slid the drawer shut and sprinted for the bed, slipping back under the silken sheets.

"Come in!" I called, trying to tidy my hair.

Seraya pushed through the door carrying a small tray of fruit and a large pitcher of water.

"Good morning, Lady Onia. I trust you slept well?"

"Yes, it was lovely."

I tried for an earnest response. But Seraya looked at me as if she knew I'd lied. Truthfully, I'd had better sleep lying in the dirt curled next to Ra. But I had a feeling that had more to do with the company than the location.

"I see you've found her favorites," she said, pointing her chin toward the silk robe and slippers lying along the edge of the bed.

"Don't worry. I'm sure she would have wanted you to have them," she said as she caught the look of guilt cross my face.

It was a nice thought, but considering Mother had left me in the human realm without so much as a token to remember her by, I doubted that was the case.

"Were you close?" I asked as I occupied my mind retwisting the root of my hair. The desert had been unkind, and the rose oil could only do so much.

"Very." Her eyes grew distant as she looked around the room, and I suddenly felt like I was disturbing the preservation of a memory standing there. "I have been your mother's right hand since the beginning. She is my greatest friend. I'm sure she would want you to have her things. You must have many unanswered questions. Being among them may offer you a chance to know her —in your own way." Seraya spoke softly as she folded the silk wear and placed it gently in Mother's trunk.

My finger knotted in a stray strand of hair as I grew distracted by her words, and I squirmed trying to free my hand.

"Stop fussing, dear. Come sit, let me," she said, patting the settee and gesturing for me to join her.

"Oh, I couldn't possibly impose. I'll be fine. I've done it on my own plenty of times," I said finally freeing my finger and moving on to the next strand.

Our eyes met in the golden-clad mirror, and she cocked her head with a brow raised.

"Nonsense. It's nothing I haven't done for *her* a million times," she said, eyeing the tapestry over the hearth. It was a simple depiction of Mother, kneeling with her arms and wings outstretched, painted onto thick linen. It was decades older than the other fabrics, and I wondered if Seraya truly meant "a million times."

I shrugged internally, getting to my feet. If I was honest, after trekking through the desert, my hair was the last thing I wanted to worry about.

"You talk as if she's still here," I said as I settled onto the settee in front of her. "Why?"

"Because she is. Perhaps not in the form I knew her. But she will be reborn, and I may one day know that form too."

My mouth opened but snapped shut before I could settle on the words. There were so many questions I wanted to ask. But it was clear Seraya was hurting. I shouldn't be so selfish as to make her relive her memories for my sake. I hesitated for a moment. Then, as if she could see the tension building in my shoulders, she said, "Go ahead, dear. I don't mind."

Her cool fingers swept my hair over my shoulders, and a pang of sadness pierced my heart.

Mothers and sons and daughters used to sit out in the spring sun as their elders gently wound and braided their hair. But that was never a moment I knew. Not that Father hadn't tried, but it was supposed to be Mother sitting here with me, and fate had robbed us of that—Ammit had robbed us of that. I took a deep breath and pushed the pain aside. Now was my chance to know her, even if it weren't in the way I'd always dreamed.

Only one question had been looming over me since the moment Ra told me of her.

"Why did she hide me away?" I asked, desperately wishing that the answer wasn't so important to me.

"Ma'at loved you dearly," she said, and I watched her reflection as she worked a balm in her hands. "It broke her to leave you and your father, but they met when the divine had already withdrawn from the human realm, and they couldn't remain together. Ma'at couldn't abandon the Hall, and your father couldn't cross into this plane. At least, not while he still lived. Atem would never have allowed it." She rolled my hair between her fingers, working with expert dexterity. "Your mother knew the danger that would come to you. Her power was greater than most. Some say even greater than Atem. Yet others still vied for her kan, trying to claim her power and make it their own. She didn't want you to face the same fate." I watched in the mirror as a sad and apologetic look settled on her flushed cheeks.

I'd walked right into the very path Mother had been shielding me from.

I twisted around to pull her into a tender hug. It wasn't much, but it was all the thanks I could offer. Her arms came around me, and she held me close as she whispered, "There are things in this Hall that threaten you. Keep your wits about you, and do not offer your trust lightly."

I jerked back, startled by her candor. "What do you mea—"

The words stuck in my throat as a familiar spirit peeked through my thoughts. It was focused and stern, and I turned to the door as a light rapping sounded from the other side.

"You may enter," Seraya called.

Before I could finish my question, Ra strode into the room, looking hot and tense. Seraya patted my shoulder, signaling my release, and made herself busy straightening.

"Good morning, Seraya," he said, offering her a subtle bow of the head.

His spirit softened as he cast a hungry look in my direction, and I realized how little the thin fabric of Mother's nightgown hid. The muscle in his jaw twitched in frustration as my nipples stiffened, but I didn't move to cover myself. He waited until he'd drank his fill before he spoke.

"Good morning, Lady Onia." He bowed low, bending at the waist.

Lady Onia?

My brows wrinkled before I remembered Seraya standing close behind me. I hoped this was for her sake and not meant to become a regular occurrence. One person calling me "Lady" was more than enough.

"I'm here to escort you to the library."

"Give me a moment," I said, picking up the clothing Seraya had laid out.

His eyes followed me to the vanity, and I caught his reflection, standing with arms crossed, watching me closely.

Our eyes met in the mirror and soundless words passed between us.

I would take you now if I could bear the consequences. His said.

I would let you, despite them. Mine answered.

The heat of his stare burned into me as I fought the urge to rise from my seat and cross the floor into his arms. But neither of us moved, and all he said was, "Sot nesu, you may wish to wear pants." Then he bowed slightly, shutting the door softly as he exited.

Seraya didn't look up from her work, and I guessed our conversation had ended. I dressed quickly, taking Ra's advice on the pants, and when I opened the door, he was leaning against the wall, eyes closed and hands loosely clasped in front of him.

CHAPTER 33

RA

My spirit was getting the best of me, and I was playing with fire, as it was. Ever since my revelation in the library, I'd been consumed by the thought of her. Even as I slept, I saw her face, and now that she was in front of me, I wanted nothing more than to tell her—to bind myself to her as I knew we had before. But I couldn't possibly say it out loud. To place something of that nature on top of her already burdened shoulders...it would be cruel. Instead, my jackal was running rampant, and the sight of her had sent me spiraling. Standing there with sleep in her eyes in a gown that clung to her curves—the dark, vanilla shade of her nipples staring back at me.

A Goddess...

I could smell her need blossoming and I had to step away to stifle the erection growing in my pants. I wouldn't subject her to my impulses.

She was walking beside me in silence, having found a comfortable rhythm in walking just to my right. I knew she only did it as a courtesy to me; otherwise, I had no doubt she'd be walking out in front—if she knew where she was going.

"You know you could just tell me where the library is," she huffed as we rounded another corner.

"And risk you being lost? No, thank you."

"Couldn't you just sniff me out?" she quipped, giving me a sidelong glance.

The jackal perked up at her smart reply, and I couldn't help but give in a little.

"Yes, but there are other ways to raise my heart rate if that's what you're aiming for."

I watched her closely as a chill ran over her, and I knew she was holding back as she bit down on her lip.

We rounded a corner, and the lofty, arched entrance of the library came into view. I pulled the iron handle, swung the door open, and stepped aside for her to enter. She turned back to look at me as she stood in the doorway.

"You're not coming?" she asked.

I wished I could, but Abraxas was gathering people for questioning as we spoke, and a few hours of her absence was well worth eliminating the risk to her soul.

"I have a security matter to see to."

I was careful not to lie outright in case her view into my spirit was keener than I knew. "But you are in good hands. Shu is good company. Someone will escort you to the training room when you are finished."

I offered her a small smile in reassurance. But when that didn't work, I scooped up her hand and pressed it to my forehead, bowing deep and letting the sensation of our kan meet. This simple touch would have to do; it would calm her when I couldn't. With a deep breath and a nod, she disappeared behind the stacks of scrolls and leather-bound books.

"Next!"

The door swung open, and Abraxas directed another guardian to sit before closing it loudly to come and stand beside me. The room I'd selected was small and stifling. The perfect place to garner the uncomfortable feeling that led people to vomit up their truths and ensure the aroma of their stress, fear, and anxiety couldn't dissipate. Between the two of us, we took up enough space that the only option was to sit.

I took a deep breath, dissecting the sweaty aroma of the guardian before me. She was tall, wide, and another new addition to our ranks. Apparently, Father had "removed" more than just his personal guard while I was gone. Abraxas couldn't tell me exactly how many we'd lost to his fits of rage, but it was enough that I had many new faces to learn. This one was one of them.

"What is your name?"

"Ayesha, my Lord."

"And your house?"

"Horus, my Lord."

"Dual spirit?"

Many of the descendants of the two-spirit gods, like Father, carried some version of the animal spirit they harbored. Horus's falcon spirit was particularly devious. Less brutal than the jackal but certainly more sly with an observant eye. It would be an asset to someone with a duplicitous agenda.

"No, sir. I don't possess the falcon. My lineage is too far removed from Horus," she said, shifting on the hard wooden chair and staring at her fingers.

I leaned forward, wrapping my hand around her wrist and pulling her closer.

"Look at me," I ordered.

She lifted her head to meet my eyes, and the heady scent of bold desire filled the room. Abraxas cleared his throat loudly, but I ignored him and Ayesha's lust-filled face.

"Did you have a hand in the Empress's passing?" I asked, holding her gaze and feeling the steady thump beneath my fingers.

"No, I couldn't possibly!" she blurted.

Her heart was steady, and her eyes didn't shift. I released her.

"You may go," I said, dismissing her with a hand.

She stood quickly, swiping moisture from her palms, and I waited for the door to shut before turning to Abraxas.

"What a fragrance!" he praised, taking another deep breath.

"Anything else?" I asked as I tried to remind myself why I'd agreed to his presence.

"You mean other than the scent of heat between her legs?" He stifled a laugh. "No. Maybe a bit of anxiety, but I still think that was mostly your doing."

I nodded. That seemed to be a problem with a few of the guardians. Finding anything of value through the thick scent of lust and desire was more difficult. *That* was why Abraxas had joined me. Two noses were undoubtedly better than one, even if his jackal was more wonton than my own.

"Not interested?" he asked, jerking a thumb toward the door.

"Hardly."

It wasn't that Ayesha wasn't pretty; she was prettier than most. But the scent had done nothing more than remind me of the woman I wanted yet couldn't have. "Who's next?" I asked, pushing Onia's sweet face and watchful eyes from my mind.

"Seraya."

"Send her in."

Seraya inched into the room, carrying herself lightly and nodding to us. She sat in the stiff chair and crossed her ankles as she met my eyes.

"What can I do for you, Ra?"

"What do you know of the Empress's murderer?" I asked.

"Why, nothing dear. Why would you think—"

"Do not lie to me, Seraya!" Fear wafted from her in waves, but it was bitter, tainted, mixing with palpable anger. It wasn't on my account. I hadn't done anything to warrant such feeling. "Have you forgotten that very little escapes these ears? I heard the warning you gave to Lady Onia. Now, tell me—what do you know?"

"Please, Ra. I know as little as you," she pleaded.

It was a lie—and a good one at that. But her eyes gave her away, pupils widening like the new moon as the words left her lips. I gripped her wrist as I'd done with Ayesha.

"Did you have a hand in Ma'at's death?" I asked.

"How dare you!" she said, twisting her arm to yank it free.

I tightened my hold as she fought against me. The jackal stretched to life at the thought of a struggle, and I reeled it back in. It's power wasn't needed here.

"Enough!" My voice echoed loudly in the small space, and Seraya stiffened. Beside me, Abraxas's eyes flicked between us, shocked by my callousness. "Answer...the question."

After a moment's hesitation, I was prepared to send her into the lower levels, but then she spoke—barely a whisper.

"No..." she said, tears welling in her eyes as she dropped her gaze.

The truth.

I released her. Her shoulders jerked from tears as they streamed down her face, and Abraxas helped her from the chair.

"Come," he said, but he didn't rush her.

A gentle palm settled on her back as he led her from the room. He returned, shutting the door tight before turning on me.

"That was harsh," he chided.

"I'm aware."

"I understand our urgency. The longer we take to find Ma'at's killer, the longer the danger remains. But it's not like you to act in anger," Abraxas added, reminding me he was more observant than we often gave him credit for.

I wished I needn't behave like a terror storming through the Hall—like my father. But Onia's life hung in the balance, and I wouldn't rest until she was safe.

"I don't have time to be gentle. There is a killer lurking in these halls. You don't think they'll want Onia next." Her image swept through my mind—emerald eyes blinking up at me as she stood arms crossed, trying to suppress her vibrant smile. My reservations vanished. "Seraya's hiding something. I know you smelled it."

He drew in a breath, closing his eyes to sift through the aroma.

"She's scared of someone," he said, opening his eyes and creasing his brow.

I pinched the space between my eyes. The noxious gas of fear and anxiety pouring out of every guardian and assessor was giving me a headache.

"Watch her closely," I said, and Abraxas nodded. "Send in the next one."

CHAPTER 34
ONIA

I stepped into the domed room and audibly gasped as I took in the collection on the walls. The library was more extensive than it appeared from the outside, made to look smaller by the lack of windows, which was saying something considering the size of the entrance. Cubed shelves held row after row of papyrus. Leather-bound parchment was stacked high on the floor and piled atop tables; every inch was flawlessly adorned with ornate symbols and precious metals. Small brass wells were set on the stacks, filled with ink and falcon quills, reminding me of Father's decorative mess. I closed my eyes to breathe in the familiar smells.

He would have loved it.

I followed the intricate tile to stand in the center, tracing the pattern with my eyes as I went. Carefully etched feathers stretched out from a golden ring forming a perfect circle, framing a saying in Kemi that I knew all too well.

"Osiris laid those stones himself," Shu called from the back of the library. He was hunched over a wide wooden bureau, examining an old scroll. "He had quite the infatuation with your mother. Although, that could be said of a fair few." He chuckled to himself.

"'Know thyself deathless and able to know all things,'" I read aloud. "My father used to say that all the time."

"Then your father was a wise man. It's a gentle reminder that the soul is everlasting and the quest for knowledge never complete." He gestured around the room with wide open arms before shaking a thick finger in my direction. "Now, what can I do for you?" he asked, coming to stand beside me.

I shifted on my feet, mildly uncomfortable with the prospect of burdening him with my ignorance. But Ra was insistent that I learn the extent of my power. He was certain I could do more with proper instruction.

"Ra says I must learn to use my kan."

"And?"

And what? I'd just told him.

He stared at me in silence, his brows lifting higher on his face. He was determined to make me say it. He watched me squirm until I broke.

"And...I need your help to achieve it." I sighed.

"Very well, that shouldn't be a problem," he said, resting a fat hand on my shoulder before turning to dig through the loose parchment on his desk. "Your kan is necessary to feed the Hall, to keep the cycle churning. The energy it draws from the Empress ensures that the souls find their way here and onward," he said with a wave of his hand. "Your kan takes after your mother, you see. As the souls pass through, they are weighed against the feather. Those that do not tip the scales will continue their cycle. Those that do, head to the Pit—to be consumed by The Demoness, never to be reborn again." I nodded, wondering why he was telling me things I already knew. "Your particular talents are designed to read the souls when the scales fail." He ducked down, disappearing behind a stack of texts. "You see, every once in a while, a soul will balance perfectly with the feather. But it must still have a path. And when the scales do not know which to choose, *you* will." *Me?* His muffled voice rose into the rafters. "This is your duty as

Empress of the Hall. To serve as judgment when the scales cannot," he said, breaching the surface and slapping a single sheet onto the table.

I leaned over, peering at the paper between his fingers. It was an artful depiction of Mother standing in full regalia, looking powerful and determined—a long thin blade in the shape of a feather in one hand, the scales in the other, and wings that made her look as if she might take flight off the page. I stared at her, wishing I could have seen her in all her glory and imagining her wielding the feather with lethal force.

"Of course, we are only born with so much kan. *Some,*" he said, giving me a pointed look, "more than others. But some have grown greedy and wish to garner more for themselves. To add to their own. Your power is unique, and it will be a target to many. Ma'at was very well versed in the use of her kan, able to hold fast to her power in the face of greed. We will need to ensure you are capable of doing the same."

"And how do we do that?" I asked. I'd never honed my kan for strength, only precision.

"Practice. Come! Show me what you've mastered!"

I balked at his bold confidence in me.

"Mastered is not the word I would use."

If I was a master of my power, I'm sure I would have managed to block Ra out by now.

"Ah, nonsense! I cannot teach you if I do not know where we are to begin. Come, come." He gestured for me to join him, holding out his arms, offering himself for a reading. I stood in the center, feeling out of place standing before a man who had watched the first sunrise. My life was but a moment compared to the centuries he'd seen, and I couldn't help but feel inadequate.

Shu cleared his throat, his gentle demeanor growing impatient, and I shook myself. I'd done this a thousand times before.

With a deep breath, my shoulders dropped, and I shut my eyes, clasping his outstretched hands and focusing on opening my kan.

In an instant, the surface of his spirit came into view. Like a dull wave, it ebbed and flowed. Similar to my own and nothing like the wild torrent of Ra's carefully caged energy. It reminded me of Father scooping me up off the pavement after I'd been knocked to my knees in the marketplace—gentle and nurturing.

I wonder if this was what Mother's kan would have felt like.

I slipped down further, feeling the heavy calm wash over me and my mind begin to empty. My kan continued its sifting, only to plunge into a hollow core, where something had been ripped free. A dim light shone at the bottom, and I reached deeper, trying to latch on to it. But a bitter and angry sensation snapped back, and I jerked free of Shu's spirit, afraid his aching loneliness may swallow me next.

"Forgive me, my dear…I was not expecting you to dive so deep. You are more skilled than you claim to be."

"I'm so sorry," I whispered, and I was, for the intrusion, but mostly for whatever had created the chasm of longing in his heart.

Shu nodded, waving a hand.

"Unearthing such pain can be difficult. Hence, why I've buried it so deep," he said, tapping at his chest.

I watched him closely, unsure how to tell him it wasn't buried as deep as he thought.

"What is it?" I asked.

He pulled in a deep breath to let out a heavy sigh, and I felt the weight of it before words even formed.

"That is my tether. What is left of her anyhow."

"Your what?"

"Tefnut—she is my soul tie. A magnificent, bright, and fiery woman who, for a time, I was lucky enough to call mine. When we were young, we tied a knot that cannot be broken, binding our kan into one and forming a tether between our spirits, uniting our power." His fingers laced together in front of him in demonstration. "But I ignored her wishes one too many times over the centuries, and in the end, she walked away from me… She is still here, of course." He rubbed at his chest as if trying to soothe the pain. "She always will be. In this life and every life after. Once a tether is made, it cannot be broken. Even in rebirth our spirits will call to one another." His hand rested on his chest. "But she does not appreciate when I pull from her power. You must have startled her when you pulled the end of our thread."

"I'm sorry. I didn't know—"

"Nonsense." He held up a hand. "I should be thanking you. It has been a long time since I've felt that light. I think she likes to forget I am still on the other end," he said with eyes full of regret.

He reached out to squeeze my hand lightly, and I realized the spark of my kan was notably absent. I gripped his hand to be sure. Shu's eyes landed on me, a questioning look in his eye, and I released him.

"Everything alright, dear?"

My mouth gaped like a fish as I hesitated.

"Why can't I feel your kan?" I asked in a whisper—mostly to myself.

"Pardon?" Shu asked, cocking his head.

"Oh, I just mean...when Ra touches me, I can *feel* it—his energy. Like lightning across my hands. But I just realized you and the others...there's nothing."

"Ahh, yes. Kan has been known to do that...when drawn to one another," he said, eyeing me closely.

"Drawn?"

Am I drawn to Ra?

A warm sensation coursed through me as I remembered Ra's effort to protect me, his tender touches and longing glances, and the way he spoke my name with pride in his heart...

Of course, I'm drawn to Ra. But what does my kan have to do with it?

"That is enough for today," Shu announced, interrupting my reverie. "You did well. Come back tomorrow, and we will begin in earnest. We'll need to work on your stealth. It's no use if everyone can feel you reading them, now is it," he said, eyes crinkling in a sweet smile as he let out a hearty chuckle.

He ushered me toward the door and my pace quickened as he shooed me out.

"We have much work to do," he muttered.

And before I could turn to ask him, the door shut behind me and I was standing out in the hall.

CHAPTER 35

ONIA

A man was waiting propped against the wall as I turned, confused by Shu's hasty retreat.

"Afternoon, Empress," the man said, scarlet, feline eyes catching the light as they landed on me. "Lord Rabassam has sent me to escort you to the training room." The man spoke low and slow, flashing a pair of lethal canines and several gold rings hanging from his lip, nose, and ear—a delicate chain connecting them across his face.

He blinked back at me expectantly, and I saw the ink of markings painted over his eyelids.

"Oh, hello. Thank you...uh..."

"Tarik, Empress." He bowed at the waist.

"Thank you, Tarik. You do know I'm not Empress yet, right?" I pressed, hoping he would take the hint and stop using the formal honorific. It was bad enough people had taken to calling me "Lady;" I certainly wasn't ready to be elevated to "Empress."

"Yes, but you will be soon. The title is yours to claim—when you are ready." Tarik shrugged.

And when would that be? I wondered. Anxiety fluttered in my

183

chest as I realized how unprepared I was, and I changed the subject.

"What house do you belong to, Tarik?" I prompted, hoping he liked talking about himself as most people did.

"House of Khonshu and Tefnut," he murmured, seeming somewhat disinterested in the topic.

Tefnut would account for the feline features. She was dual-spirit like Ra, a lioness in her other form, and Khonshu explained his unique coloring. Hair, white as the moon, was braided back in rows, joining together to drape down his back in one long, thick strand. With skin pale as ash it was as if a phantom stood before me.

He moved like one too, slinking through the hallways with little urgency—hands stuffed into his pockets, stepping in stride with one foot in front of the other like a cat on a ledge. Heads turned as we passed a group of assessors, and I hiked up a brow, meeting their gaze until the shame of their gawking caught up to them. They'd have to contend with my eyes watching them if they wanted to stare.

A man with sandy hair swallowed hard before jerking his face forward, and I was thankful for my piercing gaze.

"Don't let them bother you. Gods can be gossipy, just as humans are. Sometimes more so," Tarik muttered under his breath before making a face at a passing assessor.

"I suppose you run out of things to talk about after a while." I shrugged, turning my head to catch a few craning back to look at me.

Tarik chuckled.

"Lord Rabassam put an end to it last night. With the guardians, at least."

"*Excuse me?*"

Tarik cleared his throat and stifled a smile.

"He gathered all the guardians and threatened to have their

eyes removed if he caught them gawking at you like you had two heads again." He laughed then, like he found the idea genuinely amusing. Admittedly, that sounded like Ra. "I'm sure he'd speak to the assessors if you asked."

I'd sooner tear my own eyes out than ask Ra to scold forty assessors in my name for making me feel uncomfortable. I could handle a few ill-mannered onlookers.

Tarik must have misread my hesitation because his next words came out in a whisper.

"Don't worry, he's nothing like his father. I doubt he'd ever do it."

"What do you mean like his father?" I asked.

Ra had spent a week of walking refusing to tell me much of his family except to hang their bloodlust over my head. I'd seen what he'd done to Ra, but how much worse could it be?

"Anubis is known to be quite vicious with those in his command." Tarik made an effort to speak quietly. "Many have lost their lives to his temper. Apparently, he went on a rampage after Ma'at died. The guardians thought he was going to kill Lord Rabassam. It wouldn't be the first time he'd done such a thing to his own children."

"His own children?" I gasped, then jerked around to ensure the hallway was still empty. It was only Tarik and me now, and I turned back, eager for him to continue.

"There was an incident ages ago. Anubis cut down his eldest in front of the family." Ra had told me of Amon's death, but he'd conveniently left out his Father's involvement. "Luckily, Lord Rabassam did not meet the same fate after Ma'at. But that was only due to his siblings' fierce defense of him. Anubis cut down several guardians in his place. Rabassam may be brutal in some ways, but he is merciful in the ways that count."

The image of deep claw marks scaring Ra's chest coupled with fresh scrapes along his cheek stung behind my eyes. How could a father do such a thing? Now I could see why Ra was so adamant about setting our feelings aside. I sucked in a breath, feeling a weight settle onto my chest as I realized the path Shai had written for us. Ra and I would never be.

CHAPTER 36

ONIA

"Training room" was an understatement. Located in the outer ring, closest to the guardians' quarters, it wasn't a room so much as a hall of its own. Weapons hung along the walls, and the empty floor spanned at least one hundred cubits across—divided into smaller sections for sparring. I trailed in after Tarik, straightening to my full height to appear less out of place. Groups of guardians were already brawling with one another in every corner. I watched a small woman swing her body around a man twice her size before looping her arms around his neck. She used her momentum to bring him to the ground with a loud thud. A few onlookers cheered as she rolled and bounced back on the balls of her feet, waiting for the man to right himself. I cheered her on silently.

Ra and Abraxas were standing in the center, chatting. Ra laughed at something Abraxas said and I was happy to hear the deep rumble again. But he quieted as he turned to watch Tarik and I make our way into the center. A single hand fisted at his side as his midnight eyes swept over me, and I imagined the heat of his hands on my skin as we sparred. My spirit perked at the thought, and I averted my gaze.

Abraxas stood with a staff in each hand and turned on us with a broad smile. I had no doubt he would have waved if his hands weren't already occupied. As if we could miss him. He was the second largest deity in the room, second only to his brother. As we strode closer, he tossed a staff in my direction. I managed to catch it, although not as gracefully as I would have liked.

"Abraxas will show you how to make use of that," Ra said, coming to stand dangerously close. "And you already know what to do with this." He spun a blade in his hand and held the blunt end out to me.

His fingers brushed mine, and his jaw ticked as I took it from him, the weight lending me some comfort.

"You won't be training me anymore?" I asked, trying to hide my disappointment.

"Abraxas is very capable. He trains all our guardians. And I trained him," he added, throwing an elbow into Abraxas's side.

Abraxas beamed at his brother's show of pride, and I shrugged. Who was I to question his qualifications?

"What? Don't you trust me?" Ra asked, the muscle in his jaw jumping as it did when something was bothering him.

"With my life," I replied.

His spirit perked at my words, the jackal rising up to reach for me. But he buried it as the dimple made an appearance and he turned to leave.

"Good luck, brother; she is not an easy one!" he called over his shoulder as he swept between the wide brass doors.

Abraxas stepped forward, narrowing his eyes at me.

"We'll see about that. Nejeri!" he called.

The huddle of guardians froze before parting to reveal the small woman jumping to her feet, leaving another opponent lying defeated. She jogged forward, looking effortlessly lean and perfectly put together, not a braid out of place.

"Tarik, take a break. She won't be needing an escort in here."

Abraxas gave him a curt nod, and Tarik walked off to join the group. I watched as he stopped stooping forward to rise to his full height, pulling his hands from his pockets. He was larger than I thought at first glance. He stepped into the center of the ring to take Nejeri's place and slinked forward to crouch before his opponent—an unusual stance. But as he launched himself from the ground, the crowd swallowed him, and shouts of his name rose to the ceiling as they cheered him on.

"Ready?" Abraxas asked, handing Nejeri a staff and stepping aside.

"Ready for what?"

The words had barely left my mouth before Nejeri's staff connected with my hip.

"Aye! Are we just—"

My words were stunted as she came at me again, striking at my shoulder. Her brows drew together in concentration, and she prepared to strike again.

Fine, if that's how you want to play.

I mimicked her stance as best I could—one foot in front of the other, shoulder-width apart, with my hands resting evenly along the staff. I angled the front higher and raised my brows in challenge.

Nejeri came at me again, but this time I was ready...sort of. I managed to block her first blow, cutting the staff through the air to stop its trajectory, but she pivoted, spinning the staff and striking with the other end, hitting my hip again.

I grew tired of her taunting. I agreed to train, not public shaming. I pushed forward, jutting the staff in her direction. It connected with hers and bounced back as she recovered and lunged. I made another go at her, springing forward and sweeping the staff across my body until it connected with her leg.

She gave me a quick nod before resetting herself.

"Well done!" Abraxas shouted. "Focus your energy!"

He stood to the side, watching with his arms crossed, and I got the impression he was enjoying himself.

I tightened my grip on the staff and steadied myself for her next attack. She swung high over my head, and I lifted my staff in time to connect with hers but didn't spot the other end coming up to meet my stomach. I used the power in my legs to jump back as the bow swept up into the space I'd been occupying.

Is she trying to kill me?

"Not *that* energy. Use your kan!" Nejeri shouted over the crack of the wooden staffs meeting again.

She hardly sounded winded.

My kan?

I opened my energy to read her. Her spirit was surprisingly even given our current activity. But I pierced through the surface quickly and watched her nod as the current of her spirit coursed through her body. It moved in unison with her form, dropping low as she stepped backward to give me a moment. But a moment was all it was.

I focused on her spirit and felt the spike before she lunged. It was a fraction of a second before she was on me, but it was enough time to move my limbs out of the way. Her spirit lifted, and she moved to strike again. This time I concentrated on its trajectory and not the staff. I could feel it building in her left thigh, preparing to shift to the other. Her spirit surged into her right leg as she lunged again.

I blocked the sideways blow and pushed forward, smacking her hard where she'd just emptied her energy. She stepped back and nodded, encouraging me to continue.

She moved differently than Ra. Her movements were fluid, whereas his were quick, leaving her open longer. But her size meant she moved around me effortlessly, and I still had to work to anticipate her direction before it changed. Without my kan I would be lost.

She stepped forward, and her spirit shifted into her front leg, then pushed into her arms as she prepared to swing at me. She angled the staff across my body, cutting through the air with immeasurable speed. I thrust my own up to meet it, and before her spirit could shift for a retreat, I turned and speared the end of my staff down hard into her stomach.

"Excellent!" Abraxas cheered.

The sly smile on Nejeri's face told me I hadn't done any real damage. She was well trained, and it would probably take much more force to cause even a scratch.

I hunched over with my hand on my knee, using the staff to prop me up and trying to catch my breath.

"What...in the...balance?"

The words came out chopped up—separated by my sharp inhales.

"That was impressive. I'm Nejeri of House Sekhmet," she said, holding out a hand in greeting.

No wonder she was so skilled. The goddess of war was a force to be reckoned with.

"Nice...to meet you." I took her hand gently, and she bowed at the waist.

"Apologies for the unusual training," she said, flashing a perfect smile. "Your mother used to fight like that. We have no idea how she did it, but Ra figured if we threw you in, you would figure it out no problem."

I'd have to thank him for that brilliant idea later.

Her face was now a stark contrast to the fury I'd witnessed only moments ago. Her eyes were a slanted almond shape, small and keen, but friendly when she wasn't scowling at you. Their color fit her face—the warm-oak irises brightening her sandy skin and giving her a sun-kissed appearance.

"And what was the alternative? Keep hitting me until I pass out?"

The look on her face told me my guess wasn't far off.

"Ha! Yeah, right. As if Ra would ever allow that," Abraxas interrupted. "He knew you wouldn't go down without a fight." Abraxas was excited to see that their theory had panned out.

I sat in the center of our sparring square and crossed my legs. Abraxas squatted beside me while Nejeri sat across from me, looking like she'd hardly lifted a finger. I took a few deep breaths to steady myself and wiped at the sweat that had collected on the back of my neck. Nothing really hurt other than my lungs, I supposed.

"Mother used to fight?" I asked, trying not to sound like an eager, young child.

Abraxas nodded. "She was deadly with that staff of hers. Struck me down more than a few times." He laughed as he said it but rubbed at the back of his head like he could still feel the sting of her staff. I pictured her wielding it expertly, wings beating through the air as she descended on her opponent.

"Good," I said.

The rest of the sparring groups were too engulfed in their sessions to spend time gaping at me, and I decided this wouldn't be a poor place to pull my mind from its misery.

I caught a glimpse of Tarik's lily-white hair between a huddled group and watched as his fierce feline features sharpened, and he lunged for his opponent, bringing a knife to her neck and flashing his fangs in a teasing smile. The woman threw up her hands and stepped away, blushing as Tarik welcomed another.

"Ready?" Nejeri asked, standing over me with her arm outstretched.

She pulled me to my feet with surprising strength before stepping back to take her stance.

With a stiff nod, she came at me again.

We headed for the dining hall after Nejeri had thoroughly knocked the last bit of air from me, but not before I'd managed a few sweeps of my own.

Abraxas was teasing her as we walked, asking Tarik who he'd bet on given a week's time.

"I'll consider myself a successful teacher if Onia can take me down in under a month," Nejeri called.

"With your help, I think I can take Abraxas in a week," I joked.

Tarik laughed, and Abraxas narrowed his eyes before pulling his head into the vice of his arm. Tarik pushed and shoved him as Nejeri rolled her eyes, stifling a laugh.

"And what about me?" Ra's deep, husky voice echoed across the ceiling as he stepped out from the shadows. He looked me up and down with a smirk, and I suppressed the urge to reach out and touch him.

"Give me a day," I challenged.

His eyes narrowed on me.

"Oh, I doubt you even need that long."

CHAPTER 37
RA

"Which of you dare train her?" I could hear Father's shouts echoing through the corridors as I made my way to his den. When I stepped through the door, Ananiah and Abraxas stood silent with their eyes downcast, facing Father as he loomed over them. His face was contorted with anger. Mother sat lounging in the chair, utterly unfazed by Father's words.

Abraxas took a breath to confess his supposed crime, and I shut the door loudly, forcing the words to stall as he looked up to see me enter.

"I did," I said, walking forward to meet Abraxas's eyes.

He quieted, and Ananiah knew better than to step in. I took my position between them and Father and waited for the impending rage.

"You shall remedy this immediately!" he shouted. I had no doubt the assessors could hear him all the way in the west wing.

"I will do no such thing," I answered and watched as Ananiah's eyes jerked to Father's face before lowering once again. Onia had been training under Father's nose for weeks. Apparently, someone had seen fit to tell him. Otherwise, I doubt he would have ever noticed.

"Nonsense, she needs no skill beyond her readings!"

I kept my eyes forward, focusing on the stone in front of me. "I am her guardian. Her safety is *my* concern. And she must be able to protect herself."

Truthfully, I had no issue giving my blade and my body to her. But I knew Onia wouldn't feel safe until she could stand on her own, even if I were there to catch her. Years of rescuing herself had left her bitter and weary of aid, and I wasn't going to deny her the strength of her power because *he* deemed it unnecessary.

"I don't see an issue. Ma'at was well trained; perhaps even more deadly than you or I." I threw my barb with little regard for how it would land. Mother made a muffled sound of contempt, but I ignored her. "Or would you rather she ends up like her mother?"

Father called on his jackal as his eyes landed on me. His wrath for Abraxas and Ananiah melted away, and I met him head-on, hoping I hadn't taken it too far. I could nudge him toward the edge of his patience—the trick was not to push him over. His eyes narrowed on me as the jackal's head formed on his shoulder and Abraxas took a quiet step back.

"Do not speak of Ma'at to me," he ground out. I caught the rare flicker of pain before it was smothered in anger. "I had hoped for an Empress more...*malleable* this time." He chose his words carefully, but I heard what he left unsaid. He knew now that if Onia were made dangerous, she would be an Empress he could not break.

Mother rose from her position by the hearth to voice her opinion. "Or at least one less entitled," Mother said, rolling her eyes and looking bored.

My jackal heated to a fever pitch. *Entitled?* Onia was anything but entitled. The constant whisper of doubt in her mind made sure of that. I held tight to my composure and thanked the balance she wasn't here to feel the fury flying beneath the surface.

"But it looks as though we're bound for quite the boorish child. I suppose the fig doesn't fall far from the tree," Mother added with a huff.

"Nephthys! Do not speak ill of Ma'at!" Father barked. "She was the greatest power this realm has ever known! You will show her your respect, even in death!"

I'd almost forgotten Father's reverence for the late Empress. His disregard for Onia made it difficult to remember.

"Hmph," was all Mother said before pouting and dropping back into her chair.

Father began pacing before the hearth and the silence stretched on. I glanced at Abraxas and Ananiah, and they took the quiet moment to slip out unnoticed.

"Do you require anything further?" I asked after the sound of his grinding teeth began to grate on my ears.

He moved across the room in a hurry. "No. That will be all. Tell the boy at the door to fetch Shu."

His mind had dismissed me already as he was craning over his desk, writing in a furious script. I strode from the room without looking back but stopped as I caught Onia's scent floating through the corridor. Roses and lavender mixed with her natural aroma as if she'd just bathed. My body ached at the thought of her bare skin, and I breathed it in, wishing I could bottle it. She was somewhere in the west wing, and I quickly moved toward the east. Hopefully, the distance would be the barrier we needed.

CHAPTER 38
ONIA

I spent the next few weeks splitting my time between the library and the training room. Mornings were for practicing my readings with Shu and afternoons for training with Abraxas and Nejeri, with Ra and Tarik shepherding me back and forth. My kan had progressed to the point that I could manage simple acts on the things and people around me, and I could now take in multiple spirits at once, but I was nowhere near proficient at reading without detection. Each time I reached Shu he would shake his head in quiet disappointment before encouraging me to try again. Working my spirit so hard I learned to appreciate the strength it took for Ra to master both his spirit and his jackal's. It was no wonder he was always so stern. He likely needed great control to harness them both.

My time in the training room proved more fruitful. Tarik, Nejeri, and Abraxas took turns sparring with me, and I'd managed to sweep all of them on more than one occasion. Ra tried his hand once. But after I ended up trapped against his sweat-covered body with his scorching erection pressing into me, we decided it was best he sit out. Instead, he would come and stand by the entrance to watch in silence—desire and admiration blending in his spirit and pulling at my concentration. I'd collected a fair number of bruises from his distraction, but I wasn't the only one.

Other guardians would stop to smirk and whisper as he stood there, arms crossed, looking heated. They clearly didn't know he could hear them. Once I'd caught him staring at me openly, and Nejeri had asked, "Why does he look at you like that?"

"Like what?" I'd asked, turning to see his dark eyes fixed on me, a quiet yearning coursing through him. "Like he'd cut down anyone who dared to touch you," she'd said. I couldn't help but laugh a little because I was practically certain Ra would do just that. A blush had crept up my chest as I'd dropped my gaze.

I'd tried to cover my answer by telling her he was simply a dedicated guardian, but I don't think she believed it. Ra stopped coming after that.

My lesson with Shu this morning hadn't been all that productive. He'd been fussing with his scrolls all morning, and eventually, I'd asked if we should pick up again tomorrow to which he'd mumbled a curt "yes" without looking up.

I hadn't bothered to wait for Tarik. Abraxas wouldn't be in the training room until noon, and I was sure I could find my way on my own. I headed to the right, thinking it would lead me in the general direction of my room, but quickly realized my mistake as the light of the sconces grew dimmer and the stone ceiling dipped closer to my head. I continued, trying to find my way back but the corridor grew darker and darker until I was certain I was lost.

I was tracing a small crack in the wall, that I couldn't be sure I hadn't seen twice before, when a hushed voice floated up from the darkness at the end of the hallway.

"I've done as you asked. I can't find it. Please," it pleaded. "I won't speak a word. *Please.*"

The sound of a stinging smack pierced the darkness, and I flattened myself into the shadows, straining to listen.

"You *will* find it. Or I may find something of *yours* to take instead." A second voice hissed. The words were muffled, distorted by the stone walls and low ceiling, but it still managed to send a chill down my spine.

"No, please, *please*...I'll look again," the first voice begged. It was a woman's voice, speaking through soft sobs.

Another slap cracked through the air.

"Quiet. Begging is not becoming of you. I do not make idle threats," the second said.

I crept through the corridors trying to get closer but realized I was moving further away when the voices began to dim.

Heavens, this Hall is impossible!

I stopped, straining to hear the voices. *Maybe I can read them from here.* My reach had improved drastically, but I couldn't tell how far they were from where I stood. If I was lucky, they weren't too far off.

Before I could open my kan a sharp voice startled me out of my skin.

"Lost?" it asked.

I spun to see Ananiah standing much too close—the dull flame reflecting in her eyes as she glared at me. I jerked back a step only to find myself pinned against the wall.

"I uh, no. I was just exploring," I said quickly, hoping she couldn't sniff out my lie.

"Find anything interesting?" she asked, stepping forward and raising a finely arched brow.

I gave her a strained smile.

"Not particularly."

"Hm,"—she let out an unamused chuckle—"you really shouldn't wander about on your own, you know. It's not safe. What with a killer on the loose."

My face must have paled because Ananiah cracked a wide grin.

"Oh, he didn't tell you?" she asked, disingenuous. I bit down on my lip until blood trickled over my tongue. But Ananiah caught the scent and the smirk solidified across her rouged lips. "Typical."

I swallowed hard.

"You mean to tell me Ammit is wandering these halls?" I asked, incredulous.

She laughed like one would laugh at a child. "No, Onia," she cooed, reaching out to twirl a loc of my hair around her elegant finger. "The Hall knows every spirit that enters these walls. It's housed in the Hall records. The night Ma'at passed through, no one came or went. Except, Ra, of course." She eyed me sideways, waiting to see if that would also send me into shock. But I already knew that. He'd told me of the guilt he carried. As misplaced as it was, he'd confessed it to me anyway. Yet, *this* he chose to hide?

I snatched my hair back to keep her from toying with me.

"Whoever it is has been here for quite some time. We've had many new guardians. It's probably one of them." She shrugged. "But don't worry,"—she smiled sweetly—"I'm sure Ra is handling it."

Her easy tone wore on my nerves, and I pushed away from the wall, forcing her to step out into the light.

"I'll be sure to ask him about it," I declared, but my confidence wavered.

Why would Ra keep such a thing from me? Did he not trust me to keep out of trouble? Suddenly, his insistence on escorting me around the Hall was much less endearing.

Ananiah interrupted my thoughts as her sharp tone echoed across the ceiling.

"Come. Father wishes to see you in the Crypt."

I tried to hold in the grimace that crept up on my face. I didn't need Ananiah to like me, but I couldn't be certain she hadn't just threatened someone, and I didn't want to find out firsthand whether *she* made idle threats. I had a feeling the answer was "No."

"Lead the way," I said, rolling my shoulders back and claiming an air of false confidence.

I gestured for her to continue the way I'd come, but with a flick of her hair, she pushed past me to continue toward the darkened end of the corridor.

"It's this way," she said dryly.

I gulped down some air and did my best to calm the pounding in my chest as I followed her into the dark.

CHAPTER 39
ONIA

Ananiah led me through a slew of eerie passages until I began to think following her had been a mistake. I was about to stop and go back the way we'd come when she turned abruptly and disappeared down a flight of narrow steps. I idled at the top, watching her disappear beneath the landing.

"Quickly, I don't have all century!" she called.

I sucked in a breath, feeling foolish for not carrying a blade, and followed her down.

The path was poorly lit and damp, the only light coming from the landing at the bottom, and I took in the scent of wet earth as we descended into darkness. The stairway emptied us onto a lower level where walls were barely an arm's width apart, and if I reached up on my toes my head would touch the ceiling. I inched my way forward.

"I didn't know there were lower levels," I muttered as we made our way deeper into the dank and shadowed passageway.

Ananiah scoffed.

"There are a lot of things you don't know," she retorted, throwing the comment over her shoulder without looking back at me.

"What is that supposed to mean?" I snapped. I was growing tired of her snide comments. I'd done nothing to deserve her hostility.

She whirled on me. "It means you don't know this place. And you shouldn't be so naïve as to think you will within a day, a month, or even a year." She pointed a slender finger at my chest. "And you're foolish to go about so blindly!"

Her finger tapped into me, and I was prepared to move it, but a door swung open at the end of the corridor, and Ra stepped into the hallway.

"Ananiah, enough!" he shouted, projecting his voice for my benefit.

She sneered at him before tossing a fiery glare in my direction and breezing through the doorway.

Ra didn't acknowledge her comment. Instead, his gaze hooked on me, and he ground out a question.

"Why isn't Tarik with you?" His judgmental tone sparked irritation. How dare he take that air of superiority with me when he'd been lying all this time.

"I don't need Tarik to find my way around," I snapped back.

Evidently, that wasn't true. But I wasn't about to tell him that.

His jaw flexed in response, anger building up under the surface. "Onia, you cannot—" he paused, glancing back into the room, and I felt a frenzy of desperate worry creep into his spirit. My temper simmered as his eyes searched my face. "Never mind," he muttered.

I pushed past him, ignoring my kan's excitement as my shoulder brushed against his bare arm.

The room was dark, and I paused, waiting for my eyes to adjust. Shadows began to take shape as I stood in awe of the cavern before me.

The Crypt was a vast cave whose stone walls had been left untouched, as if it had formed naturally, without the aid of gods or men. What little light there was came trickling in from a cascade of water sprouting out of a crack in the ceiling into a fissure in the floor and back up again. The light of souls shifted and shimmered in the clear water, drifting about in no particular order as they floated through the strange cyclical waterfall. I craned my neck to look for the water's origin. A quiet gasp escaped me as a shining orb moved from the floor up to the ceiling, where it collected in a glimmering pool above us.

"Are we under the entrance hall?" I asked, looking at Ra.

He nodded silently as I watched the souls pour back into the earth.

"What is this?" I asked breathily.

"This is the Fall of Souls," Anubis answered with a hint of irritation.

"Every soul passes through the Fall when traveling into the Hall and out," Ra said, stepping in when Anubis didn't elaborate. "Upon death, they gather here." He gestured where the Fall met the soul pool and the spirits collected. "After weighing, they are deposited back into the fall for the balance to carry them to their next place." He pointed at the crack in the ground, and I watched a bright blue orb slip under the earth.

I stared in awe as the water shuttled the souls between the pool above and the gap below. As I looked at the souls continuing on their journey I wondered if Father had passed through already.

"Do you notice anything *strange* about it?" Anubis snapped, his voice shattering the peaceful aura.

I turned my attention to him. He wasn't wearing his jackal's head today, and I was starkly reminded how much Ra looked like his Father.

I watched the Fall repeat its pattern—water sprouting up from the ground like a spring and pouring back into itself as it carried souls on their journey. A gap opened as it moved toward the ceiling, a dark spot where no souls collected—a hole.

Anubis caught the confusion on my face and interrupted once again. "So you see it. You see the void forming."

"Void?" I asked.

"The black spot." He pointed out the dark patch. "The fall is *dying*...and with it, this Hall."

"Dying? How can the Hall be dying?"

Anubis turned to face me, his eyes boring into me with burning irritation. "The Hall relies on the Empress's kan to keep itself in motion," he said, impatient with my questions. "Surely, you've been told this." I nodded, trying not to take offense at his tone. "It can only sustain itself for so long without someone from House Ma'at to feed it. If it dies, the cycle will follow. Souls will cease to be reborn—all souls, of every kind." He gestured to the opening in the ground. "Even now, it takes in less."

I didn't need to ask where they were going instead. If they didn't come to the Hall, there was only one place they would go. This must be why Ammit wanted Mother's seat to remain empty. If I was not there to fill it, the cycle would die, leaving every soul to take the path to the Pit, giving Ammit an endless supply of souls.

"The balance will suffer, and at some point, it will cease. We can no longer wait for you to become comfortable with your place." The words left his mouth grimly, and I realized why I'd been summoned here. "You will ascend to your mother's seat in three days' time—when the cycle renews. The Hall cannot wait any longer," Anubis ordered. "We will seek Atem's blessing in the morning. See she is prepared." Anubis ignored my presence and spoke only to Ra.

Before I could ask a single question, Anubis turned to Ra, muttering his orders. Ananiah had already left the room, presumably to make preparations of some kind, and I stood there on an island of ignorance wishing someone would acknowledge my presence. My eyes found Ra's face. He was standing with Anubis, nodding in agreement, but holding my gaze. Fierce flames burned through his spirit at the back of my mind, and I watched the tension take hold in his shoulders.

"What does that mean?" I blurted.

Ra flexed his jaw before nodding to Anubis one final time. He slipped past me, snagging my wrist to pull me from the room.

"Aye!" I yelped as he yanked the door open.

"Not now," he muttered through clenched teeth.

His eyes darted to Anubis, who was no longer concerned with me, or anyone else.

The hallway wasn't wide enough to walk side by side, and Ra pushed me ahead, hurrying me up the stairs and snagging my hand as we reached the top. He pulled me along, his steps quickening.

I followed along in silence until I noticed a familiar path to my chamber. I would not be returning to my room until I had answers.

"Ra." I planted my feet and yanked my arm free of his hold. "What is happening? And do not lie to me," I demanded.

"Lie to you?" His brow creased in confusion. "Why would I ever lie to you, tey sot nesu?"

A flutter ran through me at his hushed words, but I found my resolve. Right now, I was not his princess. I crossed my arms in front of me, drawing my invisible boundary.

"I know about Mother. I know her killer still walks these halls." Ra's broad shoulders tightened as they took on more tension and his spirit blazed to life. The flames crawled up from his core to swallow his composure. Someone who didn't know him well enough might think me foolish for testing his patience. But I knew his jackal would sooner gnaw its own tail off than threaten me. "When were you going to tell me?" I snapped. "Before or after they tried the same with me?"

His face turned dark as he reached for me. I stepped away, trying to keep my distance—we both knew what happened when our bodies met—but he followed me forward, backing me into the hard stone and propping a fist on the wall beside my head. He gazed down at me with hooded eyes, and his voice was a grating whisper when he spoke.

"Do not suggest that your life means so little to me," he growled. "Not when everything I do is in service of you."

"Out of guilt!" I spat.

"No, Onia! Out of love!"

His big hand gripped my hip, digging his fingers into my skin as if he were straining under the weight of his words.

I gaped.

How dare he? How dare he make such a statement now—when he knew nothing could come of it.

His hands moved to my waist as he stepped into me, pressing his forehead to mine. Our kan ignited and my heart beat faster as he struggled to reign in his desire.

"That's no excuse to hide things from me," I said firmly.

I pushed lightly on his chest, but he didn't move an inch. Instead, he heaved a sigh and buried his face in my neck.

"Perhaps not to you, but it is reason enough for me," he whispered, pulling away to look at me. "You deserve peace Onia. Peace I cannot offer you. But I refuse to add to your burdens. And you are too stubborn to allow me to shoulder them, so if I must do so in secret, I will."

My heart hammered and I pushed at him until he stepped back. I couldn't stand in front of him any longer. As angry as I was, all I wanted to do was cry. And the longer I stood here the closer I was to giving in. I wrapped my arms around myself to push away from the wall. His sculpted arms pulsed with frustration, but he let me pass, following close on my heels as I trudged down the hall.

"Onia."

The tears were already welling in my eyes, so I ignored him.

"Onia, please."

He reached for me, but I skirted back, careful not to touch him.

"Goodnight, Ra."

"Sot nesu," he pleaded.

"I said goodnight," I repeated, reaching for the door.

"Princess, do not be stubborn. You must come to dinner."

"I will do no such thing," I said, swinging the door open and shutting it in his face without looking back.

———

Tarik arrived a few hours later, trying to coax me into a meal. No doubt, Ra's idea. But I sent him off unsuccessful. I couldn't bear to be in Ra's presence, not now. My heart was much too tender to play at polite conversation. Instead, I sat curled on the bed reading through Mother's letters, not bothering to sift for anything in particular. My heart clenched as I unfurled a page to find Father's bold and sweeping handwriting.

My Dearest Love,

I put this quill to parchment in hopes of convincing you to stay. But I fear I haven't the right words. So, instead, I shall tell you of the things I shall miss the most.

The scent of your hair in the early morning after a night of well-deserved rest.

The glint of your eyes as you watch the sunrise.

And the sweet song of your voice.

But perhaps most of all, I shall long for your spirit, for it is all that fuels me.

I pray the balance will bless Onia with the same strength of judgment and tender heart as her mother. If she cannot know you, I hope she is granted a piece of you to carry. But rest assured I will do my best to leave your mark in your absence.

Forever Yours,
Omari

I tucked the tear-stained parchment back into the envelope and swiped a hand across my cheeks. I opened a few more and sat reading them with tears falling down my face until I tired myself and the air stung my eyes. Eventually, I fell asleep clutching the parchment to my chest and dreamt of a world where the balance didn't punish those who found love.

CHAPTER 40
RA

I knocked on the door and stood waiting. When she didn't answer I knocked again, eager to see her face. I'd gone all evening without so much as a glance, and I feared my words might have been too brazen last night. But I couldn't go on pretending, especially if it meant she may hate me instead. For me, that was a fate worse than death.

I waited a while longer, listening to her quiet breathing, but eventually my jackal urged me into the room.

She looked content curled on top of the bed with parchment crumpled in her delicate fist. I hated to disturb her.

"Onia," I whispered, leaning over her and brushing my hand down her bare leg. Her nightgown had bunched up around her thighs and I couldn't help but savor the sensation of her skin on mine. Images of her curled in the warm sand flitted through my mind, and I wished for a simpler time.

The soft prickle of our kan sparked her awake, and she sat up looking dazed.

"What?" She blinked up at me. "What are you doing in here?" she squeaked, eyes half open.

"We need to go," I pressed, as I pulled the nightgown further down her legs.

I dreamt of burying my face between those thighs each night, tasting her until she lay spent, wrapped in my arms. Seeing her so close to my vision was too much, even for me, and I wasn't sure we would ever leave this room if she didn't send me away immediately.

She gasped, shooting up from the bed and pushing past me to stand in front of the vanity.

Her hair was spilling out of its silken wrap, trickling down her back and brushing just past her shoulders. I sucked in a shot of air, calling on my strength as she began to fuss with it. She spun, ordering me out. I was prepared to obey, if only to save us both from my blatant desire, but I stopped mid-step as I noticed her red-rimmed eyes starkly inset in her face. Ignoring her pushy demands, I stepped forward.

"Have you been crying?" I wasn't sure why I asked. The answer was clear on her face, and I knew she would deny it in the stubborn way she always resisted my love for her.

"What? No. I had poor sleep," she lied, swiping her fingers under her eyes. "Go, I need to dress." She shoved at my chest.

She was right; we needed to be moving. But any thought of Atem fell away as I pulled her into my arms. She shuffled for a moment, trying to wriggle out, but I held fast, and eventually, she wrapped her arms around me, pulling in a ragged breath. Her pride wouldn't let her cry, but it didn't stop her from burying her face in my chest and letting out a small whimper. I pressed my palm to her back and trailed slow circles across the thin fabric until she was breathing deep and even.

We were on her time now. Atem be damned. He wouldn't dare provoke House Anubis over something as trivial as time. My jackal perked at the idea of tearing his shimmering face from his body, and I bit back the overpowering energy, knowing she would feel it if I let it linger.

She clutched me close, and I rested my chin on her head,

holding her as I should have yesterday. Several minutes passed before she pulled back to peer up at me through damp lashes. Her eyes were misty but resolute as her armor slid into place.

"I'm—"

"Don't you dare," I practically barked, but she didn't jump. "I do my best to keep my jackal in order, but if you apologize *one more time*, I swear on the scales, heads will roll. None of this is your doing."

She balked then, remembering who she was talking to and no doubt conjuring up images of me ripping through shabti to lay them at her feet. I lowered my head until she could feel my breath on her skin and watched with shameful satisfaction as a chill swept over her, and the scent of desire blossomed between her legs.

"Not yours, tey ib."

This name would be my new favorite—an old phrase for "my heart," more encompassing than any she'd have heard. It was too old to be a phrase she knew, even with her knowledge of Kemi. The humans never found much use for it with their superficial, finite relationships, and so they'd abandoned it. But in this realm, it was the only acceptable declaration of love.

"I don't know what 'ib' means," she admitted. "But I do know that *I* am not *yours*."

"Please do not remind me," I muttered.

A blush crept up on her chest and I stepped away.

"I will wait outside."

I stepped out of the room, listening to her scuffle around. When she swung the door open, she was draped in a bright linen dress that cinched around her waist, making her hips look perfectly full.

I groaned, wondering why the balance was testing me so.

"Is there anything I should know? About Atem?" she asked as we made our way to the rotunda.

His name sent a shiver of rage through me, and she reached

out a gentle hand. Her touch refocused my mind and I swallowed my anger.

"He is a greedy, greasy, selfish fool, who I'd never subject you to. If it were up to me, I wouldn't have you within five hundred cubits of the Obelisk," I confessed.

Her brow bent up in horror. "Then why are we going?"

"As the first primordial god, Atem's taken up a station above the others. Most dote on him to stay in his good graces, and his approval is mostly a formality. But the other houses may not recognize your claim without it. It would leave you vulnerable in the long run, which I cannot have."

She leveled her knowing eyes on me. "But?"

Heaven, why does she have to look at me like that?

"But his kan is...unique. He may demand a viewing—a chance to *see* who you are. He claims he must ensure you are 'worthy' of your station, but truly it is just another way he subjects us to his whims. But make no mistake, we'll need him to like you, just not too much. Or he may try to *keep* you."

"Keep me?" Her soft voice turned panicked.

I brushed a finger under her chin to soothe her.

"Yes. He likes to have his favorites close to him. Some feel it is an honor, a symbol of their status, but mostly they are his pets. Just pay your respects and *try* not to provoke him."

That was easier said than done when it came to her.

CHAPTER 41
ONIA

We stepped out of our passage onto an intricate tile with a bronze sun spanning the floor, and the words "keeper of light" etched into the middle. A golden staircase pierced through the center of a watchful eye painted on the ceiling.

"He isn't subtle," Ra muttered behind me, and I took note.

He led me forward, gesturing toward the stairs. Anubis stepped up first, then me, and Ra took up the rear.

"Couldn't we take a passage up?" I asked quietly, after at least twenty floors.

"A passage cannot be opened on the other levels. Only the bottom," Ra answered.

Naturally.

"Well, are we going to the top?" I quipped.

"Yes," he uttered with curt seriousness, and I closed my mouth.

Best to conserve my air.

We climbed for what felt like ages, and I counted fifty levels before Anubis stepped out onto a landing. A slate of marble sprawled out under our feet, sleek and seamless as if it was carved from a single stone. It shone so brightly I could see my warped reflection moving in unison with me. I followed Anubis out of the stairwell and glanced up to see the soaring peak of the Obelisk rising far above us. An opening in the ceiling projected a beam of sunlight across the floor and onto a seat at the top of a small set of stairs. In it was Atem himself. There wasn't a single chair aside from his own, and I knew it was nothing less than intentional.

Anubis stopped several cubits in front of Atem's throne to bow forward, hinging at the hips until his back was parallel with the pristine floor. Ra only bowed at the neck as Atem sat crossing and uncrossing his legs, bored. I decided to split the difference, presenting him with a chest-high dip of my head.

Atem stood to drift down the stairs. His form shifted and stuttered, moving with the light that flooded the room. He shuddered across the floor until he stood before us, and I stepped backward, startled by his unnerving movement.

"Jackal," Atem said, turning his head in a gliding motion and leveling his eyes on Ra.

"Atem-Min," Ra responded.

I caught the word he tacked on the end but wasn't sure of its meaning. Evidently, it wasn't an insult because Atem didn't bristle.

"Step aside. I must meet the newest Lady of the Hall."

When Ra didn't move, I laid my hand on his arm, and he moved to my side. Atem took a furtive glance between the two of us, and I saw the spark of interest in his eyes.

"Pleased to meet you..." Atem shifted suddenly, and I blinked, seeing the space in front of me now empty. "Onia, is it?"

His voice came from beside me, and I jerked around. I hadn't registered his movement, and his face was hovering close to my own when I found him standing to my left.

"Pleased to meet you as well," I said, trying not to stare at his unusual image.

There was a golden sheen laid on his skin, like a thin piece of fabric had been held up in front of him, distorting his face to perfection.

"I was sorry to hear of Ma'at's passing. She was one of my favorites. Never did manage to bring her to the Obelisk."

His eyes grew wistful, and I wondered if Mother would have approved of my being here.

"Thank you. I'm proud to take her place," I responded, hoping to turn the conversation toward our reason for being here and expedite our exit. His elusive movements were making my skin crawl.

He shuddered and shifted, and his voice came from behind me when he spoke again.

"Ah, yes. You wish to become Empress," he chimed before blinking out of sight to appear beside Ra.

I started to turn my head but realized that this must be some game he enjoyed playing. I didn't know if it was my patience he was testing or Ra's. But the more I played into it, the longer this would take. I lifted my gaze, fixing my eyes on the throne ahead and speaking into the empty space.

"Yes. I wish to take my rightful place as Empress of the Hall."

"Hmm. And how do we know you are fit for the honor?" he asked.

I held my tongue. I'd learned from Shu how to use silence to my benefit, and I wouldn't give him any ideas. We waited in silence for a long while, but once he accepted I wasn't offering anything to prove myself, he appeared in the space before me to disrupt my concentration. I blinked and ground my teeth as I came to focus on his face. He was taller than he looked—once he stopped shimmering around the room. His eyes were big and warm like someone dipped them in honey, and he was immaculately dressed in a flowing robe that covered him from chin to toe. His image flickered as he stood before me, and his illusive form suddenly made sense.

I reached out a tentative arm. When he didn't move, I

continued, reaching my hand into his face to watch it pass through, unencumbered. I wiggled my fingers, peering at them through his honey-glazed eyes and feeling the heat surround them before I pulled my hand free. The sun was feeding his image life, manipulated by his kan, and I wondered if he was actually here.

"I'd like to speak to you *in person* if you don't mind," I requested of the projection.

"Ah, just like your mother, I see." A voice echoed through the room, but I couldn't find its source. "Quite observant," it called with a hint of irritation. The voice waited until the echo faded.

"And impossibly pretty," it whispered.

A man of solid form stepped out from a hidden place behind the throne to saunter down the steps. He moved in one fluid motion, and I knew this was the source of the vision we'd seen—Atem's true form. This time he came to stand in front of me as the projection shimmered and stuttered once more, leaving me to face only him. The beam of sun flickered before it was snuffed out, and the room became a shaded grey—less enchanting than the image Atem had provided.

"Pharoah, forgive her. She does not know of our custom," Anubis pleaded—most likely for his sake and not my own. "She will not touch you again," Anubis blurted, and if I wasn't mistaken, there was a hint of fear in his voice.

Touch him? I hadn't touched anything.

Atem held up a hand, silencing him.

"Nonsense! Ma'at was never bound by those rules." He smiled softly, turning his attention to me. "She was one of my favorites," he reminded me.

A brief sadness flicked across his face before he returned to his cheery visage.

"Now, for your ascension. I'd like to *see* for myself if you don't mind."

Ra's muscular arm cut out in front of me, forcing Atem to

step back. A sneer of disgust plastered on Atem's sharp features as he jumped aside to avoid Ra's touch.

"Is that necessary?" Ra tested.

"I wish to know our newest member of the realm before I offer my blessing. But *the Lady* must decide, jackal," Atem spat the words from his mouth like poison.

"If I agree, you will recognize my claim."

It wasn't a question. Whatever Atem wanted I wouldn't take the chance of coming out on the other side with anything less than his full blessing.

A snarl spread across his bony face, and I suppressed a cringe.

"Certainly."

I pictured the Fall drying up, leaving the souls trapped on the path to the Pit with no alternative. I saw hordes of shabti as Ammit promised them time in exchange for their service. And I saw the Hall falling into darkness, sitting abandoned and devoid of life.

"Deal," I said before I could think on it much longer.

Atem spun on his heel, clapping his hands, and letting out a sharp laugh.

"Wonderful! We will have a viewing tomorrow morning," he announced to no one in particular. "Tonight, a feast! I'm sure the others would love to see who has come to visit."

My eyes grew wide and sweat beaded on my forehead. I hadn't bartered well enough.

Tomorrow morning? A feast?

Ra stepped in close to my side as burly men sauntered in from somewhere behind the throne. They bounded down the stairs and Ra's spirit flared. A tall man with eyes like sapphires stepped forward to grip me by the arm. Ra nearly sliced off his finger bringing a blade down in front of me. The man's hand retreated, and he turned to speak to Ra.

"Careful, Safar. That dog bites," Atem called, snickering at his joke.

The man, Safar, didn't reach forward again.

"I will show her to her quarters," he offered.

"Not alone, you won't. And you will not touch her," Ra countered.

I stepped into him, making it clear that Ra's demands weren't for debate.

The man moved away, dipping his head and muttering, "Very well."

Ra looped an arm around my shoulders, and I hoped Anubis was too busy fawning over Atem to notice.

CHAPTER 42

ONIA

Safar had led me to an overly opulent room and directed me to wait. Ra only left at Safar's insistence that he receive his own quarters for the evening. After my reassurance that I would be fine in my decorative cage, he had vowed to return as soon as possible. I'd watched his spirit trickle down in my mind as the door shut and he continued down the hallway. Eventually, it had dimmed into nothingness, an uncomfortable quiet I hadn't felt in weeks. I'd grown used to having Ra's spirit there, a strong and persistent presence on my side. I pulled my eyes away from the door and surveyed the room to keep myself from counting down the minutes until his return.

If this was a room for guests, I couldn't imagine what Atem's personal chambers were like. Every detail was gilded. Even the doorknobs and hair combs were cast in gold. From the way Atem was preening himself in the floor's reflection as we left, I wouldn't be surprised if every wall of his chamber were lined with mirrors. When Safar returned, he only stood in the hallway stretching his arm out to pass me a glittering gown of pure silk before shuffling away without any further instruction.

I took it as an indication that this was to be my wear for the feast Atem had planned, and after slipping it on, I was almost certain he was preparing for a show. The dress was impossibly tight and intricately woven. Complex draping guided your eye toward my breasts and butt. It wasn't a matter of discomfort; I knew my body was beautiful. My breasts were full and my hips were plush, but I did still enjoy the art of walking.

After a few more hours of constricted pacing, Ra's spirit re-formed in my mind, and I knew he was near.

"Come in," I called when I could feel him standing just outside my door.

The door swung open and he stepped in, mumbling something about my safety, but I wasn't listening. Whoever had selected his outfit had outdone themselves. Black linen trousers hung from his chiseled hips, billowing around his legs, and a golden wesekh lay across his bare chest, glinting in the room's reflection. My spirit warmed at the sight, and I could feel his rising in a rush—his heart and jackal reaching for me. He stopped talking to let his eyes wander over me openly.

When he spoke, there was a husky lust in his voice that he didn't try to hide. "Do you wish me dead?" he asked, fists balling at his sides. "Or am I simply cursed to see your body on display and never know it for myself?"

His words ignited a fire between my legs, and I pressed my thighs together as I felt the moisture beginning to collect. He sucked in a deep breath, tossing his head back and closing his eyes.

"Heavens, that smells delicious," he groaned.

Heat crept into my face, and I dropped my gaze. But Ra caught my chin, forcing me to meet his eyes.

"You must calm yourself, tey ib. You may not be mine, but that scent is for me and me alone."

I didn't correct him. Instead, I just closed my eyes and tried to force the flush from my cheeks.

Curse Atem and his taste in clothing.

"I have something for you," he said when my heart finally

steadied itself. He pulled a blade and holster from behind him and offered them to me. "Just in case."

I took them, weighing the blade in my hand and running the leather through my fingers. It was simple, unlikely to attract attention, but well made, with a delicate "O" stamped into the handle.

It was perfect.

"It's beautiful, Ra. Just what I needed," I said, trying to lift my dress higher to conceal it. I struggled with the ill-fitting fabric until Ra let out a chuckle and I shot him a look.

"Allow me, tey ib."

I handed him the blade and holster, crossing my arms to see how much better he would fare.

He dropped to one knee and snaked a hand underneath the hem of my dress. His palm burned into me as he gripped my ankle tight, and before I could ask what he intended to do he cut into the dress, tearing his way up to my hip to give me more room. The fabric split apart with ease, and my breath hitched as he came dangerously close to my core, brushing his fingers along the dampness inside my thigh. His eyes found mine and I stilled as he took hold of me. I waited, fixed in placed while he strapped the blade down.

"Feel better?" Ra asked when he was finished, sucking the bit of wetness from his fingers.

"Not. Hardly," I said, ignoring the trembling in my legs.

Ra led me back down the stairwell, stopping at a small landing with a singular door. He hesitated—his hand hovering over the doorknob. I stilled beside him, waiting for him to open the door. But he paused to face me with a stern look in his eyes.

"Sot nesu, don't let anyone touch you."

Before I could ask why he was suddenly so possessive, he swung the doors open wide, and I took a startled step back. No one had prepared me for the number of deities filling the room. At least a hundred people were milling about the dining room, each of them dressed immaculately in a presentation of shimmering fabrics and fine jewels. It appeared Atem felt the need to invite every emperor, empress, and high master to witness his show of power.

They all turned to stare as we entered. Some of them even breaking their necks to get a glance. The pressure of their collective gaze caused the harsh edge of insecurity to cut through my stomach, but Ra's palm settled against my back as he ducked his head to whisper, "You belong here. Don't let them convince you otherwise."

He was his usual self, walking tall, striding forward—unwavering. He glanced down at me, meeting my eyes for the briefest moment, before turning his focus back to the small crowd that had gathered. I took his cue and wrapped myself in composure, mimicking a posture of poise as best I could. I straightened my spine and lifted my chin, rising to my full height and dropping my shoulders as I strode forward. Whispers sprouted up around us, but I'd grown used to that since arriving in the Hall, and I continued with as much grace as I could muster.

"Nicely done," Ra said once we'd settled in an empty corner of the room.

But his voice trailed off, and I followed his eye-line to see someone following us through the sea of gods now chattering amongst themselves. Chishi was moving in our direction, draped in sleek, flowing robes and trailing after a tall woman with glittering amber skin. She was dressed in an immaculately white gown with a cape, fastened by gold clips in the shape of crocodile heads, hanging from her sharp shoulders. Her hair was piled high on top of her head and wrapped in gold, creating a crown of fabric. I stiffened as her eyes settled on me.

Chishi smiled softly with her arms outstretched as she stopped in front of us.

"Evening, Rabasssam." She practically sang his name. "Onia," she snipped.

She reached a slender hand forward in greeting, but I didn't take it. I doubted Ra would mind, but I would. Besides, I'd become too engulfed in the woman beside her to take much notice of Chishi.

"Hello, Chishi," Ra said.

A wide smile spread across her face and she rolled her eyes at his dismissive tone.

"Onia, I don't believe you've had the pleasure of meeting my mother. Mother, thiss is Onia, our newesst Lady of the Hall. Onia, Ammit, Empress of the Pit," she cooed.

Neither of us moved to bow; instead, we stood there, trying to decipher each other before one of us could blink. Ammit's irises bore into me, a deep swirling of green and yellow, like water moving under the shade of her long lashes. A secondary lid passed over her eye as the yellow coloring moved to the forefront, almost glowing. She was aiming for shock value, and admittedly she succeeded a little, but I held steady, unflinching.

"So...you are to be our next Empress of the Hall?" Ammit asked, pursing her lips and eyeing me from head to toe.

"Yes, I am."

She reared back to look at me, a slight grimace knitting her brows together and slowly rolling her eyes from my feet back up to my face.

"Are you sure you're Ma'at's?" she whispered, leaning in as if she didn't want the others to hear.

My face contorted against my will.

Is she serious?

She must have seen my hesitation because the grimace fell away and was quickly replaced with a subtle smirk. I decided not to acknowledge her question.

"Please accept my deepest condolences for your loss. My house and I wish you balance in your time of mourning." She spoke the rites with conviction, and I wondered how she could say such a thing, knowing what she'd done.

"And what would you know of my loss?" I spat.

I decided to open my kan. Taking a loose hold as Shu had taught me until I could feel the thin thread of emotion winding together in her spirit. Anger shifted to jealousy, then pain, then sadness as her face twisted in disgust. I waited for her to show herself. But an unexpected sadness coiled in her spirit as she stepped in close.

"Your mother and I may have been naturally opposed, but she was my *oldest* and dearest friend. Do not assume that I know nothing of your loss." The thread knotted into a ball of anguish and my mouth fell open at her candidness. "We have lost more than you know."

I was reminded once again that I hadn't known my mother. Every image of her spirit I had conjured up was nothing but my imagination. But how could she have been friends with this woman? Her practices were so vile with her tumultuous heart, flitting from feeling to feeling. I watched as Ammit's spirit grew pained. I wanted to deny it, but I could see it was genuine. She held love in her spirit for my mother, and I couldn't deny that I'd hardly knew Mother enough to judge its reciprocation.

"Are you reading me, dear?" Ammit asked with a sly smile after I'd taken too long to respond.

"And if I am?" I pressed.

"Then perhaps you are Ma'at's after all." The smile pulled wide as she lifted a perfectly arched brow.

We sat staring at each other a moment, waiting for the other to speak. She was looking at me as if we'd done this many times before. I felt her spirit swell as her eyes found mine, and I knew it wasn't *me* she was looking at. She'd found Mother in my eyes, just as everyone else had, and was trying to pull her free—detangle her from the unfamiliar face. The chatter of the room fell away, and I let her.

"I imagine it's hard seeing her face in the mirror..." She wasn't asking.

"Yes, it is." I didn't know where the confession had come from, but her spirit turned tender as she saw *me* again.

The threat in her voice lifted as she tore her eyes from my face. "Enjoy the meal. Do not let him take hold of you," she said. It was a motherly tone—at least, I imagined it was—and she turned, Chishi close behind as they dove back into the crowd without another word.

"Are you alright?" Ra asked once she'd disappeared into the herd.

I nodded. "Why are they here?" I asked.

"The same reason we are. Atem demands an audience." His hand fell away from my back before he answered, and I felt the tension of his worry return. "Do not worry; she would never try anything here. Not now."

"She's nothing like I thought she'd be," I muttered.

Ra took a questioning glance at me.

"What do you mean?"

"She's...sad," I said, landing on the word before I could spend too much time thinking about whether it encompassed what I'd seen. "She's vicious, hungry, and cunning, but also *lonely*..."

She hadn't killed Mother—I was sure of it.

CHAPTER 43

ONIA

The tinkling of glasses floated throughout the room as a thundering voice announced Atem's entry. The crowd went silent as he stood idling in the doorway, waiting for his attendees to turn their attention to him and him only. Once we'd all redirected our focus, he began a slow and methodical trek through the dining room, weaving through the crowd with an unrestrained air of importance, waiting for them to bow low as he passed. But Atem wasn't the only one putting on a show. Every few steps, someone would step forward from the crowd to draw his hand to their forehead as they bowed deeply.

Anubis found his way back to us, squeezing through the crowd in a rush and stepping in front of me as Atem's parade came close. He stopped before us, smiling contently as Anubis bowed. I bent at the waist, hoping not to worsen my favor for tomorrow's viewing. Ra's spirit was tight with resentment, but he eventually bent his neck before returning to his towering position over us all.

When he straightened, Atem's eyes settled on my face, penetrating and intense, and I silently wondered if this was how people felt when I looked at them.

"You look lovely. Just like your—"

"My mother, I know," I finished, wishing people would stop telling me that.

"Yes..." His eyes grazed over my body, spending much too much time around my chest. "So pretty..." His voice was heavy with lust, and I met his eyes, not caring if they bore a hole in me, knocking me dead right where I stood.

"With a few minor adjustments, your selection fits perfectly." I stuck out my leg and settled for thinly veiled defiance instead of a thorough verbal lashing. I doubted my sharp tongue would garnish me any favors, but I felt Ra's kan brighten as the words landed as intended. The flash of my blade strapped to my thigh added to the overall effect.

"More insolent than she ever was...but you'll do," Atem retorted, flashing his teeth in some version of a smile bordering on a snarl. He looked me up and down one more time before turning in a flurry of white silk.

We spent the remainder of the evening avoiding Atem and Ammit, Ra redirecting our path through the crowd away from the people vying for Atem's slightest attention—Anubis chief among them.

Dinner went by without issue. By the grace of someone unbeknownst to me, I was sat at the table between a seemingly mute man with eyes like fire and a beautiful, big woman who had captured the attention of every man within a five-cubit radius. Save for Ra, who was seated directly across from me, carefully eyeing the man beside me and barely touching the plate in front of him. Atem sat at the head of the table, and Anubis's fawning had earned him a position just seven seats to his left.

Once Atem finished his meal, people scrambled to their feet to bow and bid him goodnight as he stood. After his equally dramatic exit, the crowd began to leave. I waited for most of them to flood through the door before making my way around the long, narrow table to find Ra. He was standing with his eyes fixed on the door, and I turned to see Anubis cheerfully fling an arm around a short blonde woman with copper skin, gripping her hip, and pressing his mouth to her neck.

My mind got stuck in what I was seeing until a narrow shoulder slammed into me and shook me out of my gawking. Chishi threw her hair over her shoulder and shot me a glare as she slipped past the rest of the people crowding in the doorway. I didn't bother voicing the words that came to mind. She was leaving without issue, and I wasn't going to stand in her way.

The crowd began to thin with most attendees venturing back to the first floor to step through their passages, scattering throughout the realm to their respective domains. I had the unfortunate fate of heading higher into the obelisk, back to my golden-clad room.

Ra led me up the stairway with a protective hand on my back.

"Are you going to tell me what that was?" I asked, spinning to face him as he shut the door behind us.

I was expecting a fight. I didn't think he'd offer up his father's sins so freely. But I was surprised when he spoke without hesitation.

"Father is not known as the most faithful of men." He shrugged. "Nor is he the most discrete. No one hardly bats an eye anymore. It wouldn't be so offensive if Mother hadn't already voiced her distaste for it."

"Nephthys knows?"

"They have been together for millennia; of course, she knows." His tone was clipped, and I had a feeling this was a conversation he'd become accustomed to—answers forming before I even opened my mouth to ask. "I suppose she allows it because he always returns to her. But it is not without its casualties."

His spirit lurched, and I stepped in close, the heat of his anger drawing me in.

"What does that mean?" My words came out slow and silky.

"I have many half-siblings. I used to have many more. And Father's trysts aren't exactly *long-lived*."

His voice trailed off, and I felt shame wash over him as understanding churned my stomach. *That* sounded like the Nephthys I knew; the one Ra had so adamantly warned me against. Suddenly, I had the urge to reject my dinner onto the perfectly polished floor, but I couldn't pull away.

"Mmm, that's awful," I murmured.

"It's disgraceful," he corrected.

My hands found their way to his chest, roaming over his markings as the deep vibration of his voice tickled my fingers.

My arms had wrapped around him, and my fingers were absentmindedly running over the muscles in his back.

"Sot nesu..." he warned.

I should stop.

"Tey ib."

Why can't I stop?

I tried to pull away, but as my hands lifted from his chest, my eyes hooked on the glisten of his dark skin in the dimly lit room, and I lost myself. My lips found his skin, warm and tingling to my touch, while my hands, no longer my own, sought every hard surface they could find.

Am I supposed to stop?

CHAPTER 44

RA

She made a cute little muffled sound of pleasure as her mouth left a trail of kan across my chest and my length hardened. She was roaming my body freely, brushing her fingers over me and pressing her hands to every inch of bare skin until she stilled between my legs, gripping the evidence of my affections.

"Tey ib, please. I have very little strength left," I commanded as her hand squeezed me gently. Here, alone, in a place not of Father's control—there was little left keeping me from ripping the dress clean off her.

She was reaching up to meet my lips, ignoring my gentle warning, and I couldn't find the strength to stop her. She let out a quiet whimper and I cracked. Her soft, swollen lips brushed mine—her taste prickly and sweet, just as I remembered. I traced my tongue along her lips, encouraging her to open for me. Her kan responded as her lips parted, every bit of skin heating at my touch and craving a release. I pulled her into me, pressing her sensual curves tight to my body, unable to resist. She moaned a sweet sound and hooked a finger in my pants, brushing the base of my shaft.

I'd relived our moment in the desert every night since, but

nothing had prepared me for the sensation of her fingers gripping me tight. Her kan swept down my length, and I stiffened in her hand until I was sure I'd come undone.

"Tey ib, what do you do to me..."

Her nipples pulled taught, brushing against my chest, and I reached up, grazing it with my fingers as my tongue rolled over hers. She leaned into my palm until her breast filled my hand and I squeezed gently. A desperate moan escaped her, shattering my control—for a mouth so sharp and cutting to make such sweet sounds... My hands found her thighs, pulling the blade from its holster and dropping it to the ground in a loud clatter. She was in my arms in an instant—legs wrapped around me with her head slung back as my tongue skimmed her chest. Heat pulsed from her core, and the intoxicating scent of her need clouded my head.

I would give her what she craved; I was helpless to deny her. My heart was hers, and she could do with it what she will. There was only one thing I needed in return.

My lips trailed over her breasts, planting swift kisses as she clung to me. Hearing my name roll off her tongue had been my private indulgence since the day I found her. From the first moment, I wanted her nearer to me, but even then, I knew I couldn't have her. So I'd given her the only name I could endure, and I wanted to hear her say it.

"Who do you crave, tey ib?"

My hand brushed against her sex from behind, teasing her. All she needed was to say it, and I would give her what she wanted— what *we* wanted.

"Who?" I prompted once more.

"Rabassam," she answered, pulling back to run her tongue across my jaw.

I tensed.

That wasn't my name. It was a name bestowed upon me, but it wasn't a name I claimed. I hated that name. And I hated it even more on her lips.

"Ra" was the only sound I wanted to hear mixing with her quiet cries of pleasure.

I asked again. "Who?"

"Rabassam..." she whispered.

I stilled, pulling back to look at her.

"My heart, look at me."

Her eyes fluttered open and focused on my face, hooded and sultry, but their usual sharpness was gone. Something had left them dull and dim.

"Onia. Stop."

Her hands continued to pour over me, and she brought her mouth to my neck, tracing her warm tongue across my markings. The jackal reached up to follow her and I buried it back, ignoring the stiffness in my pants. I moved her to the bed, laying her down as she continued to cling to me.

"Onia."

She ignored my pointed words and pawed at me until I was certain. This wasn't her doing. I pulled her hands from my skin, clutching her fingers to keep her at bay and forcing her to find my eyes.

"Onia, did you let anyone touch you tonight?" I demanded. "Anyone at all?"

"No," she slurred, eyes hooding as she tried to pull me back in. "The only man I want touching me is you."

"That's not what I meant...damn Atem and his theatrics." There were too many people to even guess who may have taken a swipe at her. "Who touched you?" She gazed up at me in confused silence. "Tey ib, it is very important you remember." More than one of the high masters in attendance could do irreparable damage with the brush of a finger. "Think," I pressed, wishing I didn't have to. But her eyes were growing dimmer as we sat here.

I could still feel the bright spark of her kan in my hands, and I hoped it was only someone minor.

She propped herself up on her elbows to frown at me.

"Mmmm. Chishi, but she's just jealous that I get to keep you all to myself," she said, clawing at the waist of my pants.

Her eyes were hazy, but they rolled in irritation.

I breathed a sigh of relief. Chishi's kan wasn't potent enough to cause real damage.

"Onia, Chishi's lineage affords her a very unique ability—"

"What? A lizard tongue?" she joked, chuckling to herself and falling back onto the bed as she poked her little tongue out at me.

I pulled her up to look at me, and her plump lip stuck out in a pout. I ignored the impulse to pull it between my teeth.

"No. Her father is Seth." I waited for understanding to spark but realized Chishi's kan would have eaten away at her intuition and continued. "The God of Mischief. A single drop of Chishi's kan will have you disregard all logic to seek out even your darkest desires."

She blinked up at me before she went back to running her fingers over my face and arms.

"You're so handsome," she purred. "Kiss me again, and don't stop."

Her eyes fluttered closed, and I knew she wasn't listening.

"Yes, sot nesu, and you are very handsome as well." I sighed, dropping a kiss along her brow.

Her long, bronzed legs were still wrapped around me, and I peeled her off to pull the tight dress from her body, leaving her lying in her shift and looking perfectly at ease. At least there was some benefit to Chishi's kan. It would wear off within a few hours. Until then, she could enjoy a blissful sleep, free from all thought of Atem or the Pit.

"Goodnight," I whispered as I pressed my forehead to hers. I passed some kan to her in hopes of countering the ill effects.

"Where are you going?" she whined, locking her fingers behind my neck and holding me tight to her.

"To my chamber."

"Why?"

"Because tonight is not our night."

And it may never be.

She released me, and I tried to ignore the pained disappointment on her face as I made my way to the door. The frenzy of my spirit, and the stubborn resistance of my jackal, told me I wasn't succeeding.

"Please," she pleaded. "Don't leave me here...in another strange place...alone." Her voice was barely a whisper, but my heart broke from her sobering words. I turned to see her sitting up straight, tears welling in her emerald eyes. She still had a dull look about her as she blinked up at me. Chishi's kan had moved on to different desires, pulling at her insecurities and making her seek the safety she craved but refused to acknowledge. I wasn't surprised to see where her heart had led her. She'd been wearing that armor for far too long; it was starting to weigh on her. With one look, I knew I couldn't leave her—not like this.

I discarded my wesekh and wrapped her in my arms so we lay flush together, the spark of our kan settling into a constant hum.

"Onia, as long as I breathe, you will never be alone."

"Thank you...I luhyouu, Ra," she mumbled around a deep yawn.

I pictured myself separating Chishi's poisonous fingers from her body. This admission shouldn't come this way. It should come from Onia, in her own time, in whatever way she pleased. Never mind that I already knew.

"I love you too, tey ib."

She responded with a soft grunt, but I don't think my words made it far past her ears.

CHAPTER 45
ONIA

Ra's warmth was absent when I woke, but his smoky scent was still embedded in the fabric around me. His side of the bed had been abandoned in the early morning, leaving me alone in the expanse of linen. I vaguely recalled his hands running over my body, and his lips pressed to my cheek before untangling my limbs from his.

We'd been sleeping in a knotted mess—our legs lacing together, my cheek flush to his bare chest, his hand draped across my hip. He had stripped me of the suffocating dress, and I'd laid beside him with nothing but the sheer fabric of my shift between us. His hands had found their way to my skin, and *somehow* it still wasn't close enough.

The heat of embarrassment rushed to my ears as I remembered my behavior—my frantic lust and my desperate pleading. But most notably, my quiet confession as he held me. I knew what I'd said. I'd meant every word, but I hadn't planned on sharing it with him. Not when Anubis still stood between us.

A sharp knock pulled me out of bed, and I moved quickly, knowing that Ra lay on the other side.

I swung the door open, prepared to throw him my best mock discontent at his abandoning our bed, but the words clung in my throat as Anubis and Safar stood behind him, gaping at me. Their presence reminded me of the reason I'd been tossed in with Chishi in the first place. But I didn't have a moment to dwell on it. Ra's jaw set tight, and his hands flexed as he took in my barely clothed appearance. He pushed into the room, forcing me back and shutting his father and Safar out in the hall. Ra stepped in close until my breasts were pressed to his chest and his lips were barely an inch from my ear.

"I'm not keen on anyone else seeing that," he muttered, barely audible.

I bit my lip hard to keep from abandoning my duty in favor of the bed we'd forsaken.

"Now, get dressed."

I lifted a brow at his command.

His eyes hooded, and there was a familiar spark of pleasure in them as he whispered, "please."

As fate would have it, Atem *had* prepared some additional torture for the event. Rows of chairs were set about in a wide circle, facing the center of the room where two blood-red, velvet chairs sat across from one another. A clear image of Atem's power over the other gods—over me. Although, from the faces in the crowd, it looked like most would rather be elsewhere.

Anubis led us into the room, stopping in front of one chair and directing me not to sit until Atem made his entrance. I contemplated taking my seat anyway. I was growing tired of the constant performance, and I knew of at least one person who would side with me.

Ra and Anubis left me to join the others for the "show," and I decided standing was in my best interest. My behavior at dinner had likely earned me a severe viewing. There was no sense in aggravating my circumstance any further.

When Atem entered, the crowd grew silent, standing swiftly as he passed. He swept by them, hardly acknowledging their presence, before coming to a stop in front of the empty chairs. I bowed at the neck, and we both took our places.

"Good day, young Onia."

"Good morning."

"I hope you will enjoy this as much as I."

"I doubt that, but I am curious what you wish to see."

"Shall we?" he said, reaching his arms out and offering his hands to me, palms up.

I took them without a word. I'd had enough of the waiting; I desperately wanted this to be over. Cold fingers wrapped around my palms, and Atem's eyes bore into me, staring at the point between my brows. Light gathered at his fingertips, and a cool sensation, like water trickling over warm skin, snaked up my arms to settle behind my eyes as I watched his concentration deepen. Suddenly, his eyes glazed over as if his sight had left him.

Close your eyes, my dear.

Atem's voice came loud and clear, but his mouth hadn't moved.

Close them. The voice instructed, and I obeyed.

I waited for the darkness to come but was instead met with a fire burning in the hearth of my home in Ashwana. A cheery laugh echoed from somewhere beyond, and I turned on my heel, searching for his face.

Pain pierced my chest as Father came striding out with a smile on his softly bearded face, ink dotting his fingers and several scrolls tucked under his arm.

"Where have you been?" he asked.

He stood looking at me, waiting for his answer. But I was too busy cherishing the slight echo of his voice. It was a glorious sound that I hadn't heard in quite some time.

"The Hall," I muttered, once I found my voice.

He chuckled, sweeping past me to set his ink down and wipe the droplets on his shirt.

"Don't say such horrible things," he chided before pulling me into a warm embrace.

My arms responded involuntarily. He hugged me quickly as if he'd seen me just yesterday, then pulled away to go about his work as if I wasn't there. I watched him move around in his disorderly fashion, walking back and forth each time he forgot something, setting things down as he went, and leaving them to be forgotten too. Eventually, he settled near the hearth to begin his work. I tried to move toward him. But my legs were stiff, and I could only manage to look on.

"Why did you leave me here?" I asked.

He didn't look up from his work.

Tears rolled down my cheeks, and my shoulders jerked with gentle sobs.

"Why didn't you fight?" I asked, this time a little quieter.

Is he the reason you're here? You want to save his soul from the fate of the Pit? Atem's voice asked.

But before I could speak, my surroundings changed. The rugs beneath my feet hardened into stone as the light brightened, moving high above me as the roof stretched up to a point and brass scales sprouted up from a limestone floor—the Hall.

I felt the warmth returning to my fingers as the familiarity of the Hall settled into my kan. A small smile tugged at my lips as I watched a shimmering Nejeri and Abraxas stride across the floor and pass through a corridor on the other side—Tarik slinking after them with his hands in his pockets. Others began to gather, moving about the rotunda to weigh the souls, shuffling back and forth between the pool and the scales.

My thoughts quieted as Ra stepped out from beneath an archway to cross the rotunda. His usual look of determination was splashed across his face, and my heart fluttered at the sight of him.

Interesting. Atem's voice rang in my head, and Ra stopped mid-stride, turning to face me. He flashed a striking smile as he reached an arm out, beckoning me to come to him.

Won't you go to him, dear?

I didn't move.

No? What a shame.

A crimson stain began to pool on Ra's chest, and he doubled over as blood poured from his mouth, spilling out onto the white tile. His hand reached out in a panic, begging me to step forward. I made to move, but my legs were suddenly numb, and I watched as he choked on my name. He crumpled to the floor in a heap, and his body began to dissipate.

And how about now? Atem hissed.

The Hall darkened, as a scream erupted from my body, shattering the tile around my feet and sending the stones plummeting into a shadowed abyss surrounding me. The scales clanged as their pedestal was set askew, and the ground shook from the force of the heavy metal meeting the earth. Water sloshed out of the pool, pouring between the chasm I'd opened until no souls were left. I stood alone as the ground began to shudder and the edges of my island whittled away. My knees locked, and I didn't dare move, too afraid I'd fall to my death.

A spark ignited deep inside my kan, and my eyes snapped open.

A warm hand was ripping my arm from the icy vice of Atem's grip.

"You've seen enough." Ra's voice was stern, and Atem turned on him, prepared to latch on to Ra. My arm cut across him instantly, redirecting Atem's grip for the velvet cast chair. A sneer crept onto his face as Ra pulled me to my feet. Atem's eyes stayed fixed between my brows, but the visions had ceased.

"Apparently, I have," he said. His voice shuddered with shock and rage as he rose slowly from his position to address me, loudly enough for the crowd to hear his edict.

"Should you manage to claim your place as Empress, I shall not challenge it."

"What? What does that mean? You said you would recognize my claim!"

He lowered his tenor, speaking only to me. "Yes, I did. But whether you manage to ascend is not my problem now, is it? You may be your mother's daughter, but I wouldn't be surprised if you don't survive. Your kan is weak, easily influenced. The Hall needs vast amounts of power, darling, and you—you may not be enough," he said, shrugging and giving me a dishonest pout. "Make no mistake, I do hope you survive it. It was a pity to lose one such as Ma'at. I would like to have another." He blinked, calling on a dramatic show of innocence before turning to rush from the room in a gust of arrogance and whispered words.

I didn't move. I wasn't sure I knew how.

How could my kan not be enough? Even after all the work I've done with Shu?

Ra was clutching my hand, and he pulled me to my feet, dragging me toward the stairwell.

"Where are we going?" I asked, my legs weak and struggling to keep up with his stride.

How long had I been sitting there?

"The Citadel of Peace. We need to speak to Éshe."

"That's it?" I asked.

I threw my head around, looking for Anubis. But no one had followed us out. We were the only souls moving to the lower levels.

"News will reach the other domains that you will succeed your mother. Father has already left. We need not linger. Éshe will know more about your kan," Ra said, not bothering to turn and face me as we continued rushing down the staircase.

I followed until my body began to ache.

"Ra, I can't—"

My face burned hot as I struggled to find my footing.

"My body...my legs."

He spun on me with worry etched deep into his face.

"Forgive me," he muttered.

Before I could ask why he was apologizing, he swept my legs from under me to cradle me close to his chest. My body sighed in relief as the pressure of Atem's vision lifted off my limbs. I didn't bother to tell him there was no apology necessary. I simply curled into him, wrapping my arms around his neck, and thanking the balance for bringing him to me.

Ra carried me to the bottom of the Obelisk, gripping me tight as I rested my head in the crook of his neck. His spirit surged, opening a seamless passage as he stepped through, and he didn't slow until his feet touched the soft earth on the other side.

CHAPTER 46

RA

She gasped as we stepped out onto the damp grass and I suppressed a laugh. It was easy to be enthralled by the view. The Citadel of Peace was everything you imagined when you pictured a place of divinity. It sat atop a high hill with clouds rolling across the ground and between the tree trunks. The sun was impossibly close, and the orange-red rays bled out across a sea of clouds, illuminating the sky as it slowly snuffed itself out. The clouds trickled over the ground, forming a soft white plane that made you want to test its hold and step out onto them. I'd tried to do so as a child, on more than one occasion, even after I learned they couldn't hold me.

The sun was setting in the distance, dipping below the horizon, and she shifted in my arms to scan the landscape.

"Heavens. It's beautiful," she marveled. "How is this possible?"

"This was Shu's vision when he built his domain, so this is what he created."

"Shu did this?" she asked, trying to imagine his round form exerting enough kan to make a place so magnificent.

"Yes, and if you're not careful, I will tell him you think him a lazy old man," I teased.

Her green eyes found my face and my spirit relaxed as she melted into me.

"Ra, I think I can walk again. You can set me down."

Whatever Atem had deigned to show her had left her on edge, and I had no plan to release her until my heart was content.

Shu's domain came with a particular benefit that I'd counted on from an early age, one I hoped would ease the tension in her shoulders, even if only for a while. No violence could be had here, none, not even in training. The energy that Shu had carved the Citadel from wouldn't allow for such behavior, so it remained quiet and...peaceful. Which meant I was free to hold her as long as I pleased.

"I'm aware of that," I said, gripping her thighs a little tighter.

With a huff, her eyes rolled, and my jackal swelled in excitement.

"Then would you care to explain your insistence on carrying me?"

"Right now, I'm not prepared to let you go." My ears were still ringing from the sound of her screams and the only thing keeping me from snapping was her energy mixing with mine. "So, will you please allow me this pleasure? It is all I have."

She nodded in stunned silence, and I longed to kiss her again. To feel her honey, brown lips on mine and taste her spirit on my tongue. But instead, I hugged her close, leaving her to rest until we reached the Citadel steps.

I carried her across the clouds and didn't slow until Zhaur's smiling face came into view. He sat propped against a column and pushed away to greet us with open arms.

"My friend!" he shouted as he came forward. "We were not expecting you." He paused, eyeing Onia, still wrapped in my arms. "Is everything alright? Has Father sent you?"

I shook my head, setting Onia on her feet.

"I'm sorry to disturb you, my friend, but we need to speak to Éshe."

Onia pulled away, trying to separate herself so I could greet Zhaur properly, but I snagged her hand and drug her back in until she was practically leaning up against me. Zhaur took my free arm, grasping it just below my elbow with a broad smile, before moving his gaze to Onia and taking her hand from me to press it gingerly to his forehead.

"Cousin, it is a pleasure to finally meet. Father has told us much about you. Zhaur, Head of House Shu. I'm afraid a more formal introduction will have to wait. Please, follow me."

Zhaur set out ahead of us, and we followed close behind, Onia stepping in perfect stride with her body nudging against me. I let my hand find its way to her hip, and she turned in surprise. We had nothing to fear here. Zhaur and I were as brothers were; he would never betray me. We followed him through the double glass doors toward the small dining room Éshe only used for "special guests."

Of course, she'd seen us coming.

CHAPTER 47
ONIA

Ra was being uncharacteristically physical as we made our way through the carefully adorned halls, but I wouldn't question it. After what I'd witnessed at Atem's hands, I welcomed his touch. In whatever way he offered. I leaned into him, allowing him to prop me up as we wound through the finely decorated halls of the Citadel.

It was larger than I'd imagined from Shu's stories, but I had a feeling that was due to the warm interior filled with art and incense. It was as a home should be. The Hall had felt almost vacant at times, with its windowless walls and darkened corridors. Whereas the Citadel had light streaming into every corner, with windows every few feet and open-air corridors leading from wing to wing. I followed silently, taking in the space until Zhaur led us into an intimate dining room with warm rugs covering the floor and a simple wooden table already set for four.

"My sweet flower, you did not tell me we would have company tonight," Zhaur called announcing our entry.

A plump woman with violet eyes and skin like the night looked up from her work around the table as we entered.

"Oh, you know I couldn't be sure. I figured best to wait and see." She waved Zhaur off before sweeping around the table to greet us. "Ra, darling! Good to see you." She stepped into him, and they placed swift kisses on each other's cheeks before she stepped away to bow in my direction. "Onia, I am so glad to finally meet you," she chirped. "Éshe, eldest daughter to Shai, God of Fate. Shame about the circumstances, but we always have time for family." She smiled sweetly, offering a hand.

Éshe made her way back toward the opposite side of the room and began pouring wine from a large gold pitcher that seemed out of place in the little room with no frills. Zhaur moved to join her, taking the pitcher and pulling her in close for a sensual kiss. It was an intimate moment that I ordinarily would have shied from, but I wasn't looking at either of them. My eyes were focused on the space between them. Each time they parted, a shimmering light, like a golden thread, would stretch out in the open space, running from Zhaur to Éshe and back again, growing fainter the further they separated. I watched as it burned brighter, snuffing out once they pressed together again.

They were tethered.

"Can you see it?" Ra said, tightening his hold on me. "I can't, but I know it's there. You'll have to tell me what it looks like. They've been tethered for ages." He stopped whispering then. "It can be quite annoying, actually!" he mock shouted, and Zhaur shot him a look.

"Now, my friend, envy is not becoming of you," he said, breezing from the room chuckling to himself.

Éshe laughed brightly, like a songbird on a spring day, and I felt Ra relax again.

I glanced back to see him taking the jab in stride, smiling and carefree. My heart clenched at how easily he fell into a natural rhythm, and it ached as I saw how the Hall deprived him of such freedom. I tried to commit the image to my memory, unsure when I'd see it again.

"Oh, I have nothing to be envious of," Ra retorted, peering down at me.

He placed a lingering kiss to my temple, and I bristled, glancing at Éshe. She seemed unfazed by Ra's open affection, moving about the room as if she hardly noticed us standing there, and I decided to let go of some of the tension in my shoulders.

Zhaur returned with large plates of food and dismissed our offer to help as he set the table. When the room had filled with fragrant notes of spice and oil, Ra pulled out a chair for me to take my seat before settling in beside me. He placed a possessive hand on my thigh and began tracing small circles with his kan.

"How are things in the Hall?" Zhaur asked as he took the seat across from Ra.

Éshe took her place beside him and began pouring out hefty servings of wine. The three of them fell into easy conversation, as if they'd only just spoken yesterday. Eventually they turned to reminiscing—as all friends did after too much time apart—and Ra and Zhaur took turns trading stories. Éshe would jump in every once in a while to tease them both for their wild ways. My ribs began to ache from laughter as Ra recounted their many attempts to thwart the Citadel's prohibition on violence.

"We tried everything we could think of!" Zhaur said, throwing his hands up.

"We couldn't even play guardian versus shabti," Ra huffed. "Shu had thought of everything."

"Then what did you do?" I asked. Two young boys with all the time in the realm? I'm sure there was a whole world of trouble they'd managed to sow.

"Terrorize Father," Zhaur said, a wide smile on his face.

Ra laughed, stroking his hand along the inside of my thigh as if it was the most natural thing. I sat listening, content to absorb their tales and admire the bright smiles that had Ra's dimple blazing to life. They laughed and joked until our plates had been picked clean and the candles had withered to the end of their wicks. Zhaur's face grew sober as he drew in a labored breath.

"As much as I cherish your company, you would not come unannounced with your woman in your arms for the food alone. Now, tell me what brings you to our door?" Zhaur asked, leaning back to drape an arm over his wife's shoulders.

Ra's spirit burned a bright satisfaction at the words "your woman." Admittedly, mine did the same. I was faintly aware of Ra answering Zhaur's question, but eventually I stopped listening. A prying sensation, like wood splintering under a heavy weight, was pressing at the edge of my mind, and my head shot up to see Éshe gazing back at me.

"What are you doing?" I asked.

Zhaur and Ra quieted to glance at her.

"Darling, don't be rude," Zhaur chided, but Éshe ignored him.

"That explains so much," she muttered, looking back and forth between Ra and I.

"What?" I asked, confused.

"I imagine you feel better having filled that hole in your heart," Éshe responded. But she wasn't looking at me. She was looking at Ra, who was staring at her with a blank face. His spirit burned with delight as he lightly squeezed my fingers.

"Yes, much," he responded.

Clearly, I was missing the subtext of this conversation, but before I could ask, Éshe spoke again.

"What would you like to know?" she asked, holding my gaze with a deep concentration. "That is the reason for your visit, yes? You'd like to know your fate?"

"I-I don't—" I stuttered, feeling rude for inviting ourselves into her home only to seek her services.

"Nonsense." She waved a hand in the air. "I'm happy to help. Just tell me what it is you need. Though, I must warn you, fate is a fickle thing. What is true today may not be true tomorrow."

I blinked at her, then glanced at Ra, but he merely waited in silence for my answer. This was my decision to make, and he was leaving it to me. I swallowed hard and met Éshe's gaze head-on.

"Is my kan strong enough to ascend as Empress of the Hall?"

She focused on my eyes, and I dared not blink.

The room filled with nervous silence—all of us waiting for her to speak.

"Hmm. Interesting," she mused, and I held my breath.

"There is nothing here," she confessed after several agonizing minutes.

"Excuse me?"

Éshe shook her head, tousling her hair around her elegant shoulders. "I see your ascent, but I cannot see past it. It is...*empty*."

"What do you mean? Empty?"

"Usually, when there is nothing..." Éshe paused, drawing in a deep breath and reaching her hand across the table. "It is because there is no future to be seen."

My mind fractured and Ra's spirit burned with fury as the jackal tried to reach the front, as if it could save me from this too.

"You mean? I-I—"

I stuttered before closing my mouth.

I couldn't say it.

Éshe's eyes softened, and Zhaur shifted in his seat, uncomfortable with the dark turn in dinner conversation.

"Your ascent may mean your death," Éshe concluded but continued quickly as she watched the tears well in my eyes. "But I cannot be certain. Fate changes as you, and everyone around you, make their decisions. You may still walk a different path," she said, trying to encourage me.

"But you can't be certain?" Ra asked after I'd been rendered mute.

Éshe answered him with silence, and I gulped down the lump in my throat.

"You'll have to excuse us," Ra said, standing and reaching for my hand.

I didn't question where we were going; I simply took it—happy to be anywhere but here.

"Will you be staying the night?" Zhaur asked as I stood, barely aware of the words passing around me.

"No, we will leave before sunrise. Otherwise, Father will wonder where we've gone," Ra answered for us both. "Thank you, and apologies for the intrusion."

"Not at all; you will always have a place here at the Citadel—both of you." It was Éshe who responded, eyeing me intently, but Zhaur nodded as if she'd spoken his mind as well. I managed a small bow before Ra pulled me from the room.

CHAPTER 48

RA

I led her through the dimly lit corridors to the other side of the Citadel, where the gardens bumped up against the back steps. My jackal was writhing at the surface, awakened by the news Éshe had delivered. She was right. Ever since finding Onia, the hole in my heart had dwindled, but it would forever remain unless she were made mine. I couldn't let Father stand in the way any longer, not with Atem's revelation and Éshe's vision hanging over our heads.

Her hand was in mine, and she'd taken up a fierce grip on her lip—her fear gathering with each silent step. I paused, pulling her around to face me.

"Onia, there is nothing to be afraid of," I said, planting a soft kiss on her knuckles.

"How can you—"

"You doubt yourself too much. You need not ascend until Éshe's vision changes."

"But Anubis, he's demanded I make my ascent tomorrow, and the Fall is dying—" She heaved a sigh, the tears threatening to spill over.

"Father and the Hall will simply have to wait. I will see to it that you do not ascend until you are ready." She must be truly blind to the depth of my affections if she thought I would allow Father's pride to cost her life. I would gladly face his wrath for her. "You will not ascend until Éshe's vision changes."

I could tell she wanted to argue, as was her nature, but she quieted as I pushed my kan forward, sending the mahogany door at the end of the hallway swinging open for her to step through.

"What's this?" she asked, stepping over the threshold into the darkened room. "Where are we?"

"This is my home. Or, at least, it was when I was a child." I watched as she turned slowly, taking in every corner. "Shu used to bring me to the Citadel when I was young. After Amon passed through, he thought I should be around other children. That was before my siblings, and he and Tefnut had just created Zhaur, so, rather than training with Father every waking moment, Shu would sneak me here." She glanced back at me, and I made myself comfortable by the door. "I'd spend days wandering the grounds with Zhaur." I paused to see her eyes glint in the reflection of the light, Éshe's vision suddenly forgotten. "That was until Father began to prepare me for the guard. Now, I just come when I can. But Zhaur and Éshe are kind enough to preserve my memories."

She stopped to finger the brass dagger that sat along the mantle beside several scrolls and an ink well.

"That was Amon's. I snuck it here after he passed through."

Her face fell as she turned to me.

"What happened?" she asked.

I hesitated. This wasn't a tale I enjoyed, but Onia deserved to know the dangers of house Anubis.

"Father happened. As he always does." The image of his vile sneer as he stood over Amon's body made my jackal twist in agony. "Amon threatened to abandon our house. Father had become too harsh with him, and Amon had no interest in serving him for the rest of his days. The day he chose to leave was the day he lost his life. I was too young to stay Father's hand, and Mother was too weak, though she gave it a valiant effort." I could still remember Shu carrying me away from the bloodshed as I beat my small fists into his back. "She was never quite the same after that."

Onia's eyes blazed with the same bitter fury I felt.

"That's shameful."

I nodded.

"I trained the others myself to keep them from Father's reach, but we've all suffered at his hand. I would do anything to ensure you can't say the same."

"Ra..." she said, a sad smile on her beautiful face. "Is this where you were that night—when Mother died?"

I nodded. I'd come here, trying to clear my mind. But all it'd earned me was the burden of guilt.

"Father had one of his tantrums. Mother had given him an earful after catching another of his lovers sneaking from the Hall. She pressed him too far and he took it out on a young guardian who happened to be standing too close. I'd peeled him off the young man and spent a few hours cleaning up his mess. Too much blood had been spilled in the rotunda—I couldn't bring myself to give the order to another. But the lingering scent of fear was overpowering, and I needed to clear my head. When I left, your mother's night guard was in his usual position, but when I returned, he was dead and so was she—thanks to my weakness."

"Your tender heart is anything but a weakness," she corrected, that familiar frown crinkling her brow.

"What's this?" she asked, pulling down her father's shirt to unfold it carefully.

It wasn't unmarked. Tarik had done an excellent job, but nothing could clear away every speck of blood. Now, it was an off-white hue with a few brown patches creeping up the left side.

"That is for you," I said. "Forgive me for having bloodied it, but I figured it was better than no memories at all."

She spun, latching her arms around my neck, and pulling me into a fierce hug. I responded without question, wrapping her in my arms, and holding her tight to me. My jackal sighed in relief, thankful to hold her once again.

She whispered into my chest, "Thank you."

I pressed a kiss to her soft, full lips, and a floodgate opened between her thighs—the scent of her desire perfuming the air. My hands fisted into her dress as I restrained myself.

Not yet.

"My heart, there is something you must know."

CHAPTER 49
ONIA

R a took a step back as I reached my hands out to his chest, and I sobered.

"About?"

"About us," he said.

After a moment of loaded confusion, he breathed a deep sigh, and his spirit dipped with worry.

"There is a reason our kan reacts as it does," he said, brushing a hand down my arm, as if to demonstrate. "A reason you can see my spirit always, and a reason my jackal would give its last life for you..." My heart began to beat faster, until I was sure it would break through my chest. "The hole that Éshe spoke of, it's you—you're the reason it's been filled." I stared up at him blankly, unsure of what he was confessing. His hands moved to my face. "Onia, we, in our past life, were tethered to one another."

I gaped at him. *Soul ties?* My thoughts clotted into a nervous knot, so potent I could feel it in my stomach.

"What?"

"I am sorry for not telling you sooner, but I—"

"How long?" I asked, pulling my face from his grip. "How long have you known?"

His dark eyes fell on me, rich and filled with dread.

"Since our first night in the Hall. After you told me you could see my spirit. I had my suspicions after our night in the desert, but I didn't know for certain."

I suddenly felt the need to shield myself and brought my arms up around my chest. Misery overtook him as I stepped away to give myself space, threatening to snuff out the joy in his spirit.

"And you're only telling me now? Why?"

"Because of this." He gestured between us frantically. "I had no plans of seeking you out. I had every intention of leaving you be. But I cannot resist you any longer. I had to tell you. If anything happened...." He shook his head. "This life will be my last; you know that. I needed you to know that no matter what happens, you will have my heart—always." His spirit flashed with anger—a sour sensation of bitterness and regret—and my heart curled in on itself.

"Then why are you so angry?" I asked, trying hard to keep from shouting. "Do you...you don't *want* to want me?"

Ra looked at me as if I'd slapped him.

"What? No. Onia, can you not see?"

He pulled me close, and I let him—his kan settling me, even now.

"My heart belongs to you. And I have no shame in it." I opened my mouth to speak, and he brought a finger to my lips. "But you're right, I am angry... I'm angry with *myself*, for failing you, for failing Ma'at, for letting Father keep you from me. And every time I see your beautiful face, I'm reminded that *I'm* the reason you're here, the reason you've faced such pain, such discomfort, and loneliness." His hands moved down my body, looping his arms around my waist until they spread across my back. "And every time I'm reminded of this, a small part of me is pleased by my mistakes, for without them, I would never have found you. *This* is my only shame. And it is mine alone. *You* are perfect." He finished his confession by dipping his head low and planting his lips on my neck, causing my body to react, and sending the heat flooding between my legs. When he pulled away, his eyes found mine, hooding briefly as a wicked smile tugged at his lips—the scent of my need having caught him.

As I stood there in the wave of his admission, the aching loneliness I'd been feeling all my life suddenly made sense. No matter my efforts, I'd never found the reason. Even when Father had loved me so completely, even when I'd found my way home to the Hall and collected the missing pieces of my life, it wasn't Mother that was missing. It was Ra.

My heart moved me, and I reached my arms around his neck, bringing his mouth down to mine. He responded gently at first, kissing me as if for the first time. Then our spark ignited—stronger than we'd ever felt, and more present than before. Ra pulled at the fabric of my kalasiri, and I struggled to be free of it until the dress fell away, leaving me bare. With his hands gripping my waist, he brought his mouth to my chest, licking his way up until he pulled away to speak between ragged breaths.

"Forgive me. I couldn't manage it any longer. I needed to feel you. All of you." He breathed as he took in my naked form. "You're even more magnificent than I'd imagined."

He brushed a stray loc over my shoulder, and I pressed my hands to his chest. My bare body was propped up by his own. The current of our kan wove back and forth as light gathered in his markings and began to seep into me. His fingers gripped the flesh at my hips, wrapping my legs around him and carrying me backward to lay me on the warm bed.

I kissed him freely, every inch of me waiting to be possessed by him. But he pulled away to study my face.

Why is he stopping?

He watched me for a moment, eyes pulling me deeper.

"If we do this, you are mine," he said. "Do you understand?"

"Tethered?"

A soft smile spread across his thick lips.

"No, tey ib. That requires a bit more intention. But there will be no others after me. I'll make sure of it."

The dark depths of his eyes swallowed me, and I felt the hollow space inside my spirit shrink into nothingness. I arched my body up, bringing my mouth close to his ear and splaying my fingers across his warm skin.

"Ra..." My voice was breathy and desperate. He stilled on top of me, waiting for my permission. "I love you." The words came out in a heady moan, and his mouth was on me again, moving across my body and making its way back to my lips. He kissed me desperately, no longer hiding his own need. I felt a distinctive pressure against my inner thigh and shifted until my core pressed firmly against it. He sucked in a sharp breath before diving for my chest, cupping my breast in his sizeable grip and covering the stiff peak with the warmth of his mouth. Heat and moisture began to collect between my legs, and I spread them wider, giving him all the permission he needed.

He settled himself between my hips, and my opening throbbed in response, begging for the heat of his touch. His fingers ran through my wet folds until they dripped with heat, and my body clenched in anticipation. We'd been fighting the pull for too long, and I couldn't contain myself any longer. A tortured moan echoed through the room as he slid a finger into me.

"You don't know how long I've been waiting to hear that sound," he grunted.

His voice was gruff as he worked another one out of me—muscles tightening around him as his mouth joined in to drive me higher. His tongue rolled out to sweep between my legs, stopping at the head and pressing gently. The fire built between my legs as his fingers pumped into me in unison, and his name left my lips in a pleading moan.

"Ra..."

His kan responded, surging upward, and sending a soft sensation, like feathers, brushing across my skin. He paused, whispering words against my sensitive flesh.

"Let it out. There is no one to hear but me."

My hesitation fell away, and I gave myself over to him. A soul-shattering moan filled the room as his fingers worked a spell on me—his mouth sucking and prodding. I felt his kan building alongside my own until a searing ecstasy began to pour into me where our bodies met. The sensation of his spirit streamed into my core, sending me over the edge as my body clenched, only to shatter in release as his name rushed from my lips. His hands gripped my thighs, pining me to the bed as he worked another out of me. And another. And another. My breath came fast and hard as I clung to him, waiting for the waves to stop crashing over me. Suddenly, his mouth was on mine, drinking in my moans as I settled into the sheets.

We lay there for a while in a blissful silence—his arm wrapped tightly around me and neither of us moving to separate. After a few moments, he planted a tender kiss between my breasts and propped himself over me.

"We must return. We must tell Father of our decision," he said, running a hand up my leg.

"What if he doesn't take kindly to it?" I asked quietly, wishing we could just lay here in the tranquil quiet of the Citadel forever.

"Just leave him to me..."

CHAPTER 50
ONIA

R a demanded I allow Nephthys to look over me. Even after I'd insisted I felt fine, he wouldn't hear otherwise. I only agreed after he told me Atem's kan could be lingering in my spirit. The last thing I wanted was some piece of him latched on to me for the rest of my days.

Muffled shouting turned sharp as we drew closer to Nephthys's study.

"Everyone saw you!" Nephthys shouted, only to be answered with silence.

Ra pulled me back a step as Anubis burst through the door, fists clenched tight, and sour impatience splashed on his face. He rushed past us without a word, followed closely by Nephthys—her hair whipping around her face as she yelled down the corridor. Guardians scurried out of Anubis's way as he pushed past.

"Don't feel sorry for her when she meets her fate! You'll have no one to blame but yourself. *You* brought this upon her!" she screeched.

Anubis only lifted a hand, dismissing her shouting as he continued through the Hall. Nephthys flung her shoulders back to stalk back into her study, shouting choice words as she slammed the door closed.

Ra didn't knock, but he stepped in first, taking the brunt of her anger.

"Out!" she hollered without looking up. "I wouldn't care even if your head were in your hands!" she snapped, furiously sifting through her herbs.

"Mother," Ra said, a scolding note in his voice.

She froze, turning only when she'd managed to reaffix what I now knew was a façade of grace and dignity. Her head cocked to the side as she forced a smile across her face. There was pain in her eyes when she finally acknowledged us. I could see it pierced her soul more than she wanted to admit.

Her heart must be broken.

"I'm fine, dear. Thank you for asking," Nephthys answered, a bitter sarcasm streaking across her face before she swiftly replaced it with an innocent look of teasing. "What can I do for you?" she asked, speaking only to Ra and ignoring me entirely.

"Lady Onia is in need of your services."

Her golden eyes flicked to my face, and I wondered if I'd done something to upset her.

"Of course, she does. Have a seat." She waved a hand at me, gesturing vaguely toward a stool in the corner.

Nephthys's study was small, tucked away between the guardians' chambers and the training room since they most frequently sought her services. But what it lacked in size, it made up for in warmth. Candles of various sizes were burning a gentle flicker—stacked on every surface, lining the shelves and covering corners of the floor. Incense burned heavily, an herbaceous aroma of musk and kyphi filling the room. It was a strange atmosphere given her cold and bitter nature.

"Rabassam, out," she directed, and my head jerked over to him.

"I—" we both started, but Nephthys whipped around before either of us could finish the thought.

"Rabassam, I will not have you hovering. Now, out!" she demanded.

His eyes searched my face and I offered him a gentle nod. I would be fine. He'd only be standing on the other side of the door.

"Very well. Onia, I will wait outside." He hung his head in a quick bow before slipping from the room silently.

"Can't have him ripping you off the chair if you start screaming now, can I?" she said dully. "Now, what's the problem?" She lit an incense and waited for it to burn down before blowing out the flame to set it aside.

"Ra wants to ensure Atem's kan has no long-lasting effects—make sure it isn't lingering."

Her face twisted. "Well, if *Rabassam* insists," she corrected. "Sit."

I wasn't sure what I'd done to earn her loathing. But I did as I was told, unwilling to risk angering her further.

"Close your eyes," she ordered as she came to stand in front of me. "This may hurt." She grabbed my face before I could protest, pressing her thumbs into my eyelids while her hands gripped my skull. "If Atem's kan is lingering, I'll need to pull it free so it doesn't take root."

I managed a stiff nod, clenching my eyes shut tight and bracing myself.

I can do this.

A kan, unlike any other, pierced my mind, and I jolted backward. But Nephthys kept a firm grip, and I hardly moved an inch. Her energy felt like a blade cutting through my veins, slashing and burning from the inside out—a scorching pain. It was nothing like the tender warmth when Ra poured into me, but rather an itching sting that made me want to claw at my skin. Even Atem's kan, however unsettling, had taken a gentler path.

This was the touch of a healer? It felt more like she was pulling me apart than putting me back together.

I bit down on my lip, finding the embers of Ra's spirit and latching onto them to pull my mind from the pain. Moments turned to minutes, and I sat bracing my mind under the pressure of Nephthys's kan. My hands balled into fists as I stifled a whimper, biting down on my cheek instead.

"You may open your eyes," she muttered.

I exhaled, feeling my muscles release all at once, and shook her energy from my mind. I wouldn't be doing that again. Whatever healing I needed, Ra would just have to manage on his own.

Nephthys was still standing before me when I looked up, eyeing me with suspicious curiosity.

"So like your mother...surprisingly durable," she said in a whisper.

I don't think she meant for it to spark a response, but I answered on instinct. "I wish people would stop saying that."

"Oh, but why?" she sang. "She was *perfect*, after all," she added, with a distant look in her eye.

"It's impossible to be perfect," I muttered, staring at the floor.

Nephthys ticked her tongue at me. "Oh, you'd be surprised. I mean, look at you." She jabbed her long fingernail into my chin, forcing me to meet her eyes. "Such beauty. So bold and strong. I doubt you even need a guardian. Yet, my son can be found trailing after you, tripping over his own blade." Her face fell into a cold stare, and I was grateful when she snatched her hand back. "Your mother was the same—men and women flocking to her feet. Even Atem himself.... We all saw it. It was hard to miss their groveling." There was a quiet hint of disgust in her voice, and a sour pang of jealousy. "I have faith you'll be just the same," she spat. For the first time, a crack opened in her elegant mask, and I saw what she truly was—angry.

I blinked back at her, not sure what to say. I couldn't blame her for her feelings. Centuries of rejection from the man you loved would leave any woman bitter. To be alone for so long…I could only imagine. Looking at her, all I could feel for her was pity.

"Nephthys, I—"

"Mother, that's enough." Ra's voice came from the door, and she jerked around—my presence forgotten. "Are you alright?" he asked, helping me down from the uncomfortable stool.

Nephthys's eyes crinkled as she smiled at me. "No one else but you in there," she concluded in that sickly cheerful tone that made me want to retch.

"Yes, apparently, I am."

Yet, still not enough for the Hall. I reminded myself.

CHAPTER 51
RA

I knew I shouldn't have left her with Mother on her own. Full-fledged guardians paled at the thought of a visit to Mother's hands, and I could hear her veiled threats whispering through the air as I sat waiting on the other side. Mother's resentment for Father had always clouded her judgment, but Onia had no part in her pain. I should have gone with her.

She was walking beside me, our hands brushing against one another as we stepped in unison, the crack in my spirit narrowing with every stroke. Our time at the Citadel had righted my spirit. I'd tried to take her slowly, but my hands had disobeyed, and my lips, and my mouth...until I'd found her lying beneath me. I had pulled away, to see if she would send me off. But her answer had come in a heated whisper, and whatever cares I had disappeared. I needed her; it was a fact I could no longer deny.

"Are we going to tell Anubis?" she asked.

"No, Mother's already eaten away at his patience. We will tell him in the morning. Besides, there is something I'd like to do first," I said, running a hand down her back until her ample behind was in my grip.

"Ra!" she scolded as she squirmed, letting out a girlish squeal and frantically scanning the hallway.

There were no souls but us, but I no longer cared if there were. I would have her, in every way I knew possible, and she wouldn't be free of me until I'd tasted every inch of her.

"Yes, my heart?"

She bit down on her perfectly plump lip, shying at my words.

Fascinating how a couple words could render a woman so bold completely silent.

I didn't need to be a reader to know she took great pleasure in those words. I could see it on her face each time I said them, no matter how she tried to hide it.

I lifted her into my arms, and her thighs clamped tight around me. Her hands pressed to my chest as she angled her face upward, a silent request I wouldn't dare deny her—perhaps ever. I dropped my head to her chest, prepared to devour her as I pushed through the door to her room. But I didn't have the chance. She was scrambling out of my arms as soon as we stepped inside.

Her chamber was in a state of chaos. Feathers were pouring out of slashed pillows to cover the floor, furniture was set on its side, and clothing had been thrown from corner to corner. The rug had been rolled off to the side, and several slash marks were etched into the wooden desk as if someone had tried to hack it open.

She unsheathed her blade and prepared to step forward, but my arm swung out.

"Don't move."

She froze without argument, and I stepped around the mess piled onto the floor.

"Why would someone do this?" I asked.

This wasn't methodical. It was impulsive and chaotic. Whoever had done it moved quickly—too quickly to think about the things they touched. Everything was upturned. Her hair oils and incense, even her ink quills had been thrown across the room.

When I turned back to her, she was gripping her knife with a vengeance, and her words came steady and controlled.

"I have something Mother's killer wants."

"What?"

My jackal rose to the front, eager to protect her.

"Yesterday, I heard voices—in the corridors...she—"

"She?"

"Yes, a woman. Threatening someone to find...something, or she'd take something in return. I couldn't tell who it was, and I didn't know what she meant then. But now..." She gestured around the disaster before us. "They must be one and the same."

I lifted a pillow to my nose. Fear and desperation leaked out of the fabric, clouding Onia's familiar scent. Fragrant citrus was ingrained in it, separate but distinct, and I recognized its owner.

Seraya...

Her scent was on everything as I inspected the damage—laced in her clothing, leaking out of her trunk, and wafting up from the bed. But that wasn't unusual. She'd likely touched every item more times than Onia herself.

Before I could speak, Tarik burst through the door gasping for breath. We both whipped around, readying ourselves. My claws came to a point, and Onia leveled her blade as he skidded to a stop. His hands came up on instinct as he caught the snarl on my face.

"You—" I was prepared to scold him for not bothering to knock, but quiet screams reached my ears through the open door, and I cut him off. "Show me!"

He spun on his heel without a word and sprinted from the room. I moved to follow him. But Onia caught my hand, gazing up at me with those enchanting eyes.

"Please," I begged, squeezing her hand briefly. "Stay here." I planted a soft kiss on her knuckles and chased after Tarik, hoping she would listen this time.

We were sprinting through the corridors when the smell hit me. A heavy metal tinge hung in the air, mixing with palpable fear.

Blood rolled through the hallways growing stronger with each step.

Balance, that's a lot.

I pushed past Tarik, moving faster than his body would allow, and followed the scent and the sound of muffled sobbing.

I rounded a corner and skidded to a stop, taking in the scene before me. Seraya sat kneeling, hunched over a crumpled mass of blood. Underneath her, Cyrus was laid out on his back, eyes open, and mouth gaping. His blood was pooling around his body, covering the stone beneath him and soaking into Seraya's skirt. She had wrapped herself around him and was sobbing into the blood-soaked fabric of his shirt. The assessors had gathered a few feet away, silently gawking, while the guardians did their best to direct them away from the scene.

"Please step back! Give her some space," Nejeri ordered, pushing through the crowd.

They shuffled back several feet, and I crouched low next to Seraya.

"Seraya?" Sobs wracked her body as she clung to Cyrus's limp form. I tried again, placing my hand on her back, hoping to get her attention. "Seraya...can you come with me? Seraya."

She broke away from him and let out a tearful shriek. I hugged her close, standing slowly, and inched her away from where Cyrus lay.

Abraxas broke through the cluster of assessors still huddled further down the corridor. He took in the sight in a single glance and met my eyes, waiting for my direction.

"Tarik, take Seraya to Father. We need to know what happened here." His eyes fixed on Cyrus lying in a pool of his own blood. But he steeled himself as he took Seraya into his arms. "Nejeri!" Her head whipped around. "Find Shu. He'll be able to bring her some peace." She nodded silently. Her eyes hardened, and she was gone before I finished speaking.

"Abraxas, you handle this. Clear the corridors. All of them."

Abraxas only nodded once before turning to address the other guardians.

Damn!

I turned, sprinting back the way I came.

I shouldn't have left her, not now, not ever...

Balance help me; if she is whole, I never will again.

CHAPTER 52
ONIA

I was still running a trench into the floor when I felt his energy surface again. It was pulsing with fear, and I froze, turning in time to see him tear through the door. A violent streak of scarlet was smeared down his front. His eyes turned wild and frantic as they searched my face. He kicked the door shut in a hurry, striding forward, and crushing me to him as he kissed me with a fervent need.

Our kan blazed to life as our lips met, a searing heat building under our skin, and he pulled at me possessively, gripping my hips and clutching my breasts as if trying to draw in every bit of me. Eventually, he grew tired of the barrier and reared back to rip my dress to shreds. His bloodied shirt met the same fate as he tossed it aside before reeling me back in.

"Never again," he muttered between heated kisses.

"Hmm?"

"I will never leave you again," he professed, pressing his forehead to mine and passing his kan between us.

His hands moved lower, caressing my body until he reached the curls between my thighs and parted the wet flesh, slicking a finger in my arousal.

"Ra..." I pleaded.

"I know, tey ib. I've kept you waiting too long, forgive me."

My core throbbed, begging him to fill me as he worked a torturous path with his fingers. He was right. We'd waited too long, and now my body savored even the simplest touch. I would forgive him for keeping us apart, so long as he righted it. He moved from my opening to my clitoris and back again, teasing me. Only pausing to lay me on the savaged bed. When he pulled away, I could see his thick head straining against the fabric of his pants, and I reached for him. He caught my hand in his, gripping my wrist and pressing it into the bed.

"I will pleasure you first as the balance intended," he whispered, sending a shudder through my legs and causing the moisture to seep down my thighs.

His lips found my breast, and he placed a trail of gentle kisses across my chest before pressing his hand to my center and slipping his fingers into a gentle rhythm. I clutched the sheets as his fingers moved inside me and his thumb swept out over my bundle of nerves. A needy moan escaped me, and his spirit swelled to life.

His name slipped past my lips, and his mouth was on me again, trailing down my front and between my hips until his tongue found its mark. My body bucked beneath him, and the spark of his kan spread across my thighs as he held them open to devour me. My breathing grew desperate, and my hands fisted in the fabric around me. His tongue worked my body, and a satisfied groan sounded against my wet skin. Stars burst forth behind my eyes, and my back arched toward the ceiling, muscles tensing and releasing as a shuddering orgasm coursed its way through me.

He pulled away from me after the waves receded to free his own desire, and I couldn't help but stare. He was thick and long, just as I knew he'd be, with deep veins coursing along his shaft and a smooth head begging for my touch. The pattern of his markings trailed down along his length, and I reached out, tracing the linework to the swollen tip. He was shockingly firm in my hand, throbbing and eager to thrust into me. I pumped him slowly, drawing out a trickle of his seed as he knelt over me. A gentle hand halted my work, and I blinked up at him.

"You tease me too sweetly. Unless you prefer I finish onto you and not in you?" he asked gently.

My mouth hung open at the thought of his seed spreading across my stomach, and I could only manage to shake my head.

Gripping my ankle, he hooked my leg over his broad shoulder, hinging my hip open wider to make more space for himself. I reached up, pulling him to me until his scorching erection slid against my core, poised to enter. I stilled, gripping his powerful arms and meeting his eyes.

"Creating life is an intentional act for us; you need not worry." His voice was soft and patient, barely a whisper, and he waited for me to nod before pushing into me.

My eyes slammed shut, and my name rose into the rafters as he breathed a sigh of relief. His kan spread across my body, rippling out from our point of connection. I could feel his energy passing through me, and I pressed my hands to his bare chest so that he would know my yearning too. My kan slipped out in waves, desperate to find his.

He stroked me gently until my fingers gripped his skin, trying to drive him deeper, then harder as the jackal rose up to meet me. I watched my kan spread through him, and his eyes slid closed as he let out a blissful groan and penetrated deeper, driving himself to the hilt and sending my body hurtling toward its peak.

His composure vanished as he drilled into me, and the gentle glow of his markings filled the room.

"Let go, my heart." He groaned, and I knew he meant more than just the tension building where our bodies met.

I faltered. He caught the hesitation in my eyes and began to slow, moving inside me with intention—a singular goal. Ra wanted me to be free from *all* burdens and troubles, and he would gladly shoulder them for me—in whatever way possible. At that moment, that meant giving me the sweetest release.

"You are safe here, in my arms." The deep rumble of his voice echoed through me. "Let go," he demanded.

I obeyed.

My energy poured from me, passing into him as he wrapped me in his kan. I shattered then, my spirit sprouting up around me, wracking my body with the current of release, and clenching down around him. He waited until I reached a climax before joining me in a torrent of ecstasy.

Ra didn't dare release me until he was sure I'd been satisfied. Once we'd spent ourselves, no longer able to discern where my kan started and his ended, we settled into comfortable silence. We lay there, among my savaged bed, feathers poking out of my hair and clinging to his sweat-covered skin until a knock sounded at the door. I stiffened. But Ra remained—breathing deeply and brushing his fingers across my stomach.

"Ra," I said in a tense whisper, nudging him.

The knock sounded again, but he didn't move to stand.

The angry staccato knock sounded again.

"Whoever knocks next will lose their fingers!" he shouted, arms still draped across me.

"Ra?" I prompted. I would have been perfectly pleased to lay there for eternity, but not if it meant guardians would come barging in thinking we'd passed through.

"Yes, my heart?"

"The door..."

He heaved an irritated sigh, standing to gather himself. I shuffled out of bed to grab a kalasiri that the intruder had dumped onto the floor, wrapping it quickly as Ra stepped to the door. He glanced back to check that I'd righted myself before swinging it open and ripping the man on the other side off his feet.

Tarik's eyes bulged as Ra's arm came across his neck, pinning him to the wall.

"Ra!" I shouted.

Tarik bared his fangs, and his eyes began to glow an iridescent red as he prepared to defend himself.

"What do you want? You've interrupted something very important to me." Ra's voice was husky and angry, betraying how tired he truly was.

"Yeah, I see you two really went for it," Tarik joked, eyeing the mess still scattered around the room. He caught the lack of amusement on my face and continued. "Master Anubis would like to speak with you. Immediately."

"What happened?" I blurted.

I'd been so preoccupied with my own selfish desires that the image of blood smeared across Ra's shirt had already left me. I glanced back at it, still lying crumpled on the floor. It wasn't as much as I thought, but it was clear someone had been injured.

"Cyrus," Ra answered.

"Is he?" I couldn't manage to say the words. Enough people had died around me; I wasn't sure I could handle another.

"Yes," Ra said, with a not-so-subtle tone of guilt.

The name conjured up an image in my mind—curly auburn hair, toffee-colored skin, and a sweet smile dotted with freckles. I had only spoken to him a few times, but his energy had been warm, happy, and inviting. He was popular with the assessors and...Seraya.

"Oh no, Seraya..." I muttered.

Seraya and Cyrus were especially close. She'd brushed it off when I'd asked her about him, but you could see the anticipation on her face whenever he was around. The feeling had been mutual, as far as I could tell. She would be heartbroken...

"She's with Shu and Father," Ra said.

"For now," Tarik corrected him gently.

"What do you mean *for now*?" Ra asked, his temper flaring.

"Anubis has ordered she be moved to the lower levels...to the cells," Tarik said with a grimace.

Cells? There were cells underneath the Hall?

"Why?" I asked.

"He must think she's more involved," Ra said.

"As in...*killed* Mother? No, that's impossible."

"I agree. She didn't kill Ma'at. But Cyrus..." Ra shrugged. "I can't be sure. Very well, I'll be there in a moment. Tarik, stay with her," he said, rummaging through the pile of clothes until he found a suitable tunic that hung a tad too high.

"He, uh...he wants to speak with you both," Tarik said, avoiding our eyes and waiting for Ra's reaction.

What could he possibly want with me? He'd made it abundantly clear that he thought very little of my presence or power. I was merely a means to an end for him. I was sure if he didn't need me to feed the Hall, I'd be back in Ashwana, lying dead in the street.

"We'll be right there," I said before Ra could protest.

CHAPTER 53

RA

She strolled beside me, looking more at ease than I'd seen her since Ashwana, and I was glad to have been the cause. As soon as her lips met mine, my spirit had latched on, reaching across the expanse, and consuming every inch of her. I had no doubt I would be buried in her now if Tarik hadn't interrupted us. I bore down on my spirit as the image of her smart mouth wrapped around my length ran through my mind.

Her fingers laced with mine as we walked through the empty halls, and I reveled in it.

Finally, she was mine.

***

Father wasn't the only one in the den when we entered. Shu was seated in an oversized chair next to the hearth, watching the crackle of the fire. Mother sat behind the desk, projecting perfection even at this hour, and Abraxas and Ananiah were leaning against it with their arms crossed, looking very much like Father with their angry stares. Their eyes were fixed on the person standing in the center, still soaked in blood with tears streaming down her face—Seraya.

The room was unearthly quiet, and I glanced at Shu, but his attention was still fixed on the flames. He wasn't the reason the den had been draped in silence.

"Nice of you to join us," Ananiah snapped.

"I don't take kindly to being summoned at this hour. What do you need?" I asked, ignoring her and speaking directly to Father.

I was pushing the boundary of his tolerance, but I didn't care. He'd already toppled mine when he left Onia to be violated by Atem for the sake of formality.

His lip curled. "We need to know what our dear Seraya has been up to," Father said.

"I've already questioned her. We received nothing of use. She's too afraid of what may happen to her. I've told you this."

"Not you, Rabassam. Her." He pointed a long, crooked finger in Onia's direction.

"Me?"

"Yes, dear. Surely you can tell us what she knows," Mother said, her cheery tone somehow sweeter than usual.

Onia shifted on her feet, irritated with Mother's demanding tone.

"I-I can only read her emotions. I can't always tell you where they come from. I will only know if she lies. I can't force her to tell you anything."

"Well, try!" Father shouted.

Seraya jerked at the sound of his voice, and Onia's hands balled into fists.

"Fine," she said, stepping forward to take Seraya's hands. "Ra?"

She glanced at me and I nodded. I would ask for her, giving her more room to concentrate. She bowed her head as always and closed her eyes. With a gentle nod, I knew she was in.

"Did you kill Ma'at?" I asked.

Seraya shook her head, more tears coursing down her cheeks.

"She lies! Look at her," Mother interjected, and we all did. It was hard not to. Seraya was still caked in Cyrus's blood, and her hands were tinted an orange-red color as if she'd tried her hardest to scrub it off but eventually gave up.

Seraya was no killer. She couldn't stomach it.

Onia shook her head, confirming what I already knew.

"Do you know who intruded on the Lady's chambers?" I asked, changing tact.

Several faces around the room screwed up in confusion, but I didn't stop to explain.

Another nod.

"Who?" I asked.

"It was me," she whispered, her confession barely audible.

I was sure Onia, Shu, and Mother had to strain to hear it. Onia's shoulders fell as she raised her eyes to look at Seraya, the hurt clear on her face.

"Why?" she asked.

Seraya shook her head, and the sweat-filled fragrance of fear exploded through the room. So potent, Abraxas had to steady himself against the desk, and Ananiah coughed to clear her senses.

"Do you know who killed Ma'at?" I asked.

Seraya nodded. Mother gasped. Father's face contorted with rage, and Shu just went on looking pensive.

"Who?" Onia pressed.

Seraya only responded with tears, her shoulders jumping up and down from the force of it and a sad wailing pouring out of her mouth. Father stepped forward, and a heavy slap landed across her face.

"Aye!" Abraxas and I shouted in unison as Onia shoved Father back a step.

"Do not touch her!" she shouted.

I stepped between them as Father's teeth ground together and his markings began to glow. His jackal was too close to the front, and I wouldn't chance him unleashing it—not with Onia standing so close.

"Ask her again," he ordered through clenched teeth.

Onia tried a gentler tone.

"Seraya, you can tell us. We will protect you."

Seraya's eyes were fixed on her feet as she shook her head. She knew that wasn't a promise we could keep. We all knew. Although perhaps Onia believed it.

"There's nothing here but fear. It's too much to feel through," Onia said, dropping her hands.

"She's right. I can smell it." It was Abraxas this time, his nose scrunching up. "You won't be getting anything else from her."

"But we know there's more. Perhaps I should try," Mother offered.

Seraya flinched, and no matter how Mother tried, she couldn't hide the spark of excitement at the prospect of unleashing her most authentic self.

"No." Onia stepped in front of Seraya. "She just needs time. Place her in the cells. Once she's calmed, I will try again."

"And what do you propose we do until then?" Mother asked, flailing her arms.

"I don't know, but I won't stand by and watch you torture her," Onia said, her back strong and her voice filling the room with a subtle sense of power.

There she is.

A deep admiration filled me, and I didn't bother to stamp it out. She should see it. She had every right to know how I felt about her. But the moment of bliss was stunted as Father made his decision.

"You shall ascend. Tomorrow, as planned. Come sunrise; the ceremony will take place," he declared.

CHAPTER 54

RA

Onia's eyes grew panicked, and her scent shifted toward fear, but I was already prepared to deny him.

"No," I growled.

Father's head jerked around at the sound of my challenge. "What did you say, boy?"

"I said no." My body ached with the need to protect her, and I wrapped an arm around her waist, pulling her in close. She bristled but didn't move away. Father's eyes bulged as they passed between us—his jackal mere inches from the surface.

"Who do you think you speak to?" he roared.

Mother flinched, and from the corner of my eye, I could see Abraxas stepping in front of Ananiah. Wise. He knew I couldn't shield them all. It was time they understood Father's selfishness. For Onia's sake, I wouldn't hide it for him any longer. She meant more to me than my duty ever would. For all I was concerned, my duty was to her and her alone.

"Onia will not ascend until *she* decides," I countered.

"For what reason do you believe this decision is hers to make?" Father asked.

Onia looked at me, her emerald eyes swirling with alarm.

"She is the Lady of this Hall, not you! And I will not allow you to risk her life so you may continue playing at Emperor!"

Father's face grew dark as the light swelled beneath his robes. Claws protruded from his hands, and his jaw grew long and pointed as dark fur covered his face. Pointed ears rose on his head, and his eyes clouded with rage. Mother stood on instinct, preparing for a swift exit.

His jackal had replaced him.

"What do I care of *her* life?" he snarled between his teeth.

"What good am I to this Hall if I am dead?" Onia's sweet voice was suddenly sharp.

"Dead?" Father barked.

"If I ascend as I am now, the Hall will drain me of my kan. I will die! You'll have nothing left to feed it."

Father let out a harsh laugh. "Ha! You won't be dead, stupid girl; you'll be vacant!"

My grip tightened around her as if fate might try to rip her from me at that very moment.

Vacant? For a god to be vacant was a fate worse than death. A "life" of nothingness while your spirit lay trapped for eternity in the walls of your mind—nothing to feed it but the memories of a life once lived. No wonder Éshe hadn't seen anything. There was nothing to be seen. Her soul would be empty. Without her kan, she'd be nothing but a shell.

"The Hall doesn't need you conscious! It simply needs you *breathing*. Shu, tell her!"

My neck cracked in Shu's direction. "You knew of this?" I asked, trying not to grip Onia too tight in my anger.

Shu's eyes were on the fire, and he didn't face me when he spoke.

Coward.

"It is true. I knew from the first day your kan might not be strong enough. But I've studied the record. The answer is clear. You need only breathe to feed the cycle. As your kan regenerates, the Hall will siphon it from you in an endless cycle. Whether you live or not, is...immaterial."

Onia's body began to shudder against me, tears pouring from her as Shu dealt the final blow. Father's betrayal was expected, but Shu...

"And what of the souls that balance the scales? Who will decide their fate?" she asked.

"I will." Father shrugged. "What does it matter what path I choose? All I need is pick one," he said simply.

"I don't understand why. Why now?" Onia's eyes were pleading, but we both knew Father would take no pity on her. He never did.

"We know not when you will be ready, if ever! Yet, this Hall is *dying*! And a killer walks these halls with your blood on their mind. Clearly, Rabassam is incapable of doing his duty." My jaw nearly snapped from the pressure of my teeth grinding together. "I will not risk this Hall for you. If you die before you make your ascent, we have assured an eternal *death* for us all. Your life is nothing in favor of all others." Onia recoiled. "You *will* ascend tomorrow. Whether you are prepared or otherwise."

I'd stopped listening to his tirade to stare at Onia. Her strength shone brightly even now. Her shoulders were pulled back and her hands had fisted at her sides, even as the tears rolled down her cheeks and her body shook with quiet sobs.

"Omar! Please escort Lady Onia to her chamber! Ensure she does not leave!"

The brawny guardian burst through the door. He was new— evident from the confusion on his face and his ignorance of the people around him. Any guardian worth their salt wouldn't dare touch her, but as he stalked forward, he reached out a meaty hand to grab her, and my jackal broke free of its hold.

My claws scraped down his arm as I placed myself between them. "Do not touch her."

I could feel a snarl building in my chest. He would be victim to much worse if he reached for her again. Blood leached out of his arm, and he scanned the room, looking for someone to defend him.

No one moved.

Father grew impatient as Omar stood clutching his arm to his chest and questioning whether he should try again. I turned to Onia, leaving Omar to his own devices. Father could lob off his head for all I cared.

Hot tears streaked down her face, and her eyes had swollen from the strain. My hands cupped her face, and I swept my thumbs across her cheeks, steeling my nerve.

She will feel it.

She had to.

"Onia, you need to go with Omar."

"What?" Her eyes blazed with pain, and her head shook violently. "Ra, no! I can't—"

"Onia, Father is right." I nearly choked on the words.

Focus. Focus on her. You must show her.

"One life for the sake of all others... My duty is to my house and the Hall...there is no question. The cycle must continue."

"Ra, please..."

"I know I have failed you. But we must ensure the safety of the cycle."

She clung to me, hanging her head, and sobbing into my shirt. But I took a decided step away, widening the gap and making my position known. Mother huffed a satisfied noise as I came to stand beside Father.

She stood there for a moment, letting the tears stain the stone beneath her, and then she was gone. She shoved past the guardians outside the door and raced out into the hallway. I listened closely for the sound of her steps as she headed for the west wing.

Father turned on Omar.

"Don't just stand there; follow her!" Father barked.

I left Father to his own arrogance, knowing full well he wouldn't question my allegiances, not after I'd denied her so openly. He was too blinded by pride to think he'd been deceived. I took a moment to thank the balance for his self-important nature. For once, it would serve in my favor. Now, all that remained was to save Onia from the fate Shai had dealt.

I was moving quickly through the guardians' quarters with Abraxas hot on my heel. Heads turned as I passed through the common room, and they scrambled to stand in time to bow before I reached them. Most of the guardians followed Father out of fear, but a few would follow me, regardless. I searched their faces until I found who I was looking for.

"Nejeri." She came forward without hesitation. "Tarik!" I scanned the crowd until I caught his stark-white hair moving toward me. He'd managed to make a reputation for himself in his short time here, and the others skirted out of his way. He rose to his full height, meeting my eye. "Come with me."

They fell in step, knowing better than to ask questions in the open.

"What's happening?" Tarik asked as we stopped in front of Abraxas's chamber.

Abraxas gestured for us to step inside, and I swung the door open.

Guilt cut me deep as I took in his space. His room was barren, just as empty as my own...

I should have defied Father long ago.

"Onia needs our help," Nejeri offered an answer, and I glanced at her, wondering what she knew.

"You wouldn't be running about the Hall with that look on your face for anyone but her," she said, and I wondered if my affections had been so obvious.

"Father's confined Onia to her chamber. He intends to

perform the ceremony tomorrow." My explanation was met with blank stares, and I realized they still didn't have the revelation we'd had. "If Onia ascends now, the Hall will take her kan...*all* of her kan. She'll be left..." I couldn't bring myself to say the words. The image of her hollowed form was more than I could bear. Bile rose in my throat, and Nejeri's face turned up in horror as Abraxas filled the word in for me.

"Vacant," he said.

"So what do we do?" Nejeri asked, looking at me expectantly.

"We get her out," Abraxas said firmly, reminding me how similar we were.

"Precisely. Abraxas, I need you to delay the changing of the guard this morning. Father may suspect my involvement. It must come from you. Just make sure the rotunda is empty. Nejeri, make sure she is armed." They both nodded in agreement.

"Tarik, Father will place a guardian at her door. You'll need to *relieve* them of their duty." His eyes flashed a cruel intention.

I wouldn't dictate his methods, especially if it was Omar.

"Yes, Lord Rabassam." He bowed.

"You may call me Ra," I offered with a stiff nod.

"What will you do?" Abraxas asked as I turned to leave.

"I have my own task."

CHAPTER 55
ONIA

R a's spirit had been clear. I wasn't to believe a word he spoke.

It'd taken a moment for me to see. His first words had cut too deep, and I wasn't watching him closely enough. The embers of his spirit had shrunk back as my mind overflowed with grief, and for a moment, I thought I was alone again. But when I saw his eyes, I'd seen the distinct spark of deception filling his spirit even as his body portrayed a different truth.

I'd played my role as best I could, but someone would catch on the longer I lingered, so I made for my chamber, speeding through the hallways, not waiting for the guardian to catch up to me. If he lost track of me, he'd have to answer to Anubis, and that wasn't my concern.

I paced until my legs began to ache.

Why am I waiting here? What is Ra planning?

My mind jerked as a heavy crash sounded against the door, followed by a loaded silence.

"Who's there?" I called, pulling my blade from its holster.

Minutes passed before a knock came. But I didn't answer; instead, I pushed my kan forward, hoping to go unnoticed but not really caring either way. Anyone wishing me harm wasn't deserving of privacy. A sharp and discerning light answered the call of my kan—spirited and unwavering. I knew that light, even having never seen it before. It was daring and sprightly—a perfect match for only one.

Nejeri...

The door cracked open, and a dainty hand inched through.

"It's me," she called, waving.

"Do you wish me dead?"

How many more times would I ask this question? I wondered.

"Never," she declared. Just as I knew she would.

"Come in."

She slipped through the doorway, shutting it behind her and lifting her robe aside. She pulled a long dagger from between her thighs, and thrust it toward me.

"Nejeri, what is this?" I asked, not taking the offered weapon.

"You're leaving... We've taken care of everything. The path has been cleared." She was whispering between deep breaths, and I realized she must have run here. "Take this; we don't have much time. The guards will change soon." She jutted the knife in my direction, offering the holster with it. I took it, looping the leather around my free thigh, and watched as she reached behind to pull a short staff from between her shoulder blades, passing it to me without question.

"I can't leave yet," I said, and Nejeri's face contorted. "I need to talk to Shu."

I wouldn't leave the cycle to decay. What good was my escape if I couldn't manage to strengthen my kan? If anyone knew how to achieve it, it was Shu. Even after his stinging betrayal, I trusted him to tell me the truth.

"Yes, Ra has seen to everything. He will meet you in the rotunda. Your guard has been replaced," she said, shooing me toward the door.

I nodded, feeling an aching knot take hold in my throat as I fought back more tears. Nejeri stared back, her friendly face and bright eyes suddenly sad.

We stood there a moment. There wasn't much to say now, other than goodbye, and neither of us was ready.

Nejeri cracked first. "She would be proud of you," she proclaimed, pulling me into a fierce hug. "Goodbye, Empress. Return to us." Nejeri's words were charged with defiance, and I didn't bother to correct her. She was right. The Hall was my domain as far as I was concerned, but I couldn't claim it if the void was my only option. Every soul deserved better than the flip of Anubis's coin.

Nejeri hurried from the room silently, and I gathered myself to leave, taking a moment to bid Mother a silent goodbye.

When I stepped out into the corridor, Omar lay in a crumpled heap by my feet, and Tarik was leaning against the wall with a satisfied grin. His eyes were still burning an iridescent red from the struggle, but if I knew Tarik, and if I'd heard correctly, there hadn't been much of one.

"Decided not to let them cage you, huh?" he asked.

"Not in this lifetime."

Or any other for that matter.

"Is he..." I gestured to Omar's limp body.

"No, but it will be a while before he wakes. And we'll both be long gone before that happens." He pushed away from the wall and nodded toward the empty corridor laid out in front of us. "Go. I'll remain here until you've gone."

"Thank you," I said.

"It's been an honor, Empress." He bowed deeply, and I took off sprinting down the hallway before he righted himself.

I moved quickly at first, knowing that few people wandered through the western wing. The only things on this end were a few chambers and the altar, but as I edged closer to the center, I slowed, opening my kan to feel around me. Two guardians stood close together down the hallway to my right. Someone was moving toward the dining room far ahead of me, and a few assessors were heading in my direction. I sprinted for the closest alcove and ducked inside, concealing myself in the deep shadows. The group passed by, too consumed by their conversation to consider someone lurking in the dark.

As soon as the group was out of earshot, I moved from my hiding place and sprinted through the corridor, running the length of the hallway as fast as my legs would carry me.

CHAPTER 56

RA

The familiar cloak of silence blanketed the library. Shu was hunched over his parchment-covered desk flipping through a large leather-bound text when I entered. The panicked scent of fear filled the room, so thick I could practically taste it.

"Tell me why I shouldn't cut you down where you stand!" I shouted as I bounded into the room.

"You are too honorable to take up arms against the defenseless," he declared, not looking up from the text as he flipped through the pages furiously.

I bore down on my kan, shoving the jackal back into his cage. Shu was right, although the longer he ignored my presence, the less certain I was of my own character.

"Do not feign indifference!" I bit the words out to keep from striking him.

"Indifference?" he shouted, and I took a step forward, the jackal piquing at his outburst. He settled himself quickly, running his thick hands over his front as if smoothing the outside would somehow soothe the inside as well. "I have been trying, and failing, since the day she arrived to ensure her survival. While you and your father play at your petty politics."

I stepped in close, unsheathing my blade, holding it tight to his fat throat, and shoving him into a nearby shelf. He was testing my well-honed patience. The jackal might show itself this night, and I had no mercy for those that stood in its way.

"Do not take me for the same sort as my father." The words came out through gritted teeth and a low growl.

"Forgive me...forgive me, my boy!" He choked out the words. "I know you better than that. I fear your father has pushed me to my limits." His hands came up in a sign of goodwill, and I stepped away from him, knowing I wouldn't act against him. There was no honor in staking him down, not when he refused to take up arms in return.

"You and I both," I murmured, dropping my blade. "Why, Shu? Why didn't you tell her?"

His eyes fixed on the parchment in front of him. The scent of shame wafted over him as he spoke.

"Anubis wants the Hall to himself. If she is vacant, there would be no one to stand in his way...." He sighed, barely able to admit it. "He offered me a prize too precious to deny."

Tefnut...

My anger heated to a fever pitch.

"Shu, she is gone! And you have betrayed Onia for this?"

"I am not proud of what I've done. But you may one day understand the plight of love...perhaps then you will see why I kept this secret from you."

He didn't need to speak to me of love as if I was a child. I knew all too well the pain love brought, and I would do worse than keep secrets in her name.

"Tell me what must be done, and I shall do it," I demanded.

"There is nothing for you to do, my boy," he said, clapping me on the arm. "The task is hers and hers alone." He skirted around me to return to his papers. "If our young Empress can harness enough kan before the ceremony, she may prevail." He swept a tense hand across his sweat-stricken brow. "I may have found a way, but I fear it will not be easy..." He sifted through the papyrus until he found what he was looking for and offered it to me.

It was an ancient scroll with instructions for a particular form of meditation designed to lead the reader toward their markings.

"She must be *marked*. And greatly. If she can perform a significant renewal of her spirit, it may give her the power she needs," Shu finished.

Markings required skill beyond even the greatest gods. Without Shu's guidance, I doubt I would have any myself. But what choice did we have? If this was the only path, then so be it. I would do all that I could to show her, and we would not return until the work was done.

I snatched up the scroll and headed for the door.

"Good luck," Shu muttered under his breath as the doors slammed shut behind me.

We would need it.

I slipped out of the library, listening closely to the movement of people. The heavy footfalls of guardians heading toward the rotunda echoed in the distance. The shift change would take place any moment, and if I had any hope of slipping out undetected, I would need to move at break-neck speed. I sprinted through the corridors, narrowly avoiding them. But as the rotunda came into view, our paths converged, and the encounter was inevitable. Shouts broke out behind me, and a knife flew past, slicing through my shirt and grazing my arm as I ducked. I could see the light of the soul pool emanating from the end of the hallway.

Not much further.

I pushed myself harder, calling on my markings for added speed, not slowing until I saw her. The rotunda was empty, and she was standing before a gleaming passage, waiting with her eyes wide.

"Onia, go! Go, now!"

Her eyes met mine as she realized what I was asking of her, and her bold defiance promptly ignored my demands.

Her blade flew past me, and I spun, taking the opening to cut down a guardian as she met her mark. Another guardian slipped past, but before I could turn for him, I heard the distinct sound of bone breaking and the scream of a fallen man. I left her to it, confident she could handle him, and set my sights on the one still standing before me. My jackal rose to the front, unwilling to part from her without a fight, and I shifted midstride, spinning to meet the fool who dared to separate her from me. I disarmed him quickly, bringing him to his knees in suffocating pain. It wasn't elegant, but Onia was waiting for me, and it would have to do. The crunch of bone dissipated, and I turned for her, pumping my legs as fast as they would move.

Angry steps sounded as more guardians burst into the rotunda.

The slice and sting of a knife finding its mark met my ears.

My feet faltered, and my trajectory ended before I could reach her.

"Ra!" Her voice was pain-stricken as I craned my neck to see her tear-streaked face. She wasn't moving, and the knife lodged in my back kept me from shouting anything more than, "GO!"

I met the cold hard stone beneath me, and the sound of guardians racing up beside me jerked my kan awake. If she wouldn't listen, I would see to it myself. I gathered enough energy, expelling it in a rush. My kan hurtled toward her with enough force to knock her from her feet and send her through the open passage. Her voice rang out as she called my name, and I watched, helpless, as the passage swallowed her. The hole in my chest cracked open, and my jackal tumbled out, destroying every ounce of my control in favor of vengeance.

They'd taken her from me, and I wouldn't deny myself the satisfaction of blood.

Surging to my feet, I reached around to yank the blade from my back, spearing it into the throat of a traitorous guardian. I stepped around his crumpled form, laying in a pool of his own blood and gasping for breath. I turned to find the one responsible for my wound. He stepped forward—brave, but stupid. My claws savored the tension of flesh tearing from bone as he hit the floor. As he fell I turned my attention to the last of them. She stood frozen in place, wondering if fleeing would save her hide from a similar fate.

It wouldn't. But I didn't bother telling her; the jackal always thrilled at a chase.

Arms came around me I stepped in her direction.

"Brother, enough!" Abraxas held me tight, gathering his strength to keep me from separating the young guardian from her head. "She'll be alright. She can take care of herself."

His words cut through me, and I broke his grasp, spinning to face him and shoving him back a step.

"You don't think I know that! Only a fool would underestimate her now! Of course, she can take care of herself, but she shouldn't have to!" My voice peaked as assessors began trickling in to gawk at the carnage.

"For your sake, I hope that is true." Father's voice echoed across the high ceiling as he strode forward, followed by several guardians.

I centered myself preparing to meet him with fang and claw, but before I could move, Shu's gentle kan reached me from afar, wrapping me in a quiet ribbon of peace and causing the fight to trickle out of me. His energy pushed up against me, and my mind settled on the image of her face—her sweet, full lips and the warmth of her emerald eyes soothing my kan into my usual composure.

Father's voice droned.

"Take him to the cells," he directed, not bothering to address me and stepping over the blood-soaked stone. "And have this cleaned!" he barked, disappearing into the shadow of the eastern corridor.

CHAPTER 57
ONIA

When I landed on the other side, the tears were already streaking down my face. I was lying in the grass clutching my staff with my knees pulled to my chest as hard sobs racked my body. My shoulders heaved, and my lungs strained for air. A tremor ran through me as the sound of his voice, pleading for my escape, cracked through my memory. He was gone. He'd given me everything he'd had, and he was gone. The tears came strong and steady, but I didn't care to stop them. It was the only reminder that death hadn't caught me yet—despite the gaping hole in my heart.

I lay there, letting the salt of my tears mix with the dewy air until hiccups replaced the sobs and my eyes stung from exertion.

Every inch of me ached from my encounter with the guardians, and my spirit was drained from the strain of opening a passage. I could feel my body pulse as my kan slowly restored itself. My eyes closed as the sun's amber rays shone down to warm my face, and I sat on the damp earth, feeling the clouds roll over me and watching the sun move across the sky until my hips were sore and I had no choice but to get up.

I gripped the staff so hard my nails cut into my palm and used it to right myself. A thick fog covered the ground as a cloud rolled over the hilltop to settle between the trees. The Citadel was the only place that had come to mind as I went hurtling through the passage. With its quiet greenery and sun-filled corridors, it was the one place that felt safe, even knowing what Shu had done.

Éshe was sitting atop the stairs with a pained expression marring her face as I made my way to the steps. The light of day had come and gone as I lay in the grass piecing myself back together, and a dusky glow had settled across the alabaster stones, creating a calming aura.

I see why he came here.

"You knew I was here?" I asked as I staggered up the stairs.

Éshe answered with a slight nod and a sad smile. "I figured you'd join us when you were ready," she said.

With a sigh, I plopped down beside her. "Did you know?" I asked.

I wished I could go on not knowing, but I couldn't help but wonder if she'd hidden this fate from us. Had she seen my ill-fated escape? Did she know what would come of our plans, only to keep it to herself?

Another small shake of her head. "I only saw you arriving a few hours ago. Something must have changed since you left."

I knew exactly what had changed. Anubis. His decision to force my ascent had launched us onto this desperate path, and now I was bound to walk it alone.

Éshe looped an arm around my shoulder, pulling me in close.

Well, perhaps not entirely alone.

"I need your help," I said as we watched the sun disappear behind the clouds.

I stood in the doorway of the small library, conscious of the mud clinging to my feet and stamping into the rugs that lay by the door.

"Darling, sit," Éshe said, ignoring my tattered state.

She'd led me inside after my tears finally stopped. But I was still covered in dirt and mud, and I scanned for an appropriate place to sit. But Éshe simply snatched my weapons from me and pointed at a plush chair by the hearth.

"Give me these. You just sit," she ordered, and I obeyed—thankful for her direction.

My mind had stopped turning an hour ago. It was all I could do to get my feet moving.

Zhaur came bounding in a few moments later to fuss over me.

"Do you need tea? Wine perhaps? Are you hungry?" I opened my mouth to tell him I was fine, but he answered for me before I could get the words out. "Never mind. Don't worry. I'll bring some of everything." He hustled from the room.

Éshe eyed me as he breezed through the door. "You'd think the eldest son of the god of peace wouldn't be quite so anxious." She shrugged, laughing lightly. "You'll have to excuse him. He worries," she said, blushing sweetly.

I watched their tether stretch and shrink across the room as he swept in and out, and my stomach knotted, knowing I would never know that feeling. A few hours ago, I was wrapped in Ra's warm embrace, listening to the heavy thump of his heart beneath my fingers, and now the hole had been returned to my spirit—bigger than before. Gone was his gentle flame, replaced by the memory of his strangled cry.

Zhaur returned with a plate piled high and every liquid he could think of. Neither of them pressed me to speak, and we sat for a long while in complete silence. I watched the sky turn to night before eventually clearing my throat.

"You were right Éshe."

They listened in silence as I told them of Anubis's plans for me and my frantic exit from the Hall. Éshe's face grew darker and darker as my tale continued, and when I finished, she was rubbing wide circles across my back, while Zhaur had begun pacing in front of us.

"So, how do we ensure your survival?" he asked, rubbing at his lightly bearded chin. With the deep concentration on his face, he looked like Shu when he sat frowning at some old papyrus. "Did Father say what you were meant to do? He must know something."

I'd decided not to tell him of Shu's betrayal. I had no idea why he'd done it, but it would do no good for Zhaur to share my pain. So, I simply shook my head.

"All I know is my kan is not strong enough to withstand the ascent."

"Then we must strengthen it until Éshe sees differently," he concluded.

We all nodded, but there was one piece we were still ignoring.

"How do I do that?" I asked.

"Renewal," Éshe answered. "Isn't it obvious?"

Zhaur and I stopped our pondering to frown at her.

"What's the easiest way to garner strength in your kan?" she asked.

"Markings," Zhaur answered when I sat staring blankly.

"That's the *easiest* way?" I asked. "Doesn't it take centuries to achieve such power?"

"Yes, but..." She paused, and I felt the splintering feeling at the edges of my mind.

I didn't stop her. Whatever she saw, I wanted to know.

"Perhaps this is the path you're meant to take."

"You mean the one where I end up vacant and feeding the Hall for eternity?" I asked, feeling a little guilty for my sarcasm. She was only trying to help.

"Unless you're looking to take another's kan...what choice do we have?" My face screwed up. That was out of the question. So much so that Éshe continued without even pausing to consider it.

"A single renewal, if substantial enough, could provide you with what you need. Shu kept plenty of texts." She waved a hand at the shelves around us. It wasn't as extensive a collection as the Hall, but it was more than anyone could read in a lifetime—any human, that was. "I'm sure there is something here that could tell us. And Zhaur has a few markings himself."

Zhaur nodded enthusiastically. "I'm not as versed as Father, but I will do all that I can."

I sat there, glancing between the two of them—grateful for their company and hopeful outlook.

"We will find the answer," Éshe said, soothing me with a tender hug, and I wished she meant it as more than mere words of encouragement.

<hr>

Éshe led me through the Citadel until we reached the deep mahogany door.

"We have plenty of empty rooms if you'd rather not—"

"No, this is perfect," I said, stepping inside and breathing in his warm scent filling the room. "Thank you."

"Rest. We'll fight fate in the morning." She laughed, a gentle fluttering sound, and bowed briskly before shutting the door behind her.

I closed my eyes to find my breath. Ra's essence surrounded me as I stood in a perfect reflection of him. Without his distraction, I could see all the details I'd missed before—the scrolls piled on top of his desk, the ash of incense burned long ago, a small blade tucked beside the bed, the handle glinting in the candlelight. I laughed. Of course, he would bring this here, even though it would be of no use. Then I remembered the dagger stuck in his back, and I tucked the blade back where I'd found it. If he were here, he would insist it remain.

Every corner held reminders of him, and I ran my hands across the mantle, gently touching each item as I wondered what memory went with it. I collapsed on the bed, savoring the scent of our bodies still covering the sheets from our earlier encounter. The last time I was here, he'd held me in his arms. Now, I sat here wondering whether he lived. I shut my eyes and tried to release my hold on the image of blood sprouting from his back as the passage closed around me.

I would not mourn him without evidence. Ra would fight with every breath to return to me. I must do the same.

"Close your eyes. Take a deep breath and focus on your spirit," Zhaur instructed as he had every day for the last three days.

We'd come to the same spot every morning since I landed at the Citadel. A small patch of grass in the center courtyard, no bigger than thirty cubits on either side.

Zhaur was kneeling in front of me with his hands resting gently on his lap. I mirrored his position, folding my legs under me and laying my hands on my thighs. I glanced up to see his eyes were already shut, and I quickly followed suit.

"Can you feel your kan coursing through your body?" Zhaur asked quietly.

I nodded, then remembered his direction and answered, "Yes."

"Have you found the strand you wish to restore?"

I dug down deep, finding the thread I'd selected on our first day. It was a decaying piece of my spirit, fading into oblivion and tainted by some portion of my memory. I focused on the thread, pulling it taut until it was close enough to the surface for me to examine.

"Yes," I said as I watched it curl and twist in my mind's eye.

"Remember, you must isolate the strand and strip it of the dead energy to encourage it to regenerate. Like one would cull a bad crop. Once the regeneration takes place, it will renew itself—stronger than before."

I grunted in acknowledgment.

He'd told me this many times. I followed his instructions precisely each time, but my spirit needed more encouragement than I could manage. Zhaur quieted, sensing my impatience grow as he recited his instructions, and I took a steadying breath. He wasn't as patient as his father, but he was being gracious with his time and energy. I saw a flicker of Shu in him each time I progressed. He was as determined to achieve a result as I was.

My spirit strained under my focus as I began to peel away at the decay, digging for what lay underneath. As I coaxed it open, prying at it until I felt the energy unravel, a bright bundle of spirit peeking out beneath its shell. My eyes creased as I tried to remember everything Zhaur had taught me.

"As we go about our lives, we retain the negative energy we encounter within us. It builds, collecting in our spirit and infecting pieces of it until they start to die. In order to be marked by the balance, you must first find the decaying pieces. Then you must peel back the energy so it may breathe again. Once it is free, your kan will restore it, giving it new life and strengthening it."

I opened my eyes and tossed my head back. My breath came shallow and fast, exhausted from the effort of my concentration.

How had Ra done this so many times?

"Should we stop for today?" Zhaur asked.

I met his eyes with a hard stare. He knew better than to ask me that. We'd spent the last three days in this very spot, honing my spirit. I wouldn't walk away simply because I was tired.

"No. I'll continue until sundown." The sun was already clear across the sky, and it would soon dip behind the clouds. "But you don't have to stay. You've done enough," I offered.

He nodded, getting to his feet and bowing slightly.

"I will tell Éshe to expect you late for dinner." He smirked, knowing I would likely be in this same position well after nightfall.

I offered him a soft smile. "Thank you," I said.

I would need to find a new way of thanking them. Words didn't feel sufficient any longer. Before trying again, I waited for him to step under the sunny archway and make his way out of the courtyard. I rolled my shoulders and took a deep breath.

You can do this.

CHAPTER 58

RA

The night she left was filled with panic and rage. Father had ordered a search of the Hall, and Tarik and Shu had been taken in for questioning. Tarik hadn't put up a fight. Nejeri had moved to their defense, but Shu, ever the peacekeeper, had stepped out willingly. I don't think he anticipated what was in store for him. If he had, I doubt he would have gone so freely. I suspected neither would fare well in this.

Abraxas had snuck me to Mother's care before depositing me in my cell. He'd sat me down on her stone slab, and I'd found myself complying with every direction. I knew the calm running over my emotions was not my own doing, but I didn't want to wash away Onia's image, so I just sat there, letting Shu's peace claim me. The anger had started to build again when the cloud of his energy lifted, but by then, I'd managed to regain my composure.

Father had ordered me contained to the lower levels indefinitely and had stripped me of my titles. Mother was outraged, scolding me like a child for my insolence. But she knew she held no persuasion over me, and she eventually resigned herself to seething quietly as she mended the gash in my back. All the while mumbling foul words under her breath as if no one could hear her.

Abraxas returned to Father's den as soon as he'd locked my cell behind him. Father had instated him as commander, disregarding Ananiah's seniority and skill, as expected. So, for the time being he needed to remain in Father's good graces. If Shu and Tarik had any hope of surviving this ordeal, they would need someone with a level head to intervene when Father inevitably snapped.

My new quarters were nothing more than a box. The stone floor carried up to the stone walls that arched over into a stone ceiling. I could reach out and touch both sides with little effort. It was dark and cold, with no light and no life. Father's men, the ones that remained faithful to him at least, arrived twice a day at the same hour to bring what I could only assume was intended as food. Now and then, Nejeri or Abraxas would sneak into the dark of the lower tunnels to tell me of Father's behavior and how his mind grew ever-closer to shattering—teetering on the edge of sanity.

Shu was being held in a cage like my own, and I guessed that the quiet sobs followed by the shrieks of pain were his. Seraya had been handed to Mother for questioning, and no one had seen her since. The guardians and the assessors were no longer allowed to congregate, and meals were held separately for each. In only a few days of my absence, Father had managed to alienate my men and bring his authority into question beyond the Hall.

There was talk in other domains that he was losing his hold, and news of Onia's absence had reached Atem. All the while, the cracks were progressing beyond the crypt. I could hear the shifting of brick and the rumble of stone breaking overhead. Eventually, one of Father's personal guards came to tell me Abraxas was no longer available.

There wasn't a familiar face after that.

Instead, Father's new men came to risk their lives. At first, I found it difficult, cutting them down. But after a while it became easier, and I decided that if Father wanted me dead, he would have to do it himself.

Onia's long legs straddled me as I gripped the flesh around her hips, letting my kan pass through her to seep in wherever we touched. Her head fell back, and I let my thumbs sink into the fold of her skin where her hips met her thighs, gripping tighter as I moved inside. She planted her hands on my chest, and a satisfied moan left her lips, tangled with my name. Her muscles tensed, and her breasts pressed together as her fingers dug into me. Powerful wings unfurled at her back, stretching wide. I could feel her walls pulsing in rhythm with my every thrust.

She was almost there.

She met my gaze and her eyes clouded over. Her mouth moved, but I couldn't hear her words. A tear rolled down her cheek, and the bed began to swallow me. The sheets wrapped around my arms and tore my hands away from her body, pulling me deeper until I sunk into the shadows. I struggled against the fabric as her body drifted further and further from me. My vision went black, but somewhere high above me she was screaming my name.

The darkness receded abruptly, and the fabric was gone. Onia's body lay crumpled at the top of the marble steps in front of me. She lay at a disturbing angle—the beautiful curve of her frame distorted by death. Her name left my throat in a mangled cry, and I lurched forward. Blood was pooling on her chest and her hair was sprawled out behind her. I felt something snap, and the darkness consumed me before I could reach her.

Dried blood chipped off my sweat-covered body as I sat up, gasping, in the tight quarters of my cell.

She's safe. I told myself. *I made sure of that.*

"Get up!" A voice shouted from the darkened hallway.

I didn't answer. Whoever it was, I didn't recognize the voice. Which meant it was one of Father's new guards—the dumb ones he'd found to replace the ones with sense.

"I said get up!"

"Aye! I said—"

I snatched a hand through the small opening in the door, gripping the man's chin and letting my claws sink into his cheeks. His words died in his throat as he let out a whimper.

"You know, you're dimmer than you look," I said, snatching my hand back as he sucked in a stinging breath from the scrape of my claws.

"Master Anubis wishes to speak with you." He groaned, rubbing his face and pulling away to stare at his bloodied hand.

"Then tell him he can come down here," I snapped.

I wasn't under his command any longer. I wouldn't move simply because he requested it.

"Now, Rabassam, is that any way to treat your fellow guardian?" Father's voice came loud and harsh in the small quarters, and the guardian flinched at the sudden noise.

I groaned. "I am no longer a guardian. Besides, I don't know this one," I said, moving to sit at the back of my cell, as far away from him as I could manage.

"Had enough of your fall from grace?"

"Eh, it's quieter down here." I shrugged.

"I can change that," Father said, and I remembered the sound of Shu's screaming fading into agonizing groans as the night went on.

"Go cast your threats at someone else. I no longer care what you do to me."

"Oh, my threats are not for you," he said as he yanked Abraxas out of the shadows to showcase his handiwork.

An angry, raised scar had been cut into his face by a hand I knew all too well.

"Brother, are you alright?" I asked, standing to get a closer look at him.

Abraxas nodded.

"Nothing more than a scratch," he responded, squaring his shoulders and meeting my eye.

Father grunted in dry amusement. I knew better than to think this was all he had planned. This mark would only be the first of many, and Abraxas wasn't used to such treatment. I'd always shielded him from it.

"You *will* tell me where she is," Father said.

"I've already told you. I don't know where she's gone."

My hands fisted until blood seeped out of my palms. My jackal rose to the front, and Abraxas shook his head. Father's men had come asking this question every day since the night she left. But none of them believed my answers. Once their tactics turned cold, it cost them their lives. I liked to think I knew her well enough to know where she'd gone, though I couldn't be sure. Especially when I'd sent her flying through the passage without warning.

The memory struck me—her arm stretching through the light as she reached for me, begging me to follow—and a low growl emanated from my chest.

There was one place I knew she wouldn't return without me.

"The human realm."

I let the lie leave my mouth, watching Abraxas closely in my periphery. He didn't even blink, and I felt pride in having trained him well. The silent pressure hung in the air as I waited for Father to bend. The sound of a fissure opening in the ceiling cut through the silence, and he looked up, the fear of his declining hold prompting him to act.

"Send a company to the human realm. She cannot be far from Mahatnaten," Father dictated.

Abraxas and the guardian shuffled quickly out of the room, leaving Father and me alone, staring at each other in the dark.

"Make no mistake. If you've lied to me, it will be your end." He spoke from his chest, and I knew he believed his words. But it didn't matter to me. I would gladly die a traitor in her name.

CHAPTER 59

ONIA

My body hummed as I sat in the grass with my eyes closed, focusing on the energy I wanted to mend. I steadied my breath, sifting through my spirit until I found a battered stream of kan coursing through me. It was slow and labored, burdened by something achingly heavy. Who knew what had caused it? My spirit had sustained too much damage to really know. But as I concentrated on encouraging it to shed its sorrows, memories came flooding through. Ra's agonizing scream. His blood-stricken body falling to the floor. Heat rose in my chest as I tried to re-center my kan, pushing it down and wrapping it in my intention. Hot tears ran down my cheeks when the image wouldn't leave me.

My concentration broke, and I glanced down at my hands. In the past three weeks, I'd only managed to mark my hands. Zhaur suggested starting with something small until I got the hang of it, and the delicate lines tracing down my fingers were all I'd been able to produce. They were different than I'd expected, softer. Ra's markings were swirling and bold, clearly stamped into his skin. But mine were faint, neat, little lines etched underneath. There were no symbols yet. According to Éshe, those only came with a substantial renewal.

I shifted in the grass, preparing to dive back into myself when a panicked voice shouted across the courtyard.

"Onia! Onia, come quickly!" Éshe yelled, sprinting down the back steps and gripping her skirts in her hands.

"What's wrong?" I shouted, standing from my place on the ground.

"It's Anubis! He won't release him until he speaks with you!" she cried.

Tears were clogging her throat, stunting her speech.

"Release him?" My stomach flipped. *Release who?*

"Just hurry!"

I sprinted across the clearing and up the stairs, following after her without any further questions. I read her kan quickly. If she couldn't tell me what lay ahead, I would have to see for myself. I was met with a thick fog surrounding her spirit, covering it in a heavy blanket of emotion. Nothing much was passing through, only fear running from her surface to her core.

The sound of heated shouting pierced the air as we rounded the corner.

"You dare enter my domain with such demands?"

"Your domain means nothing to me, boy!" I recognized the harsh words of Anubis's tone as he berated Zhaur.

As we stepped into the room, Éshe began to sob quietly, and I braced myself for what came next.

Anubis stood hovering over a mass of dark fabric crumpled at his feet. Metal clanged against metal as the clump shifted, lifting up a little higher. My heartbeat stuttered as Shu's gaunt face looked up from beneath a tattered cloak. A whimper escaped from Éshe, and she buried her face in Zhaur's chest.

"Onia, I am so glad to see you. You've been quite difficult to find. I've searched almost every domain looking for you," he sneered.

"What have you done?" I whispered.

"What have *I* done? I have done nothing... You did this, my dear. This is what happens when you abandon your duty." His snide melodic tone made me want to slap him, but the Citadel wouldn't allow it. So, I simply clenched my fists until I thought my hands might bleed.

"Let him go." I bit the words out through clenched teeth.

"Of course. As soon as you fulfill your duty. I cannot force you to follow, not here in this worthless place," he spat. "But I'm happy to provide some encouragement. There are plenty more where this came from," Anubis said, reaching down and yanking Shu to his feet. His limp form hung from the fabric in a hideous display of brutality. This man couldn't be Shu. His normally plump face was hollow in the cheeks, and his cheerful, curious eyes were shadowed and distant as if he was reliving some wretched horror. Anubis released his hold, and metal irons clashed against the wood floor as Shu collapsed at his feet.

"What do you want? You want me to lie vacant for the rest of my days? Is that it?" I dug into my resolve to keep my voice from shaking.

His lip curled, and I took pleasure in his frustration. It would soon be replaced by his smug and satisfied face. My heart wouldn't allow me to play his game much longer.

"Come home, Onia...*Ra* misses you terribly." His eyes narrowed, and he angled his head, a sneer spreading across his lips as he bared his teeth.

"What have you done to him?" I snapped.

"Oh, nothing, my dear. He's waiting for you..."

His gaze dragged over to the bloody mess of Shu's body and my insides twisted. An image of Ra stripped to scraps with his kan dwindling into nothingness scolded me like hot iron. My kan flared, and I had to remind myself where we were. Beside me, Zhaur's spirit was swirling in a pool of loosely contained rage; evidently, he was not as attached to his father's pacifism. Éshe whimpered as her beautiful face contorted in pain. Pain that reflected the terror of our circumstances. Pain that I could end.

I settled my kan and swallowed hard.

"Fine."

"Onia, you don't—" Zhaur began.

I'm sure whatever he was about to say were encouraging words of perseverance, but I wouldn't know. I cut him off.

"It's alright," I said, holding up a hand.

I stooped down to offer Shu my arm. His frail fingers wrapped around my wrist, and his eyes filled with tears. Zhaur and Éshe rushed forward, bracing his weight on either side. Éshe released him once he was securely in Zhaur's arms, turning in her vibrant skirts, now damp with tears, and pulling me into a fierce hug. She pulled away, holding my hands in hers and bending at the knees to press her forehead to them. She displayed her reverence openly, and I recognized it as a small act of defiance. Over her shoulder, Zhaur closed his eyes and bowed, hanging his head low.

When Éshe released me, a sheet of swirling light had already appeared at Anubis's back, and he reached an arm forward to guide me. I took a deep breath, finding my confidence, and strode past him into the light.

Dust and rubble shifted underfoot as I stepped out onto the other side. Darkness enveloped us as the light of the passage faded away, and I stepped forward hesitantly, unable to see the path before me. I stood in the dark of the rotunda, confused by the shadows filling the room.

"What's wrong? Don't you recognize your home?" Anubis's snide voice sounded from the darkness somewhere to my right.

The light of the soul pool was dull, leaving only a faint shimmer to guide the way. The scales sat askew—the slab of stone beneath them missing a significant portion of its base, so the plates hung slanted to one side. I stepped around a pile of fallen rock and listened as stone shifted overhead. The Hall crumbled further with every step, and I stopped to gape at the destruction.

"You see what you've made of it?" Anubis called.

"I-I didn't know—"

"Didn't you?" I felt him lurking close behind me. "You're a very observant young woman. Didn't you see it? Couldn't you feel the energy fade? Tell me, Onia, is this what you wanted?" He stepped forward, spreading his arms wide and turning to make a show of the disaster before us.

A lump found its way into my throat. I had never imagined this was the fate of the Hall in just a few weeks of my absence.

"Is it..." I began, stepping into the rotunda, the shuffle of dust rising as I bent to grasp the remnants of an elegantly engraved column in my hands.

"Dead?" Anubis filled in the word with a sense of finality. "No. But we no longer have time for your insolence. The ceremony will take place in the morning."

Guilt wrapped its icy fingers around my stomach, but shame smothered it down.

"Where is he?" I turned on Anubis.

He turned, silently directing me to follow.

The dim light faded as we plunged into pure darkness, making our way through the lower levels, delving deeper than I'd ever gone before. The air grew thick with moisture, and my breathing grew labored as my lungs worked to find what little air was left down there. The stench of excrement wafted from every direction, and I prayed it wasn't Ra's. Although, I had a feeling I'd already seen its source at the Citadel. My heart wrenched for Shu once more at the thought of how I'd failed him.

Ra's spirit returned to my mind, burning hot as the flames reached high and his anger settled into a steady blaze. A low growl emitted from the passage on my right, and I stepped out in front of Anubis, not waiting for him to lead the way. As I came closer the growling ceased. I stopped in front of a heavy door with a small opening at eye level to peer through to the other side.

Ra's jackal stood on all fours, poised for violence in the center of the cell, hackles standing high and ears pinned on alert.

"Ra?" I whispered.

He shifted in an instant, or what would have been an instant if not for his injuries. As it were, his body changed slowly. Bones stretching, claws retreating in unison, and his eyes held on to the reflective glint until the last of his jackal was gone, and he stood stark naked before me. He ducked to keep from hitting the ceiling —his massive form barely contained by the cage they'd put him in.

"No." His voice was hoarse from disuse. "No."

"It's okay." His flame grew frenzied as his eyes locked onto me. "Open the door," I demanded, turning on Anubis.

He stared at me with a blank expression before gesturing toward the circular key hanging beside the door. I fumbled with it in the dark, holding my breath, and focusing on the newly formed scars.

"It's alright," I repeated under my breath until the key slid into place.

He was on me before I could pull the door aside, sweeping me into his arms and lifting me up in one swift motion. His breathing grew ragged as he pressed his bare chest into me and pushed me back into the wall.

"Ra. It's alright," I said again, trying to convince myself.

His powerful body was scarred all over—the evidence of blunt force against flesh and fresh cuts melding slowly laid across his skin. I searched for a place to lay my hands but settled on his face after finding no inch free of Anubis's punishment. Ra's lips found mine and his tongue passed through, rolling over my own as he gripped my body tight. I ignored the pinch of his fingers on my skin, latching on to savor the feeling instead. I'd gone without his touch for too long, and I would cherish every sensation.

He drove our kiss deeper, spreading his hand across my hips

and breathing life back into me, only pulling away for breath of his own.

"You can't be here, tey ib."

His eyes were pleading, and I felt the whisper of his breath on my face as he silently begged me to run.

Glancing at the deep wound running along his neck, I knew I couldn't. No one else needed to suffer for my failings, and one of us had to live to see the end.

"Ib?" Anubis barked an incredulous laugh. "No wonder you've become so weak. You betrayed this House for the comfort of a woman?" he cackled. As if he hadn't betrayed Nephthys a thousand times over for much less.

Ra ignored his words to clutch me closer, holding me to him and stalling my lungs. But I would rather him take my final breath than let me go. My weeks in the Citadel without him by my side had left the hole to grow, and his silent ministrations were mending me from the inside out.

"I'm taking him," I asserted, not bothering to look at Anubis.

It wasn't open for discussion. If he wanted me to go along peaceably with his plan, Ra was leaving this cell.

"It does not matter to me what comes of him now. He has served his purpose. But Nephthys will not help him," Anubis said before shrugging and turning toward the darkened steps.

I waited until I couldn't hear his heavy footsteps, then kissed Ra again. Once he was certain we were alone, his hands found the swath of skin beneath my dress, and his kan crept over me, slow and tender. Our lips crashed together as we desperately tried to devour one another. I knew we should be going. His kan was growing wild and eager, and I worried he intended to take me on the cold, damp floor. Not that I would stop him in ordinary circumstances, but blood was oozing out of deep wounds as his muscles clenched and released around me.

"Ra." I breathed in the scent of smoke and blood, and waited until he met my eyes. "My love, let's go."

CHAPTER 60

RA

I read the fear on her face and pulled away. The image of my battered body was too much for her. I lowered her back to the ground and stepped away to give her space, but kept a gentle hold on her wrist, savoring the familiar sensation of her kan. She took up a position in front as we made our way through the corridors, shielding my unclothed groin from the people we passed. Although, each time we came upon someone, they averted their eyes—likely from the obscene amount of blood and not my nakedness.

Her chamber was exactly as we'd left it, clothes and pillows strewn across the floor with every bit of furniture still out of place, and the faint scent of our bodies in the sheets. She snatched a random piece of fabric from a pile nearest the bed and snagged the jug of water that sat on her vanity.

"What happened?" she asked, gesturing for me to sit.

Her eyes flicked over me quickly, unable to look at the carnage as she dampened her rags. She knelt before me to brush my skin tenderly, starting with the shallow cuts along my thighs and making her way up to my chest. Dried, caked blood flaked off each time I shifted, dusting the carpet, and I kept as still as stone. I had no concern for the fabric, but I knew she would blame herself if I so much as flinched, and I wouldn't give her heart any more reasons to ache for me.

"Father grew tired of looking for you in distant places," I said, finding her eyes to pull myself away from the scratch and sting of my raw skin. "Luckily, I am much more durable than Shu. Is he dead?"

"No, why would you think that?" She glanced up beneath her dark lashes.

My hands fisted into the bed to keep from touching her.

"When his screams stopped, I suspected he'd succumbed to his injuries. Where is he?"

She reached for my chest, and I angled myself closer to ease her work. "He'll be okay. He's at the Citadel with Zhaur and Éshe."

"He did well," I said, hoping to lift away some of the guilt that crossed her face. He'd lasted longer than I thought he would have.

"Where is everyone else?" she asked once she'd rubbed off most of the clotted blood.

"Abraxas commands the guard now. Tarik and Nejeri are still with him. Nejeri returned to her chamber before you left, and Tarik moves like a shadow. Omar had no one to blame for his misgivings."

"Did Anubis kill him?" she asked, hesitant.

I nodded. Father had seen fit to "release" Omar from his duty.

A pained expression crossed her face before she went back to scrubbing at my skin.

"And he did this? Anubis?" she asked quietly, struggling to get the words out.

"His men, yes. But these wounds are old. The guardians stopped coming after the eighth one died."

Tears began to well in her eyes, and she ducked her head.

"Why aren't they healing?" she asked.

A hiss of pain escaped me as she swept across a ragged gash in my hip. She winced, pulling the wet cloth away.

"Sor—"

"You know how I feel about that word," I said, gripping her wrist and halting her progress. I pulled her closer, forcing her to meet my eyes. "Who are you?" I asked, confused by the woman looking back at me.

"W-what do you mean?"

"I mean, who are you? You're not *my* Onia. My heart knows better than to apologize for the things she cannot control—not to me. And she knows better than to hide from me," I said, wiping away a stray tear and dragging her up until she was firmly planted in my lap.

"Ra! You're—" she panicked.

"Do not cry for me."

"But I can't—"

She quieted as my fingers snaked into her hair and I pulled her mouth to mine.

A soft moan escaped her, and I breathed it in, relishing the rush of kan on my tongue. I pulled away, but only for a moment as I shifted beneath her so she sat straddling me. Heat blossomed between her legs as her body responded, and I drew in the delectable fragrance.

"Ra..." she breathed.

"Hush," I ordered.

The scales and a thousand shabti couldn't stop me from finishing what I'd just started. I longed to hear her little cries of pleasure as I stroked into her. But this time, I wouldn't release her until she was crying out in ecstasy for all to hear. This realm would know she was mine.

Her core pulsed as she ground into me, and my shaft grew painfully firm. I pushed my hands under her skirt and stilled as I fingered the leather holster strapped to her thigh. She sucked in a breath as I pulled the dagger free, swiping the broad side against her hot skin. The blade was one of my own—one I kept in the

Citadel due to my overly cautious nature and Father's relentless training.

Smart woman.

Her skirt gathered, billowing around her hips, and shielding her body from me. I lifted the blade and used it to cut her free before discarding it on the bed. She moaned quietly as my hands found her dark nipples, and I rolled one between my fingers, eliciting a soft gasp from her sweet mouth. My body filled with the aching need to claim her, and I gripped her hips, pulling her down and burying myself in the heat of her body.

Her name left my lips as I felt the familiar strain of her wet flesh yielding to me.

"Tey ib, you take me so sweetly."

I moved inside her, sending my kan coursing through her body —pouring into her legs and snaking into her stomach. A strangled cry tore free from her throat, and I knew my markings were doing their work. She would feel every scorching inch of me as I stroked her to completion, and my markings would increase the sensation tenfold. Soon she would be but a puddle in my arms.

She gripped me tight to steady herself as she met my every thrust.

"Ra!" she pleaded, no longer shying from her desire.

My sac tightened at the sound. That mouth of hers would be my undoing, I knew. But I wanted to watch her unravel first—to see that blissful look in her eyes as she shuddered and shattered on top of me.

"Take what is yours," I commanded her, and she ground into me, working my body for her pleasure.

I felt her flex around my length, throbbing as she threw her head back to take in my seed. I poured into her and held her close as her body tensed and released, again and again.

CHAPTER 61
ONIA

I opened my eyes to see him gazing at me, his precious dimple winking back at me in appreciation. He was hovering above me after tearing into me in more ways than I could count. He pressed his forehead to my own in a silent display of affection, and I accepted his declaration, passing a bit of my kan back to him. We no longer needed words—they wouldn't suffice.

"I'll draw a bath," he said, pushing up from me.

"No," I groaned as I pulled him back down.

His arms came around me as he wrapped a loc around his finger, tugging gently.

"I'll only be a moment. You can join me if you'd like." He winked and tapped at my temple before pressing a kiss to my brow and breaking the illusion of our bliss.

I stared openly at his hard, naked body, and I longed to feel it pressed on top of me again. We'd spent the last few hours exploring each other, but as I watched him move about the room, I realized I wasn't ready to let him go.

"Okay, but please put clothes on," I said, mimicking his signature tone that said, "this request is an order."

"Jealous, tey ib?" He lifted a brow before dropping his expression and taking on the stony appearance he usually wore. He wrapped a bolt of fabric around himself, leaving it hanging low on his chiseled hips, and disappeared into the hallway. As the door swung shut behind him, I focused on the steady flame at the back of my mind. He was still basking in the memory of our bodies melding together, and a smoldering satisfaction burned bright in his spirit. I held tight to it as he moved about the Hall, and it never dimmed, not once—no matter how far he wandered from me.

I took the moment of solitude to sort through my confession —as if the right words would ease the pain. But I knew, no matter how I said it, I would break his heart. After all he'd done—just to give my life away. It would shatter him.

When he returned, he announced to every guard placed outside my door that he wasn't leaving my side, and if any of them took issue with that, they would need to remove him by force. A few of them had started to speak against him but thought better of it after seeing the determination on his face and remembering the ill fate of their brethren. I watched his body flex with heated anger, trying to commit it to memory. If memories were all I'd have for the rest of my days, I would take as many as I could gather.

I waited quietly as he filled the copper tub with steaming water before stepping in and calling me to him. I took his hand and settled between his legs as we waited for the water to settle. His arms gripped me tight as he nuzzled my hair. The scent of rose oil and eucalyptus floated around us, calming my nerves, and eventually I found the courage to say it.

"This isn't a terrible way to spend your last day."

Ra's spirit flared, and his arm tightened around me involuntarily. "Last day?" he asked.

I sucked in a deep breath and shut my eyes. "I don't know that I'll be seeing another one come morning." I spoke to the water, muttering to keep from establishing a truth I already knew. His spirit jerked, the flame flickering as he struggled to make sense of my words.

"Tey ib, speak plainly," he demanded, his big hand spreading across my belly.

I squirmed, and after a few moments of strained silence, I realized he was going to make me say it—unable to admit it himself. I twisted in his arms to see his face. "Ra…" I gripped his hand and launched into my explanation. "I haven't achieved the power I need. Éshe's vision remains the same."

"You don't need to explain yourself. I can handle the guards. Gather your things; we won't have much time." Water sloshed out over the rim of the tub as he made to stand, but I planted my hands on his chest, and he looked at me with mild irritation as I sat on top of him, unmoving.

"Onia, we need to leave." His voice was gentle, and I wasn't sure if he was truly confused or remaining willfully ignorant to the hand we'd been dealt. The jackal rose close to the surface, prepared to defend me at a moment's notice. But it wouldn't be necessary.

"Ra, I can't."

"Yes, you can. And you will," he said. He glowered at me, using his dark and menacing gaze to intimidate me, apparently having forgotten we knew each other better than that.

"Please. My heart can't do this anymore. Not when I could make it all end," I begged, hoping he would see how tired my soul truly was. Watching people and the Hall fall victim to my failure had become more than I could bear.

"At what cost?" he shouted. But I knew his words weren't directed at me. I didn't doubt that if he could curse Shai to his face, he would.

"I know the cost. That's why I have to. We tried—you tired, but I'm not strong enough. That's why I'm asking you to help me through it. I can't do this alone."

His midnight eyes softened as he abandoned his posturing to take my hands in his. "Onia, you know there is nothing in all the realms I could ever deny you. I would count the sands of time if it would give us even one more day. But now, you ask too much of me. I cannot stand idly by and watch you give up your life."

His tone turned pleading, and I reached for him, holding his face in my hands.

"And whose life would you rather give? Yours?" His silence was the only confirmation I needed. "Ra, it has to be me. I am the only descendant of House Ma'at. There is no other choice."

His hand reached up to cradle my cheek, and I leaned into the comfort of his kan.

"Tether yourself to me," he whispered, holding me close to his body as if he would tie me to him literally.

I knew this would come. I knew he would give anything to see me through the other side. So, I'd asked Éshe the very same question, because I wouldn't risk us both without knowing.

"We can't know that it will be enough. Mother was *primordial*. Her kan was likely greater than the pair of us combined. I will not leave us both vacant and alone for eternity." His jaw flexed under the pressure of his pain, and I watched his eyes fill with tears. "And someone needs to watch over the Hall. You know as well as I do Anubis will abuse whatever power he obtains. You mustn't leave everyone to their own defense." My mind thought of Shu, lying in a bloodied heap, and I found my conviction. "If I am vacant, and you are not here to stand in his way, he will have had his every wish granted."

He hung his head, and I watched his gentle tears fall into the water.

"I can't do this without you. Please, Ra, I've already decided." I choked out the words, speaking around the knot in my throat. I was aiming for understanding but decided I would settle with quiet compliance. If I had to walk the path ahead on my own, I wasn't sure I would even make it there.

When he lifted his head, his fierce and consuming gaze met mine, unwavering.

"I couldn't leave your side even if I wanted to."

CHAPTER 62
ONIA

We awoke to a firm beating on the door. For a while, neither of us moved, and we sat tangled together, taking comfort in the warmth of each other's bodies, knowing they wouldn't dare enter uninvited. After several long moments, the thudding stopped, and I decided we'd taken up as much time as fate would allow. I moved to discard the sheets and address our visitor, but Ra stayed my movement.

"I'll get it."

He freed his hand from mine and made for the door, pulling it open swiftly, causing the young man on the other side to jump backward.

"M-m-morning, sir. Master Anubis requests Lady Onia's presence for the ceremony," he stammered, and I could see Ra's kan growing agitated.

"Does he now..." Ra pressed, and I saw the confusion on the young guardian's face.

"Ra, stop that," I scolded. His anger was misplaced, and he knew it. I walked toward the open door so the young man could see me. "We'll be out in a few moments."

Ra's kan was wild as I slid the door closed, and I turned on him.

"You promised..."

"I promised you I'd stand by your side. I said nothing about resisting the urge to tear through every last person along the way."

"Well, you're not helping," I said, slapping him lightly on the arm.

He caught my wrist on its way back and dragged me in, kissing me hard. His arms wrapped around me, and I fought back tears. I pulled away, rubbing at the tightness in my chest.

"That's not helping either," I said—my voice barely a whisper.

I dressed slowly, not wanting to rush the inevitable.

Just when I thought I was ready, I got caught in the mirror. A woman was staring back at me, looking full of pride and strength. Her brow was set high with knowing, and her chin ended in a soft, dignified point. Perceptive eyes watched me as I gathered myself. Who was this woman? I almost asked her out loud. It'd been a while since I'd really seen myself, and this woman looked different than I remembered. The fullness in her cheeks had been chiseled into resolve, and something menacing and dangerous lurked behind her eyes. She was, without a doubt, divine—poised for whatever came next.

"Ah, so you finally see her."

I don't know when Ra came to stand behind me, but he was gazing at the woman with open adoration.

"Excuse me?" I said, unable to tear my eyes from her.

"Her. The woman you've been so uncertain of. The one with the fire in her eyes. I've been watching you, waiting for you to realize."

Realize what?

His arms came around me, and his lips found my neck. In the mirror, he embraced the woman—their spirits swelling in unison.

"It's a pretty good mask if I do say so myself," I said.

But even as I said it, the words felt wrong, and Ra corrected me.

"No, tey ib. *That's* no mask. That's just you," he added before turning for the door and holding his hand out to me in offering.

"Ready?"

We walked to the rotunda in silence. Ra wrapped his arm around my waist for added balance as we stepped over the larger debris that had been brushed to the side. The darkness had lifted, and someone had corrected the scales, so they sat upright and even.

Anubis sat under them with his jackal's head squarely on his shoulders. Nephthys and Ananiah flanked his makeshift throne. Guardians were posted every few feet, one under each archway and lining the path to the soul pool. I spotted Nejeri, Tarik, and Abraxas among them. I made my way forward, walking slowly until I stood in front of Anubis.

"Taking your time, I see," Anubis sneered through big, inhuman teeth.

Beside me, Ra loosened his hold on his jackal.

"The fate of the Hall and your house is in my hands. Do not push me." I leveled my threat, hoping he wouldn't see through me. But one thing I wouldn't tolerate was his smug satisfaction at having bent me to his will. This choice was still mine to make, and he would live with the knowledge that his power had been mine to give and take away.

With a grunt and a fisted hand, he nodded for me to continue. A man in long, flowing black robes stepped out from a shadowed archway, gesturing for me to follow. Ra continued with me, crushing my hand in his grip as we made our way toward the soul pool.

Ananiah offered me a slight nod as I passed. Nephthys hung

her head, avoiding my gaze, and I guessed she didn't care much for goodbyes.

Nejeri and Tarik caught my eye, and I recognized the hardened look on their faces. I was wearing a similar one myself. Abraxas looked his usual self—calm and composed as his brother had taught him. But he hesitated as I grew nearer, looking more nervous with every step. As I stopped before them, Abraxas dropped to his knee, hanging his head, and placing his blade on the ground.

I turned to Ra, unsure what this gesture was meant to be. But my question was answered when Nejeri and Tarik did the same, followed by several others around them. Suddenly bodies bowed, one after the other, lining the rotunda and placing their weapons on the ground. The ones that remained standing stood shifting on their feet, uncomfortable with the fact that they were now outnumbered.

The news of my fate had likely filled the Hall moments after my escape. They all knew by now that I was walking a path of desolation. I turned slowly, taking in the number of guardians kneeling before me, and fixed my eyes on Anubis, checking to see that the message had reached him. He stood seething but said nothing.

The cloaked man pressed on, and I turned my back on Anubis, striding forward until we came to the water's edge. The man gestured for me to join him, and I took a definitive step forward but was pulled backward as Ra gripped my wrist, halting my progression.

He looked at me with desperate eyes and all I could say was, "I'm sorry."

He stepped into me, and I angled my face upward, expecting him to kiss me one last time. Instead, he pressed his head to mine and began pouring his kan into me without restraint. I startled, realizing what he was doing, but his hands gripped my waist and held me to him, forcing me to take in his energy. My eyes slid shut as he directed it into my chest and enveloped my heart—a warmth blossoming as it settled. My power surged as my kan drank him in.

"You have my heart. Please bring it back to me," he whispered before pulling away, leaving barely a drop left for himself.

"I'll try."

He stepped away with his hands fisted at his sides and nodded for me to continue.

The old man stepped in close, signaling me to stand in front of the shallow pool. I glanced down at the water and watched as a small cluster of souls drifted to the surface. What had once been a bright swirling of tangled souls filling the pool, was now a patchwork of light with giant gaping holes. I turned to face the man with my back to the pool and waited for his instruction.

He stood in front of me, arms outstretched with his hands hovering around my face.

I closed my eyes, bracing for the moment the Hall latched on to me. The old man pressed his thumb to the space between my brows, pushing firmly against my head and causing my balance to falter. Then, I was falling. But I didn't flail. My body fell like a stone—backward into the pool, and my mind splintered as I hit the water. Shallow waves lapped around my face as the current pulled at me, separating my spirit from my physical form, and sending me spiraling down into the Fall.

CHAPTER 63

RA

I watched helplessly as her body hit the water—souls moving about her form. I resisted the urge to cover her as the water soaked her clothing, leaving it clinging to her skin. The old healer turned to face the room, nodding once toward Father, and taking up a fortified stance at the front of the pool. She wasn't of this realm any longer, and I watched as the pool filled with light and souls surged upward from the fall beneath. Gasps sounded from the guardians and assessors that had gathered around the archways as the Hall began mending itself. Debris turned quickly to dust and moved about the room, settling in the wide crevasses that had split open, filling them, and solidifying once again. The flame of the sconces burned brighter, and the water in the pool filled until her body lay fully submerged.

Father stood, craning his neck to peer into the water, but the souls began to flow and cover her body until she was practically gone from view. I swallowed hard. She had given herself for this Hall; now, I would do the same.

I made my way to Father, who was now sitting in his chair with an arrogant look about him. I glanced at the still-standing guardians, waiting to see if they'd intervene, but none of them moved to stop me, and I continued until I was only inches from his face.

"I challenge you for the seat of Master of House Anubis," I whispered my words for his ears only, and watched with quiet pleasure as his would-be brows came together and his face distorted with unbridled rage. His teeth flashed as he snarled, hands gripping the arms of his chair so hard the wood began to crack.

"You dare dishonor the House of Anubis?" He spat the words at me, a sprinkle of saliva landing on my face.

"There is no honor to be had in this house. Not while you remain at its head."

My eyes flicked over to Ananiah and Abraxas. How many times had we all suffered at his hand? How many more would know the same pain?

"You have no second." He offered his excuse, knowing it was empty as he said it, but hoping it would stick.

"I second this challenge!" Abraxas shouted, standing from his position on the floor.

Father's ears pinned as he realized his hold on this "family" was waning.

He changed tactics.

"Her life lies with the balance, and you wish to play at master?" he asked, dangling her fate in front of me.

"Do not feign concern for her! Everything I've done, I have done for her! This will be no different." I freed my blades from their holsters, gripping one in each hand. "No matter what becomes of her, I will not let her sacrifice be for nothing. This Hall will not be yours. Take up your arms!"

He rose to his feet, stripping off his robes until he stood bare-chested and growling. He claimed no weapon, confident in his skill. But the memories of everything he'd taken from me clung tight to my spirit—the sound of Amon's screams as his spirit was ended, Shu's tortured cries piercing the stone walls for hours on end, and Onia's gentle sobs as I held her just last night. All of it originated from Father and his insatiable need to consume.

No longer.

I backed away, waiting for him to join me. He idled for a moment, and I waited, knowing he needed time to come to terms with the circumstance he'd created. He'd grown too comfortable and had failed to realize that the people around him had cast him aside long ago—only doing as he demanded out of fear. But there was nothing left for him to destroy. I had no reason to continue under his command.

"Come, Father!" I taunted before shifting mid-way, letting my hands sharpen into claws, and my mouth pull into a long snout—a mirror image of him.

Father strode forward, wasting no time. He struck out in a wild frenzy, swinging his arms at my head only for me to block each strike in turn. I brought my knee to his chest, barely grazing him as he swept backward. But I didn't slow as he slipped beyond my reach. I charged forward to cut through the air, aiming for his neck. Father jerked away as I dropped to the ground sweeping out a leg and catching him in his retreat. He tumbled to the earth, and the struggle continued.

He dove over me, his jaws gnashing at my throat as he trapped me beneath him, and my jackal thrilled as we watched the plan playing out as anticipated. Father had always fought with poorly executed plans, never thinking past his next move. His impulsive nature would feed him thought after thought until he was overtaken by rage as his foresight failed him. But I'd learned that one carefully crafted decision was more valuable than a hundred thoughtless ones.

I brought my blades up, crossing them and slicing a deep X into his chest. He recoiled as my blades met his skin and released a low growl as he pushed up to his feet. His markings began to burn bright along his arms, telegraphing his intention, and I rolled to my feet to gather what little kan I had left.

My body hardened in time for his fist to connect, but his strength sent me stumbling back, and he took his opening. He swung again, and again, and again, striking me mercilessly until blood bubbled up in my throat. Old wounds split apart as his hands tore into me. I pushed my spirit into my legs, calling on my markings to give me speed. Father struck out again, missing his mark as I finally managed to sidestep him. His control was lurking close to the edge, and I decided to push him further.

I spun on my heel, bringing my elbow into his jaw through my rotation and sending his body staggering backward. He righted himself and slashed at me, carving a wide slice of flesh from my arm. My kan reached up to close the wound but only managed to stem the blood flow after giving most of it to Onia. My breathing grew labored as I avoided each attack. I couldn't maintain this indefinitely. He was still skilled after all his years of idle posturing, and I couldn't risk much more. My kan wouldn't be able to heal me. If I had any hope of beating him, I would need all his sense to be lost before my spirit gave out.

I turned to face him and drove a fist to his jaw. His bones cracked under the pressure, and I watched as his hold snapped. His canine eyes grew wide with fury, and a chilling roar exploded from his chest as his jackal took control. He swept his claws through the air and what followed was a series of chaotic and reckless blows—each of them more desperate than the last. I tried to sidestep his aimless rage.

But Father saw red, and his claws came across my face, stinging and hot as his knee connected with my stomach. Blood spurt from my mouth as I doubled over, and I held tight to my jackal, biding my time for the moment I needed it most. Father took his opening, bringing his fist to my face repeatedly. My left eye swelled shut as he continued his barrage. Onia's beautiful face rose from the depths of my memory—her brown skin glinting in the sun, a gleaming smile spread across her face as she looked at me. My body broke as Father dealt his final blow, and I clung to her.

"Brother!" Abraxas's voice shattered the tense silence.

"This is no brother of yours!" Father shouted.

His voice came from far above me, and I slowly registered that I was now lying in the rotunda in a puddle of my own blood. My eyes cracked open to see Father's feet retreating to his throne, satisfied I wouldn't recover.

"If I am vacant and you are not here to stand in his way, he will have had his every wish granted." Her trembling voice reminded me of my purpose.

I was her guardian, and I would not fail her.

I released my jackal, calling on its power and letting it take my place. My kan surged as I raised my blades and let them fly.

Deep gashes sliced the tendons behind Father's knees, sending him to the ground. Light gathered beneath his skin as he worked to heal himself. I only had seconds before he would stand again. I latched on to every ounce of my spirit, feeling it pulse into my legs as I launched myself across the floor. Father jolted as my claws hooked around his neck. But the jackal acted in an instant.

Blood sprayed across the freshly mended stone, staining it red in every direction. The thud of his skull rolling from his shoulders and landing in a crimson river echoed softly through the rotunda. My chest heaved as I strained to mend my wounds. Blood was pouring from my body, collecting on the floor with Father's, and I prepared myself to join her. My eyes slid shut as I swayed on my feet, and my balance faltered as my kan grew weaker. I exhaled in relief and waited.

Before Osiris could claim me, a shoulder was propping me up. Abraxas jerked me upright, wordlessly placing a hand on my back and passing me his kan. I took it graciously and bowed as it swept through me—a similar sensation to my own, albeit less bitter. Nejeri appeared beside him, handing me a cloth as I straightened. I knelt before Father's remnants to cover his face as the last of my wounds mended themselves.

"Thank you," I said, turning to Abraxas and drawing him into a rough hug.

His hand beat against my back as the shock ran through him. But when I pulled away, his usual easy character had already fallen back into place.

"Where is Mother?" I asked, scanning the room.

"She left when you issued your challenge."

I only nodded. I didn't think she would stand in my way, but I hadn't expected her to abandon Father so easily.

"Ananiah, too," he added, confirming what I'd suspected. She was nowhere to be found, and I assumed she'd gone with Mother. I wouldn't stop her. She was free to do as she pleased now.

"Clear the rotunda. They don't need to witness the Empress's —" I turned to the pool, but the words were cut short as I realized her body was no longer lying beneath the surface. "Where is she?" I demanded of the old healer.

"She has passed through," he answered softly, seeming unbothered by neither her absence nor the display of violence he'd just witnessed.

"What?" My voice ruptured through the chamber. "Passed through? She was to be vacant!"

"She must first join with the Hall. Her body and spirit will return; whether her kan returns with her is a different question."

I was prepared to berate the old man for not having told us of this sooner when a thunderous crack sounded beneath us. The guardians and assessors scurried about, with most of the assessors making a swift exit, apparently having seen enough. Tarik sprinted forward to join Abraxas, Nejeri, and me in the center.

"Go, we'll stay and watch the pool," Nejeri offered.

"What should I do with Father?"

I glanced down at him. He was kneeling in his own blood with his head at his knees.

"I no longer care what comes of him," I said, nodding to

Father's cloth-covered face. "But the rest of our house may wish to pay their respects. He will have a proper burial."

Abraxas nodded.

"Gather all the new guards. I will need to speak with them when I return."

Without waiting for anything more, I turned and sprinted for the crypt.

CHAPTER 64
ONIA

ater flowed over me, moving upward, dragging me slowly through the current as souls drifted over my head. I swept an arm aside, trying to displace the water or feel for the spirits' warmth as they passed, but they moved through me without faltering, continuing their course.

I sat there, enjoying the impossible stillness that had befallen my body. For a moment, it felt like peace. Not the kind that comes to you when you stop to breathe, or the kind that creeps over you right before you fall asleep, but true stillness. Something so infinite, not even Shu could've conjured it. Even the subtle rise and fall of my chest had stopped, and it occurred to me that the steady current of worry that plagued my mind was gone, leaving nothing but silence. But as I sat there, the quiet calm turned to mild panic. I dug down, trying to find the remnants of my spirit, but came up empty.

Why am I here?

An empty silence answered my question.

Where am I?

I tested my limbs, lifting them out of the water until I sat with my knees to my chest. I was sitting in a wide river that seemed to stretch on forever in both directions. A sandy bank marked the edge of the water on either side. But there was nothing beyond it. Only sand as far as the eye could see. I got to my feet, wondering if I was meant to stand here for eternity. Or perhaps I was meant to pick a direction? Souls were moving both ways, darting around my feet. But...

Which way is the Hall?

"I knew you'd find your way." A soft voice called from the bank.

My head whipped around, startled by the break in the silence.

A woman stood at the edge of the water with wings spread open—her face shrouded in a golden light.

"Come, you can't stand there too long. The current will snatch you up." The woman stretched a hand in my direction, beckoning me to join her on the shore. "Come." She stepped out of the light and strode forward, her hips swaying ever so slightly as she bent down to offer her hand.

"Mother?" The word came out all on its own.

My face fell into a quiet shock as her fingers wrapped around my palm, lifting me from the water with ease.

"Yes, darling?"

My own face stared back at me, holding my gaze, unblinking. She was beautiful—light green eyes and smooth golden skin. Her wings were large, spreading out behind her several cubits in each direction.

"Where are we?" I asked, glancing up and down the river as I came to stand beside her.

"This is the path to the Hall." She waved an elegant hand at the water.

"You mean they're...passing through?" I asked, glancing at the lights flowing up the river.

"Yes, dear."

I stood on the bank, watching the light bend and twist as the water pulled them along, forcing them on their path of life. There were no holes that I could see. The Hall was already pulling from my kan—healing itself. That would explain the draining emptiness I was feeling. But my mind was slowly filling with the thoughts that had been so notably absent, and I latched on to the first question that lifted from the fog.

"How did you end up here?" I asked.

"The same way we all do," she said solemnly. "I died."

She knew that wasn't what I meant. But she didn't elaborate. Instead, we stood there a moment staring at one another sifting through all the words we wanted to say.

Mother found her's first.

"I'm sorry," she whispered. I shook my head, but she held up a hand. "No, darling. This is my doing. I hoped by leaving you and your father behind we could avoid this—that you could enjoy your life without divine intervention," she said, cupping my cheek. "But it seems I was wrong. I see that now. Perhaps, if I had stayed, I would have been there to guide you—perhaps then you would have been prepared for this. Even if my own fate stayed the same," she muttered.

I swallowed back my tears as she brushed the hair out of my eyes to hold my face in her hands.

"Can you forgive me?" she asked.

I blinked back at her.

"I already have," I said. "Seraya told me everything. I understand."

Mother sat down along the bank, hanging her bare feet in the water, and I joined her. We sat in the warm sand, taking comfort in having finally found each other. She draped a wing over me, shielding me from the sunlight that appeared to originate from no particular direction.

"Who did this to you?" I asked, shattering the silence.

Mother offered me a dejected smile—a pitiful look.

"I had hoped this wouldn't be left for you to ponder, but I take it Anubis has failed in finding the culprit?" I nodded, and

Mother sighed, meeting my gaze, and reaching out a hand to cup my cheek.

"Who in the Hall do you know that carries a sadness in their spirit so dismal it's a wonder their heart doesn't bleed? A spirit so wretched it bolsters itself against the pain of others? A soul scorned a hundred times over?"

I thought of the people in the Hall—Abraxas and Tarik with their playful nature, Nejeri and her bright-eyed wit, Ra's commanding yet tender heart, and Ananiah with her sharp and unabashed opinions. But even *she* knew joy from time to time. Shu refused to raise a hand in violence, and Anubis was too consumed by thoughts of himself to know anything of sadness. In fact, he might be the only soul in the Hall that felt nothing other than bliss and anger. That left only one...

"Nephthys..."

Mother nodded.

As her name left my lips, the image fit—her cold and vile kan, the snaked-eyed cheer, and her vicious words. All of it, coupled with her shattered heart, it was a wonder she smiled at all. I had no doubt every threat she'd ever laid had been made real. But she'd spent centuries in Mother's Hall. What reason would she suddenly have to cut her down?

"Why?" I pressed.

"Why does Nephthys do anything?" Mother shrugged her delicate shoulders. "Anubis. He asked for my hand." My face must have screwed up because she laughed softly before adding, "It wasn't the first time he'd done so. It's been a regular occurrence since House Anubis joined the Hall. I always suspected she knew, but I suppose my continuous denial of him gave her enough security to stay."

That didn't surprise me. Centuries of betrayal hadn't prompted Nephthys to leave, so why would this?

"What changed."

"He did...when he offered to tether himself to me."

My mouth gaped open. Asking for her hand was one thing, but a soul tie...

"Did you say yes?"

Mother's beautiful face contorted with stunned confusion. "I couldn't possibly. My heart has always belonged to one." She glanced upriver, and I wondered if she knew where Father had gone. Mother and Father hadn't been together for over two decades, but the thought of her moving on left a sour taste in my mouth. Perhaps because Father never had.

"No," she continued. "I denied him as I always have. But Nephthys already knew of his proposal. She must have found his letter before it made its way to me."

Letter?

My mind recalled the deep slash marks in Mother's vanity as realization dawned. Poor Seraya, she'd been pulled into Nephthys's scheming, and it had cost her dearly.

"Anubis never would have told her. He was fond of his secrets," Mother added.

Yes, that I knew firsthand.

Her eyes filled with sympathy as she remembered Anubis's callous treatment of Nephthys. I'd seen how he disregarded her so easily, setting her aside for his own selfish needs the same way he did everyone else. I wondered why he didn't simply free her. What value did she serve in such a state—bound to him by pain alone? As quickly as I asked myself, I knew the answer—her power. Even untethered Nephthys was a force Anubis could wield in his favor, and why waste a soul tie on a lesser power when *the* Empress Ma'at was available?

"Did you fight?" I asked, wondering how Nephthys had managed to take Mother's life.

She clicked her tongue at me as if I'd insulted her. "Of course I did, darling. But heartbreak is a very powerful emotion. One I hope you will never know for yourself."

It was a bit too late for that. But I'd tell her about Ra later. We had plenty of time now.

Nephthys's heart had been broken beyond repair. Anyone could see it. She'd spent centuries pining for a man who didn't love her, watching as he took woman after woman to his bed, only to offer his tether to another. I was surprised she hadn't cracked sooner.

"Have you seen Father?" I asked as I watched a dark and murky soul drifting by.

"Yes, my dear. I will join him soon. In another life." She smiled sweetly, and her voice quieted as she stared at me. "Forgive me. You look so like him."

I laughed loudly. "He says otherwise." As did everyone else.

"How was it? Without me?" She asked.

I smiled at her concern. I'd never doubted her love for me, Father had made sure of that. But it was still a comfort to know she cared. We sat there a while, telling each other of all the things we'd been holding on to. I told her of the life I'd lived and the love I'd found with Ra, and she told me of her and Father and her painstaking decision to leave.

"Your Father was covered in ink," she chuckled, the corners of her eyes crinkling as she recounted the day they met. "And I was apologizing profusely. Of course, I'd run into him on purpose," she added, winking. "I would never be so clumsy. But he was truly handsome, and I didn't think anything would come of it."

"Obviously, fate had other plans," I said, eyeing her.

She smiled sweetly and shrugged.

"We spent every waking moment together. It felt as if our love grew stronger every day. Until one day, we decided to give it a life of its own, and we created you. I knew Omari would give you all the love he could offer. So, when the time came, I did the same and left. And I have cherished our secret every day since." She smiled at me.

"Will you tell him I miss him, if you can," I muttered. I'd said it every day for years, but I think it'd been a long while since he really understood.

Mother nodded, reaching for my hand to hold it in her own.

We laughed and cried together, and by the time we were through, we'd managed to pack two lifetimes into what felt like two hours. But I had no concept of how long we'd been sitting there. I suppose it didn't matter; I'd likely spend the rest of my "life" on this bank, watching the water drift by as the Hall fed from my kan.

As I sat there trying to come to terms with my new existence, Mother's voice pulled me from my misery.

"I'm afraid you must go now, dear. The longer you're here, the more difficult it will be to return you."

"Return me?" I asked.

"Yes, dear. You didn't think I'd let you stay here, did you?" My face confirmed my defeat, and she shook her head, disappointed. "Oh darling, never. The Hall needs you. They need you," she said, gesturing at the water. Her gentle tone swept over me, and I met her eyes.

"But how? My kan isn't strong enough. I tried," I said, lifting my hands in front of my face to show her my meager markings. "But it was no use."

A mischievous glint sparked in Mother's eye as she tilted her head to one side.

"What greater renewal is there than to pass through the Fall and appear on the other side," she said, leading me back to the water. I opened my mouth to question her, but she held up a dainty hand to silence me. "Onia, trust your mother now." I quieted, gulping down my words and scrambling to my feet. "I see someone has given you their kan to bolster you. Please give them my thanks; it is likely the only reason the current didn't carry you off immediately."

Ra's face flashed in my mind, and my heart warmed—grateful for his stubborn persistence.

"Close your eyes, dear." I did as I was told. "Now, take a deep breath." I sucked in a big breath of air. "I love you," Mother whispered.

Tears rolled down my cheeks as she pressed her fingers to my head and pushed gently.

I felt the current of water passing over me, and my eyes opened to see the dark of the Crypt and the souls moving freely. My body began to reawaken, and my lungs suddenly begged for air. I struggled against the current as I floated, suspended in the Fall, stuck between. I gathered my kan, feeling it rush up in a frenzy, and pushed it from my body aimlessly. My energy disrupted the current, and my body hurtled toward the floor faster than I expected. I flailed and landed with a loud crack as the wall of water burst open, spilling onto the floor, and knocking me loose.

I inhaled sharply, trying to steady myself, but my chest struggled under the weight of something pressing on my back and drooping down around me. I straightened as best I could and surveyed my body with my kan. Wet feathers smattered the floor, glistening in the glow of the Fall. My energy pulsed as I realized what was jutting out from my back.

Powerful wings hung around my shoulders, and I pressed my kan outward, straightening them and pushing them down around me. They were a tawny brown, like a hawk, and I pumped them once more, sending the loose feathers floating up from the floor.

I plucked one out of the air, examining it closely. Small, black markings were inked onto them—tiny messages from the balance, each different from the other. The Kemi symbol for love and life glared back at me from the ones I'd gathered in my hand. But I didn't have time to ponder them. The clamor of footsteps sounded from above, and I pulled myself to my feet, preparing to face

Anubis. My hands fisted at my sides, and my kan flooded me as I braced myself.

Before I could take a single step, the warm flicker of a familiar spirit burst through my mind, and I was racing up the dark and narrow stairs. I stumbled under the weight of my wings, trying to fit them into the narrow hallway. But Ra's spirit burned brighter with every step. He was sprinting for me. I could feel it. I pushed myself to reach him.

I burst out of the darkness and into the light of the small landing at the top, only to run smack into his chest. The scent of smoke and musk filled my senses as I clung to him. His strong arms came around me as best they could, maneuvering awkwardly around my wings.

"Tey ib?" he asked softly, as if he couldn't be sure I wasn't a mirage.

I blinked up at him as he pulled away to eye me tenderly.

Dried blood covered his body once again, but the wounds had healed from what I could see, and I gripped him tight, rising on my toes, answering him with a kiss. He sighed a deep relief as our lips met, and I kissed him until my lungs begged for air.

"I thought—" he sputtered, gazing at me in awe.

"You asked me to return, remember. I couldn't deny such a request."

He crushed me to him, burying his face in my hair and carrying me from the Crypt.

CHAPTER 65
ONIA

Nephthys's disappearance didn't come as a surprise. After all this time, I now understood her version of protection was simply self-preservation. But Ananiah's absence shocked me. Ra had given her freedom from her father's reigns, but she'd chosen to hand them to her mother instead.

I supposed she had her reasons.

Ra was insistent that we find them both. If only to know what Nephthys had done with Seraya. The guardians had completed a thorough search of her chambers and study, but Seraya was nowhere to be found. I planned to ask Atem to act against Nephthys once we found her. Mother had given me what I needed to force his hand, and with it, I would honor her memory.

Mother hadn't just saved Anubis's proposal to tether themselves, but she'd saved every letter he'd written her over the centuries. Page after page of requests for her hand, each of them as eloquent as the last. And there, buried at the bottom of the pile, under everything else, was the single piece of proof that Nephthys had seen fit to end Mother's life over.

"Do you think he loved her?" I asked Ra as we sat, sifting through Anubis's confessions.

"Ma'at?" he asked, looking up from a page.

"Nephthys."

He shrugged. "I doubt he even knew what that word meant."

"You really mustn't hide them. They're beautiful," Ra chided, brushing his fingers across my feathers.

I focused my kan as he had taught me and cloaked my wings beneath my energy.

"I know. They're just a bit large, and I haven't gotten used to the movement."

He shrugged.

"Suit yourself," he said, offering me his arm.

I took it, sliding my hand down the bulk of his bicep, so my hand rested lightly along his forearm. His kan prickled in response and I clutched him a little closer. He led me toward the rotunda where the other emperors, empresses, and high masters were waiting. Ra had suggested I make my ascent known to the other houses by inviting them to the Hall for a "celebration"—a subtle show of power designed to dissuade them from acting against me. I was confident I could hold my own, especially now that my spirit had been renewed by the Fall, but if I could spare myself the energy, I would abide.

I entered the rotunda feeling every bit an empress as Ra ushered me through the room with Abraxas, Nejeri, and Tarik walking purposefully behind. Hundreds of gods and goddesses had gathered to pay their respects, and I made the obligatory greetings, moving from person to person with a smile until there was all but one left.

Ra's energy tensed as Ammit headed in our direction. I could feel him preparing to step in front of me, and I gently placed my free hand on his tightly wound muscles. He was right to be concerned. She may not have killed Mother, but she was still responsible for chasing me through the desert. She couldn't be trusted. But here, in my domain, I had nothing to worry about. She was greedy, but she wasn't foolish.

Ra looked down at me, and I silently requested a moment alone with her. He hesitated before relaxing his energy and gently removing his arm from my grip. He caught my hand as I pulled away and turned it over, pressing a kiss to the center of my palm before straightening and striding forward with his usual air of authority. His public display caught me off guard. But the message was clear. I remained under the protection of House Anubis—to threaten me was to threaten them. Considering I caught several eyes lingering on me followed by frenzied murmurs, the message had been warranted. I'd have to thank him later.

I watched him move past Ammit, refusing to acknowledge her presence beyond a curt nod, to join a small cluster of assessors standing near the soul pool. He was chatting politely, but I knew he wasn't listening, not to them anyway. If I knew him, he'd be eavesdropping. I didn't bow as she approached; instead, I dropped the veil of kan that shrouded my wings, letting her see me as I was —no longer caring if I took up too much space.

She followed suit, and her kan fell away, creeping across her face until her beautiful visage was covered in glittering scales. Her eyes were a piercing reptilian yellow rather than the mystic green I'd seen before, and it struck me that they were oddly mesmerizing —pretty even. She waited until I was close enough to touch before addressing me.

"Congratulations on your ascension, my dear." Her voice was insincere—she practically hissed it at me. Part of me suspected that she would have if we weren't in full view of the entire realm.

"Thank you."

"Though, I wouldn't get too comfortable. This crowd can be quite...insatiable," she said, smirking and glancing around.

"Let them. I have no intention of releasing my dominion," I said, crossing my arms over my chest.

"Hm. That makes things more difficult."

She ignored my presence to ponder her options. But I interrupted her, tired of her taunting.

"Do you wish me dead?" I asked, hoping she would have enough respect for my life to tell me outright.

"I did." She confessed. "But now… Let's just say I haven't decided." She shrugged. "I do not know you well enough to decide." Her eyes narrowed as she considered me.

Apparently, her care for my mother started and ended with her. It struck me as odd how many people had placed her spirit on my shoulders, expecting me to uphold a woman I never knew, but all the while dismissing *me*. I decided at that moment that if my mother's reputation wouldn't do me any favors, perhaps my own would.

"Very well, then. You may want to reconsider your assessment of me." Her brow piqued. "You're right; you do not know me. But I assure you I am more dangerous than you may think." I leveled my threat, ensuring she would know it wasn't empty. There was very little in this world that I had left to claim as my own, and I wouldn't stand idly by as it was swept away from me by someone else's greed. "These souls are not yours, and they never will be," I said with finality.

She eyed me curiously. "Who said anything about souls, dear?"

What?

If it wasn't souls she was after, why did she insist on terrorizing me?

"Whatever you're after, I wouldn't count on getting what you want," I said, hiking a brow and wishing to be rid of her.

"I am a very patient woman." She spoke slowly as if proving her point.

"I'm not."

We locked gazes, and neither of us dared to look away.

"Hm," she mused after a moment. "You are your mother's child after all," she said, looking me over once more before turning quickly and heading into the crowd. I watched her leave—the air around her feet sweeping up the train of her cape with her long stride. The thought came to me that she moved with intention—always—never wasting her energy where it wasn't needed.

"Ammit!" I called, and she whirled. "Who told you? About me?"

She frowned, mildly amused.

"Your mother, of course," she called before sweeping through the crowd.

"Would you like me to remove her head?" Ra's hushed voice came close to my ear, and my eyes slid closed as his arms looped around me.

A slow drumbeat sounded near the end of the soul pool, followed by a languid flute, and my hips began to move in tune. "Perhaps another day," I said. "For now, dance with me."

He bent his knees until his body fit flush with mine, and his hands trailed down to my thighs, finding the sliver of skin between the fabric and sending his kan coursing into my legs. Our bodies moved in unison as the rhythm quickened and a song rose into the rafters.

"As you wish, my Empress."

ALSO BY R. A. MOREAU

COMING SOON

THE RISE OF KEK

THE BOOK OF KAN - BOOK TWO

"It was my turn to take, and I would wrestle my life from the hands of fate no matter the cost."

AVAILABLE NOW

CELESTIAL BODIES:

THE SUN SERPENT'S DAUGHTER

This high-stakes fantasy romance offers a unique take on star-crossed lovers amidst a one-of-a-kind magic system with a diverse cast of characters, including a Black heroine and a deaf male love interest.

ABOUT THE AUTHOR

R. A. Moreau focuses her work on Black romances in fantastical settings. She hopes that by sharing her work, more women will have the opportunity to see themselves in the stories they love.

When she isn't working, she loves spending time with her two dogs and eating more bread than any healthcare professional would recommend.

SOCIALS

www.moreauwrites.com

GLOSSARY

The following is descriptive of the roles these characters and groups play in The Fall of Souls. Artistic liberties have been taken for the purposes of the story and some roles may be a departure from traditional mythology.

Abraxas (Ah-brax-iss) — Youngest son of Anubis and Nephthys. Member and Trainer of The Dead Guard.
    House: Anubis
    Rank: Guardian

Ammit (Ah-mit) — A funerary deity dwelling in the underworld, known as The Pit. Ammit claims and devours the souls that fail the test of Ma'at. She is traditionally said to have the head of a crocodile, the forequarters of a lion, and the hind parts of a hippopotamus.
    House: Ammit
    Rank: Empress
    Titles: Devourer of Souls; Eater of Hearts

Ananiah (Ann-uh-nye-uh) — Eldest daughter of Anubis and Nephthys.
　　House: Anubis

Anubis (Ah-nu-bis) — A funerary deity overseeing death, mummification, embalming, and the afterlife. Tasked with guarding the dead as they journey through the afterlife. Traditionally depicted with the head of a jackal.
　　House: Anubis
　　Rank: High Master

Assessors — The group of deities responsible for weighing the souls against The Feather of Ma'at. Traditionally, the assessors are representative of forty-two minor deities charged with helping to judge the souls in the afterlife.

Atem (Ah-tem) — The first ever deity with power over the light.
　　House: Atem
　　Rank: Pharaoh

Chishi (Chee-shee) — Daughter of Ammit and Seth.
　　House: Ammit

The Dead Guard — The group of deities tasked with guarding The Hall and the souls of the dead as they pass through The Hall.

Éshe (Eh-she) — Wife of Zhaur, Daughter of Shai, and Lady of The Citadel of Peace.
　　House: Shai

The Hall — The gathering place of souls. All souls begin their journey in the afterlife at the Hall, where they are weighed against the feather of Ma'at and judged to be worthy of rebirth or sent to the Pit to be devoured by Ammit.

Kan (Kah-n) — The inherit energy that feeds your soul, present in all living things, but stronger and more powerful in those of divine nature.

Khepri (Keh-pree) — The deity responsible for raising the morning sun.

Konshu (Kon-shoo) — The deity with power over the moon.

Ma'at (Mah-aht) — A primordial deity and personification of balance and justice; responsible for overseeing The Hall.
    House: Ma'at
    Rank: Empress

Nejeri (Neh-jeer-ee) — Member of the Dead Guard.
    House: Sekhmet

Neme (Neh-meh) — Striped headcloth traditionally worn by pharaohs.

Nephthys (Nef-tis) — A primordial deity known as "The Housewife," and associated with protection and guardianship.

Omari (Oh-mar-ee) — Father of Onia and husband of Ma'at.

Onia (Oh-nye-uh) — Only daughter of Ma'at and Omari, and heir to the House of Ma'at.

Rabassam (Rah-bah-sahm) — Eldest living child of Anubis and Nepthys. Commander of the Dead Guard. Also known as "Ra."
    House: Anubis

Sematawy (Sem-ah-tah-wee) — "Lady of two lands"

Shai (Sh-ay) — A deity with the power over fate.

Shu (Sh-oo) — Primodial deity and personification of peace. Emperor of the Citadel of Peace. Brother to Ma'at and Uncle to Onia.
Rank: Emperor

Soul Tie — An individual to whom one has tethered their soul.

Sot Nesu (Soh-t Neh-soo) — "Princess"

Sunu (Soo-Noo) — A healer.

Tarik (Tah-reek) — Member of the Dead Guard.
House: Tefnut

Tefnut (Tef-nuht) — A deity with power over the rain and traditionally depicted with the head of a lioness.
Rank: Empress

Tether — The connection that establishes the relationship between soul ties.

Tey Ib (Teh Eeb) — "My heart"

Tey Sot Nesu (Teh Soh-t Neh-soo) — "My princess"

Wesekh — A broad ornamental collar worn by elites, deities, and others of high rank.

Zhaur (Zah-ur) — Emperor of The Citadel of Peace. Son to Shu and Tefnut.
House: Shu
Rank: Emperor